George Wilson

Portrait Gallery of the Chamber of Commerce of the State of

New-York

George Wilson

Portrait Gallery of the Chamber of Commerce of the State of New-York

ISBN/EAN: 9783337098629

Printed in Europe, USA, Canada, Australia, Japan

Cover: Foto ©Raphael Reischuk / pixelio.de

More available books at **www.hansebooks.com**

INTRODUCTORY NOTE.

THE collection of portraits possessed by the Chamber of Commerce has increased to such an extent within the last three years as to warrant the publication of a catalogue, together with a brief biographical sketch of each subject.

The first portrait in the collection was painted for the Chamber one hundred and eighteen years ago. It is a full length life size of Lieutenant-Governor CADWALLADER COLDEN, then Acting Governor of the Colony of New-York. The Chamber of Commerce was organized by twenty-four merchants April 5th, 1768, and incorporated March 13th, 1770, by GEORGE THE THIRD, through the kindly offices of Lieutenant-Governor COLDEN. It was for this act of friendship in obtaining the Charter as well as for the interest he had manifested in the affairs of the Chamber, that the portrait was painted.

In 1792 a companion portrait, that of ALEXANDER HAMILTON, then Secretary of the Treasury of the United States, also full length and life size, was painted by JOHN TRUMBULL, for the merchants of New-York, admirers of that great statesman, and by them presented to the Chamber of Commerce.

These two portraits, which formed the nucleus of the collection, have passed through many vicissitudes. That of COLDEN originally hung in the great room of the Exchange, which stood at the lower end of Broad Street, where the Chamber held its sessions from 1769 to 1775. At the close of the Revolution it was found in the possession of the family of Lieutenant-Governor COLDEN, and by them restored to the Chamber in May, 1793. It was then placed on the walls of the room used by the Chamber in the Merchants Coffee House, on the southeast corner of Wall and Water Streets, and was afterwards removed to the rooms occupied by the Chamber in the Tontine Coffee House, on the northwest corner of Wall and Water Streets. On April 15th, 1817, the portraits of Colins and Hamilton were loaned to the Academy of Fine Arts, and, for many years, made a part of the exhibition of the Academy

On May 1st, 1827, the Chamber of Commerce having taken rooms in the Merchants' Exchange, then standing on the site of the present Custom House, the portraits were again in its possession, and remained until the great fire of December 16th, 1835. On the morning of the second day of the conflagration which consumed the Exchange, the portraits were removed and deposited for safe keeping in the loft of a building at the lower end of Wall Street, where they remained unrecognized for eight years. On their recovery they were hung in the Directors' room of the Merchants' Bank until February 6th, 1844, when they were deposited with the New-York Historical Society. October 1st, 1868, they were again reclaimed by the Chamber, and now, in a good state of preservation, find a permanent place in its hall on Nassau Street.

It was not until 1865 that measures were taken to procure portraits of the Presidents of the Association, and there now remain but four of the earlier and five of those of later years to be obtained to complete the full number of twenty-six who have filled that office since its organization.

The rule confining the collection to the Presidents of the Chamber was relaxed several years ago, and the gallery now contains eighty portraits and four bronze and marble busts, embracing those of men of national and even world-wide reputation ; great merchants who led the Colonies in their opposition to the tyrannical acts of the British Parliament, whose names are inseparable from the history of the Republic ; statesmen, whose fame is known in every land ; financiers, who met a Nation's emergencies with unparalleled skill and success ; patriots, whose fidelity to

their country was never doubted; philanthropists, who conse-
crated their wealth to the elevation of their fellow men, and
others who originated or were identified with many of the great
enterprises of the nineteenth century.

Of the portraits painted for or purchased by the Chamber,
there are two, besides those of COLDEN and HAMILTON, which
deserve special notice, both for the great personal worth of the
subjects and their relation to the State and the Nation. One
of these is that of DE WITT CLINTON, who, to his great merit as
Mayor of this City, and thrice Governor of the State, added that
far more enduring title of founder and creator of the Canal system
of New-York, which gave to our City her great commercial
supremacy. The other, that of JOHN SHERMAN, who, as Secretary
of the Treasury, in the second great epoch of the Nation's financial
history, became "the restorer of the public credit, and the successful funder of the national debt." The resumption of specie payments, without disaster or financial disturbance, also accomplished
by him, was an act worthy of the Nation's gratitude.

Two other portraits in the gallery are also entitled to special
notice here, as showing the breadth of the Chamber's sympathies ;
they are those of RICHARD COBDEN, the friend of the United States
and the great apostle of the English system of free trade, and of
JOHN BRIGHT, the advocate and defender of the Union in our civil
war, who fought single handed in our behalf, against the nobility,
gentry and Parliament of Great Britain, and won a moral victory.

To one of the bronze busts, presented in connection with the
recent Centennial of the Inauguration of the First President of the
United States, in this City, that of GEORGE WASHINGTON, by
BARBEDIENNE, the Chamber feels that special attention should
also be called. It was a graceful and appropriate act on the
part of the donor thus to connect the memory of WASHINGTON with
an Institution, several of the officers and prominent members of
which were his steadfast and loyal friends, who aided him by their
fortunes and by personal service in achieving the Nation's liberty
and independence.

The purpose of this collection has not been so much to gather fine specimens of the art of portraiture in painting or sculpture, although many of the works were executed by some of the most eminent artists of their time, but to preserve the lineaments of those men who for more than a century have illustrated the commerce of New-York. In their features they show those types of enterprise and judgment which have raised the character of the New-York merchant to its high standard, and carried their fame to the uttermost ends of the earth.

In the preparation of the biographical sketches printed in this volume the Secretary has availed himself of the authentic and valuable information contained in the records of the Chamber of Commerce. He has also consulted, as far as practicable, the families or near relatives of the subjects in reference to matters within their personal knowledge. By this method great accuracy is believed to have been secured. The sketches, though necessarily brief, embody, with few exceptions, all the important events of each life.

CHAMBER OF COMMERCE,
New York, *March 15th*, 1890.

CATALOGUE.

CATALOGUE.

PORTRAIT No. 1.

JOHN CRUGER, First President of the Chamber of Commerce, 1768 1770. Painted in 1865, by THOMAS HICKS, after an original in miniature. Biographical Sketch, page 17.

PORTRAIT No. 2.

HENRY WHITE, Fourth President of the Chamber of Commerce, 1772 1773. Painted in 1867, by HENRY PETERS GRAY, after an original, by JOHN SINGLETON COPLEY. Biographical Sketch, page 20.

PORTRAIT No. 3.

THEOPHYLACT BACHE, Fifth President of the Chamber of Commerce, 1773-1774. A crayon drawing executed in 1867, by VINCENT COLYER, after an original drawing by ST. MEMIN. Biographical Sketch, page 24.

PORTRAIT No. 4.

WILLIAM WALTON, Sixth President of the Chamber of Commerce, 1774 1775. Painted in 1868, by HENRY PETERS GRAY, after an original, by an unknown artist. Biographical Sketch, page 28.

PORTRAIT No. 5.

JOHN ALSOP, Eighth President of the Chamber of Commerce, 1784 1785. Painted in 1865, by THOMAS HICKS, after an original, by an unknown artist. Biographical Sketch, page 30.

PORTRAIT No. 6.

JOHN BROOME, Ninth President of the Chamber of Commerce, 1785 1794. Painted in 1889, by CHARLES C. MARKHAM. Presented by his great grandson, GEORGE COCHRAN BROOME. Biographical Sketch, page 225.

PORTRAIT No. 7.

COMFORT SANDS, Tenth President of the Chamber of Commerce, 1794-1798. Painted in 1890, by THOMAS W. WOOD, after a pastel, by an unknown artist. Biographical Sketch, page 193.

PORTRAIT No. 8.

JOHN MURRAY, Eleventh President of the Chamber of Commerce, 1798 1806. Painted in 1865, by DANIEL HUNTINGTON, after an original, by JOHN TRUMBULL. Biographical Sketch, page 33.

PORTRAIT No. 9.

CORNELIUS RAY, Twelfth President of the Chamber of Commerce, 1806 1819. Painted in 1889, by OLIVER LAY, after a miniature. Presented by his granddaughter, Mrs. N. E. BAYLIES. Biographical Sketch, page 177.

ROBERT LENOX, Fourteenth President of the Chamber of Commerce, 1827 1840. Painted in 1865, by DANIEL HUNTINGTON, after an original, by JOHN WESLEY JARVIS. Presented by his son, JAMES LENOX. Biographical Sketch, page 34.

ISAAC CAROW, Fifteenth President of the Chamber of Commerce, 1840 1842. Painted in 1865, by HENRY PETERS GRAY, after a miniature. Biographical Sketch, page 36.

JAMES GORE KING, Seventeenth President of the Chamber of Commerce, 1845 1847 and 1848–1849. Painted in 1865, by THOMAS P. ROSSITER. Biographical Sketch, page 37.

MOSES H. GRINNELL, Eighteenth President of the Chamber of Commerce, 1847 1848 and 1849–1852. Painted in 1864, by J. O. EATON. Presented by his son, IRVING GRINNELL. Biographical Sketch, page 44.

ELIAS HICKS, Nineteenth President of the Chamber of Commerce, 1852 1853. Painted in 1867. Replica by THOMAS HICKS. Biographical Sketch, page 47.

PELATIAH PERIT, Twentieth President of the Chamber of Commerce, 1853–1863. Painted in 1864. Replica by THOMAS HICKS. Biographical Sketch, page 48.

PORTRAIT No. 16.

WILLIAM E. DODGE, Twenty-Second President of the Chamber of Commerce, 1867 1875. Painted in 1884, by DANIEL HUNTINGTON. Presented by his family. Biographical Sketch, page 53.

PORTRAIT No. 17.

GEORGE W. LANE, Twenty-Fourth President of the Chamber of Commerce, 1882 1883. Painted in 1887, by E. WOOD PERRY. Presented by his daughters. Biographical Sketch, page 57.

PORTRAIT No. 18.

JAMES BOORMAN, Vice-President of the Chamber of Commerce, 1839 1841. Painted in 1856, by THOMAS P. ROSSITER. Presented by HENRY F. SPAULDING. Biographical Sketch, page 198.

PORTRAIT No. 19.

JONATHAN STURGES, Second Vice-President of the Chamber of Commerce, 1863 1867. Painted in 1889, by DANIEL HUNTINGTON. Presented by his son, FREDERICK STURGES. Biographical Sketch, page 59.

PORTRAIT No. 20.

GEORGE OPDYKE, Vice-President of the Chamber of Commerce, 1867 1875. Painted in 1886, by HARRIET C. LANE, after an original, by CHARLES L. ELLIOTT. Presented by his family. Biographical Sketch, page 60.

PORTRAIT No. 21.

SIMEON B. CHITTENDEN, Second Vice-President of the Chamber of Commerce, 1867 1869. Painted in 1890, by DANIEL HUNTINGTON. Presented by his son, SIMEON B. CHITTENDEN. Biographical Sketch, page 212.

PORTRAIT No. 22.

WILLIAM H. FOGG, Second Vice-President of the Chamber of Commerce, 1882–1884. Painted in 1887, by EASTMAN JOHNSON. Presented by his widow, Mrs. WILLIAM H. FOGG. Biographical Sketch, page 64.

PORTRAIT No. 23.

MATTHEW MAURY, Secretary of the Chamber of Commerce, 1849–1853. Painted in 1885, by JULIAN SCOTT. Presented by his family. Biographical Sketch, page 65.

PORTRAIT No. 25.

ALEXANDER HAMILTON, American Statesman and the first Secretary of the Treasury of the United States. Painted in 1792, by JOHN TRUMBULL. Biographical Sketch, page 69.

PORTRAIT No. 26.

JOHN SHERMAN, American Statesman and Secretary of the Treasury of the United States, 1877–1881. Painted in 1880, by DANIEL HUNTINGTON. Biographical Sketch, page 76.

PORTRAIT No. 27.

DE WITT CLINTON, American Statesman and Governor of New-York, 1817–1823 and 1825–1828. Painted in 1807, by JOHN TRUMBULL. Biographical Sketch, page 83.

PORTRAIT No. 28.

DE WITT CLINTON. Painted in 1843, by HENRY INMAN. Presented by SAMUEL B. RUGGLES.

PORTRAIT No. 29.

JOHN A. KING, American Statesman and Governor of New-York, 1857-1859. Painted in 1859, by ROBERT HINCKLEY. Presented by his family. Biographical Sketch, page 90.

PORTRAIT No. 30.

EDWIN D. MORGAN, American Statesman and Governor of New-York, 1859-1863. Painted in 1882, by G. P. A. HEALY. Presented by his grandson, EDWIN D. MORGAN. Biographical Sketch, page 95.

PORTRAIT No. 31.

CADWALLADER COLDEN, Lieut.-Governor of the Colony of New-York, 1761-75. Painted in 1772, by MATTHEW PRATT. Biographical Sketch, page 99.

PORTRAIT No. 32.

FRANCIS EGERTON, Duke of Bridgewater. Painted in England in 1844, by HENRY INMAN, after original authorities. Presented by SAMUEL B. RUGGLES. Biographical Sketch, page 100.

PORTRAIT No. 33.

RICHARD COBDEN, British Statesman. Painted in 1860, by J. FAGNANI. Presented by MORRIS KETCHUM. Biographical Sketch, page 102.

PORTRAIT No. 34.

JOHN BRIGHT, British Statesman. Painted in 1865, by J. FAGNANI. Presented by SIMEON B. CHITTENDEN. Biographical Sketch, page 105.

PORTRAIT No. 35.

GIDEON LEE. Painted in 1832, by GEORGE W. TWIBILL, JR. Presented by his son, W. CREIGHTON LEE. Biographical Sketch, page 110.

PORTRAIT No. 36.

AMBROSE C. KINGSLAND. Painted in 1887. Replica by DANIEL HUNTINGTON. Presented by his family. Biographical Sketch, page 114.

PORTRAIT No. 37.

ANSON G. PHELPS. Painted in 1835, by WALDO & JEWETT. Presented by his daughter, Mrs. WILLIAM E. DODGE. Biographical Sketch, page 116.

PORTRAIT No. 38.

GEORGE T. HOPE. Painted in 1870, by HENRY PETERS GRAY. Presented by HIRAM H. LAMPORT. Biographical Sketch, page 119.

PORTRAIT No. 39.

JEREMIAH P. ROBINSON. Painted in 1888, by MORGAN RHEES. Presented by his family. Biographical Sketch, page 122.

PORTRAIT No. 40.

THOMAS B. CODDINGTON. Painted in 1886, by EASTMAN JOHNSON. Presented by his daughters. Biographical Sketch, page 125.

PORTRAIT No. 41.

GEORGE W. BLUNT. Painted in 1878, by his daughter, Mrs. MARY S. RATHBONE. Presented by the Board of Commissioners of Pilots. Biographical Sketch, page 127.

PORTRAIT No. 42.

WALTER R. JONES. Painted in 1885, by GEORGE H. STORY, after an original, by JAMES BOGLE. Presented by JOHN D. JONES. Biographical Sketch, page 134.

PORTRAIT No. 43.

LORING ANDREWS. Painted in 1886, by ROBERT GORDON HARDIE. Presented by his family. Biographical Sketch, page 137.

PORTRAIT No. 44.

JOSHUA BATES. Painted in 1865, by HENRY PETERS GRAY, after an original, by E. U. EDDIS. Biographical Sketch, page 140.

PORTRAIT No. 45.

PETER COOPER. Painted in 1886, by HENRY A. LOOP. Presented by his son, EDWARD COOPER. Biographical Sketch, page 146.

PORTRAIT No. 46.

JOHN DAVID WOLFE. Painted in 1886. Replica by DANIEL HUNTINGTON. Presented by his daughter, CATHARINE LORILLARD WOLFE. Biographical Sketch, page 150.

PORTRAIT No. 47.

BENJAMIN B. SHERMAN. Painted in 1886, by FRANK B. CARPENTER. Presented by his family. Biographical Sketch, page 153.

PORTRAIT No. 48.

PRESERVED FISH. Painted in 1886, by JULIAN SCOTT, after a daguerreotype. Biographical Sketch, page 155.

PORTRAIT No. 49.

DAVID LEAVITT. Painted in 1887, by VIRGINIA TUCKER, after an original, by JARED B. FLAGG. Presented by his family. Biographical Sketch, page 156.

PORTRAIT No. 50.

FRANCIS SKIDDY. Painted in 1887, by EASTMAN JOHNSON. Presented by his daughter, Mrs. CHARLES P. FISCHER. Biographical Sketch, page 158.

PORTRAIT No. 51.

GUSTAV SCHWAB. Painted in 1889, by JULIUS GEERTZ. Presented by his family. Biographical Sketch, page 159.

PORTRAIT No. 52.

ELLIOT C. COWDIN. Painted in 1886, by J. W. ALEXANDER. Presented by his widow. Mrs. ELLIOT C. COWDIN. Biographical Sketch, page 162.

PORTRAIT No. 53.

KINLOCH STUART. Painted in 1840, by A. B. DURAND. Presented by Mrs. ROBERT L. STUART. Biographical Sketch, page 166.

PORTRAIT No. 54.

ROBERT L. STUART. Painted in 1886, by SEYMOUR J. GUY. Presented by his widow, Mrs. ROBERT L. STUART. Biographical Sketch, page 167.

PORTRAIT No. 55.

ROBERT McCREA. Painted in 1835, by WALDO & JEWETT. Presented by his daughter, Mrs. ROBERT L. STUART. Biographical Sketch, page 169.

PORTRAIT No. 56.

JOHN JACOB ASTOR. Painted in 1890, by JACOB H. LAZARUS, after an original, by GILBERT STUART. Presented by his grandson, JOHN JACOB ASTOR. Biographical Sketch, page 170.

PORTRAIT No. 57.

SAMUEL B. RUGGLES. Painted in 1882, by DANIEL HUNTINGTON. Biographical Sketch, page 174.

PORTRAIT No. 58.

ROBERT RAY. Painted in 1886, by OLIVER LAY, after an original, by DANIEL HUNTINGTON. Presented by his daughter, Mrs. N. E. BAYLIES. Biographical Sketch, page 178.

PORTRAIT No. 59.

JOHN C. GREEN. Painted in 1878, by DANIEL HUNTINGTON. Presented by his widow, Mrs. SARAH H. GREEN. Biographical Sketch, page 179.

PORTRAIT No. 60.

CHARLES H. MARSHALL. Painted in 1864, by RICHARD J. NAGLE. Biographical Sketch, page 183.

PORTRAIT No. 61.

JAMES STOKES. Painted in 1884. Replica by DANIEL HUNTINGTON. Presented by his son, ANSON PHELPS STOKES. Biographical Sketch, page 187.

PORTRAIT No. 62.

PAUL SPOFFORD. Painted in 1890, by THOMAS W. WOOD. Presented by his family. Biographical Sketch, page 189.

PORTRAIT No. 63.

THOMAS TILESTON. Painted in 1865, by THOMAS HICKS. Biographical Sketch, page 191.

PORTRAIT No. 64.

JOHN J. PHELPS. Painted in 1885, by HENRY ULKE, after an original, by DANIEL HUNTINGTON. Presented by his son, WILLIAM WALTER PHELPS. Biographical Sketch, page 200.

PORTRAIT No. 65.

MARSHALL O. ROBERTS. Painted in 1872, by THOMAS HICKS. Presented by his widow, Mrs. SUSAN L. ROBERTS. Biographical Sketch, page 203.

PORTRAIT No. 66.

RUFUS PRIME. Painted in 1886, by OLIVER LAY, after an original, by DANIEL HUNTINGTON. Presented by his daughter, CORNELIA PRIME. Biographical Sketch, page 205.

PORTRAIT No. 67.

GEORGE T. TRIMBLE. Painted in 1857, by W. SERGEANT KENDALL, after an original, by DANIEL HUNTINGTON. Presented by his son, MERRITT TRIMBLE. Biographical Sketch, page 206.

PORTRAIT No. 68.

ISAAC SHERMAN. Painted in 1863, by THOMAS HICKS. Presented by his widow, Mrs. ISAAC SHERMAN. Biographical Sketch, page 209.

PORTRAIT No. 69.

HORACE B. CLAFLIN. Painted in 1880, by A. A. ANDERSON. Presented by his son, JOHN CLAFLIN. Biographical Sketch, page 217.

PORTRAIT No. 70.

JEREMIAH MILBANK. Painted in 1889, by J. W. ALEXANDER. Presented by his family. Biographical Sketch, page 224.

PORTRAIT No. 71.

ROBERT H. McCURDY. Painted in 1885, after an original, by an unknown artist. Presented by his son, RICHARD A. McCURDY. Biographical Sketch, page 227.

PORTRAIT No. 72.

JOHN CASWELL. Painted in 1890, by THOMAS W. WOOD, after an original, by EASTMAN JOHNSON. Presented by CHARLES S. SMITH. Biographical Sketch, page 229.

PORTRAIT No. 73.

JACOB BARKER. Painted in 1885, by H. DIEGENDESCH, after an original, by HENRY INMAN. Presented by his family. Biographical Sketch, page 232.

PORTRAIT No. 74.

DANIEL DRAKE-SMITH. Painted in 1889, by JARED B. FLAGG. Presented by his family. Biographical Sketch, page 234.

PORTRAIT No. 75.

ALFRED S. BARNES. Painted in 1889, by GEORGE W. MAYNARD. Presented by his family. Biographical Sketch, page 235.

PORTRAIT No. 76.

JAMES BROWN. Painted in 1856, by THOMAS P. ROSSITER. Presented by HENRY F. SPAULDING. Biographical Sketch, page 238.

PORTRAIT No. 77.

CORNELIUS VANDERBILT. Painted in 1887. Replica by JARED B. FLAGG. Presented by his grandson, CORNELIUS VANDERBILT. Biographical Sketch, page 242.

PORTRAIT No. 78.

WILLIAM H. VANDERBILT. Painted in 1887. Replica by EASTMAN JOHNSON. Presented by his son, CORNELIUS VANDERBILT. Biographical Sketch, page 245.

PORTRAIT No. 79.

HANSON K. CORNING. Painted in 1889, by CARL L. BRANDT. Presented by his children. Biographical Sketch, page 248.

PORTRAIT No. 80.

MOSES TAYLOR. Painted in 1888, by DANIEL HUNTINGTON. Presented by his widow, Mrs. CATHARINE A. TAYLOR. Biographical Sketch, page 261.

SCULPTURE.

GEORGE WASHINGTON. Bronze bust, executed in Paris in 1889, by BARBEDIENNE, after an original made by HOUDON at Mount Vernon in 1785. Presented by CHARLES S. SMITH. Biographical Sketch, page 250.

JONATHAN GOODHUE. Marble bust, executed in 1849, by HENRY K. BROWN. Biographical Sketch, page 129.

GEORGE GRISWOLD. Marble bust, executed in 1844, by J. BATTIN. Presented by his daughter, Mrs. SARAH H. GREEN. Biographical Sketch, page 132.

ROBERT B. POTTER. Bronze bust, executed in 1888, by W. C. NOBLE. Biographical Sketch, page 263.

BIOGRAPHICAL SKETCHES.

BIOGRAPHICAL SKETCHES.

JOHN CRUGER.

AN eminent American merchant and patriot, born of English parents in this City, July 18, 1710. JOHN CRUGER belonged to a family of successful and enterprising merchants. He and his brother, HENRY, were owners of a number of ships engaged in general trade, principally with Bristol, England, and the West India Islands. Their place of business was on CRUGERS' Wharf, on the east side of Whitehall Slip, on the East River. The great fire of 1776 broke out there, and the buildings belonging to the CRUGERS were wholly destroyed. JOHN CRUGER was honored in his day with positions of the highest trust in the gift of his fellow-citizens, having been Mayor of the City and Speaker of the General Assembly of the Colony. In all his public career, covering many years, he never forfeited the respect and confidence of the people, and his administration of the various offices he held was characterized by the highest ability and integrity.

In 1765, when the odious Stamp Act was imposed upon the Colonies, the merchants of New-York were among the first to oppose its enforcement, and it was mainly due to the influence of JOHN CRUGER, then Mayor of the City, that the revolt which the Stamp Act engendered did not result in bloodshed. The protests of the people against its enforcement did not avail. The merchants thereupon resolved upon the more effective measure of non-importation from Great Britain, and it was this determined opposition that compelled the British Parliament to repeal the Act.

It was during this exciting period that JOHN CRUGER

2

and a few of the leading merchants met at BOLTON & SIGELL's Tavern, (yet standing on the corner of Broad and Pearl streets, and now known as WASHINGTON's Headquarters,) on the 5th day of April, 1768, and there organized the New-York Chamber of Commerce. Mr. CRUGER was the first named of its founders, and was elected its President. On the 2d of May, 1769, he was again unanimously chosen, and at that time, while serving as Speaker of the General Assembly, he was charged by that body to convey to the merchants of this City and Colony "the thanks of the House for their repeated disinterested, public spirited and patriotic conduct in declining the importation of goods from Great Britain until such Acts of Parliament as the General Assembly had declared unconstitutional and subversive of the rights and liberties of the people of this Colony should be repealed." Thus, in the infancy of this metropolis, the patriotic devotion of its merchants to the cause of popular rights was clearly recognized and upheld. And it is a source of just pride to-day that the Chamber of Commerce, the merchants' representative body, has lost none of its ancient spirit, as its records from 1861 to 1865 will abundantly show. JOHN CRUGER retained the office of President of the Chamber until it had received its charter from the Crown and its permanent existence fully assured. In May, 1770, he declined a re-election.

In all the early difficulties which the Chamber had to encounter, resulting from differences of opinion in regard to measures affecting the trade of the Colony, Mr. CRUGER stood steadfastly by the Chamber and earnestly contended for its interests.

JOHN CRUGER exercised great influence with his fellow-citizens, and did much to moderate their passions and harmonize the conflicting opinions of the opposing parties which existed at that time. His course during the eventful period of 1775, when patriotic blood boiled at fever heat on receipt of the news of the Lexington outrage, was marked by a calm, dignified courage and self-reliance; and while he did not take an active part in the beginning of the contest, from conscientious scruples which his official

position imposed upon him, his sympathies were nevertheless with the people in their efforts to secure redress for
the wrongs done them by the mother country.
He never swerved from the dictates of conscience. His
judgment was sound ; his mind free from bias. Although he
was as anxious as the strongest revolutionist to wage war
upon any arbitrary measures of the king, yet his course
was always dictated by prudence, caution and firmness.
When asked to subscribe to the Articles of Association entered into by the citizens of New-York on April 29th, 1775,
which proposed "to adopt and carry into execution whatever
measures may be recommended by the Continental Congress
or by the Provincial Convention for the purpose of preserving
our Constitution, and opposing the execution of several arbitrary and oppressive acts of the British Parliament." Mr.
CRUGER, in a joint letter with JACOB WALTON, refused,
"because," said he, "as we were elected Representatives
in General Assembly for the City and County of New-York,
we conceive that the faithful performance of that important
trust requires of us a free, unbiased exercise of our judgment. To submit this to the control of any power on earth
would, in our opinion, be deserting that trust : but to
engage implicitly to approve and carry into execution the
regulations of any other body, would justly expose us to
the reproach of our own consciences, the censure not only of
our constituents, but of the whole world." This is the
language of a man who believed in reason and conscience.
He logically adds : "In our legislative capacity we have
already transmitted to the King and both Houses of Parliament representations of our grievances.   *   *   * As the
signing of this Association, therefore, would, in effect, be to
deprive ourselves of our legislative powers, we cannot but
suppose, from the tenor of it, an exemption of us is implied
in it." We may be pardoned for dwelling a little longer
upon Mr. CRUGER's character. Moderation and firmness
in him were beautifully combined. He was in no sense a
servile subject of the king, but he steadily opposed violent
or incendiary words or action. He endeavored to modify
the anger of the revolutionists, in the hope that the king

would ultimately exhibit that justice which the people demanded. Evidence of his earnest desire for peace is shown in his letter to General GAGE, the British commander. This letter, drawn by Mr. CRUGER, is dated May 5th, 1775, and is signed by fourteen members of the Assembly. It urges General GAGE, "that as far as consistent with his duty, he would immediately order a cessation of public hostilities until his Majesty can be apprised of the situation of the American Colonies;" and the same letter also expressed the wish, "that no military force might land or be stationed in this Province." Shortly after, however, the British army took possession of the City, just prior to which Mr. CRUGER retired to Kinderhook on the Hudson, where he appears to have suffered from the infirmities of advancing age and the need of those necessities which the condition of affairs deprived him of. He returned to this City after peace was declared in 1783, and here, on Tuesday, the 27th of December, 1791, died, at the age of 82 years.

How touching is the following tribute, which was printed with a notice of his death in the *New-York Journal and Patriotic Register:*

> " It may be truly said of him, that he was
>   The upright man,
>   Beloved of all his friends ;
>   And of whom an enemy
>   (If he had one)
>   Could speak no evil."

HENRY WHITE.

HENRY WHITE came of Welsh birth and origin, and possessed in an eminent degree the loyalty, thoroughness and integrity of his race. In May, 1756, we find him as a petitioner for leave to supply bread to South Carolina for the use of the Navy. The New-York *Mercury*, of December 12th, 1757, makes the announcement, that " HENRY WHITE has just imported from London and Bristol a neat assortment of goods, fit for the season, which he will sell for ready money or short credit, at his store in King-street." On May 13th, 1761, he married EVA VAN CORTLANDT. daughter of FREDERICK, and grand-daughter of JACOBUS VAN CORTLANDT. This connection secured for Mr. WHITE a fortune. One year later he became the owner of the sloop "Moro," which, like all the craft sailing from New-York at this time, was armed. The "Moro" carried ten guns. The war with France was then ended on land, but still continued on the seas. An example of his enterprise and honesty is found in a brief notice in WEYMAN's *Gazette* of March 21st, 1763, wherein he announces his intention to sail for England, and "invites those to whom he is indebted to call for their money." Mr. WHITE was, undoubtedly, a very ambitious man; and persistent and attentive as he was in business, he seems to have been desirous of political preferment. In 1769, for example, he sought and obtained from the Governor of the Colony a seat at the Council Board, made vacant by the refusal of Mr. DE LANCEY to take office. This position he retained during the remaining period of English rule in this country. His increasing business compelled him, in 1769, to change his location from CRUGERS' wharf to the house of the then late ABRAHAM DE PEYSTER. This house stood between the "Fly market and the coffee house," where, according to HUGH GAINES' New York *Gazette and Weekly Mercury*, he was prepared to sell "nails of all sizes; Bohea and Congo teas; 6 by 8, 7 by 9, and 8 by 10 window glass; English sail cloth; from No. 1 to 7, Russia do.; writing paper, English cordage, Bristol beer, blue duffils, spotted rugs; Newkirk and Dutch oznabrigs, Madeira wine." This, to some extent, is an interesting contrast to the nature, volume and variety of the importation to be found in a modern well stocked store. It is more pertinent, however, to record Mr. WHITE's connection with our struggle for independence. He was, undoubtedly, a man of strong convictions, and his unquestioned loyalty to the king in those stormy days resulted in his leaving the country for a brief period. Mr. WHITE was one of the consignees of the tea shipped to

America in the winter of 1773 to 1774, which caused so much turbulence along the Atlantic coast. The feeling against the English Government was then so strong that it was resolved to pay no duties. At Charleston the merchandise was refused by the consignees and allowed to rot in the store. Three ships with similar cargoes arrived at Boston, but the tea was thrown into the sea. One cargo arrived at Philadelphia, but "brotherly love" at that time could not restrain the Philadelphians from gathering in town meeting, and exacting a promise from the captain of the vessel to return to London with his ship and cargo the following day.

HENRY WHITE would not consent to these manifestations of disapproval with the king's decrees. He and two other consignees, on December 1st, 1773, addressed a memorial to Governor TRYON to protect their importations. When these arrived, April 18th, 1774, Captain LOCKYER was allowed to bring his vessel to the city, but the crew had to remain aboard. From the New-York *Gazette* of April 25th, we learn that a Vigilance Committee, on the morning after the arrival of the ship, conducted the captain to the house of "the Hon. HENRY WHITE, Esquire, one of the consignees, and there informed Captain LOCKYER that he should not presume to go near the Custom House." The captain shortly after left the city. In 1775 Mr. WHITE seems to have incurred the displeasure of those who resisted the king's orders, for the Committee of Safety had placed before them an intercepted letter, addressed by Governor MARTIN, of North Carolina, to Mr. WHITE, asking for the shipment of a marquee, "with the royal standard." About this time Mr. WHITE considered his liberty was jeopardized, and probably left the City, somewhat hurriedly, for, in the summer of 1776, according to Governor TRYON's account, he was in England. He returned to New-York in the fall of 1776, when the British had resumed control, and his name appears among the signers of the loyal address to Lord HOWE in October following. During the war he gave material assistance to the king's troops, sold captured vessels and cargoes, distributed prize

money among British war vessels, and in other ways
endeavored to uphold and continue British authority and
influence. SABINE says, that on October 9th, 1780, Mr.
WHITE appeared before the Surrogate to prove the will of
Major ANDRÉ, and testified that he knew his signature and
handwriting well. When the war ended, Mr. WHITE left
the City, returning to England with the British who evacuated New-York in the fall of 1783. His estates were
confiscated in 1779. His mansion in 1786 was occupied
by GEORGE CLINTON, New-York's first Governor. All of
the property was vested in the people of this State, as the
advertisement reads, "by the attainder of HENRY WHITE,
Esquire, late one of the members of the Council of the late
Colony of New-York." Mr. WHITE was elected Vice-
President of the Chamber of Commerce May 1, 1770, and
President May 5, 1772, and served in that capacity until
May 1, 1775. He died in Golden Square, London, on
December 23d, 1786, his wife surviving him nearly half
a century. She died at her residence, No. 11 Broadway,
on August 19th, 1835, at the ripe age of ninety-nine
years. By her Mr. WHITE had thirteen children, seven
of whom lived to be twenty-one years old. Of these, HENRY
married ANN VAN CORTLANDT, and lived and died in this
country. JOHN CHAMBERS WHITE entered the British
Navy, and was knighted after attaining the rank of Vice-
Admiral. He married CORDELIA FANSHAWE for his first
wife, and Miss DALRYMPLE for his second. FREDERICK
VAN CORTLANDT WHITE entered the British army in 1781 as
an ensign, and rose to the rank of general. He married
first SOPHIA COORE, and after her death Miss DAVIDSON.
WILLIAM TRYON WHITE, another son, died in this country.
Of the daughters, ANN married in 1787 Dr. JOHN McNA-
MARA HAYES, (afterwards Sir JOHN,) of Golden Square,
London. She died in England. MARGARET married PETER
JAY MUNRO, and died here, and FRANCES, who married
Dr. ARCHIBALD BRUCE, also lived and died in the United
States. The portrait of Mr. WHITE, belonging to the Cham-
ber of Commerce, is from an excellent picture by COPLEY, in
possession of AUGUSTUS VAN CORTLANDT, a great grandson.

THEOPHYLACT BACHE.

The stormy days of the Revolution naturally engendered the bitterest feeling between the Revolutionists and the Royalists. But there were men who, while acknowledging their allegiance to the king, did not hold the theory that the "king can do no wrong." They, however, opposed the movement to cut loose from the mother country, and sought to bring about a reconciliation between the opposing forces. THEOPHYLACT BACHE, the subject of this sketch, was one of these men of peace. Of noble and generous instincts, sterling integrity, fine, dignified presence, he was a friend to all, and while lamenting the rupture between the king and the revolutionists, he accepted its results, and lived through the early years of the republic, devoting a large share of his time to charitable objects and public pursuits, beloved by all who knew him. THEOPHYLACT BACHE was born in the town of Settle, in the West Riding of Yorkshire, England, on January 17th, 1734-5 (old style.) His father was an excise collector. THEOPHYLACT arrived in New-York September 17th, 1751, and acted as assistant to PAUL RICHARD, a successful merchant of that day, who had been Mayor of the City. Six years after his arrival he appears in the public prints of that day as the seller of "a choice parcel of Madeira wine, Cheshire cheese, spermaceti candles," and other European stock; and in 1757 records show that he was a partner with LEONARD LISPENARD as a merchant and owner of the ship "Grace." About this period his business as an importer increased so rapidly as to warrant a change of location, and in 1760 he was again compelled to seek more commodious quarters. On October 16th of that year he married ANN DOROTHY, daughter of ANDREW BARCLAY, a wealthy gentleman from Curacoa, who had established himself as a merchant in New-York. This connection proved valuable to him. Of his wife's sisters, CATHERINE married AUGUSTUS VAN CORTLANDT; SARAH, ANTHONY LISPENARD; ANN MARGARET, FREDERICK JAY; HELENA,

Major MONCRIEFF, a British officer, and CHARLOTTE AMELIA, married Dr. RICHARD BAILEY. THEOPHYLACT was one of a large family, his brother, RICHARD, being the eighteenth child. RICHARD had also come to America, for as early as 1760 he was established in business at Philadelphia, and with THEOPHYLACT conducted an underwriting agency for vessels and cargoes. A policy is still in existence issued by the two brothers at Philadelphia, dated May 31st, 1764, on a shipment from that port to Havana by the brig "Success" for a 3½ per cent. consideration. RICHARD was married on October 29th, 1767, to SARAH, the only daughter of the illustrious BENJAMIN FRANKLIN.

The name of THEOPHYLACT BACHE is of peculiar interest to the Chamber of Commerce, seeing that he was one of its organizers when its members first assembled to give it the name it has borne for one hundred and twenty one years. In 1770 he was chosen its Treasurer; in 1771, Vice President, and in 1773 he was elected its President. He was also a petitioner for the incorporation of the Marine Society, and one of the incorporators of the Society of the New-York Hospital, in 1771. To what extent Mr. BACHE took part in the great opposition to the Stamp Act in 1765 there is no clear record. It is almost certain that he took no prominent part. He was a man of domestic tastes, and his business seems to have absorbed nearly his whole attention. That he was highly esteemed is evident from the fact that while he did not seek political distinction, his high standing and undoubted integrity led the citizens to regard him as one of their most trusted advisers. When the Committee of Fifty-one was organized in May, 1774, Mr. BACHE proved himself a valuable member. He was a willing promoter of the first Continental Congress, and was one of two appointed to oversee the election of Deputies. This Congress did nothing more than adopt a "Declaration of Rights," and recommend to the Colonies a non-exportation and non-importation Act. The peaceful proclivities of Mr. BACHE were plainly shown in 1775, when the news of the battle of Lexington reached New-York. He regarded the war as a conflict between friends and kindred. In New-York the lines between the king's adherents and the patriotic party were becoming more sharply drawn. Attempts were made to break up the middle party and compel the neutrals to define their position. Mr. BACHE's family in America were divided in their choice of king and country. His brother, RICHARD, was a strong Revolutionist. Mr. BACHE's attempts to remain impartial were of little avail, but the following unsigned letter, said to have been written by him to Major MONCRIEFF, discloses some phases of the character of the man :

NEW-YORK, *September* 3, 1775.

DEAR MAJOR :

I wrote to you a few days ago by the transport which sailed from hence. I hope you have received it. It is now decreed by the Congress criminal to speak, and as it would be equally so to write, not knowing into whose hands this may fall before this reaches you, I am determined not to transgress. I wish to remain in this country as long as I can, and not to do anything that may cause a banishment, or the punishment of being sent to the mines of Syms-bury, which are punishments daily inflicted on those poor culprits who are found, or even supposed, *inimical.* Don't think of returning here while the unhappy contest continues. You will be ferreted and exposed to insults I would wish you to avoid. I will take care of your wife as much as a brother or a friend can do. She is as well and as happy as can be expected. I expect that she will lay in at Flatbush, as I think it would be dangerous to bring her to town. The late firing of the "Asia" has been fatal to many women in her situation. The family join me in love to you, and believe me to be, dear MONCRIEFF,

Yours,

——— ———

To Major MONCRIEFF,

Boston.

THOMAS MONCRIEFF had married HELENA BARCLAY, the sister of Mrs. BACHE, in 1774. This letter caused trouble to Mr. BACHE, for he was summoned before the Committee of Safety for examination. Through a friendly hint, however, he left town. In 1775 he was again cited to appear before the Committee, but he replied in a characteristic letter, that he was deeply concerned at the charge that he was inimical to the cause of America. He declared the accusation against him was unwarranted, and was made by those unacquainted with his sentiments. "I sincerely hope for a reconciliation," he wrote, "that this once happy country may enjoy the blessings of peace." About this period he retreated to the British lines, and during the war divided his time between this City and his Flatbush residence, a favorite country seat with New-Yorkers. During the conflict he maintained a strict neutrality, but on the night of June 15th, 1778, he was carried off by force, with Major MONCRIEFF, to Morristown, N. J., where they underwent a nominal confinement for a short time. During the war he did his utmost to alleviate the distress. In 1784 his interest in the Chamber of Commerce was again made manifest by his efforts to re-admit to membership all those who had been absent during the war. With other parties, Mr. BACHE, in 1770, had become interested in large tracts of land, and in 1785 he was interested with JAMES BARCLAY in a claim to a tract of 18,000 acres on the west side of the waters which flow into Lake Champlain. When peace was restored he re-commenced business at his old place, No. 38 Hanover Square, which, from 1794 to 1801, is described as 122 Pearl street. Mr. BACHE erected the buildings on Water-street, then known as Nos. 85, 86 and 87. In 1802 Mr. BACHE occupied No. 87. As the "river front" became further filled in, four more houses were added on Front-street, and on its final extension to South-street he erected two fine warehouses, known as 44 and 45 South street, which were subsequently accepted as models for similar structures. These were destroyed in the disastrous fire of 1835. Here, on the ground floor, JONATHAN GOODHUE, the founder of the old and well known house of GOODHUE & Co., occupied an office. No. 45 was the office of the late MOSES TAYLOR, the distinguished merchant whose portrait adorns the walls of the Chamber of Commerce. In 1803 Mr. BACHE took his son ANDREW into partnership, the firm becoming THEOPHYLACT & ANDREW BACHE. The business was not prosperous during the latter part of Mr. BACHE's career. The period was one of commercial disaster. The whole world was, so to speak, armed to the teeth. Mr. BACHE died on October 30th, 1807, in the 73d year of his age, and was buried from the house of his friend and kinsman, CHARLES McEVERS, in Wall-street, on the following Sunday. Mr. BACHE was a Governor of the New-York Hospital from 1785 to 1797, and President from 1794 to 1797, and second President of the St. GEORGE's Society in 1786. Revolutionists and Royalists alike seem to have regarded him with great respect, for he was made Vice-President of the Chamber in 1788, and was re-elected yearly until 1792. He was a vestryman of Trinity Church for many years. By his wife, ANN DOROTHY BARCLAY, whose death occurred in 1795, he had a numerous issue, several of whom lived to maturity.

WILLIAM WALTON.

WILLIAM WALTON, one of the founders of the Chamber of Commerce, and successively its Treasurer, Vice-President and President, came of English descent, though early in the eighteenth century his ancestors played an important part in the maritime and commercial history of America. His uncle, WILLIAM WALTON, realized a fortune from his fleet of vessels plying to southern ports. He controlled the carrying trade of St. Augustine, the Spaniards being especially friendly towards him. WILLIAM WALTON, the subject of this sketch, was the son of JACOB WALTON, a brother of WILLIAM just referred to, and was born in this City in 1731. His uncle, WILLIAM, regarded his nephew with great favor, and early took him into the business he had found so lucrative. The uncle had no

children of his own. As the young man grew up he enjoyed all the advantages which a fine physique, business
success and glowing prospects could give him. On October
3d, 1757, the record of New-York marriages announces his
alliance with the influential family of the DE LANCEYS, for,
on that date, he married MARY, daughter of Lieutenant-
Governor JAMES DE LANCEY. The DE LANCEYS had inter-
married with the VAN CORTLANDTS, one of the most
powerful families in the province. In 1768 WILLIAM
WALTON, the uncle, died, and WILLIAM, the nephew, with
his brother, carried on the business under the style of
WILLIAM & JACOB WALTON & Co. JACOB had married
a daughter of HENRY CRUGER, and was a member of the
New-York General Assembly. In 1772 the two brothers
owned large tracts of land at Socialborough, in the northern
part of the State, and also were engaged in manufacturing.
WILLIAM was a man of great public spirit. Even in those
primitive days he saw the need of an association of a body
of merchants, by whose united efforts the commercial and
maritime interests of the country could be advanced. He
accordingly helped organize the Chamber of Commerce in
1768, was its Treasurer in 1771, its Vice-President in 1772,
and President from 1774 to 1775. He was also a petitioner
for the incorporation of the Marine Society, and was a
warm supporter of the measures adopted by the merchants
in opposition to the Stamp Act. He was also a member of
the Committee of Correspondence of Fifty-one, which was
formed soon after the receipt of the news of the closing of the
Port of Boston. Mr. WALTON was also one of the Committee
of Sixty, appointed to carry out the non-importation and
non exportation order adopted by the Continental Congress
of 1774, and records show that he was a prominent member
of the Committee of Safety of One Hundred, chosen in
1775. Like many others, Mr. WALTON's sympathies were
with the patriotic party, but family ties probably modified
the course he personally would have chosen.

The DE LANCEYS were nearly all adherents to the Royalists' cause, while the WALTONS were inclined to be neutral
in the conflict. About this time Mr. WALTON went to his

residence in Jersey, intending probably to stay there until something was definitely settled, but finally returned to the City when the British authority was restored. Soon after his Jersey estates were confiscated.

During the war he resided in New-York, employing himself in alleviating the distress and in mitigating the severities the war occasioned. When the Chamber of Commerce resumed its sittings, June 21st, 1779, Mr. WALTON became a regular attendant, and in 1783 he was again chosen Vice-President. Though he continued to reside in the City, Mr. WALTON did not resume active business. He died August 18th, 1796, in the sixty-fifth year of his age. His wife died May 16th, 1707. Mr. WALTON left three sons, who inherited his estates. Their names were WILLIAM, JAMES DE LANCEY and JACOB. JACOB, after serving a term in the British Navy, became a Rear Admiral. DANIEL CROMMELIN VERPLANCK married the daughter, ANN. The old name is still directly preserved by the Reverend WILLIAM WALTON, a son of JACOB, the British Admiral. The WALTON family has been an honorable one. It should be added, that the old Walton house, continuously held by the family since 1752, was standing until within a few years, in Franklin Square, and was known as 326 Pearl-street. This old relic had been the scene of many an important gathering in the old Colonial days. WILLIAM WALTON, the uncle of the subject of this sketch, built the homestead, and at his death bequeathed it to his nephew, WILLIAM. Many notables shared the hospitalities of this mansion, and its historic connections will always be found of interest.

— —

JOHN ALSOP.

THE family of ALSOP in America is descended from RICHARD ALSOP, who emigrated from England towards the close of the seventeenth century, and under the patronage of THOMAS WANDELL, a brother of his mother, settled at Mespat Kills, since called Maspeth, and afterwards known as Newtown, Long Island. Mr. WANDELL, dying without issue, left his estate in Newtown to his nephew, who continued to reside upon it until his death. By his wife, HANNAH, daughter of Captain JOHN UNDERHILL, a famous Indian fighter, he left a numerous issue. His third son, JOHN ALSOP, was bred to the legal profession, and early located himself at New-Windsor, in Orange County, New-York, but soon removed to the City of New-York, where he was admitted a freeman in 1749. He continued in the practice of his profession until his death, in 1761. He married ABIGAIL, daughter of JOSEPH SACKETT, of Newtown, by whom he had two sons, JOHN and RICHARD, both of whom survived him.

JOHN ALSOP, the subject of this sketch, was the eldest son of JOHN ALSOP and ABIGAIL SACKETT. The precise date of his birth is not known. He was brought up as a merchant, as his name appears signed JOHN ALSOP, Junior, to the agreement entered into by the principal merchants of the City, in December, 1753, "not to receive copper half-pence otherwise than fourteen for a shilling." About this time he engaged in business with his brother, RICHARD, under the firm of JOHN & RICHARD ALSOP. Their partnership was dissolved on the 30th of September, 1757, RICHARD removing to Middletown, Conn., and JOHN continuing the business in New-York in his own name. He soon reached the first rank among the merchants of the City. During the period which preceded and followed the passage and repeal of the Stamp Act, in 1765 and 1766, he was active with his fellow merchants in measures of resistance to the oppressive laws of the British Parliament, and in May, 1769, was chosen to read the acknowledgment of the merchants of the resolution adopted by the Assembly, thanking them for their faithful observance of the Non-Importation agreements. He was then a member of the Chamber of Commerce, which he had aided in founding the year before. In 1770 he was one of the Committee of In-spection to enforce the agreements which were still continued. When the news of the passage of the Boston

Port Bill reached New-York, in May, 1774, and a Committee of Correspondence was raised to concert measures of resistance, JOHN ALSOP was the first named of the fifty-one members; and, on the organization of the Committee, was chosen deputy Chairman. In the summer of the same year he was elected one of the New-York delegates to the First Continental Congress. In May, 1775, he was one of the Committee of One Hundred chosen by the citizens to take charge of the Government till a convention could be assembled; the following year he was re-elected to Congress. On the adoption of the Declaration of Independence, Mr. ALSOP and his colleagues, representing the State of New-York, were recalled, the State not being prepared to ratify the Declaration of Independence. In a letter to the convention he expressed surprise and indignation at the slight put upon the New-York delegation, in leaving it without instructions on this point, although such instructions had been repeatedly sought for. Withdrawing to Middletown, where his brother's family was settled, he resided there until the close of the war. On his return to the City, in 1784, he renewed his connection with the Chamber of Commerce, and was one of the petitioners for a confirmation of the charter from the State in April of that year. On the re-organization of the Chamber he was the unanimous choice of his fellow merchants for the Presidency of that body—a high tribute to the integrity of his character and the fidelity of his attachment to his native land—from men who had not always agreed with him in opinion. In 1785 he declined a re-election, owing to his failing health and advanced years, and he gradually withdrew from business.

Mr. ALSOP was for many years a Vestryman of Trinity Church, President of the Society of the New-York Hospital from 1770 to 1784, and also served as Governor from 1781 to 1788. He was one of the incorporators of the Hospital.

Mr. ALSOP married, on the 8th June, 1766, MARY FROGAT, who died on the 14th April, 1772, at the early age of 28 years, leaving to his care an only child, MARY, who was married March 30th, 1783, to Hon. RUFUS KING, then a delegate from Massachusetts to the Congress sitting in New York. Mr. ALSOP died on the 22d November, 1794, at an advanced age.

The descendants of JOHN ALSOP were well known in New-York. They were the Hon. JOHN ALSOP KING, formerly Governor of the State of New-York; the Hon. CHARLES KING, LL. D., President of Columbia College; the Hon. JAMES GORE KING, of the great banking house of PRIME, WARD & KING, who represented New-Jersey in the 31st Congress; and who was also President of the Chamber of Commerce from 1845 to 1847, and from 1848 to 1849.

The name of ALSOP, extinct in the line of JOHN, is sustained by descendants of his brother, RICHARD. His grandson, RICHARD, was a distinguished merchant of Philadelphia, and the founder of the great house of ALSOP & Co., which, with its connections on the west coast of America, carried the name of ALSOP to the four corners of the earth, and made it a familiar sound on the commercial marts of the eastern and western hemispheres.

JOHN MURRAY.

JOHN MURRAY was of Scotch parentage, born in the town of Swatara, Pennsylvania, in 1737. Early in life he came to New York City and entered the counting-house, or store, as the merchants of that day modestly designated their places of business, of an older brother, ROBERT, with whom he was at a later period associated in partnership, under the name of ROBERT & JOHN MURRAY. The house was later continued under the styles of JOHN MURRAY, JOHN MURRAY & SON and JOHN MURRAY & SONS.

He was a man of quiet and unobtrusive manners, and plain, simple habits, particularly averse to display of any kind; as a citizen, among the foremost in the support of all the religious and philanthropic institutions of the day;

3

in his religious belief a Presbyterian, and for many years
an elder in Dr. Rodgers' church.

As a business man he was comprehensive in his views,
of strict integrity and successful.

He took no prominent part in public affairs, and is not
known ever to have held any office. In his political
opinions he was a Federalist, and among his most intimate
friends were RUFUS KING and ALEXANDER HAMILTON.

During the later years of his life Mr. MURRAY was much
engaged in acting as referee and arbitrator in cases of mercantile differences, and an appeal was rarely taken from
his decisions.

Mr. MURRAY was admitted to the Chamber on the 3d of
August, 1779. In 1788 he was elected Vice-President of
the Institution, and in 1798 advanced to the office of President, which he held continually until 1806.

Mr. MURRAY died at his country seat on New-York
Island, then three miles from the City, now that part of it
known as "Murray Hill," on the 17th of October, 1808,
aged 71.

ROBERT LENOX.

THE mercantile career of ROBERT LENOX is best summed
up in the words of a resolution adopted by the Chamber
of Commerce at his death, which occurred on December
13th, 1839, at the ripe age of 80 years. In that tribute
he was declared to be "an eminent merchant who, for
a period beyond the ordinary course of human life, had
been distinguished for great prudence, a clear and sound
judgment, and unblemished reputation." Mr. LENOX
was born in the town of Kirkcudbright, Scotland, in December, 1759, but came to this country when very young.
After attending school for a brief period at Burlington,
New-Jersey, he accepted a position in the office of an
uncle, with whom he remained until the close of the war
of the Revolution. After his marriage, in 1783, he re-

visited the scenes of his birth and childhood, and in 1781 returned to New-York, where he at once commenced business in a moderate way, conducting it with that skill and prudence which characterized him throughout life. Dr. CHARLES KING, historian of the Chamber, says of him, " that he was one of the most extensive, as well as successful merchants in the United States, and such was his prudence and sagacity that it is believed there was not a year during the whole period of his actual mercantile life in which he did not find his property greater at the close than it had been at the commencement." This estimate of Mr. LENOX's character and ability is undoubtedly a just one, and, in view of the danger at that time to American commerce, occasioned by the depredations of maritime belligerents, Mr. LENOX seems to have escaped those reverses which befell other merchants of that day. He became a member of the Chamber of Commerce on March 7th, 1786, and was rarely absent from his seat at the regular meetings. The records show that he was one of the most active members after the revival of the Chamber in 1817, and his name is found on several Committees, charged with the consideration of important questions. It is peculiarly interesting to record the fact, that the Chamber of Commerce was then interesting itself in the promulgation of the principles of free trade. A protective tariff was considered by many of the members as a "delusion and a snare." Mr. LENOX seems to have been impressed with free trade doctrines, for he appears as one of the delegates of the Chamber to the celebrated free trade convention held at Philadelphia in the fall of 1820, of which WILLIAM BAYARD, then President of the Chamber, was President. In January, 1824, Mr. LENOX was appointed Chairman of the Committee of Correspondence, organized to oppose the increase of the tariff, which was then threatened. The interest shown by Mr. LENOX, in matters affecting the mercantile prosperity of New-York, prompted the members of the Chamber, in 1819, to elect him Vice-President, which office he filled until the fall of 1826, when, upon President BAYARD's death, he was unanimously elected to fill the vacancy. He continued to hold the office of President until he died, in 1839. In this brief sketch it is impossible to enumerate all the important questions of public interest which the Chamber discussed, and took action upon, during Mr. LENOX's official term. It earnestly sought to influence Congressional action in favor of free trade, and Mr. LENOX was, undoubtedly, an uncompromising free-trader in its widest sense, and lost no opportunity of impressing his views upon his colleagues. By virtue of his office as President of the Chamber, Mr. LENOX was a trustee of the Sailors' Snug Harbor and Chairman of the Board, and helped carry out many practical reforms in that noble institution. Permission was given to change the site of the hospital, the Staten Island property being purchased for that purpose ; part of the building was erected, and the humane work of caring for old sailors began : and, in fact, the Sailors' Snug Harbor commenced to assume proportions which, since then, have become consolidated into one of the most beneficent organizations of the world—a noble monument to its founder, Capt. ROBERT RICHARD RANDALL.

ISAAC CAROW.

ISAAC CAROW belonged to an old Huguenot family that settled in New-York about 1655. He was born at St. Croix, in the West Indies, March 29th, 1778, his father, ISAAC CAROW, being a merchant in the West Indian trade. His mother's name was ANN COOPER. ISAAC CAROW, the subject of this sketch, moved to New-York in 1793, and married ELIZA MOWATT, his cousin, June 30th, 1803, by whom he had eight children. He was deeply interested in public affairs, and devoted considerable time and money to charitable purposes. He was Warden of St. Mark's Episcopal Church, a Governor of New-York Hospital, a prominent member of the Bible Society and a warm promoter of the Society Library. He visited Europe in 1815, and again in

1827. During the latter visit he was the guest of LAFAY-LETTE, in France.

His upright character and standing as a merchant led the members of the Chamber of Commerce to elect him their presiding officer, and Mr. CAROW served in that capacity from 1840 to 1842. Dr. CHARLES KING, the historian of the Chamber, says: "Of Mr. CAROW, who has since paid the debt of nature, we have not succeeded in obtaining any details that might aid our own recollection of him as an old acquaintance—a fellow passenger under trying circumstances on a voyage to Europe towards the close of the war of 1812 and as a man of mark upon 'Change, though of the greatest modesty and simplicity, Mr. CAROW was of a very retiring disposition and habits—yet of very clear perceptions and decided convictions—amiable and gentle, though with a short, quick manner occasionally, that might be taken for impatience, but for the kind smile which so usually accompanied it. He was diligent, cautious and exact in business, and therefore successful, and at his death left behind him no enemies and a spotless name."

Mr. CAROW died in this City September 3d, 1850. The firm of which he was the head, and the one succeeding it bearing the CAROW name, are now extinct.

JAMES GORE KING.

JAMES GORE KING was the third son of RUFUS KING and MARY ALSOP, his wife. He was born in the City of New-York, on the 8th of May, 1791, at the residence of his grandfather, JOHN ALSOP, No. 38 Smith-street, afterwards known as 62 William-street.

He entered Harvard University, Cambridge, Mass., in 1805, and graduated from it with honor in 1810.

In the summer of 1814, when a very large militia force was called out by the General Government and stationed in this City, JAMES GORE KING was selected as his Assistant Adjutant-General by Major-General EBENEZER

STEVENS, who commanded in chief the whole militia contingent, in subordination to the general officer of the United States Army, to whom was assigned the command of the military district, and especially the defence of the City of New-York. The troops were disbanded at the commencement of the winter of 1814-15, and with the peace which was concluded at Ghent in December, 1814, closed his military service.

In the year 1815 he established, under the firm of JAMES G. KING & Co., a commission house in this City. In the year 1818, however, upon the recommendation of his father-in-law, Mr. GRACIE, he broke up his business in this City, and went to Liverpool, and there, with his brother-in-law, ARCHIBALD GRACIE, established the house of KING & GRACIE.

During a residence of nearly six years in this chief of English seaports, with a large business, and encountering heavy responsibilities, Mr. KING so skillfully steered his bark, that in despite of the wide-spread calamities which, both in England and America, marked the years 1822, 1823 and 1824, he maintained his own high character, fulfilled all the responsibilities of his house, and on leaving England, in 1824, in compliance with advantageous arrangements made for his future residence in New-York, left behind him an enviable name and reputation for urbanity, intelligence, promptness and integrity. He made many fast and valuable friends while abroad, and retained their good will and confidence unabated to the day of his death.

While in Liverpool he was brought into relations of business and much personal intimacy with the late JOHN JACOB ASTOR, who was on a brief visit to Europe; and such was the impression made upon that sagacious observer and almost unerring judge of character, by the business tact and promptness of Mr. KING, and his general character, that, upon his return to the United States, Mr. ASTOR invited him to come to New-York, and take the chief direction of the American Fur Company, with a very liberal salary. This offer Mr. KING declined, but Mr. ASTOR continued his fast friend always, and had another occasion of proving his friendship about the close of 1823. Consulted by Mr. PRIME, then at the head of the house of PRIME, WARD, SANDS & Co., as to his knowledge of some fitting person upon whom Mr. PRIME might safely devolve a portion of the business of his house, Mr. ASTOR at once suggested the name of JAMES G. KING, and accompanied it with such eulogies as to determine Mr. PRIME, who it seems, from some business intercourse between their houses, had himself thought of Mr. KING, to invite him to become a partner in his house.

This proposal Mr. KING accepted, and came back to New-York, and on the 1st of May, 1824, became a partner of the house of PRIME, WARD, SANDS, KING & Co., which then consisted of NATHANIEL PRIME, SAMUEL WARD, JOSEPH SANDS, JAMES GORE KING and ROBERT RAY.

In 1826 the death of Mr. SANDS caused a dissolution of the firm, which was reconstituted under the name of PRIME, WARD, KING & Co., consisting of all the surviving partners of the firm, with the addition of EDWARD PRIME, eldest son of the senior partner.

In 1831 he became warmly interested in the success of the great undertaking the New-York and Erie Railroad—then all but hopeless, so great was the indifference of the public to its claims, and so general the distrust of its feasibility.

After considering the subject well, and satisfying himself both of the practicability and the advantages of such a road, in 1835 he consented to accept the Presidency of the Company—declining, however, to receive any salary. A new subscription was started, with gratifying success. Mr. KING, in the summer of that year, visited and inspected the whole line of the road, new surveys were made, and a considerable portion of the road along the Delaware was put under contract, and in the following year, 1833, the Legislature of the State, moved thereto in no slight degree by the high character of Mr. KING, under whose management it was felt that whatever aid might be appropriated by the State would be faithfully applied, granted to the Company

the credit of the State to the amount of three millions of
dollars.

In 1837 failures of largely extended houses, commencing
at New-Orleans, spread throughout the land. New-York
had its full proportion. In London, too, several houses,
chiefly connected with the commerce of the United States,
were brought to a stand. The Bank of England set its
face against a further extension of credit, and this policy
re-acted with great intensity in New-York.

The seasons, too, had been unfavorable to agriculture,
and, for the first time in our history as a nation, even
wheat was imported from abroad for our own consumption.
Nearly a million and a half bushels of wheat were brought
from Europe into New-York in the course of the spring of
1837. In that year the banks of the City of New-York, after
a long and honest struggle, came to the conclusion that a suspension of specie payments was unavoidable, and, indeed,
indispensable, in order to avert the necessity of further
sacrifice of property by the struggling merchants in the
effort to meet their engagements.

Accordingly, after deliberate consultation among the
officers and directors of the banks, on Wednesday, 10th of
May, the following notice was issued :

"NOTICE TO THE PUBLIC IN RELATION TO THE BANKS.

"At a meeting last evening of all the banks in this City,
" except three, it was

" *Resolved*, That under existing circumstances, it is ex-
" pedient and necessary to suspend payments in specie.

" In the mean time, the notes of all the banks will be
" received at the different banks as usual in payment of
" debts and on deposit ; and as the indebtedness of the
" community to the banks exceeds three times the amount
" of their liabilities to the public, it is hoped and expected
" that the notes of the different banks will pass current as
" usual, and that the state of the times will soon be such as
" to render the resumption of specie payments practicable."

The merchants and traders of the City met the same day at the Exchange, in pursuance of a call numerously signed by leading men of all parties and pursuits; James G. King presented himself, and after reading the call, enforced its objects with great power and effect. He concluded by moving the following resolutions, which were seconded by Nathaniel Prime, and adopted:

" *Resolved*," (after reciting the resolution of the banks just given,) "That relying upon the above statement, we have full confidence in the ultimate ability of the banks of this City to redeem all their bills and notes, and that we will, ourselves, continue to receive, and we recommend all our fellow citizens to receive them as heretofore.

"That in an emergency like the present, it is alike the dictate of patriotism and self-interest to abstain from all measures tending to aggravate existing evils, and by mutual forbearance and mutual aid to mitigate as far as practicable the existing difficulties, and thus most essentially to assist in the restoration of specie payments."

These resolutions were put separately, and each was unanimously adopted. The sanction thus given by all the leading men of business produced an instantaneous effect; a sense of relief was felt, as if a heavy pressure were removed. Stocks and other securities rose in price, and business became more active.

It is a coincidence which at the time was gratifying to Mr. King, and in the retrospect is now not less gratifying to his family, that on occasion of suspending specie payments by the banks in 1812–13, during the war with England, Rufus King was called from his retirement on Long Island to urge the same views as those presented by his son in 1837, and that in each case the speaker carried his hearers and the country with him.

Throughout the summer of 1837, Mr. King, with others of like views, was earnest in preparing measures for the speediest possible return to specie payments.

When in London, whither he went in October of that year,

he undertook to show to the leading capitalists and to the Bank of England, that in their own interest, if from no other view, they should aid the Americans struggling to extricate themselves from embarrassments and to return to specie payments.

In conformity with these opinions of Mr. KING, the Bank of England resolved to confide to his house the consignment of one million pounds sterling in gold, upon the responsibility of his house and the guaranty of BARING, BROTHERS & Co.

The first shipment of eighty thousand sovereigns was made by the bank the next day, per packet ship "Gladiator," and Mr. KING himself soon followed, with a much larger sum. The solicitude of Mr. KING to hasten resumption by the banks of New-York and throughout the United States, which has been already dwelt upon, lay at the bottom of this great operation, and he was naturally and reasonably elated at his success.

The anticipation of Mr. KING, that with the aid this opportunity fortunately brought to them, the banks of New-York would resume and maintain specie payment, was abundantly realized.

As the coin from the Bank of England arrived, it was disposed of on easy terms to the banks here and in Boston— a large sum offered to the Bank of the United States of Pennsylvania was at first declined, but afterwards availed of—and thus the City of New-York, which had seen itself compelled to lead the way in suspension, had the great honor and satisfaction to lead the way itself in resumption, and to smooth the way for others.

The signal confidence reposed by the Bank of England in the house of PRIME, WARD & KING, in this important transaction, was fully justified by the event, as were the sagacious provisions of Mr. KING, as to the good results to be effected by such a use of the bank's treasure.

It is satisfactory to be able to add, that a concern of so large import, entered into not without high motives on the part of the Bank of England, and conducted with equal skill and fidelity by the New-York house, was wound up without loss and with great promptness.

In the autumn of the year 1839 SAMUEL WARD died, but the partnership, according to its tenor, was continued, the eldest son of Mr. WARD, and the son-in-law of Mr. KING, DENNING DUER, having been admitted as partners in the previous month of May.

In 1844, A. GRACIE KING, son of JAMES G. KING, became a partner, and the house then consisted of JAMES G. KING, EDWARD PRIME, SAMUEL WARD, DENNING DUER and A. GRACIE KING. A diversity of views as to the proper scope and business of the house led, in 1847, to its dissolution. JAMES G. KING, with his son-in-law and son, continuing business under the firm name of JAMES G. KING & SONS, in which firm his eldest son, Judge JAMES G. KING, subsequently became a partner.

Mr. KING was elected a member of the Chamber of Commerce April 15, 1817. In 1841 he was chosen first Vice-President, and annually re-chosen for four years, when, in 1845, he became President, and served in that station three years.

He took his seat in the House of Representatives, at Washington, as a member of the 31st Congress, on Monday, December 4th, 1849.

On a bill for the collection of the revenue, his efficiency and his practical ability were specially manifested. The House had talked over and cavilled at and delayed a joint resolution from the Senate, authorizing the requisite expenditure for defraying the cost of collecting duties at the Custom House. The matter was urgent, for there was no appropriation, and no money, therefore, available for such uses. In consequence, the business of the Custom House was seriously embarrassed : every other desk almost was vacant, for lack of means to pay for services, and ships arriving with full cargoes were unable to discharge, because there were not officers to attend. Mr. KING, feeling the great wrong and the great suffering arising from delay, applied himself strenuously to the subject, digested the various amounts needed under specific heads, so as to

meet objections on that score, and then moved an amendment to the resolution from the Senate, in which, after
appropriating the respective sums needed for the half
year, he employed this phraseology: "and in that pro-
" portion for any shorter or longer time, *until Congress*
" *shall act upon the subject.*" The passage here marked
in italics fixes permanently, and without any fresh appropriation, the expenditure for the collection of revenues
until Congress shall otherwise order—a very important
point, since it obviates the recurrence of any like embarrassment to that the resolution was designed to cure. This
resolution was finally adopted by a considerable majority,
and became and it is now the law of the land.

His death was very sudden, and in this particular not
unanticipated by him.

On Monday, the 3d of October, 1853, he had been as well
as usual, and retired at his accustomed hour. He was suddenly attacked, and before the physician could reach the
house, or the family even be assembled, with perfect consciousness and perfect resignation, without a struggle and
almost without a sigh, he breathed out his life in less
than half an hour from the first attack of the paroxysm.

James G. King was simple in his tastes and habits, unostentatious, self-denying, considerate of others, actively
benevolent, exact yet liberal in business, cheerful and in-
structive as a companion, sought after and prized in society,
but loving home with a fondness which years rather added
to than weakened.

life a noble type of true manhood. He was one of that class who believed in honesty, not simply because it was the best policy, but because it was right to be honest. He was one of New-England's best sons. Born at New-Bedford, on March 3d, 1803, his childhood was spent among seafaring men, and at an early age he evinced a strong desire to brave the tempest, and obtain a share in what was then a profitable maritime business.

Before he was twenty years old he went from New-Bedford as supercargo to Rio de Janeiro, sold the goods there at a profit, then obtained a cargo of coffee and sailed to Trieste, at which place he sold the coffee. Here he left his ship, and, after making a commercial tour through England, returned to this country. His perceptive faculties were ever on the alert, and as he had an abiding faith in the magnificent future of America, he set about using his talents to open up and develop business intercourse with foreign lands. Naturally, his face was turned towards New-York, where there was a wider scope for his abilities and usefulness. Here he soon became known for his keen sagacity, boundless energy and unswerving integrity. He was regarded everywhere as a vigilant, enterprising and honorable merchant, and when he became a partner in a leading shipping firm, subsequently famous as the house of GRINNELL, MINTURN & Co., he and his partner soon made the firm known all over the world. Its name was a synonym for financial strength. It had two great lines of packets running from New-York; one to London and the other to Liverpool. Almost every port in the civilized globe knew the firm's vessels, all of which were of the finest construction. An authority states that the house of GRINNELL, MINTURN & Co. built more ships than any other American firm during the period when our maritime interests flourished. Mr. GRINNELL was always active in his efforts to obtain adequate internal improvements, to the end that our lakes and rivers could be utilized to the nation's benefit. As a citizen he was public spirited, and took a lively interest in all matters affecting the general welfare of the State and nation. On one or two occasions he accepted public office. In 1838 he was elected by the Whigs a member of Congress from New-York City, and it was believed by many that in 1856 he might have been elected Governor of this State, but for his refusal to accept the nomination. In that year, however, he was chosen one of the Presidential Electors at Large on the Republican ticket. In 1869 President GRANT appointed him Collector of the Port of New-York, and subsequently Naval Officer. Those who remember Mr. GRINNELL in his official capacity will recall his courteous manner and the creditable way in which he administered his important duties. His patient, painstaking industry led him to thoroughly consider the various tariff problems that came before him, and his decisions were characterized by a spirit of fairness and impartiality that won him the respect of the merchants. In other positions Mr. GRINNELL was equally appreciated. He was at one time President of the Union Club, and of the New-England Society. In 1850 DANIEL WEBSTER, his intimate friend, made one of his grandest speeches at the Annual Dinner of the New-England Society, at which Mr. GRINNELL presided. Nor did the multifarious duties of Mr. GRINNELL prevent him from taking an active part in charitable affairs. Public institutions found in him a liberal giver. For many years he was one of the Commissioners of Charities and Correction, and gave much of his valuable time to that office. His purse was ever open to the poor and needy, and his reputation for sterling integrity and practical charity led to his frequent selection as guardian and trustee of funds and estates: and banks, insurance companies and similar institutions elected him in some cases president, and in others, director.

Mr. GRINNELL was one of the oldest members of the Chamber of Commerce, and was held in high esteem by its members. He was elected on February 3d, 1829, and retained his membership up to the time of his death. As a tribute to his high standing and his practical knowledge of questions which the Chamber was so often called upon to consider, Mr. GRINNELL was elected its President in

1847, serving one year, and was again chosen for that office in 1849, retiring in 1852.

This beautiful tribute was paid by its members to his memory : " Devoid of envy and hatred, and never a bigoted partisan, he respected the convictions of those with whom he felt constrained to differ. His conscientious devotion to duty, truth and justice, his sterling integrity and freedom from selfishness, his open and manly bearing, his tender and comprehensive benevolence, his liberal and constant support of the institutions of learning and religion, shed a daily beauty over his life and diffuse a delightful fragrance around his memory. But though filling various stations of responsibility and influence in the course of an unusually protracted career, and distinguished in all of them for foresight, probity, zeal and vigor, Mr. GRINNELL will probably be the longest remembered by his fellow-citizens for the skill, munificence and enthusiasm with which he fostered the growth in this country of that 'militia of the seas'- the mercantile marine—whereon a great maritime nation must largely depend for prosperity in peace and safety in war."

This useful life was brought to a close in this City on November 24, 1877, Mr. GRINNELL being then in his 75th year.

ELIAS HICKS.

ELIAS HICKS, son of VALENTINE and ABIGAIL HICKS, and grandson of ELIAS HICKS, the founder of the religious Society of Friends, which still bears his name, was born at Jericho, Long Island, on the 12th of June, (sixth month,) 1815.

The early education of Mr. HICKS was acquired in the country, where he remained until his sixteenth year, when he was sent to New-York, and entered the office of the celebrated house of SAMUEL HICKS, then heavily interested in shipping.

From this he passed into the house of his father-in-law, ROBERT HICKS, and transacted a ship-chandlery business, under the title of ROBERT HICKS & SONS ; at a later period he formed a partnership with Mr. WILLIAM T. FROST, and conducted a large shipping business at 68 South-street, under the firm of FROST & HICKS. He soon distinguished himself by the energy of his character and his strong mercantile powers, and in May, 1852, at the early age of 32 years, was chosen President of the Chamber of Commerce, an honor sought for and prized for nearly a century by the most honored merchants of this commercial city.

Here, on the threshold of wide commercial influence, his health began to fail. His physical strength, for which he had been distinguished in early youth, rapidly deserted him, and he sank quickly under the insidious attacks of consumption. He died on the 9th January (first month) of the succeeding year, 1853, and his remains were carried to the country home of his ancestors and there buried.

PELATIAH PERIT.

PELATIAH PERIT was President of the Chamber of Commerce during a period of ten years, from 1853 to 1863, and took an active interest in all the discussions of that body, especially those which related to the financial policy of the United States at the beginning of the recent war.

The characteristics which Mr. PERIT exhibited throughout his long life illustrate the influences of heredity. He was the son of JOHN PERIT, merchant, and the descendant of one of the earliest ministers of the French Huguenot Church in New-York. His mother was a daughter of PELATIAH WEBSTER, a graduate of Yale College in the year 1746, and a merchant in Philadelphia during the latter part of the last century. As early as 1776 Mr. WEBSTER printed an essay on the Evils of an Inflated Currency, and from that time on, during the organization of the independent government of this country, his counsels were frequently given to the public upon commercial and financial questions. WEBSTER'S "Political Essays" were reprinted in 1791, and have since been consulted by the principal writers upon the history of American finance.

PELATIAH PERIT was born in Norwich, Conn., June 23, 1785. At the age of thirteen years he entered Yale College, where he graduated in 1802. His elder brother, JOHN WEBSTER PERIT, (afterward a China merchant in Philadelphia,) preceded him in college by a single year. He came under strong religious influences while he was a student, and at the close of his course expected to study for the Christian ministry, but the purpose was given up because of the partial failure of his health. In his nineteenth year he became a clerk in an importer's house at Philadelphia, in the interests of which he made several voyages to the West Indies and South America. The writer of this sketch has heard him describe the pleasure which he had in escorting ALEXANDER VON HUMBOLDT about the City of Philadelphia, on the explorer's arrival from Mexico, when he came introduced to the house where young PERIT was engaged.

In 1809 he removed to New-York, and formed, with a kinsman, the firm of PERIT & LATHROP, but the partnership did not last long, and Mr. PERIT entered the house of GOODHUE & Co., with which he remained connected until his retirement from business. The reputation of this firm is well known. They were engaged in shipping and commercial transactions with merchants in widely distant countries, and were the confidential correspondents of Messrs. BARING BROTHERS & Co., of London, Messrs. WILLIAM ROPES & Co., of St. Petersburg, and many other houses of distinction. The name of Mr. PERIT never appeared in the title of the firm, but his connection with it was well known, and the part which he had in conducting its wide correspondence kept him interested in the commercial progress of every country, and led to the maintenance of a wide personal acquaintance in different parts of the globe. His business life developed another element of his character—interest in religious and philanthropic enterprises, and particularly in everything

4

which pertained to the advancement of Christian missions and the welfare of seamen. A mere enumeration of the unpaid positions to which he was called, and to which he devoted a great deal of time, would show how varied and how consistent were his labors for the good of his fellow-men. At different times he was President of the American Seamen's Friend Society, a trustee of the Sailors' Snug Harbor, and President of the Seamen's Bank for Savings. He was a director, likewise, of many of the missionary and benevolent societies to which the Presbyterian Church, the church of his life-long preference, gave its support. For forty years he was an officer of the American Bible Society, either as Manager or Vice-President.

He held but one political office. In 1857, when the peace of the City was seriously endangered by a contest between the " Municipal " and the " Metropolitan " police, he was appointed a member of the Board of Police Commissioners, where his fairness and good sense were serviceable in the restoration of order. After this end was secured he gave up the office.

In all the manifestations of his character, social, mercantile, religious and political, he was conservative. He was never led away by radical enthusiasm. Dr. LEONARD BACON, (whose commemorative discourse is printed in *Hunt's Merchants' Magazine*, for April, 1864,) truly said of him, that " rash and one-sided schemes of reformation were ever offensive to his judgment. Perhaps he was more charmed with the idea of defending and of perpetuating and perfecting the good which has descended to us from foregoing ages, than with the idea of finding out what there is in existing institutions that needs to be reformed. Yet his sagacity, his good sense, his intelligent patriotism and his love of justice, guarded him against the error of those self-styled conservative men, who sacrifice the reality to the name, and become destructives for the sake of a false and foolish consistency. Not long before the last Presidential election there was a time when the immediate danger to the country seemed to be that the votes in the Electoral College might be so divided among four candidates as to throw the election into the House of Representatives, which would prolong the agitation from November to February, and would give to desperate men an opportunity for desperate measures. Mr. PERIT had never been an active politician. But deeply impressed with what seemed to be the most imminent peril of the country, he did not hesitate to commit himself publicly and unequivocally on the question of the hour, and as a conservative man to urge on conservative men the duty of terminating the agitation by giving their votes and their influence for the only candidate in whose behalf there was a possibility of obtaining a majority in the Electoral Colleges. So afterwards, when the long-meditated treason had become overt rebellion, and when the question was whether the national Government, without any considerable military force, with its Navy carefully disposed in the remotest seas, with its Treasury purposely empty, and its credit at a discount, could make any resistance, he was among the leaders in that movement of merchants and capitalists which brought forth millions of treasure to restore and confirm the credit of the country."

The influence of the Chamber of Commerce was very marked during the time of his continuous presidency, and especially in the early years of the Civil War. Mr. PERIT was constantly at his post as President of the Chamber, and was not infrequently called upon to lend the influence of his name and character to meetings of a more public character. Two social events which occurred during his official term were very noteworthy, and gave him pleasant recollections, the reception of the Prince of Wales (then travelling as Baron RENFREW) and the reception of the first Japanese Embassy.

A few years before his death, Mr. PERIT began to throw off gradually the cares of business and station. He sold the property at Bloomingdale, (just north of the grounds of the New-York Orphan Asylum,) where for many years he had resided, and built a house in New-Haven, Conn. That place continued to be his home until his death, which occurred, after a brief illness, March 8, 1864, in his seventy-ninth year.

When he gave up active pursuits, Mr. PERIT determined to devote his leisure to the preparation of a history of American commerce, and he began to collect and arrange the papers requisite for such a work. He solicited from his correspondents their suggestions ; he was encouraged to proceed in his plan by a formal resolution of the Chamber; he wrote many pages ; but death came before he had made sufficient progress to justify the publication of the chapters he had prepared.

Mr. PERIT was twice married, first to Miss LATHROP, and after her death, to Miss MARIA COIT, both of Norwich, Conn. He had no children. His widow survived him many years. She was the daughter of DANIEL L. COIT, of Norwich, who for a short time, in the early part of the century, was a merchant in New-York, of the firm of HOWLAND & COIT.

Mr. PERIT was nearly six feet in height and well proportioned. His manners were reserved and dignified, and gave him a commanding presence in the public meetings where he was accustomed to preside. His addresses on such occasions were brief and pointed, showing, in the conciseness of their language, the influence of his business habits ; showing, also, in their clearness and propriety of expression, the influence of the liberal education that he had received in early life. He was a constant reader of the reviews, and, to some extent, of historical and theological writings, but he is chiefly to be remembered as a man of affairs, whose mind was inspired by an intelligent and systematic interest in the progress of mankind. He was a patriot who desired that the name and influence of his country should everywhere support the best ideas in religion, in morals, in politics, in diplomacy and in finance. The Calvinism of his Huguenot ancestry, and the financial scholarship of his grandfather were apparent throughout his long career.—DANIEL C. GILMAN, LL. D.

WILLIAM E. DODGE.

WILLIAM EARL DODGE was born in Hartford, Conn., September 4th, 1805. He sprang from Puritan English stock,—his American ancestor, WILLIAM DODGE, landing at Salem, Mass., in 1629. His father, DAVID LOW DODGE, was, at one time, a large importer and jobber in New York, and took a prominent position in religious and charitable societies. His mother was a daughter of Rev. AARON CLEAVELAND, of English and Scotch descent. While still quite young he entered a wholesale dry goods store in this City, and later became a clerk for his father, who built near Norwich, Conn., one of the earliest cotton factories in the country. When eighteen, he began to visit New-York regularly to make purchases for this establishment. In 1825 he became a permanent resident here, and, until his death, February 9th, 1883, was increasingly identified with the mercantile, benevolent and religious interests of the metropolis. In 1828 he married a daughter of ANSON G. PHELPS, a leading importer of metals, and, after five years, gave up his successful business in dry goods and joined his father-in-law in founding the firm of PHELPS, DODGE & Co., now one of the oldest houses in the United States.

Mr. Dodge was also extensively engaged in the lumber trade in Pennsylvania, Michigan, Georgia, Texas and Canada. He was active in creating the iron industries of Scranton, Pa., and the brass and copper factories at Ansonia, Conn. In the early history of the Erie Railroad he became a director, and remained on the Board until the road was completed. He was one of the originators of the Central Railroad of New-Jersey and of the Delaware, Lackawanna and Western System, and also of railroads in Texas. He was among the first to encourage the construction of elevated railways, and he was a subscriber to the original Atlantic Cable Company.

He served upon the Boards of some of the principal commercial and financial institutions of the City, among them the Mutual Life Insurance Company, the United States Trust Company, and the Western Union Telegraph Company. For many years he was an officer of the Mercantile Library Association, and he joined the Union League Club soon after its organization.

In 1855 he became a member of the Chamber of Commerce, and always took an active share in its proceedings. He had a profound regard for its influential and honorable position, and for its long career of usefulness. He was elected President in 1867, and retained the office eight consecutive years. In the patriotic and vigorous efforts of the Chamber to sustain the Government during the war for the preservation of the Union, Mr. DODGE had a prominent part. Always conservative and conciliatory towards opponents, and alive to the demands of commerce and of humanity, he exerted his influence to avert hostilities." One of the last services of this character was to go as delegate to the " Peace Congress," which had been called to devise, if possible, some solution that might be acceptable to both North and South. When this, with every other proposal for just concession, failed, he henceforth advocated the suppression of rebellion at any cost.

Mr. DODGE was nominated in 1864 to represent the Eighth Congressional District, and, after a contested election of unusual length, secured his seat in the 39th Congress in time to share in the memorable deliberation relative to the reconstruction of the Southern States. In these measures he did not always vote with his party. While demanding the ratification of the constitutional amendments, he held to the wisdom of discontinuing military domination, and of admitting to office those qualified by intelligence, position and honest evidences of loyalty. At the same time he believed it best for the lately emancipated slaves not to be immediately enfranchised ; and, on the other hand, that they should not count in the basis of representation so long as they were deprived of the right of suffrage. In Congress, as elsewhere, Mr. DODGE opposed inflation of the currency, and advocated the necessity and advantages of a wise protective tariff in accordance with the "American system." He was urged to accept a renomination, but felt obliged to decline.

In the cause of temperance Mr. DODGE was recognized as a foremost leader. From early manhood he was engaged in persistent and judicious efforts to abolish the use of intoxicating liquors. During the last eighteen years of his life he was President of the National Temperance and Publication House. He stood a firm friend of the Indians, and in 1869 accepted an appointment to act as one of the Commissioners to carry into effect the "peace policy" inaugurated by President GRANT to reform the corrupt administration of Indian affairs, and to provide practical measures to civilize, educate and Christianize the long deceived and oppressed tribes. In the discharge of these duties he made an extended tour through the Indian Territory.

Mr. DODGE also labored unremittingly for the elevation of the colored people. He maintained that Christian education was indispensable in preparing the millions of freedmen for citizenship, and he therefore gave largely to institutions established for their benefit, especially to Lincoln University. He also left an educational fund to be used chiefly in raising up colored teachers and preachers.

His gifts to other institutions of learning in different parts of the country were constant and liberal, but his convictions of the immediate religious wants, particularly of the West, led him, for a series of years, to select and support personally a number of young men in theological seminaries.

What he attempted to do for institutions, churches, and almost every form of Christian effort in his own country, he desired to promote also in other lands. He was, for several years, a member of the Board of Foreign Missions of the Presbyterian Church, and for nearly twenty years the Vice-President of the American Board of Commissioners for Foreign Missions. Although, as a member and elder in the Presbyterian Church, he cherished an intelligent preference for his own denomination, he loved to co-operate with organizations of a national and unsectarian character. He was a manager of the American Bible Society, the American Tract Society and the American Sunday School Union, and President of the American Branch of the Evangelical Alliance. He took a warm interest in Young Men's Christian Associations and in undenominational City missions. He often presented in public the claims of these various societies, and his presence on any platform, whether religious or secular, was always welcome. He was a ready speaker, presenting clear, practical, timely and forcible views, in an animated manner, and with a distinct, ringing voice.

In personal appearance he was somewhat above medium height, with a lithe, vigorous frame, a brisk, erect carriage, a bright black eye, and a face full of geniality and benevolence. His bearing was frank, kindly, and without pretence. Wherever he went friends were quickly won, and those who knew him best saw most of his sincere, unselfish, attractive qualities.

He traveled widely, for business or pleasure, over all parts of the United States, and several times crossed the Atlantic. He was still incessantly engaged in a scarcely diminished variety of labors when, from heart disease, he died, almost instantaneously, in his own home, at the age of seventy-eight.

A bronze statue of Mr. DODGE was erected at a prominent point near the junction of Broadway and Sixth Avenue. Previous monuments in the City were intended to commemorate the services of military heroes or eminent statesmen. In an address at the dedication, the Hon. ABRAM S. HEWITT called attention to the fact, that this was erected "to perpetuate the memory of one whose chief claim to distinction lies in a noble character, a useful life, and, above all, in the employment of his means as a trust fund for the good of his fellow-men."

Mr. SAMUEL D. BABCOCK, Ex-President of the Chamber of Commerce, presented the statue to the City, in behalf of the Committee, expressing the hope that "it would be preserved as a perpetual reminder of an upright and influential merchant, a useful and loyal citizen, a zealous

GEORGE W. LANE.

GEORGE WILLIAM LANE, President of the Chamber of Commerce at the time of his death, was, for almost all his life, a resident of New-York. He was born near Red Mills, in the neighborhood of Lake Mahopac, Putnam County, New York, January 8, 1818, and on the borders of that lake he maintained, during the latter part of his life, a summer home. While still a boy he came to New-York, and began that career in Front-street which he followed until his death. He became one of the most conspicuous representatives of the mercantile business in which he was engaged. He died at his home in New-York City, December 30, 1883, when he had almost completed his sixty-sixth year.

For thirty years he was a member of the Chamber of Commerce. He was elected Vice-President of that body May 6, 1875, and President May 4, 1882. Among the financial institutions with which he was then connected, and to which he had devoted much attention during the later years of his life, may be mentioned the Fulton National Bank, the Merchants' National Bank, the Seamen's Bank for Savings, the Continental [Fire] Insurance Company, the Atlantic Mutual [Marine] Insurance Company, and also the Central Trust Company, of which he was one of the original incorporators.

In religious and philanthropic work he was also prominently active. He was one of the members of the Madison Square Presbyterian Church when it was organized under the pastoral care of the late Rev. Dr. WILLIAM ADAMS, and he continued to be an elder of that church and a tru to until his death. He was a member of the Board of Home Missions of the Presbyterian Church, a manager of the American Bible Society, President for fifteen years of the Port Society, Trustee for five years of the Union Theological Seminary, and President of the Managers of the Presbyterian Hospital.

He was also interested in the promotion of good government, and especially in efforts to secure an honest administration of the City of New-York. He worked efficiently in the Committee of Seventy, by which a fraudulent system of municipal affairs was exposed and frustrated. At the urgent request of his friend, Mayor HAVEMEYER, he accepted the office of Chamberlain of the City, and continued in it from May, 1873, to February, 1875. With great reluctance, in the summer before his death, he consented to become a member of the Croton Aqueduct Commission, and the arduous responsibilities of this position weighed heavily upon him.

In all these important stations he maintained the confidence of his colleagues and associates, as the numerous tributes testify which were called out by his death. Although his disposition was that of a modest, retiring man, who never wished preferment, his strong convictions, excellent judgment and abundant public spirit were so well known that his counsel was constantly sought. It was freely given to all who asked it. There are few men in any community whose opinions were so trustworthy as Mr. LANE'S, either in public or in private affairs. He had a large measure of that sagacity which sees the end from the beginning, combined with that instinctive sense of justice and righteousness which does not hesitate in forming a purpose, nor swerve from a chosen course because of its unpleasantness or want of popularity.

Soon after the death of Mr. LANE, Rev. Dr. CHARLES H. PARKHURST delivered two commemorative addresses in the Madison Square Presbyterian Church. These addresses were printed with the proceedings of the various associations to which Mr. LANE belonged. These discourses present the characteristics of the man more completely than they can

JONATHAN STURGES.

This and succeeding generations will remember JONA-
THAN STURGES as one of the old school of merchants, whose
probity and honor were as natural to them as their foresight and perseverance. The life of Mr. STURGES was of
that well rounded, symmetrical kind, and was in all that
the phrase implies good and true. It was a life worth
living. It presented the highest sagacity of the merchant
and the noblest virtues of the private citizen. There was
in Mr. STURGES a beautiful blending of modesty and wisdom, of instinctive courtesy and firm principle. What he
did was thorough. Although conducting a large business,
he nevertheless found time to devote to philanthropic and
Christian work. Truly his long life was well spent. It was
a career of principle, which leaves its impress upon a generation, and silently but eloquently bids the man of commerce
bring all his transactions to the bar of conscience. Rich as
Mr. STURGES was in this world's goods, he was richer still
in honor, and at his death he left to his family, in addition
to his earthly fortune, the priceless possession of a good
name.

Mr. STURGES was born in Southport, Conn., March 24th,
1802, entered the service of R. & L. REED, grocers, in Front-
street, in 1821, and became a partner in 1828, when the firm
name was changed to REED & STURGES. Mr. REED died
in 1836; the firm then became STURGES, ROE & BARKER,
and in 1843 STURGES, BENNET & Co., and so remained until
1865, when it was again changed to STURGES, ARNOLD &
Co. Mr. STURGES retired from the firm on January 1st, 1868.
The extensive grocery, coffee and tea business of the house
had been continued at No. 125 Front-street from 1815, when
it was first started by LYMAN REED. Mr. STURGES became
the owner of the property, reconstructed the building and

had his office there. He, with GEORGE GRISWOLD, was one of the chief promoters of the Illinois Central Railroad, and was a director up to the time of his death. He was also a director in the New-York and New-Haven Railway. It is not questioned that he was regarded as the foremost man in the tea and coffee trade, and his counsel, enriched by the experience of half a century, was often sought by the trade. As a friend he was warm and steadfast, and everybody implicitly trusted him.

Mr. STURGES was one of the oldest and most valued members of the Chamber of Commerce, served on several important Special and Standing Committees, and filled the office of Vice-President from 1863 to 1867. In an eloquent tribute to his memory, delivered at a meeting of the Chamber, held December 3d, 1874, Mr. A. A. Low said of him, " He was a recognized patron of art. In the Church he manifested the virtues of the Christian, in society the unostentatious attributes of a gentleman, in the service of his country the devoted zeal of a true patriot, as a citizen the love of the philanthopist, never forgetting his obligations to the poor, the sick and the crippled, but extending to all the benefactions of a warm heart and of an open hand. The homage we pay to the good man when living we desire to perpetuate in hallowed memories, and to this end we inscribe on our minutes the sentiments that are graven on our hearts—of gratitude for this life of uncommon beauty, of sincere sorrow for our own great loss, and of our sympathy for the family of the bereaved." Mr. STURGES deserved this warm tribute, which needs no elaboration here. His honorable career was brought to a close November 28th, 1874, by an attack of pneumonia, the result of a cold caught a few days previously while attending a religious conference in Philadelphia.

through a long line of prosperous farmers, from a Holland family who settled upon Long Island, N. Y., about the year 1650.

After having for two years attended the District School, he assumed charge of it at the age of sixteen. Two years later, in 1823, he adventurously started out into the new West, settling first at Cleveland, Ohio, and there engaged in mercantile pursuits. Later he removed to New Orleans, where he remained five years. In 1829 Mr. OP-DYKE married Miss ELIZABETH HALL STRYKER, of his native place, and in 1832 he entered into business in New-York City as wholesale clothing manufacturer, afterwards as importer of dry goods, and finally as banker. He continued in active business until his death, June 12, 1880, and passed successfully through every financial panic of fifty years. From 1839 to 1853 he made his residence near Newark, N. J., and then removed back to New-York City.

In early life Mr. OPDYKE took an active part in political affairs. Departing from the Whig opinions of his family, he became a Democrat, and a devoted supporter of the Administration of ANDREW JACKSON. He was, however, at all times heartily opposed to the extension of slavery, and in 1848 he aided in the organization of the Free Soil party, and was its candidate for Congress in the Fifth District of New Jersey, but was defeated by WILLIAM WRIGHT, who afterwards was United States Senator from that State.

At the time of the financial panic of 1857, Mr. OPDYKE exerted himself to bring about a concerted movement by the banks of New-York City to restore confidence by enlarging their loans upon securities and credits of undoubted value. He claimed that the financial crisis was largely based upon fear, the general condition of the business of the country being sound, and the only real weakness being among the prematurely extended railways in the West. He showed how the Bank of England had stemmed financial crisis by enlarging credits on good securities, instead of refusing their customers accommodation in times of greatest need. As a result of these efforts, a

Board of Currency was organized, and much valuable investigation made by the leading bankers of the City into economic questions, with a result that still influences the administration of the banks of the country.

In 1858 he was elected a member of the Assembly by the Republican party, and took an active part in advocating all measures for the advancement of the commercial interests of the City and State of New-York.

In 1860 he was a delegate to the National Republican Convention at Chicago, and, with DAVID DUDLEY FIELD and the late HORACE GREELEY, aided largely in effecting the nomination of ABRAHAM LINCOLN, of whose administration he afterwards became an active and efficient adviser.

The first public action taken in New-York City in support of the National Government, upon the outbreak of the Rebellion, was that of the Chamber of Commerce upon the resolutions proposed by Mr. OPDYKE, at its meeting, held April 19th, 1861. This was the beginning of untiring and patriotic labors on his part throughout the war, during which he gave freely of his time, strength and means, in every direction where he found he could in any way aid the nation in its great struggle. In the fall of 1861, Mr. OPDYKE was elected Mayor of the City of New-York, and held that office through the eventful years of 1862 and 1863, being the only Republican Mayor the City of New-York has chosen. His position as the Chief Magistrate placed him at the rallying point for all intelligent and patriotic zeal in the metropolis, and he was especially active in the raising and equipping of troops, and in the forwarding of them to the seat of war. The draft riots in the City occurred during his Mayoralty, and the emergency was met by him with courage and an unwavering determination to restore obedience to law without yielding to the clamor of the mob. He remained at his post of duty, and refused to listen to any measures of compromise, although he was frequently threatened with assassination, his residence twice attacked by the mob, and other of his property destroyed by fire. During the continuance of the riot, the Common Council unanimously

voted $2,500,000, to relieve from actual service all who were
drafted. This ordinance the Mayor promptly vetoed, declaring that rioters should be conquered, not conciliated,
and that the City must actually furnish the men needed to
preserve the nation. After the riot was quelled the Mayor
defeated the scheme of the Common Council, by securing
action of the Board of Supervisors, which furnished actual
men as substitutes for those who were drafted and who did
not themselves serve.

Mr. OPDYKE was a delegate at large to the New-York
Constitutional Convention of 1867–8, and a member of the
succeeding Constitutional Commission of 1872–3. In revising the State Constitution, he found work which was
most interesting and congenial to his tastes, and labored
con amore upon all the subjects which came before the
Convention and Commission. He was especially active
in all that concerned the canals and other commercial
interests of the State; in all that related to Common
School education, and especially to measures for compulsory attendance at the schools; in all that contributed to
the improved government of cities, including measures
looking to the election, by the vote of tax-payers only, of
a Board of Financial Control in the large cities; and in the
Constitutional amendment that was eventually adopted as
to bribery. He greatly regretted that the Legislature did
not approve the proposed amendment relative to Boards of
Financial Control in cities, which was first suppressed by
political manœuvres, and when again proposed by the
Charter Commission, was defeated by politicians, whose
schemes it would have effectually checked.

Mr. OPDYKE was at all times an earnest student, and
supplemented his early schooling by systematic self
instruction. He became a clear and forcible writer and a
pleasing and effective speaker. As early as 1845 he wrote
a treatise on Political Economy, which he afterwards revised and published in 1851. In this work he discussed the
theory of wages, the value of land and other questions, and
advanced many original views which have since become accepted doctrines of the science. In his treatise he demon-

strated the economic evils of slavery, and took strong
ground in favor of free trade, but was willing to accept "a
tariff for revenue only" as a practical policy for the United
States. He also advocated the issue by the National Government of an inconvertible paper money, limited by
constitutional provisions to a certain amount *per capita* of
population. When, during the War of the Rebellion, Secretary CHASE sought his advice as to the proposed issue of the
legal tenders, Mr. OPDYKE, adhering to his views formulated
in 1845, strongly urged the issue of national currency to
an amount not exceeding three hundred million dollars.
Against the subsequent enlarged issues of these notes he
earnestly objected, foreseeing the injurious effects that
soon followed the inflation of the currency.

Mr. OPDYKE published also, in 1866, a volume of "Mayoralty Documents," embracing the political and adminis-
trative history of the City during his term of office. This
volume contains his veto messages, which throw a strong
light upon the modes of City government under ineffective
charter provisions.

Mr. OPDYKE was for twenty-two years a member of the
Chamber of Commerce of the State of New-York. For
eight years, from 1867 to 1875, he was a Vice-President,
and during the period of his connection with the Chamber
he was constant in his attendance at its meetings, and
very active in calling attention to matters of public
concern, serving upon most of the important Committees, and taking a prominent part in the debates of the
Chamber. Especially was he prominent in all measures
for improving the navigation and defence of New-York
Harbor, and for securing free navigation of the State
Canals.

WILLIAM H. FOGG.

WILLIAM H. FOGG was born on a farm in the town
of Berwick, Maine, on December 27th, 1817. His grand-

father was a prominent officer in the Church, and his father was a man highly esteemed by his fellow citizens. The parents of Mr. Fogg came from genuine New-England stock. The small means Mr. Fogg had accumulated as clerk in a country store enabled him to establish, with two other young men, in Boston, the firm of Bennock, Fogg & Shannon, which continued for some time, but being unsuccessful, the partnership was dissolved. To Mr. Fogg's honor, be it said, he paid, years after, with interest the whole indebtedness of this firm. In 1847 the firm of Fogg Brothers was organized, having more or less relation with the brother, Hiram, who resided in China. The business was transferred to New-York in 1852, and the branch at Boston closed. Mr. Fogg's brother died in 1855, and the firm then became William H. Fogg & Co., the business devolving entirely upon William H. Fogg, who was then thirty-eight years of age. Energy, enterprise and honesty ensured success, and soon the firm became prominent in the China trade. When Mr. Fogg returned from his visit to that country in 1880, the firm dissolved, but the business was continued under the name of the China and Japan Trading Company, of which Mr. Fogg remained President until his death. The Company's enterpise is now a matter of history. It had branches at Shanghai, China; at Yokohama, Kobe, Osaca, in Japan; at London and San Francisco, and handled, in addition to tea and silk, large quantities of general merchandise. In all his transactions, William H. Fogg was conservative and cautious, and had the reputation of conducting the affairs of the Company on sound principles. For a quarter of a century he was an honored member of the Chamber of Commerce, and for two years prior to his death one of its Vice-Presidents. At the time of his decease he was a director in the Park Bank, and once its President, a director of the Atlantic Mutual Insurance Company, the Equitable Life Assurance Company and the Mercantile Trust Company. He was also a Governor of the New-York Hospital, and of several other beneficent organizations, all of which expressed in fitting terms their

5

sorrow at his death, which occurred in this City, March 24th, 1884.

Those who knew him would testify, without exception, that Mr. Fogg was one of the most courteous of men, possessing, in an eminent degree, that charming urbanity which smooths intercourse between men of business, and enables them to avoid many of the asperities so often encountered in commercial life. The writer knew him intimately, and often had to consult with him on important questions which came before the Chamber for consideration and action. In all cases, and at all times, Mr. Fogg showed the same unvarying courtesy which characterized his whole life. In his capacity as Vice-President of the Chamber, or as Chairman of its Executive Committee, he was ever ready to spend his time and means to further the interests and enhance the welfare of New-York. Practical, sagacious and cool, Mr. Fogg's judgment was highly valued, and his force of character much admired by his colleagues and friends. He was a man of deeply religious convictions, liberal but unostentatious in all his works of charity.

MATTHEW MAURY.

MATTHEW MAURY was born in Liverpool, England, September 29th, 1800. He descended from a Huguenot family, which settled in Virginia in 1717, and was the third son of JAMES MAURY, who, directly after the Revolution, went to Liverpool to establish an American house, and was appointed consul to that port by General WASHINGTON. He filled this office from 1790 to 1829, under the first six Presidents of the United States, reflecting credit upon his country, and commanding the honor and respect of those with whom he came in contact both in public and private life, and at a time when to be an American was necessarily unpopular. He was the first President of the American Chamber of Commerce in Liverpool, and his portrait, painted for that body by STEWART NEWTON, still hangs in its rooms.

MATTHEW MAURY was educated at Eton, and visited America for the first time in 1817. He began business with MAURY, LATHAM & CO., his father's house in Liverpool, and was made a partner soon after he came of age. They were general merchants, tobacco being their chief import, until the cotton trade grew up. The first American cotton was shipped in wooden boxes. A memorandum by Consul MAURY, of these first imports, was as follows:

In 1785, 5 in 3 vessels; in 1786, 6 in 2 vessels; in 1787, 108 bales in 5 vessels, and so on. Thus, MATTHEW MAURY grew up with the business in which he spent his life, and had a rare familiarity with it in all its details. When the present method of "futures" began, it was so distasteful to his ideas as a merchant that he could never fully enter into it. After 1822, he was constantly in America. In 1832, with his younger brother, RUTSON, he established the house of M. & R. MAURY, in New-York, changed in 1841 to MAURY BROTHERS, of which he continued the head until his death.

Born under the flag, MATTHEW MAURY was by right an American citizen, and had the strongest love and admiration for his country and her Republican Government, with a firm belief in its complete success. This did not hinder his admiring many excellent features in the working of the English Government, such as the absence of rotation in office, and the simplicity of the tariff.

JAMES MAURY, like all thoughtful men of his time, had a great aversion to slavery, an aversion he carefully instilled into his children, and charged them, when they came to this country, never to own a slave. Brought up under such influences, it is plain, that when the late war broke out, MATTHEW MAURY could be nothing else but a strong Union man, and ever remain so.

He had a high appreciation of the value of the New-York Chamber of Commerce, and almost all his public services were rendered through it. He was its Secretary from 1849 to 1853.

In the following measures he was either prime mover or a zealous co-worker:

In the establishment of the bonded warehouse system, when ROBERT J. WALKER was Secretary of the Treasury; in an endeavor to improve the banking system of this State; in the founding in 1848 of the "Institution for the Savings of Merchants' Clerks and others," in which he took a deep interest, and served always as trustee, and as Second Vice-President for twenty-one years; in an effort to establish a time and weather observatory on the Battery in this City, which failed because the authorities did not favor it; in the repeal of the cotton tax, because it was an export duty, and therefore unconstitutional. This met with much opposition, but the arguments against it were unanswerable, and the tax was at last repealed.

The resumption of specie payments he urged almost from the day the war closed. He was one of the very few who insisted that preparation should begin at once to retire the greenbacks, and bring the country back to a gold basis, believing that this would check speculation, which, he argued, would be the inevitable result of our irredeemable and inflated currency.

Though devoted to business, he read widely and was well informed upon general topics. Being fond of the sea, he studied mathematics for amusement, and mastered not only the science of navigation, but on more than one occasion navigated the ship in which he was a passenger, during the illness of its captain. Astronomy was his delight, and he kept up with its progress to the end of his life.

In 1841 he married ELIZABETH, the second daughter of JOSHUA GILPIN, of Wilmington, Del., and had two children, a son and daughter. In early life Mr. MAURY was confirmed in the Church of England, and was a constant and faithful attendant at St. Thomas' Church, and afterwards at St. Mark's in this City.

He died at his home, September 18th, 1877. The spontaneous testimony to his personal character by the mer-

chants among whom he moved was summed up and graven
upon his tombstone in the following words :

"A merchant in this City for nearly fifty years, his
stainless character commanded the respect of all his asso
ciates, and worthily upheld the honored name bequeathed
him by his much honored father."

ALEXANDER HAMILTON.

No man in our national history presents a more completely rounded character for genius, industry, intuitive
perception, integrity, ability and vast attainments than
ALEXANDER HAMILTON. As patriot, publicist, soldier,
jurist, economist, financier and statesman, he stands, in the
opinion of those best qualified to judge, pre-eminent among
the men of his time. Dying at the early age of forty-seven,
when most men have hardly reached the full maturity of
their powers, he had been before the public for thirty
years, and, in no instance, had failed to accomplish more
than his most sanguine friends had dared to anticipate.

The Prince DE TALLEYRAND, the ablest and clearest
headed of French statesmen, who had for some years been
intimately acquainted with HAMILTON, and knew all his
plans for his nation's advancement, said of him, when in
the zenith of his own power in France : "I consider
NAPOLEON, FOX and HAMILTON as the three greatest men
of our epoch, and, if I were called upon to decide between
the three, I should, without hesitation, give the first place
to HAMILTON. *Il avait deviné l' Europe.*" The full sig-
nificance of this favorite word of TALLEYRAND, "*deviné*,"
cannot be expressed in any literal translation. The thought
seems to be, that his genius had entranced Europe.

Chancellor KENT, in an address before the Law Association of New-York in 1836 said : "Among his brethren,
HAMILTON was indisputably pre-eminent. This was universally conceded. He rose at once to the loftiest heights

of professional eminence by his profound penetration, his power of analysis, the comprehensive grasp and strength of his understanding, and the firmness, frankness and integrity of his character."

The Marquis DE TALLEYRAND PERIGORD, son of the great statesman, and himself a man of great genius and learning, in his *Etudé sur la Republique des Etats Unis d' Amerique*, says: "It was to the constructive political genius of ALEXANDER HAMILTON that America owed her Constitution; it was he who furnished the essential materials which composed it; it is to him that the general plan of the edifice is due; it was he who designed the lines which made that Constitution one of the most remarkable monuments of history. By his energy, his patriotism, his marvellous intelligence and his eloquence he succeeded in directing the public mind to the necessity of a more coherent, more perfect union. Knowing how to silence the selfish views of the different States, he led them to unite in the achievement of a great work. The Constitution completed and adopted, there remained something still to be accomplished; it was necessary to give a judicial, clear, precise and lucid interpretation of this Constitution, in all those constantly recurring conditions, in which it would be called upon to guide and control public events."

Both these great boons to his country were bestowed by the genius and the extraordinary ability of HAMILTON. He had been, young as he was, a thorough student of every form of constitutional government; he had perceived the necessity of the substitution of a strong national government for the effete and outworn confederation; by pen and voice, he had demonstrated the necessity of the Constitution; he was one of the most active members of the Convention which formed it; he procured its adoption and ratification in the Convention of New-York against strong opposition; he expounded and defended it in the "*Federalist*," as well as in other publications; when our Government was re-organized under the Constitution, and he was called to administer on a bankrupt treasury, a national debt of vast proportions, and to rescue the nation from impending ruin, he devised measures, which speedily gave our country a credit abroad and at home which was equal to the best.

The City of New-York and its Chamber of Commerce are under the greatest obligations to ALEXANDER HAMILTON for what he did to revive and fully establish its credit, as well as for his previous good deeds in defending it, and rescuing it from threatened bombardment, at the beginning of the war of the Revolution. His genius and financial skill made New-York possible.

Let us, then, briefly review the career of this extraordinary man. ALEXANDER HAMILTON was born in Nevis, one of the British West India Islands, January 11, 1757. His father was JAMES HAMILTON, of a good Ayrshire family; his mother, whose maiden name was FAUCETTE, was of Huguenot stock. The father had set up in mercantile business in St. Christopher, but had become insolvent from endorsing for others. They had several sons; but only THOMAS and ALEXANDER attained maturity. The mother died when ALEXANDER was yet a small child, but he had vivid recollections of her beauty and of her superior intellect and cultivation. ALEXANDER was taken by his mother's relatives to St. Croix and put at school there, where he speedily became proficient in French and English, with some little knowledge of Hebrew. He absorbed knowledge rapidly. In the autumn of 1769, he entered the counting house of Mr. NICHOLAS CRUGER, in St. Croix. Mr. NICHOLAS CRUGER was a New-Yorker by birth and education, a nephew of JOHN CRUGER, who was so eminent in the ante and post Revolutionary history of New-York, and was the first President of the New-York Chamber of Commerce. Mr. N. CRUGER had a warehouse in St. Croix, and also one in New-York, to which his West India goods were shipped. Here he showed such diligence, intelligence and aptitude for business that a year later he had a confidential relation with his employer, and during Mr. CRUGER's absence at New-York, was put in charge of the business. He was here, as always, a diligent student in commercial science, history and the classics. In August, 1772, before his sixteenth birthday, he was in St.

Eustatia on business, when a cyclone burst upon the Leeward Islands. A full description of the storm and its effects was published in a local paper, and attracted much attention. Inquiry was made by the Governor of St. Croix for the author, and the discovery was made that it was the work of the boy HAMILTON. Arrangements were offered to him and accepted, by which he was to receive a liberal education at or near New-York. He had letters to several eminent men, among others to WILLIAM LIVINGSTON, then of Elizabethtown, New-Jersey, in whose country seat he found a home while attending the Grammar School in Elizabethtown. He was a most earnest and diligent student, and endeared himself to the LIVINGSTONS. WILLIAM LIVINGSTON was the associate editor of the "American Whig," then published in New-York, and was a liberal in politics, and from him HAMILTON, perhaps, received his first impulses toward political composition.

In 1773, HAMILTON entered King's (now Columbia) College, stipulating that he should be admitted to any class for which he was qualified, and that he might advance from class to class, as his attainments might justify. He was here a diligent student, not only keeping up with his classes, but studying political and economical science, medicine and philosophy. But he mingled, also, boy as he was, with the patriots of his time. He was one of the "Sons of Liberty," and advocated the cause of the Boston patriots as he had opportunity.

There appeared in November, 1774, anonymously, two pamphlets, written with great ability, advocating the Tory, or, as they preferred to call it, the Loyalist views of those, who, at this time, were defending the oppressive measures of the English Government: their titles were "Friendly Address to all Reasonable Americans on the subject of our Political Confusions," and "Free Thoughts on the Proceedings of the Continental Congress;" both "By a Westchester Farmer." They were from the pen of Rev. (afterwards Bishop) SAMUEL SEABURY, an intense Loyalist, and one of the most accomplished writers of the time. While the Whigs and Sons of Liberty were looking, with trepida-

tion, for some writer on their side, who could meet this able
and adroit adversary, and overthrow his specious arguments, there appeared, also anonymously, within two weeks
after the publication of the Tory pamphlets, "A Vindication of the Measures of the Congress from the Calumnies
of their Enemies, in answer to a Letter under the Signature
of A Westchester Farmer," embracing, in addition, "A
General Address to the Inhabitants of America, and a
particular Address to the Farmers of the Province of New-
York," by "A Friend of America." This reply was in no
respect inferior to the pamphlets which had called it forth;
in learning, in argument, in eloquent appeal, and in its
complete demolition of the "Farmer's" positions, it was
superior to them. Who wrote it? was the universal question. It was attributed, by both parties, to WILLIAM LIV-
INGSTON or JOHN JAY, the ablest men on the Liberal side, but
both denied its authorship. The controversy went on; the
Westchester Farmer appearing with two more pamphlets,
one addressed to the "Very accomplished writer of the
Vindication;" and to these that writer replied February 5,
1775, with a still more crushing answer, to which the Farmer
never made reply. When it was finally proved that these
powerful vindications of the Liberal cause were from the pen
of ALEXANDER HAMILTON, a student in King's College, who
had just passed his eighteenth birthday, the Tories were
confounded, and the friends of Liberty encouraged and
strengthened. We must pass rapidly over the subsequent
events of Mr. HAMILTON's wonderful career. Before graduating, he had studied diligently military tactics, and qualified himself to command a company. He had also made
an elegant and effective address to the merchants of New
York, which brought them into hearty co-operation with
the Revolutionary party.

In March, 1776, when but 19 years of age, he was commissioned a Captain of Artillery, by the Provincial or State
Congress, and served with credit at the battles of Long
Island, White Plains, Trenton and Princeton, his Company
being admirably drilled, and both they and their leader
exhibiting undaunted courage. He was at this time fair

of complexion, slender, somewhat below the average size, and though boyish in stature, and looking even younger than he was, he possessed an energy, dignity and military bearing, which produced the most perfect obedience in all his command.

A year later, when just twenty, he was made one of WASHINGTON's Aids-de-Camp, became soon his private Secretary, and assisted in planning campaigns. He remained with the Commander in Chief till February, 1781, when he was twenty-four years old. In December, 1780, he married a daughter of General SCHUYLER. In July, 1781, he became commander of a New-York battery, and captured, on October 14, 1781, a redoubt at Yorktown. After the surrender of CORNWALLIS he applied himself to the study of the law, was a member of Congress in 1782-83, and Chairman of important Committees. He returned to the practice of law in New-York City in August, 1783, and soon took the lead in his profession, though the bar of New-York was at that time very brilliant and able. He still took a lively interest in political, financial and social matters; protected the Tories from persecution; was active in establishing the Bank of New-York; helped to found an Anti-Slavery Society; studied intently the question of the Union *vs.* the Confederation; was a member of the New-York Legislature in January, 1787, and one of the delegates and the most active member in the National Convention to form the Constitution of the United States. In that Convention he advocated and carried the doctrine of implied powers, by which the Constitution was made the broad, comprehensive and enduring charter of a nation's rights, which it became. A large part of the Constitution was from his pen. He advocated and carried its ratification before the New-York State Convention; defended it in a series of essays, afterwards published as "*The Federalist*," in which he was assisted by MADISON and JAY; was appointed Secretary of the Treasury in September, 1789, and in January, 1790, presented a report and plans, which rescued the nation from bankruptcy, and became the basis of its financial system, restoring its credit at home and abroad.

He proposed plans for funding the national debt, for assuming those of the several States, for receiving and disposing of the public lands, for obtaining revenue from public lands, and from imposts by a protective tariff, for a mint, and a national bank. He remained at his post for six years, and having perfected all his plans, restored public credit, witnessed the revival of trade and industry, he resigned in January, 1795, and returned to his legal practice. But he was too much of a statesman and publicist to lay down his pen and relinquish his interest in public affairs. He advocated neutrality in the French Revolutionary struggle, and supported JAY's treaty with great ability. He assisted in the preparation of WASHINGTON's " Farewell Address." In 1797 he declined the position of Chief Justice of the United States. In 1798, in consequence of the hostile action of the French Directory, the Army was re-organized, WASHINGTON taking the chief command, and HAMILTON second in command, as Major-General and Inspector-General. On the death of WASHINGTON, in December, 1799, HAMILTON succeeded him as Commander-in-Chief, but the Army was soon disbanded.

When the House of Representatives were called to choose, in February, 1801, between JEFFERSON and BURR, the two candidates receiving the highest number of votes for the Presidency, HAMILTON advised his friends to vote for JEFFERSON; and when, in 1804, BURR was a candidate for Governor of New-York, HAMILTON opposed his election, as a dangerous man, unfit to be trusted with power. BURR was defeated, and attributing his defeat to HAMILTON, challenged him to a duel. HAMILTON was opposed to duelling, but for once in his life he made the mistake of accepting the challenge, and on July 11, 1804, met his adversary at Weehawken, was mortally wounded, and died the following day in this City. Since the founding of the Republic no man of greater gifts, of more ardent patriotism, or more untiring industry, has taken a prominent part in its councils.

JOHN SHERMAN.

In the political and financial history of our country for the last hundred years and more, there have been many masters of finance, who would have achieved high honors in any country, and who have rescued our nation from seemingly impending ruin. Among these heroes of finance we may name ROBERT MORRIS, the illustrious banker of the Revolution; ALEXANDER HAMILTON, who delivered the nation from bankruptcy, and gave it a credit unsurpassed at that time by any other nation; ALBERT GALLATIN, who remained in office for twelve eventful years, and whose financial ability was as conspicuous as his statesmanship. Coming down to a later period, SALMON P. CHASE, the projector of the national banking law, who, with his able lieutenants in the Senate, WILLIAM P. FESSENDEN and JOHN SHERMAN, provided for the bankrupt treasury the means of conducting a great war; WILLIAM P. FESSENDEN, whose nine months' service was illustrious for its reduction of the gold premium; HUGH McCULLOCH, whose management was judicious and able, looking to the rapid reduction of the national debt; and, after a little further interval, JOHN SHERMAN, whom twenty years of financial experience had made wise, in laying such foundations for the nation's wealth and prosperity as should prove permanent; the man who perfected the national banking system, funded, at low rates of interest, the remainder of the national debt, and brought about resumption of specie payments without shock or financial disturbance. Of living financiers in this country or Europe, he is easily chief, and the glowing eulogy which the late Hon. WILLIAM E. DODGE, addressed to him in February, 1879, as the bearer of a congratulatory letter to him, from the Chamber of Commerce, did not exceed his merits: "You will henceforward be known as Secretary of the Treasury of the United States, in the second great epoch of the nation's financial history, as one of the founders of the national banking law, as the restorer of the public credit, and the successful funder of the national debt."

With all honor, then, to those financial princes who had preceded him, we must give still higher praise to the right royal work of our modern monarch of finance.

JOHN SHERMAN was born in Lancaster, Fairfield County, Ohio, May 10th, 1823, being the eighth child of Hon. CHARLES R. SHERMAN, Judge of the Supreme Court of Ohio, and MARY (HOYT) SHERMAN. He was of excellent lineage, his ancestors having been for more than two hundred and fifty years in the country, and two hundred in England, of that intelligent, upright, GOD-fearing class, which has furnished our ablest lawyers, judges and professional men. ROGER SHERMAN, one of the signers of the Declaration of Independence, was from another branch of the same family. Nearly a dozen Judges of the higher Courts, as well as many eminent professional men, have honored the SHERMAN name since 1634, the date of the first settlement in this country. Hon. CHARLES R. SHERMAN, the father of JOHN, was a man of mark, both in Connecticut, where he was born and educated, and in Ohio, to which State he removed in 1811, and where he died. He was eminent as a lawyer, and was appointed by President MONROE, Collector of Internal Revenue. By the defaulting of two of his deputies he became financially embarrassed. In 1823 he was elected by the Legislature Judge of the Supreme Court of the State, but was cut off by a sudden illness, in 1829, in the sixth year of his term, and the forty-first of his age, leaving eleven children, between the ages of eighteen years and six weeks, with very limited means for their support. Mrs. SHERMAN was, however, a woman of the highest character, and of excellent capacity for business. Friends and relatives gathered about her, and offered to take her children, and bring them up as worthy descendants of the beloved Judge. Four of them were thus taken, one (afterward General W. T. SHERMAN) by Hon. THOMAS EWING, and JOHN by his kinsman, JOHN SHERMAN, a merchant of Mount Vernon, Ohio, where it was expected he would be educated and trained for business. It was

two years after his father's death, before he went to Mount
Vernon, and those years were spent under his mother's
careful training. He remained in Mount Vernon four
years, and was in school most of the time, where he made
remarkable proficiency in his studies, and became well
grounded in Latin and mathematics. From there he was
taken by his sister to Lancaster, and placed under the
instruction of Mr. S. C. HOWE, whose school was considered
one of the best in the Western States. Here he continued
for three years, and was prepared to enter the Sophomore
year in college, but he had not the means to defray his
college expenses. He engaged, therefore, as junior rodman
on the Muskingum Improvement. He remained for two
years on this improvement, gaining in health and strength
and knowledge of men, and sustaining himself. In 1839
he returned to Lancaster, and resumed his studies, but in
the spring of 1840, his older brother, CHARLES T. SHERMAN,
who was in a good practice, invited him to Mansfield to
assist him in his office while preparing for college. Here
he found an uncle, Judge PARKER, an eminent scholar and
jurist, who took a great interest in him, and directed his
studies. At the Judge's advice, he devoted the whole of
the next four years to law studies instead of entering
college. He became very thoroughly familiar with the
best legal works, and in his brother's office had considerable
practice. When he was twenty-one years of age he was
unusually well prepared for admission to the bar. For
a full year before this time, he was able to more than
pay his way, and on his graduation was at once admitted
as an equal partner in his brother's business. He remained
in partnership with his brother for ten years, and such was
his success that he became the trusted counsellor of some
of the large railroad lines, and, among others, of the
Pittsburg, Fort Wayne and Chicago, of which he was, and
still is, a director. During all this time, he laid up more
than $1,000 a year from his earnings, and made some ven-
tures in land and manufactures, which have turned out
well.

Mr. SHERMAN was married in 1848 to Miss CECILIA

STEWART, of Mansfield, who has proved to be all that a good wife should be, and has exerted an admirable influence on his character.

Mr. SHERMAN was first elected to the Thirty-fourth Congress, in 1854, and took his seat in December, 1855. He was elected as a Free Soiler, or opponent of slavery extension, by the elements which afterwards crystallized into the Republican party.

He supported NATHANIEL P. BANKS for Speaker, who was finally elected on a plurality vote, after 133 ballotings. Mr. SHERMAN was placed on the Committee on Foreign Affairs, but, as a new member, was not entrusted with the lead on any very important topics. He made a vigorous opposition to the bill for adjusting the *French Spoliation Claims*, and secured its defeat; took part, on the Republican side, in the Kansas debate, and made a powerful and fearless report on the outrages on the ballot and the murders, committed there. He was re-elected to the Thirty-fifth, Thirty-sixth and Thirty-seventh Congresses, and soon took a high position as an able, clear-headed and fearless debater, and a legislator of great skill in all financial questions, who could not be swerved, by any influence, from any position which he believed to be right. He showed very soon his thorough mastery of the questions of finance, and he became a terror to the corruptionists, then in power in the departments. He was in the minority, but his able reports showed the people and Congress what an earthquake there would be, when the Republicans came into power. In the Thirty-sixth Congress he was a prominent candidate for Speaker, having a plurality of votes, and steadily gaining till the thirty-ninth ballot, when he withdrew, and five days later, on the forty-fourth ballot, Mr. PENNINGTON, of New-Jersey, a Republican, was elected. Mr. PENNINGTON made Mr. SHERMAN Chairman of the Committee of Ways and Means. It was a trying position, in the last half of President BUCHANAN's administration, and required thorough knowledge of finance, and a fearless, but not a quarrelsome, spirit. The credit of the United States was very low; the national debt was $62,000,000; on this the Government was compelled to pay 12 per cent. interest, and a loan of twenty millions, offered at 88, could not find purchasers. A civil war, or a disruption of the Government was believed by many to be pending. Mr. SHERMAN began by retrenching expenses in all directions, breaking up, as far as possible, the frauds which, in the Navy and other departments, were drawing the life blood of the nation. Mr. SHERMAN did what he could to help the national credit, but the President (BUCHANAN) had become very much offended by the investigations into frauds in the Navy Department, and thwarted, by every means in his power, the measures he proposed. Mr. SHERMAN was re-elected to the Thirty-seventh Congress; but before he could take his seat, was elected Senator in place of SALMON P. CHASE, appointed by President LINCOLN, Secretary of the Treasury.

Here was a field for his abilities altogether new. The war had come, and there was great need of money, in large sums, while the Treasury was entirely bankrupt; not even the $12,000,000 left of the $20,000,000 loan, offered in Mr. BUCHANAN's administration, could be placed at any reasonable rate. Trade was at a standstill, and no revenues coming in, yet hundreds of millions of dollars were needed at once. Mr. CHASE was a financier of extraordinary ability, but he felt relieved to find in the Senate, some strong counsellors on whom he could lean. Foremost among these were Senators SHERMAN and FESSENDEN, both subsequently Secretaries of the Treasury. Mr. SHERMAN, thoroughly trained by his Congressional experience and his previous studies in financial matters, was ready to propose and carry through great and bold, but judicious action. SHERMAN and FESSENDEN were in perfect harmony; the latter was Chairman of the Finance Committee at this time, but SHERMAN was his prompt and able lieutenant. A bill authorizing "the issue of United States notes, and for the redemption and funding thereof, and for funding the floating debt of the United States," was brought forward, ably advocated by Mr. SHERMAN, and passed. A bill for issuing National Bonds and Treasury Notes followed; then a bill for creating National Banks, based on United States Bonds, and furnishing all the currency for the country ; and a bill for taxing all bank bills, the issues of State banks, till they were taxed out of existence. These great measures, proposed and perfected by a single Congress, were a sufficient task for the powers of any three men ; but they were completed, and the gigantic machinery of a great war kept in motion by them.

It is not necessary that we should make any comparison between the three financial giants by whom this work was accomplished ; no abler financiers have appeared in modern times, or achieved a greater measure of success ; but each worked in his own field, though in perfect harmony with the others. As the war went on, and the expenses increased from $2,000,000 to $3,000,000 a day, and yet no attempt was made to place these gigantic loans abroad, but our own people absorbed them rapidly, other nations looked on with amazement, and asked, where all this would end. Two years later our national debt had reached about $3,000,000,000 ; gold had touched 285 ; Mr. CHASE had resigned, and accepted a seat on the Supreme Court Bench as Chief Justice, and Mr. FESSENDEN had taken his place ; Mr. SHERMAN was Chairman of the Finance Committee, and indisputably the ablest financier under the Government. The problems to be solved were the funding of our bonds at lower rates of interest, the paying off of the debt, or at least reducing it more rapidly than any nation had ever done ; the enforcing of an income tax and internal revenue duties, and, though yet in the somewhat dim distance—a matter to be considered and prepared for—the resumption of specie payment within a reasonable period. To these tasks the Secretaries of the Treasury, FESSENDEN and McCULLOCH, addressed themselves, but without the aid of Mr. SHERMAN in the Senate they would have been powerless. It was thought a master stroke when the 7.30 notes were paid off from the proceeds of Five-Twenty six per cent. bonds at par ; but the changing of the latter into Five per cents (the Ten-forties,) 4½ per cents, 4 per cents and 3 per cents, caused great astonishment abroad, while the steady reduction of the debt from its

6

maximum of $2,756,431,371 ascertained debt (and over $500,000,000 of unfunded debt,) to $1,700,000,000 before the resumption, and to $1,150,000,000 since, have surpassed anything the world has ever seen. When, after sixteen years of service in the Senate, Mr. SHERMAN took his place as Secretary of the Treasury, in March, 1877, the measures looking to resumption, which he had carried through Congress for fifteen years, were all working perfectly, and the way was, in most respects, prepared. The paying off of the debt and the reduction of the interest on the bonds had reduced the price of gold to 103, and now it remained that there must be a sufficient amount of gold coin and fractional silver coin in the Treasury, to meet the demands upon it under the Resumption Act, passed in 1875, which provided for actual resumption January 1, 1879. This Act had been drawn and passed under Mr. SHERMAN's own eye. It was necessary, or at least desirable, that no bonds should be issued to purchase specie, and that no purchases of specie should be made from foreign countries to facilitate resumption. Mr. SHERMAN managed the whole business admirably. It was one of his maxims, that "the quickest way to bring about resumption was to resume," and that there would not be required a very large amount of specie for this purpose, inasmuch as most persons would prefer paper to gold, as more portable, if they were convinced that the paper could be converted into gold, anywhere and at any time, without loss. Confidence was a much larger element in resumption than coin. Still, it was desirable to have such an accumulation of specie in the Treasury as to prevent all possibility of any panic. He had accumulated in this way by the close of 1878 a coin reserve to the amount of $138,000,000. The precautions were more than sufficient. Very little coin was drawn from the Treasury, and even that little was speedily returned and deposited in the Treasury, so that in January, 1880, there was $135,436,474 of gold coin in the Treasury, only about $2,564,000 less than before resumption, while the silver coin had increased from $1,697,338 to $28,147,351 in July, 1879. But this great work of resumption, the greatest ever attempted by mortal man, was not accomplished without great labor, much violent opposition, detraction and abuse, such as few men could have withstood. Now, everybody rejoices at it. And it is worthy of remark, that during all this struggle, Mr. SHERMAN was working steadily to reduce taxation, by the repeal of the internal revenue taxes, except on liquors and tobacco, and by such modifications of the tariff as were possible. No man ever deserved more fully than Mr. SHERMAN the honors conferred on him by the Chamber of Commerce in 1879, in giving to his beautiful full-length portrait of life size, the place of honor in their collection of eminent statesmen and merchants.

In March, 1881, Mr. SHERMAN retired from the Treasury, having been previously re-elected a member of the Senate, in which he took his seat. Upon the death of Vice-President HENDRICKS, in 1885, Mr. SHERMAN was elected President *pro tem.* of the Senate, which position he resigned in March, 1887. He was re-elected to the Senate in January, 1886, for the term commencing March 4, 1887, and ending March 4, 1893, and is now in vigorous health and strength a member of that body.

DE WITT CLINTON.

IT is over sixty years since DE WITT CLINTON, the most distinguished scion of the CLINTON family, passed away; and while New-York has lost and still retains many statesmen and scholars, whose names will be illustrious while the world stands, on no one of them have more honors been bestowed, and not one of her sons has better deserved them than DE WITT CLINTON. Yet Mr. CLINTON was not, at any time in his career, a popular man. He had no personal magnetism: he had the reputation of being proud, cold and vindictive, and even his kindliest deeds were thought to be accompanied with a reserve and reluctance which robbed them of half their virtue. In the lapse of years, since his death, we have learned that many of these charges were made from partisan rancor; that a part of the allegations were the result of a personal diffidence and reticence which he had tried in vain to overcome; and that while he had cause for pride in his lineage, and in his own attainments, he was, beneath the outer shell of his reserve, a man of very kind heart and genial disposition. But he owed his success in public life— a success which, perhaps, no other man in this country has surpassed—to his extraordinary merits, in a greater degree than to his lineage.

The CLINTONS were a distinguished family. The family name was that of the Earls of Lincoln, in the seventeenth and eighteenth centuries; and the first Governor GEORGE CLINTON, Chief Magistrate of the Colony of New-York from 1743 to 1753, was the youngest son of FRANCIS, sixth Earl of Lincoln: his son, Sir HENRY CLINTON, was the British general who commanded the English army here, during a part of the Revolutionary war. It was another branch of the CLINTON family, though still connected, at an earlier date, with the Lords of Lincoln, from which DE WITT CLINTON was descended. WILLIAM CLINTON, a royalist of note in the civil war in England, was an officer in the army of CHARLES I., and after the death of that monarch, for a long time an exile on the continent. He subsequently went to Scotland, where he married, and later removed to Ireland, where he died, leaving one son, JAMES CLINTON, who spent some time in England, but returned to Ireland, after his marriage with the daughter of a captain in CROMWELL'S army. The son of JAMES, CHARLES CLINTON, the grandfather of DE WITT CLINTON, was a man of influence, property and character, in County Longford, Ireland, and at the age of thirty-nine, determined to emigrate to America, and establish a colony of his friends and neighbors in some of the newer sections of the Province of New-York. This was in 1729. There were ninety-four persons in his colony, for whom he paid passage money. They fell into bad hands. The captain of the vessel robbed them of all their goods which he could seize, and, though New-York was the destination contracted for, landed them on the coast of Massachusetts, and left them there. In 1731, Mr. CLINTON removed to

Little Britain, now within the bounds of Orange County. This was then on the frontier of civilization. The inhabitants of Little Britain were obliged to fortify their houses against the raids of the savages. Mr. CLINTON took an active part in the subsequent Indian and French war. In 1758 he was colonel of a regiment of provincial troops in the Valley of the Mohawk, and soon after joined the main army under General BRADSTREET, and assisted in the capture of Fort Frontenac. He died at his residence, in 1773, in the eighty-third year of his age, leaving four sons: ALEXANDER and CHARLES, both eminent as physicians and surgeons; JAMES, the father of DE WITT, a general in the Revolutionary war, and GEORGE, a soldier and statesman, also a general, the first Governor of the State of New-York, and who continued in that office for twenty-one years, and was subsequently Vice-President of the United States from 1801 to 1812.

JAMES CLINTON was an ensign in the Provincial Army in 1757, at the age of 21 years, lieutenant in 1758, captain in 1759, took part with his father and brother in the capture of Fort Frontenac, in the same year, and continued in service till the close of the French war in 1763. He then returned to his farm in Little Britain, where he married Miss MARY DE WITT, by whom he had four sons, ALEXANDER, CHARLES, DE WITT and GEORGE, all of whom were bred to the law, and all but one obtained high positions. The father entered with great zeal into the war of the Revolution, as did his brother GEORGE. In 1775, JAMES CLINTON became Colonel of the Third Regiment of New-York troops, and in 1776 was promoted to the rank of Brigadier-General. In 1777 and 1778, he was stationed on the banks of the Hudson, and, in the latter year, threw the gigantic chain across the Hudson, to prevent the British squadron from ascending the river. In 1779, Gen. CLINTON, with his detachment of 2,000 men, joined Gen. SULLIVAN in traversing the Indian country in Western New-York, and effectually broke up the Indian raids on the white settlements. He was called by Gen. WASHINGTON, to take the command of the Northern army, after ARNOLD's

treason in 1780, a difficult and important command, in
which he acquitted himself with honor. He retained his
connection with the army till the peace, was present at the
evacuation of New-York in 1783, and then retired to his
farm at Little Britain. After the war, he was a member of
the State Convention to ratify the Constitution of the United
States, a State Senator, a member of the Constitutional
Convention of the State, and held other important offices.
He died in 1812. His eldest son was private Secretary to
his uncle, Governor GEORGE CLINTON; the second son was
a lawyer in Orange, and the third, DE WITT, was the subject of our sketch.

DE WITT CLINTON was born at Little Britain, March 2,
1769. His early education was obtained at the Grammar
School of his native town, and he fitted for College at Kingston, where was then the best Academy in the State. He
entered the Junior Class in Columbia (previously King's) College, in the spring of 1784, the first student under the new
title, graduated at the head of his class in 1786, and commenced the study of law with SAMUEL JONES, then an eminent lawyer in New-York. The Convention which met at
Poughkeepsie, June 17, 1788, to decide whether New-York
would accept and ratify the Constitution of the United
States, which had just been promulgated, was, perhaps, the
most important Convention ever held in the State. If New-
York refused to accept it, the Constitution could hardly
be adopted, and chaos would come again; yet there were
features in it which the New-York Republicans did not
approve. Prominent among its members were: Governor
GEORGE CLINTON, its President, and Gen. JAMES CLINTON,
the father of DE WITT, both strongly opposed to the Constitution, and men of great influence and power. DE
WITT was also present, though not a member; he was
nineteen years of age, and a law student. ALEXANDER
HAMILTON and JOHN JAY, R. R. LIVINGSTON and JAMES
DUANE, all among the framers of the Constitution, were
its able defenders. The battle was long and fierce, the
debates lasting for six weeks, and each party brought to
them all the ability, eloquence and learning they possessed;

in the end, HAMILTON and his friends secured the adoption and ratification of the Constitution, which took place July 26, 1788. The CLINTONS voted against it steadily, but when it was adopted they ceased their opposition, and supported it right loyally. To DE WITT CLINTON this Convention was an event of great importance. He watched all its debates with the greatest interest, and reported them in the columns of a New-York journal, and when the Constitution was adopted, gave it his unqualified support.

On the death of his brother ALEXANDER in 1789, he was appointed his successor, as Private Secretary of Governor GEORGE CLINTON, which post he filled till Governor CLINTON's retirement, in 1795, advocating the Republican doctrines, and his uncle's administration, vigorously, in the New-York press. In 1797, he was elected to the New-York Assembly, and in 1798, to the State Senate, and was very active as a leader in both bodies. He was a member of the Council of Appointment, and, differing from the Governor on the question whether the sole power of nomination was vested in the Governor, or whether it inhered in all the members of the Council, a convention was called, and CLINTON's construction was adopted. He afterwards doubted the wisdom of that decision, and, in 1822, it was reversed.

In 1802, DE WITT CLINTON, then only thirty-three years of age, was elected United States Senator, and in that body delivered several speeches, which showed a profound knowledge of international law, and vast research. The speech delivered on the Mississippi question, on a resolution to take possession of New-Orleans, because the Spanish intendante had prohibited the free navigation of the Mississippi, was so masterly an argument, that it elicited the highest commendation from the ablest jurists in Washington, and defeated the resolution. In the summer of 1803, Mr. CLINTON was elected Mayor of New-York City, resigning his seat in the Senate to take the position. He was Mayor, by re-election, from 1803 to 1807, from 1809 to 1810, and from 1811 to 1814; and though able men have sat in the Mayor's chair, it is not too much to say that, in careful regard for all the interests of the City, in wise measures for

its development, in pushing forward as rapidly as possible
the action for the construction of the Erie Canal, to bring
the products of other States and sections to its markets,
and in the promotion of its educational, benevolent and religious interests, the City has never had a Mayor who
approached him in excellence. With the same official
powers, and an equally long term of office, one or two of
his successors might have come nearer to him than they
have done—but these factors were wanting. During six
years of this time, Mayor CLINTON was also a State Senator,
and during that time, proposed and advocated laws covering
almost the whole scope of State and City legislation. In
the summer of 1810 he, with his associates, the first Canal
Commissioners, examined the Mohawk Valley, and the
route now occupied by the Erie and Oswego Canals, for
the purpose of ascertaining the practicability of constructing a canal from the Hudson to the Lakes. The journal
which he kept during that journey, is still in print, and
is full of interest, for its exposition of the condition of
those sections of the State, nearly eighty years ago. In
1811 Mr. CLINTON was elected Lieutenant-Governor of New-
York, and in 1812, was nominated for the Presidency, in
opposition to JAMES MADISON. The contest was very bitter.
Mr. CLINTON was unsuccessful, receiving 89 electoral votes,
while Mr. MADISON had 128.

For some years after this defeat, he withdrew himself
very much from political affairs, and entered with greater
zeal and zest into literary pursuits, while he continued his
advocacy of the Erie Canal and other internal improvements
for the benefit of commerce. He was, from 1811 to 1814,
again Mayor of New-York, and wide awake to its interests.
In 1815 his enemies defeated him as Mayor and Canal Commissioner. His address before the New-York Historical
Society, in December, 1811, on the Iroquois, or Six Nations
of Indians, is justly regarded as one of the ablest and most
learned of his orations. He was one of the earliest and
most efficient friends of the New-York Historical Society,
which he aided largely, both personally and officially. Soon
after the termination of the war of 1812–14, Mr. CLINTON

again began to urge upon the people and the Legislature, the
necessity of the construction of the Canals. A large meeting
of influential citizens was held in New-York in 1816, and a
memorial of great ability, drawn up by Mr. CLINTON, was
submitted, adopted and presented to the Legislature.
On the 15th day of April, 1817, a bill committing the State
to the construction of the Canals was passed, and July 4,
1817, the work was commenced.

In the fall of 1817 Mr. CLINTON was elected Governor of
New-York, almost unanimously. In 1820 he was re-elected,
and during both terms, aside from his other duties, the
prosecution of the Canals to their completion was pressed
with vigor and success.

In 1822, a Convention was held to frame a new Constitution; the term of the Governor's service was made two
years, (it had previously been three, as it is now,) and in
the autumn of that year, JOSEPH C. YATES was elected
Governor for the following two years. In the autumn of
1824, Mr. CLINTON was again elected, and held the office
till his death, which occurred on the 11th of February,
1828. In October, 1825, the work on the Canals was completed, and Governor CLINTON passed in triumph from
Lake Erie to the Hudson, greeted all along the route with
the greatest expressions of joy, at the new impulse thus
given to the State and national commerce. His message
of January 1, 1828, breathed a spirit of the highest patriotism, and closed with this eloquent and impressive peroration: "We are inhabitants of the same land, children of
the same country, heirs of the same inheritance, connected
by identity of interest, similarity of language and community
of descent, by the sympathies of religion, and by all the
ligaments which now bind man to man in the closest bonds
of friendship and alliance. Let us, then, enter on the discharge of our exalted and solemn duties by a course of
conduct worthy of ourselves and our country; which will
deserve the applause of our constituents, insure the approbation of our own consciences, and call down the benediction
of the Supreme Ruler of the Universe." His death, six
weeks later, was very sudden, and called forth the warmest

expressions of admiration and sympathy, from all parts of the State and the United States.

The Chamber of Commerce testified its respect for his memory in a series of resolutions, adopted at a special meeting, held on the 18th of February, one of which we here quote, as comprehending, in a brief summary, the outline of an illustrious life :

" His devotion to the cause of science and literature, and to the benevolent institutions which distinguished the present day—his successful efforts to promote schools among the great body of our citizens, whereby nearly half a million of our youth receive the benefit of education - - his genius in projecting, and his untiring zeal and energy in carrying into effect, the great scheme of internal navigation, which has already united the Hudson with the inland seas of the North, and will soon lead to a similar union with the immense waters of the West, and lay open to the commerce of this City fertile countries, whose shores are not inferior in extent to the shores of Europe—all show the superiority of his mind—that it was directed to the most patriotic objects, and that its efforts have been crowned with the most splendid success."

De Witt Clinton will be known in the history of our country as the promoter of education and science, the efficient organizer of measures for the development of the City and State, the patron and helper of every form of benevolent action, and the *founder and creator of the Canal system of New-York*.

JOHN A. KING.

John Alsop King, the eldest son of Rufus and Mary King, was born in New-York, on 3d January, 1788, where he passed his early years until the appointment of his father as Minister to the Court of St. James. During the residence of the latter in London, his two eldest sons, John and Charles, were pupils in the public school at Harrow, under Dr. Drury, where they acquired a good classical education, and improved the vigorous constitution they inherited, in the manly exercises and sports of this celebrated school. After the return of his father to America in 1803, JOHN passed over to Paris, where he was instructed in the French language and mathematics. Returning home the next year, he continued his education, and, in due time, engaged in the study of law under EDMUND PENDLETON, being admitted to practice in the then Court of Chancery in 1809. In 1810 he married MARY, the daughter of CORNELIUS RAY, an honored merchant of New York, and at that time President of the Chamber of Commerce. Mr. KING made his residence in this City. While pursuing his profession, the war with England was declared in 1812, and although he disapproved of such a declaration, he felt that he had but one duty, as a good citizen, to sustain his country, and asked for and obtained from Governor TOMPKINS a commission of Lieutenant of Cavalry, in which capacity he served in New-York until the close of the war.

Possessed of but moderate means, he decided, in 1815, to remove to the country, where he bought a farm at Jamaica, L. I., near his father's residence, upon which he lived many years of his life, surrounded by the influences of a happy home, with an increasing family, and with the sincere respect and kindly feeling of his neighbors. He was a laborious and active farmer, raising large crops by his own exertions, and by the introduction of the best processes, as they were suggested by the improving knowledge on farm matters. A lover of good stock and of thorough bred animals, he was interested especially in the improvement of horses, a fact which showed itself in his efforts to promote the formation of a Jockey Club on Long Island, of which he was for many years President, and in which many of his friends were practical members, both as breeders and owners of celebrated horses. His deep interest in the political questions of the day, and his earnest and manly advocacy of the measures he deemed best for the interests of the country, soon won the confidence of his neighbors, and he was called by them to represent them

in the Assembly of the State in 1819, 1820 and 1821. These
were times when the aspects of parties were changing,
and political feelings were deeply roused by the intrigues
and schemes of designing men. The breaking up of the
Federal party, to which Mr. KING belonged, was one
of the results of these contests, and he arrayed himself,
with many others, against DE WITT CLINTON. Notwithstanding this political opposition, he was a firm
friend to the latter in the making of the Erie Canal, of
which enterprise he remained a warm advocate during his
long life. In 1824 Mr. KING was sent to the Senate of the
State, and was thus advancing on the road of political preferment, when he was appointed in 1825 by Mr. ADAMS as
Secretary of Legation to his father as Minister to the Court
of ST. JAMES. He remained in that capacity in London,
until his father's return home an invalid, and afterwards
as Chargé des Affaires until the arrival of the new Minister.
This residence was in many respects a source of pleasure,
for he was kindly received, and renewed many of the acquaintances of his former school days.

Returning to Long Island, he purchased from his brothers
the old homestead, to which he removed, passing there the
remainder of his life, beloved and respected. Political
life was again opened to him, and although he was defeated
as a candidate for Congress, under the changed aspects of
the times, he was, in 1832, sent to the Assembly, where he
interested himself in the general business of the State, but
more particularly in procuring a charter for the Brooklyn
and Jamaica Railroad, of which he became President, and
which was the beginning of the lines of road which have
opened up the Island in all directions.

In 1839 Mr. KING was sent to the National Convention to
nominate a candidate for the Presidency. Mr. CLAY was his
choice, but finding his nomination impossible he was induced
to give his vote, with that of the State, for General HARRISON.
In this and subsequent conventions, when the question of
the extension of slavery became a leading question, Mr.
KING was always faithful and earnest in his opposition to
this measure.

Having been elected to the 31st Congress in 1848, he was an active agent in endeavoring to prevent the passage of the compromise measures, which looked to the extension of slavery to the new Territories acquired from Mexico, but which resulted in bringing in California as a free State, for which he earnestly contended, and which was the first check the advocates of slavery received; but the efforts to prevent the passage of the fugitive slave law failed, though that very act was what alone was wanting to rouse every manly instinct of the Northern States to examine into the political as well as moral character of slavery, and to restrict it within its then limits. Mr. KING was a delegate to the conventions at which Generals SCOTT and FREMONT were nominated for the Presidency. At the latter convention, in 1856, he earnestly advocated the choice of FREMONT, as representing the voice of the people against slavery, which was then beginning to make itself clearly heard. He had been the year before the presiding officer of the Convention in the State of New-York, where the old Whigs and independent Democrats were fused into a new Republican party, the war cry being opposition to the extension of slavery; and in the next year, though Mr. BUCHANAN was chosen President, the State of New-York, by a large majority, gave its vote for Fremont, elected Mr. KING as Governor, and at the same time declared, as he afterwards, in his inaugural address, said he understood it to be "their deliberate and irrevocable decree, that so far as the State of New-York is concerned, there shall be henceforth no extension of slavery in the Territories of the United States;" "a resolution I most unreservedly adopt, and am prepared to abide by it, at all times, under all circumstances, and in every emergency."

The public schools, the Erie Canal and other great public measures for the benefit of the State and City, received his faithful attention, and when called upon in the case of the quarantine riots and to carry out the law creating the Metropolitan Police, he manifested such determined firmness and took such decisive steps that the public peace was preserved and the laws sustained, notwithstanding the

serious efforts which were made to render them inopera-
tive.

After the term of his office as Governor, to which he
declined a re-nomination, Mr. KING attended the convention
which nominated Mr. LINCOLN for the Presidency. and
then retired into private life, from which he was again
recalled in 1861, to become a member of the Peace Convention, to which he had been appointed by Governor
MORGAN. Hoping little from its meetings, he felt it his
duty to do what he could to arrest the serious troubles
which were threatening the life of the country. Though
these efforts were unsuccessful, Mr. KING had the happiness to live long enough to see the country, after a bloody
war, restored once more to peace, with the stain on its
escutcheon removed, and advancing rapidly on a career of
prosperity. As always in his life, the welfare of his country
was the theme upon which his thoughts were warmly turned,
and on the 4th of July, 1867, he addressed the students at
Union Hall Academy, Jamaica. L. I., which had prospered
for fifty years, largely under his fostering care, and com-
mended to them the care of the flag of their country, which
had just been presented to them, telling them that the
older men were passing away, and that to them was soon
to be committed the care of that flag, and of all it represented ; a care which must be exercised with a deep sense
of responsibility to GOD. While thus speaking he fell
back into the arms of his friends, and was carried to his
home, where, after lingering a few days, he died peacefully,
surrounded by his sorrowing family, on the 7th July, 1867,
at the age of seventy-nine.

Mr. KING's liberal and enlightened views as to the promotion of the varied interests of the State and City of
his birth, characterized his whole public life, and his advocacy of every measure to advance the commercial growth
and prosperity of the City, obtained for him recognition
from the Chamber of Commerce, which made him an
honorary member of their body. The State Agricultural
Society and the United States Agricultural Society were
both indebted to him as one of their founders and deeply

interested friends during his life, the former electing him as one of their Presidents, and the latter one of their Vice-Presidents, while the Agricultural College at Ovid, now a part of Cornell University, received much of his time and care. Long Island, especially Queens County, was constantly in his thoughts, the evidence being in his unremitted efforts to improve the roads and means of transportation, and to organize and support the Queens County Agricultural Society, of which he was many times the President.

He was an earnest and faithful member of the Protestant Episcopal Church, in which he had been brought up, and towards which his heart always turned warmly. In the Convention of the Diocese of New-York, and in the General Theological Seminary, his counsels were judicious and prudent, and he was ever ready to speak and act so as to strengthen the cause of religion and of the Church of his convictions. At his own home, Jamaica, he took an earnest part in advancing the prosperity of the educational and religious institutions, and more especially that of Grace Church, of which he was Vestryman and Warden for many years, and which received his loving care and liberal gifts, and in whose quiet yard his remains lie. Mr. KING was a member of the New-York and Long Island Historical Societies, and was a founder of the St. Nicholas Society.

Mr. KING was tall and well proportioned in person, quick and graceful in his movements, courteous and affable in manner, and a good speaker, with a clear, powerful and pleasant voice. Correct and temperate in his habits from his youth up, he suffered none of the evil effects of irregularity in life, but enjoyed health and vigor and all his faculties unimpaired to the close of a long and useful career.

EDWIN D. MORGAN.

THE career of EDWIN DENISON MORGAN, as merchant and statesman, and particularly as war Governor of the State of New-York, will always be read with interest.

EDWIN D. MORGAN was born in Washington, Berkshire County, Mass., February 8th, 1811. His father, JASPER MORGAN, was a New-England farmer, and the son, therefore, passed his boyhood days in the fields, and managed to obtain some little learning at the village school during the winter months. With a common school education, a capital of 37 cents, and a determination to win success, he started out at the age of 17 to seek his fortune. He went to Hartford, Conn., and there bound himself for three years as assistant to his uncle, a grocer of that City. Such was his aptitude for trading that before the end of his term of apprenticeship he was sent to New-York to purchase tea, sugar and corn. The last named was then an article of import instead of export, and young MORGAN proved so shrewd and successful a buyer that, at the age of 20, his uncle took him into partnership. In 1832 he was elected a member of the City Council of Hartford. In 1833 he married Miss WATERMAN, of that City, and in December, 1836, he came to New-York. He afterwards formed a partnership with a Mr. EARLE, and with their savings, and $10,000 advanced to them by a Hartford capitalist, the firm of MORGAN & EARLE, in 1837, began business as wholesale grocers. At the end of the year the firm was dissolved, and EDWIN D. MORGAN began business on his own account. His fine faculty of anticipating the changes in the market was proverbial, and all his ventures seemed successful. While other dealers ofttimes operated at a loss, Mr. MORGAN reaped profits. He soon became known as one of the largest dealers in raw sugar, and handled tea and coffee with successful results. Opportunities which others missed, he saw and took advantage of, and he was rapidly accumulating a large fortune. In 1847 he formed the house of E. D. MORGAN & Co., taking as partners his cousin, GEORGE D. MORGAN, and his two former clerks, JOHN T. TERRY and SOLON HUMPHREYS. These three partners chiefly conducted the business, Mr. MORGAN having determined upon a political career. In 1849 Mr. MORGAN was elected President of the Board of Assistant Aldermen, a body which was then composed of eminently respectable merchants and men of standing. During the cholera ravages in the City he was unremitting in his exertions for the sick and dying, visiting the hospitals and giving of his own means to alleviate the distress and suffering which then existed. In 1850 he was elected to the State Senate from the Sixth District of New-York, and served two terms in that body, being Chairman of the Finance Committee, and President *pro tem.* for both terms. He declined a third term, and in 1855 was appointed Commissioner of Emigration, a position at that time held by some of the best citizens of New-York. This office he held till 1858. In the meantime, as the Whig party, of which Mr. MORGAN was a member, had become merged in the Republican party, he joined the latter, and, in fact, was one of its founders. He was Vice-President of the National Convention in May, 1856, at which the party was organized, and was made Chairman of the National Committee, and presided a few months later at the Philadelphia Convention, at which FREMONT was nominated for President, and the FREMONT campaign was conducted under his management. In 1858 he was nominated by the Republicans for Governor of the State. He was elected to this high office, and his sensible administration is now a matter of history. In 1860 he was re-elected, and his record during his second term is inseparably connected with the history of the War of the Rebellion. When the war broke out he labored assiduously for the success of the Union cause, and will always be remembered as one of the war Governors of the loyal States. Men and money were wanted, and Governor MORGAN spent the whole of his time endeavoring to secure both. By May, 1861, he had succeeded, under a special Act of the Legislature, in enrolling 30,000 men, and by July 12th, they had been organized into 38 regiments, officered and sent to the war. The energy of the Governor was unbounded. When President LINCOLN, after the attack on McCLELLAN, called for 300,000 more troops, Governor MORGAN determined that New-York should supply her fair quota. Accordingly, a State bounty was offered, in addition to the national bounty,

7

and the Governor undertook to raise the sum of $4,000,000 for this object. It was discovered that the State had about this amount to its credit in various banks, and Governor MORGAN took this money to pay the bounties. He called for 25,000 men, and offered $50 bounty for each man. Speedily this number was obtained, and sent to the front; the Legislature in the following year legalized the expenditure therefor. "I am for continuing this war to the end," wrote the Governor, "with all the force we have in the field, with all we can raise by voluntary enlistment, and after that, if need be, by a conscription embracing all classes and description of persons of proper age." It is on record, that during his second term, Governor MORGAN enrolled and equipped 200,000 soldiers. President LINCOLN made him Major-General of volunteers, and, in order to facilitate his labors, placed him in command of the Military Department of New-York. He expended $3,500,000 in bounties to soldiers, and made contracts amounting to several millions of dollars for supplies.

In 1862 Mr. MORGAN declined a re-nomination for Governor, but was in that year elected by the Legislature Senator of the United States to succeed PRESTON KING, and he filled this office from March 4th, 1863, to March 4th, 1869. In February, 1865, he was nominated for Secretary of the Treasury by President LINCOLN, but at Mr. MORGAN's request, the nomination was withdrawn. At the conclusion of his term as Senator he again returned to his business in this City. In 1881 President ARTHUR nominated him for Secretary of the Treasury, but, although the nomination was unanimously confirmed by the Senate, Mr. MORGAN, for the second time, declined that honor.

Mr. MORGAN was elected a member of the Chamber of Commerce May 1st, 1849, and retained his connection therewith, up to the day of his death, which occurred February 14th, 1883. He served on several important Committees of the Chamber, and his ripe experience and high character were much appreciated by those with whom he acted on public questions. He was a member of several institutions, and director of financial and business corporations, and gave liberally whenever he saw opportunities for practical charity. As a patron of art, he was well known both here and on the continent of Europe.

CADWALLADER COLDEN.

CADWALLADER COLDEN, Lieutenant-Governor of the Colony of New-York, 1761-75, was born at Dunse, Scotland, February 17th, 1688, and died at Flushing, L. I., September 28th, 1776, aged 88 years. The Chamber of Commerce obtained its charter from King GEORGE III., March 13th, 1770, through the good offices and at the request of CADWALLADER COLDEN, on the petition of JOHN CRUGER, the first President of the Chamber. Mr. COLDEN early in life applied himself to the study of mathematics and medicine, and soon became distinguished by his proficiency in both. He came to this country about the year 1708, and practiced as a physician in Philadelphia for several years with marked success. He visited England, but returned in 1716 with his wife, whom he had, in the meantime, married in Scotland. Brigadier-General HUNTER, then Governor of New-York, conceived a favorable opinion of Mr. COLDEN, and requested him to leave Philadelphia and make his future home in New-York. He accordingly settled here in 1718, and the next year was made Surveyor-General of Lands, being the first to fill that office in the Colony. He was also appointed Master in Chancery. In 1720, on the arrival of Governor BURNET, he was honored with a seat in the King's Council of the Province, and in 1760 succeeded to the administration of the Government. In 1761 he was appointed Lieutenant-Governor of New-York, and held this commission almost up to the date of his death, being repeatedly at the head of the Government during the decease or absence of several Governors. The name of CADWALLADER COLDEN is quite familiar to the student of history, and the school boy of to-day is made acquainted with the fact that Mr. COLDEN, as Lieutenant-Governor of King GEORGE III., was as conspicuous for his firmness in upholding his Majesty's authority, as the revolutionists were in resisting it. When the British Parliament determined to levy a tax on the colonies, the spirit of resentment and indignation ran high, and several thousand people assembled at the Battery, near the fortification then called Fort George, determined to compel Lieutenant-Governor COLDEN to deliver up the paper which was to be distributed in this City under the British Stamp Act, on November 1st, 1765. They surrounded the fort, and threatened to assassinate Mr. COLDEN and his adherents, but he was loyal to his trust, and took the necessary precautions to defend it. Although the engineers within the fort assured him that the place was untenable, and his family implored him to regard his safety, he preserved a calm and firm demeanor, and finally succeeded in placing the Governmental papers on board a British man-of-war then in port. His carriages were destroyed before his eyes, and the angry populace also burned him in effigy. After the return of Governor TRYON, Mr. COLDEN gave up all public duties and retired to his country seat. The published writings of the Lieutenant-Governor include a number of scientific dissertations. Some of them, through the variety of hands into which they have fallen, have become mutilated and others are lost. CADWALLADER COLDEN possessed an eminently cultivated mind, and although the latter portion of his official life was of a trying and harassing nature, he had few personal enemies, and his efforts to promote the commercial interests of New-York, as well as his personal action in behalf of the organization of this Chamber, make the name of CADWALLADER COLDEN one to be honored by the merchants of this and succeeding generations.

FRANCIS EGERTON.

THIS English nobleman, bearing the title of the Duke of Bridgewater, was born in England in 1736. He has been aptly called by historians the father of British inland

navigation; and we know that his success stimulated DE
WITT CLINTON to attempt his great enterprise of the
Erie Canal. The account of his navigable canal, which,
with the exception of the Sankey Canal, was the first
great undertaking of the kind executed in Great Britain
in modern times, is familiar to many of our merchants.
An engineer named JAMES BRINDLEY was associated
with the Duke in his various enterprises. The latter
owned a large estate at Worsley, near Manchester,
which abounded in coal, and he conceived the idea that an
artificial water route between the places named would be
immensely beneficial to the development of that section.
Accordingly, an Act was passed for the scheme in 1754
and 1758, but it was afterwards discovered that navigation
would be of more service if carried over the River Irwell to
Manchester, and further legislation was therefore secured
agreeably to the new plan, and likewise to extend a side
branch to Longford Bridge, in Stratford. Although navigable subterraneous tunnels and elevated aqueducts are
now familiar with us, yet the Duke of Bridgewater and his
coadjutors appear to have been the first to introduce them,
and make it possible to carry canals over rivers and large
and deep valleys. The Duke's projects were, in those
primitive days of transportation, deemed by many chi-
merical. Results, however, justified his endeavors, for in
1761 he had the satisfaction of seeing the first boat sail
over his canal. Other gentlemen soon afterwards became
interested in the canal from the Trent to the Mersey,
and navigation by artificial waterways in Great Britain
was soon an accomplished fact, and the Duke, who had
made many sacrifices, financially and otherwise, in order
to promote his schemes, lived to see several projects of this
nature carried to successful completion.

The Duke died in 1822, at the age of eighty-six years,
leaving his vast estates to his nephew, FRANCIS HENRY
EGERTON, son of the Bishop of Durham, who succeeded in
1823 to the title; and is widely known in the religious world
for his bequest of £8.000 for the *Bridgewater Treatises*.
He was the last Earl of Bridgewater, and died in 1829.

RICHARD COBDEN.

RICHARD COBDEN was born at the farm house of Dun-
ford, near Midhurst, in the Weald of Sussex, on the 3d of
June, 1804. His early education was procured in the
Grammar School of Midhurst, which then sustained a high
reputation. While yet a lad, his father died, and an uncle,
who was a warehouseman in London, took him into his
establishment. Soon after, he changed to another house,
where he was at first a clerk, and afterward a commercial
traveler. He was very popular in this last calling, but was
then, as always, a diligent student of political economy and
political science. ADAM SMITH'S "Wealth of Nations"
was his favorite text-book. The firm by which he was employed retired from business, and disposed of their interest
and good-will to three of their employees, among whom
was COBDEN, who became the head of the firm. His business
was the manufacture and printing of calicoes. "COBDEN'S
prints" became the rage, and, at last, were worn by the
Queen herself. On commencing business, Mr. COBDEN had
taken up his residence in Manchester, where one of his
warehouses was situated. Here he soon began to write for
the press, generally on political and politico-economical
subjects, over the signature of "Libra," and soon drifted into
public speaking. After a little practice, he became an effective, though not a remarkably eloquent speaker. In 1832,
he was elected Alderman. For the next six years he was
heartily engaged in two great reforms, the extension of
borough privileges and national education, and the overthrow of the corn laws, as the first step toward free trade.
He was the founder of the Anti-Corn Law League, organized
in 1839, and one of the most liberal contributors to it, as well
as its leading orator and defender. In 1841, he was returned
to Parliament for Stockport, and distinguished himself
as a Parliamentary orator, by the extent of his information
and the cogency of his reasoning. The five or six years
which followed were years of intense labor and excitement.
Mr. COBDEN had determined to give Parliament and the

people no rest, till all the corn laws were repealed ; and to this work he bent all his energies, and all the resources of a most vigorous intellect, and an indomitable will. Opposed to him were the whole body of the Tories, the associated Whigs, the great landed nobility and gentry, the Premier and the Cabinet, and the great majority of the House of Lords. The case seemed hopeless ; only the men of the Manchester school, the dissenting ministers, and the workingmen and a few of their employers, were on his side. In the conflict he employed every possible expedient. Petitions, with scores of thousands of names, were sent in ; mass meetings were summoned ; the ministers were deluged with letters ; commissions were appointed, bazars held, and COBDEN and his colleagues exhausted all their *repertoire* of argument, railing and invective upon their opponents. It was long before they were able to make much impression ; but after the second year converts began to come in from the nobility and gentry, the land owners and the agriculturists, and, at last, the venerable Duke of WELLINGTON and a majority of the House of Lords. In May, 1846, the corn laws were repealed, and the duty on imported grain was to cease absolutely in February, 1849. It was a great triumph for Mr. COBDEN. Sir ROBERT PEEL, then Premier, gracefully acknowledged that the name which ought to be chiefly associated with the success of these measures was the name of RICHARD COBDEN.

Mr. COBDEN had carried on this vigorous conflict at great personal sacrifice and pecuniary loss. After the repeal, his friends of the late Anti Corn Law League subscribed and presented to him the munificent sum of £80,000, ($400,000,) to secure his independence, and enable him to devote his energies, henceforth, to the cause of his country. A part of this sum was invested in Illinois Central Railway securities, which, though for a time unremunerative, eventually became productive.

His subsequent labors in Parliament and out of it were devoted to peace, reform, retrenchment and the introduction of arbitration in the place of war for the settlement of inter-

national difficulties. He was urged to enter the Cabinet, by
Lord JOHN RUSSELL, but declined. He was elected, in 1847,
for the West Riding of Yorkshire, as well as for Stockport,
and chose the former seat. In 1848 he supported a motion
for the repeal of the navigation laws, making shipbuilding
free, and the next year came out for electoral reform,
secret voting and the shortening of the duration of
Parliaments. In 1849 and the following years, he urged
arbitration measures to prevent war, and the reduction of revenue and expenditure, with much of his old
force and vigor. Peace conferences, in which he was active,
were held with good effect from 1849 to 1853, and were only
discontinued during the Crimean war. In his opposition
to that war, Mr. COBDEN and Mr. BRIGHT were again working together. Their protests were earnest and dignified,
but they did not avail, and the war went on. But when
peace came, COBDEN's arbitration clause was inserted in
the treaty. On the occasion of the Chinese war, Mr.
COBDEN moved a vote of censure on the Government in
Parliament, and Earl DERBY, one of the same tenor, in the
House of Lords. COBDEN's motion was carried by 16
majority, while Earl DERBY's was defeated by 36. Lord
PALMERSTON, then Premier, went to the country on the
question, and the voters sustained him, and COBDEN,
BRIGHT and many other eminent liberals were not elected.
COBDEN had made the canvass for BRIGHT, who was very
ill, and addressing the Manchester voters, after his defeat,
he was affected to tears. COBDEN was for more than two
years out of Parliament, part of the time travelling in this
country.

On his return, he was offered by Lord PALMERSTON, in
1859, the office of President of the Board of Trade, which
he declined, but consented to negotiate an important
commercial treaty with France. This treaty was one of
the best services he ever rendered to his country. The
duties on beer, wine and brandy, and on manufactured
goods, had been so heavy as to be almost prohibitory, and
had caused much bitterness, and frequent rumors of war.
After long negotiation, these were reduced to a very low

tariff. and great relief was experienced by both countries. The treaty has been, as a whole, profitable both to England and France, and it has greatly diminished the fears which had periodically agitated the two countries lest there should be an invasion of the territory of one by the other. The adjustment of the details of this treaty, which was signed in October, 1861, occupied some time, and it was not till late in 1862, that he made his appearance in Parliament as member for Rochdale. He voted with his friend, Bright, on the American question when there was any measure of importance up, but he never spoke upon it in Parliament, addressing himself only to questions of the Government supplies or manufactures, and the reduction of national expenditures, on the only two occasions on which he addressed the Commons. His last public speech was delivered at Rochdale in November, 1864, and in this he alluded to the American war in such a way as to show that his heart was with the Union cause. In a letter, written from his sick room February 5, 1865, this is still more manifest, and he expressed joy that the Confederate cause was failing. He died on the 2d of April, 1865, of asthma. In him, England lost one of her greatest statesmen.

JOHN BRIGHT.

JOHN BRIGHT was born at Greenbank, near Rochdale, Lancashire, November 16th, 1811. His family were members of the Society of Friends. JACOB BRIGHT, his father, had set up a hand-loom in the neighborhood of Rochdale, in 1802, and thus laid the foundation of the vast cotton manufactures which have since made Rochdale famous. Young BRIGHT received a good early education, first at the excellent Friends' school at Ackworth, and later at York and Newton. At the age of fifteen he entered his father's business, but his leisure was fully occupied with political studies. In 1830, at the age of nineteen, he made his debût as a speaker on temperance; and having committed his speeches to memory, acquitted himself moderately well.

When, a year or two later, he attempted to speak against the corn laws, he was not so successful at first; his manner was awkward, his voice somewhat harsh, and his sentences ill framed. But there were still evidences, that with practice and self discipline, he would become an effective speaker, though not much promise of the eloquence, which eventually gave him the rank of the first orator in Great Britain.

In 1835 he began to plead the cause of national education, and rendered good service by his addresses. The same year he first made the acquaintance of RICHARD COBDEN, who was seven years his senior, and who was, while an active manufacturer, largely interested in national education, and in the anti-corn law crusade. For thirty years the two men worked together, and were the best of friends, often speaking from the same platform in favor of electoral reform, and in opposition to the corn laws and other oppressive measures of legislation. Mr. BRIGHT had already become a famous orator, and his addresses were, as a matter of choice, always clothed in the terse and vigorous Saxon speech, of which he was a master. He had, as early as 1838, become greatly interested in the Anti-Corn Law agitation, and when the Anti-Corn Law League was formed, in 1841, BRIGHT's name was second on the list of the Committee. From this time forward, though continuing his connection with Rochdale manufactures, Mr. BRIGHT was very active in public life. He spoke often and forcibly against the corn laws; and in Parliament, which he entered in 1843, became known as a tribune of the people. He was largely instrumental in securing the powerful assistance of Sir ROBERT PEEL, and, through his aid, in carrying the repeal of the corn laws.

As a member of the Society of Friends, he abhorred war, and, whenever it was threatened, he was active in his opposition to it, taking strong ground against the increase of armaments. In the Crimean war, he opposed the Government and his own constituents, by his brilliant and memorable speeches against its continuance. In 1856 he was not re-elected, but the next year was returned from Birmingham. His next efforts were addressed to the termination of the East India Company's charter, and the transfer of the Government of India to the Crown, and to the extension of the elective franchise in England to all householders.

It was at this juncture that our own civil war commenced, and though his own business, and that of the whole Lancashire manufacturing districts, suffered terribly from it, JOHN BRIGHT was, from the first news of the war, conspicuous in his support of the Union, while nearly every member of Parliament, and the nobility, gentry, clergy, army and navy, and most of the bankers, were bitterly hostile to the North. He was taunted with his inconsistency in advocating our war for the Union, when he had always opposed the wars in which England engaged. Very noble was his reply: "I cannot, for the life of me, see, upon any of those principles upon which States are governed now—I say nothing of the literal words of the New Testament—I cannot see how the state of affairs in America, with regard to the United States Government, could have been different from what it is at this moment. * * * * I say that the war, be it successful or not, be it Christian or not, be it wise or not, is a war to sustain the Government, and to sustain the authority of a great nation; and that the people of England, if they are true to their own sympathies, to their own history, to their own great act of 1834, (the Emancipation Act,) to which reference has already been made, will have no sympathy with those who wish to build up a great empire, on the perpetual bondage of millions of their fellow men."—[Speech at Rochdale, August 1, 1861.]

Nor did his ardor cool as the war went on, though for the first year or two, the greater measure of success seemed to be on the Southern side. He was no fair weather friend. In December, 1861, just at the time of the MASON and SLIDELL seizure, when the friends of the South in England

were urging the immediate declaration of war against the
United States, Mr. BRIGHT was invited by his fellow-
townsmen in Rochdale to a banquet given in his honor.
In his speech at that banquet he stated, with great force,
the claims of the North on Great Britain from their ties of
kindred. Millions of the Americans, he said, were either
natives of Great Britain, or of British parentage. He concluded his address with these eloquent words :

"Now, whether the Union will be restored or not, or the
South achieve an unhonored independence or not, I know
not, and I predict not. But this I think I know : that in
a few years—a very few years—the 20,000,000 of free men
in the North will be 30,000,000, or even 50,000,000—a population equal to or exceeding that of this kingdom. When
that time comes, I pray that it may not be said among
them, that in the darkest hour of their country's trials,
England, the land of their fathers, looked on with icy
coldness and saw unmoved the perils and calamities of
their children. As for me, I have but this to say : I am but
one in this audience, and but one in the citizenship of this
country ; but if all other tongues are silenced, mine shall
speak for that policy which gives hope to the bondmen of
the South, and which tends to generous thoughts and generous words and generous deeds, between the two great
nations who speak the English language, and from their
origin are alike entitled to the English name."

On the 18th of December, 1862, he spoke at Birmingham
on the war, which was, at that time, exhibiting results
very discouraging to the North ; but his faith did not fail ;
he said : "The Chancellor of the Exchequer (Mr. GLAD-
STONE) as a speaker is not surpassed by any man in England, and he is a great statesman ; he believes the cause of
the North to be hopeless, and that their enterprise cannot
succeed." After denouncing the leaders who sought to
force into the family of nations a State based upon the mon-
strous principle of the extension and perpetuation of slavery,
Mr. BRIGHT continued : "I have another and far brighter

vision before my gaze. It may be but a vision, but I will cherish it. I see one vast confederation, stretching from the frozen North in unbroken line to the glowing South, and from the wild billows of the Atlantic, westward to the calmer waters of the Pacific main—and I see one people and one language, and one law and one faith, and over all that wide continent, the home of freedom, and a refuge for the oppressed of every race and of every clime."

When the Chamber of Commerce of New-York, in March, 1862, sent to Mr. BRIGHT, through the American Minister in London, the following resolution : " *Resolved*, That the Chamber of Commerce of the State of New-York does hereby record its grateful sense of the intelligent, eloquent, just and fearless manner in which Mr. JOHN BRIGHT, of Birmingham, has advocated, before the people of England and in the British Parliament, the principles of constitutional liberty and international justice, for which the American people are contending ; and that these proceedings be communicated to Mr. BRIGHT ;" the statesman responded in a very beautiful letter. The testimonial was fully deserved. The gift sent over to his Lancashire constituents by the Chamber of Commerce in January, 1863, to supply their needs, which had been caused by the war, called out from Mr. BRIGHT one of his most eloquent addresses, closing with this glowing peroration : " From the very outburst of this great convulsion, I have had but one hope and one faith, and it is this, that the result of this stupendous strife may be to make freedom the heritage forever of a whole continent ; and that the grandeur and the prosperity of the American Union may never be impaired." Everywhere : in Parliament, against Mr. ROEBUCK and our other enemies there, he had made, on every important occasion, his powerful and effective appeals ; at the trades' unions, in the Birmingham Chamber of Commerce, at repeated calls from them, and at gatherings of workingmen and manufacturers. In all places, and at all times, he was our effective and powerful advocate. Well did he deserve the name, by which he is most widely known in this country, " The Friend of America."

We pass hastily over his history since our war. It was a noble and glorious fight which he waged in behalf of household suffrage, and it ended by his enemies yielding to his persistent demands, even more than he had asked. In 1868, he became President of the Board of Trade, in Mr. GLADSTONE'S administration, but in 1870 was compelled to resign from ill health. In 1873 he again entered the Cabinet, as Chancellor of the Duchy of Lancaster, and went out with his colleagues in 1874. In 1880 he again accepted a seat in the Cabinet, as Chancellor of the Duchy of Lancaster, but resigned in 1882, in consequence of his objection to the Egyptian war. In the autumn of 1888, Mr. BRIGHT's health began to fail, pneumonia and pulmonary congestion set in, and though he rallied after the first severe attacks, and there was some hope of his recovery, a relapse occurred in the spring, and on the 27th of March, 1889, he died, as he had lived, peacefully, honored, mourned and lamented, the world over.

At the news of his death, the Chamber of Commerce of the State of New-York passed resolutions expressing their appreciation of his great services and noble Christian character, declaring that his splendid fame as a statesman and orator were the peculiar inheritance of the English speaking race, and that his firm adherence to his convictions of right and duty was worthy of the highest honor. They also placed on record their loving tribute of gratitude to his memory for his unwavering friendship for the United States, and his powerful advocacy of the preservation of the Union during the late struggle.

GIDEON LEE.

GIDEON LEE was one of the many noted men of New-England birth who have found their way to the metropolis of the Republic in quest of occupation and fortune during the century. Having lost his father at an early age, and been thrown upon his own resources before he was fourteen, the success of his efforts to achieve fame and fortune were due wholly to his native energy of character. There was so much of him and in him that he would have distinguished himself in any calling in life to which choice or circumstances had assigned him. His intellect was so superior that it qualified him for leadership in spite of his lack of opportunities for acquiring education. We are accustomed to the phrase, "a self-made man," and the popular partiality runs strongly in favor of those who have worked their way up to position and influence without any adventitious aid. GIDEON LEE was one of the finest types of this class, and every step in his useful and honorable career may be studied with advantage by the young men of later generations who are to compete for the prizes of thrift and industry.

Mr. LEE was born in Amherst, Mass., April 27th, 1778. In his fourteenth year he was apprenticed to a tanner and shoemaker, the two occupations being at that time combined. He worked at tanning in summer and at shoemaking in winter.

After learning his trade he began business on his own account in Worthington, Mass. The first hundred dollars he earned he expended in increasing his stock of learning at Westfield Academy. He was associated with a Mr. HUBBARD, the firm being HUBBARD & LEE. In the course of business he became acquainted with WILLIAM EDWARDS, then of the firm of DWIGHT & EDWARDS, of Cummington, Mass.; and in 1807 they made him an offer of $1,000 a year to go to New-York and sell their leather, which he accepted. After acting in that capacity a year, he decided to operate for himself. Accordingly he hired an old store on the corner of Ferry and Jacob streets, and there the foundation was laid of the great house of GIDEON LEE & Co., which for thirty years thereafter was the synonym of financial reliability and commercial rectitude. Nobody ever doubted GIDEON LEE's word, whether it was oral or written. It was equally and absolutely good in either case.

In 1819 he admitted his confidential clerk, SHEPHERD KNAPP, into partnership, and they continued together till

1839, when both retired. In 1837 CHARLES M. LEUPP, Mr.
LEE's son-in-law and a clerk in the house, was accorded a
place as junior partner.

Mr. LEE took high rank among the merchants of the
metropolis at an early stage of his career and held it to the
end.

In 1822 he was elected to the lower house of the New-
York Legislature. For three years, from 1828 to 1830, in-
clusive, he was an Alderman. These were days when few
if any but men of acknowledged worth were chosen to the
municipal councils. In 1833 he was elected Mayor of
New-York by the Common Council. That was before
Mayors were voted for by the people. During his term
the noted election riot occurred, in which the State Arsenal
was attacked; it was promptly suppressed, owing to his
energy and courage. In 1834 he was elected to Congress
and served one term, from March 4, 1835, to March 4, 1837.
He declined a re-election, with the intention of retiring
from business, and leaving city life for the quiet of a rural
home. In May, 1837, the memorable panic arose, which
brought innumerable houses to bankruptcy. GIDEON
LEE & Co. held large stocks of leather in their stores and
in tanneries. It was impossible, in that momentous crisis,
to realize upon them. The firm were leaned upon by
several concerns to whom they had been accustomed to
render assistance. They were obliged, to use an expression
much in vogue in periods of financial straits, to "take care
of both sides of the bill book." Their bills payable they
met at maturity; their bills receivable they could not
collect. To fortify themselves against any and every
danger, Mr. KNAPP was despatched to Boston to negotiate
a loan from EBENEZER FRANCIS, on the pledge of leather
at half price as security. Mr. FRANCIS received the proposal with satisfaction, perceiving a good opportunity to
put some of his money where it would command good
interest. But he warned Mr. KNAPP that he should charge
him a high rate. His idea of usance, however, was something like that of OLIVER SURFACE, in SHERIDAN's great
comedy, for when he was asked, "how much?" he said,

with an evident misgiving that he would be taken for a SHYLOCK, "eight per cent. per annum." Mr. KNAPP felt relieved ; he had just come from a city where a man was considered very lucky if he could prevail upon anybody to lend him money on first class collaterals, at twelve per cent., and there were borrowers who were forced to pay thirty per cent. The bargain was closed without further parley, and leather sent on to Boston to be stored, insured and hypothecated to an amount on which Mr. FRANCIS advanced $100,000. That made the firm comparatively easy till the crisis was passed. Two years and a half later, that leather was sold for almost double what it would have brought— if it could have been sold at all—at the time the loan was procured. Eight months after it was all closed out the market price declined about thirty-three and a third per cent.

On the 1st of February, 1839, Mr. LEE and Mr. KNAPP retired, the former to remove to Geneva, N. Y., where he had purchased a fine estate, and the latter to assume the Presidency of the Mechanics' Bank, in Wall-street, which he held with so much distinction for thirty or more years. It was Mr. KNAPP who made the brief but highly effective speech at the meeting of bankers, held in 1861, to consider the appeal of SALMON P. CHASE, Secretary of the Treasury, for their co-operation to sustain the Government. "Why, of course," said Mr KNAPP, "we must support the Secretary to the fullest extent our means will allow ; if the Government is not sustained we shall not be good long ; we must stand or fall together." The force of this argument was irresistible, and from that moment there were always funds enough available for the vigorous prosecution of the struggle against rebellion. Mr. KNAPP died on the 22d of February, 1875, at the age of about eighty years.

In 1840 Mr. LEE was selected as one of the electors of the State of New-York, and voted for HARRISON and TYLER. He had been a democrat all his life until 1837. At that time he took issue with the VAN BUREN administration on the currency question, and seceded from the party, with a number of others, including NATHANIEL P.

8

TALMADGE, United States Senator. They called themselves "Conservatives," and kept up an organization for a
year or two, but gradually gravitated to and were merged
in the Whig party. That was his last official position.

He died on the 24th of August, 1841, aged 63 years.

In person, GIDEON LEE was a man of commanding
appearance. There was a blending of amiability with
firmness in his countenance which gave it a peculiar
fascination. Strangers when they met him were very apt
to look at him intently as if impressed with his striking
personality. He was tall, erect and dignified. He was
sometimes stern of aspect, but never forbidding, for there
was so much kindness in his nature that it was pleasingly
expressed in his features. He had a thoroughly generous
heart, and was always ready to extend a helping hand to
young men seeking to make their way in life, if he had
faith in their integrity. He had no toleration for anybody
who was untruthful and disingenuous. If a man deceived
him once, he wanted as little as possible to do with him
ever thereafter. His sterling uprightness was the most
conspicuous trait in his character.

He was so good, so true, so just, that if the human race
were up to his standard in an ethical point of view, the mil-
lennium would be with us. It seems hardly possible that
any human being could be more scrupulously observant than
he was of the Scriptural injunction, "Do unto others as ye
would others should do unto you."—ISAAC H. BAILEY.

AMBROSE C. KINGSLAND.

AMBROSE C. KINGSLAND was born in this City May 24th,
1804, and died here October 13th 1878, in the 75th year of
his age. He was Mayor of New-York from 1851 to 1853;
a member of the Chamber of Commerce from 1851 to 1878,
and for many years was one of New-York's representative
merchants. His father was also a resident of this City, and
was descended from a family which came from England

about the year 1665, and settled upon a tract of land situated on what is known as Barbadoes Neck, between the Hackensack and Passaic Rivers, in the State of New-Jersey. The patent for this track of land, amounting to several thousand of acres, had been obtained from the British crown. Mr. KINGSLAND was educated at the Friend's Seminary in this City, and, about the year 1820, formed a partnership with his brother, DANIEL C. KINGSLAND, under the firm name of D. & A. KINGSLAND, and conducted a grocery business at No. 49 Broad-street, within a few doors of the place occupied by the firm in later years. The scope of the firm's business was afterwards enlarged, greater risks were assumed, and the house became prominent in the shipping trade, whale oil being its specialty. This firm fitted out, and sent from this port the first ship to cruise for sperm whales. CORNELIUS K. SUTTON, a cousin of the KINGSLANDS, entered the firm in 1843 as a partner, and the firm name was then changed to D. & A. KINGSLAND & Co., which afterwards became D. & A. KINGSLAND & SUTTON. Mr. AMBROSE C. KINGSLAND married in 1833 Miss MARY LOVETT, a daughter of GEORGE LOVETT, a successful merchant of this City, over half a century ago.

The firm of D. & A. KINGSLAND & SUTTON continued until the death of DANIEL C. KINGSLAND in 1873; at that time it was transacting a large business with England, China and the East Indies, the firm's vessels being constantly employed between those countries and the United States.

Mr. KINGSLAND was the first Mayor of New-York elected to serve for the term of two years, and to him is due the credit of suggesting a large public park for the City. The development of this idea resulted in the establishment of the present Central Park. Many will remember that during Mr. KINGSLAND's term of office a proposition was made to extend Pine-street through Trinity Church Yard. The scheme was, however, strongly opposed by the Mayor and the Church corporation, and finally defeated.

Mr. Kingsland had eight children, several of whom survive and are well known in business and social circles.

ANSON G. PHELPS.

Anson G. Phelps became a member of the Chamber of Commerce May 3d, 1825, when it occupied rooms in the "Tontine Coffee House," on the northwest corner of Wall and Water streets.

His ancestors were among the first settlers of Connecticut. Two or more in the maternal line were early pastors of the Colonists one of them, Rev. Timothy Woodbridge, being settled over the First Church in Hartford.

Mr. Phelps was born in Simsbury, March, 1781. His father joined the Revolutionary army almost at the outbreak of hostilities, and served throughout the war. Much of the time he was an officer under General Greene, and he named this son Anson Greene, in memory of his old commander. Captain Thomas Phelps returned from the army broken in health, and with only worthless Continental money for his seven years' service. His wife, like the wives of many other officers and soldiers during this struggle for independence, had been compelled to support herself during most of the war. She was a woman of resolute spirit, much refinement, earnest piety and of superior education for that period.

Both parents having died before he was eleven years of age, the orphan boy was placed in the family of a minister in the neighboring village of Canton. He helped the minister in taking care of his farm, and also worked in the shop and store of an older brother of his own. At eighteen he found employment in Hartford at an establishment for the manufacture and sale of saddlery and trunks, and soon developed a marked aptitude for business. When he had reached twenty-one he was sent, during the winter, to Charleston, South Carolina, to secure a wider market for these goods. The visits were repeated for three or four seasons, and he then opened a store in Hartford for a general business on his own account, carrying it on for several years. During this time he married OLIVIA EGGLESTON, a descendant of OLIVER OLCOTT, one of the original founders of the city.

In 1815 he removed to New-York and established himself as a dealer in metals. He was unusually successful, and extended his transactions in various directions. For a long time he was agent and part owner of the old line of packets running to Charleston. Later on he formed a partnership with ELISHA PECK, and the firm of PHELPS & PECK, to aid in paying for the metals they imported, became large purchasers and shippers of cotton to England. They also manufactured wire at Haverstraw on the Hudson. In 1832 their warehouse, at the corner of Fulton and Cliff streets, fell in from excessive weight of tin and cotton, and several clerks and workmen were killed. Soon after this catastrophe the firm was dissolved, and Mr. PHELPS associated with himself his two sons-in-law, WILLIAM E. DODGE and DANIEL JAMES, the latter going to Liverpool to carry on the business under the title of PHELPS, JAMES & Co., while the New-York house took the name of PHELPS, DODGE & Co. A copper mill in connection with the business was established at Birmingham, Conn., and subsequently the advantageous water-power of the Naugatuck River was utilized somewhat above this point, and a mill planted there for the manufacture of brass kettles.

This was the beginning of the present flourishing town of Ansonia, so called from the given name of Mr. PHELPS. The original factory has grown into larger establishments, one of which is the "Ansonia Clock Company." In addition to his other undertakings, Mr. PHELPS became also extensively interested in pine lands in Pennsylvania.

When he first came to New-York he resided on Broadway, near Fulton-street, and opposite St. Paul's Church. He afterwards moved into Beekman-street, for greater quiet, and to enjoy a spacious fruit garden. Still later, he occupied a dwelling-house in Cliff, between Fulton and John streets, at that time a retired neighborhood, devoted exclusively to private residences.

He made large purchases of real estate in the upper part of the City, on the East River, at the foot of 30th to 34th streets. On a portion of this property there stood the old Hossack mansion, surrounded by gardens, which ran down to the bold and rocky bank of the river. Here Mr. PHELPS spent the last years of his life, and here, not long after returning from a journey to Europe for his failing health, he died, November 30th, 1853, at the age of seventy-three.

Mr. PHELPS was not only known as a merchant who had enjoyed a remarkable career of prosperity, and acquired large wealth, but he had also a wide reputation as a public benefactor and Christian philanthropist.

He was President of the New-York Asylum for the Blind, and also the Branch of the Colonization Society, established in the State of New-York. He took a special interest in the Republic of Liberia, and believed it could be made an effective instrumentality in carrying Christian civilization into the interior of Africa.

He was a manager of the American Bible Society, the American Tract Society, the Seamen's Friends Society, and of the Peace Society. He was likewise a liberal promoter of Foreign and Home Missions, of Temperance, Sunday Schools and similar organizations. His will contained bequests for charitable and religious purposes exceeding $500,000.

He was a man of simple habits and wholly averse to display. He loved to accumulate, both from an ambition to achieve large results, and also because it was his distinct purpose and pleasure to use his means for the good of his fellow men and the promotion of the Kingdom of God. He was long a member of the old " Brick Church," standing on the site now occupied by the *Times* building, and then under the charge of Rev. GARDINER SPRING, D. D. He subsequently aided in founding the Mercer-street Church, whose pastor, at the time of Mr. PHELPS' death, Rev. GEORGE L. PRENTISS, D. D., describes him as having a strong and original character, remarkable for self-reliance, an iron will, solid and comprehensive judgment, a sagacious power of combination and forecast, untiring perseverance, good common sense, and possessing a constitution capable of immense labor and endurance.

He had a broad, firmly knit frame, with a commanding presence, and a face full of mingled firmness and benevolence. His domestic life exhibited strong and tender affections, intelligent and pervading piety, and a solemn sense of personal responsibility to God.

He left an only son, bearing his father's name, and four married daughters. His wife survived him a few years.

GEORGE T. HOPE.

GEORGE T. HOPE, a distinguished Underwriter, born September 20th, 1818, in the town of Hopewell, Orange County, N. Y., where he passed his childhood and early youth, died July 27th, 1885, at his home in Bay Ridge, Long Island.

From his father, REUBEN HOPE, born in England, of Huguenot parentage, and his mother, a daughter of a soldier of the American Revolution, the subject of our sketch inherited qualities of mind and heart which were the antecedent possibility of his subsequent distinction. While yet a youth his family became resident in the City of New-York, where his business career was accomplished. He was married in 1844 to Miss AMELIA HAYS, who, with their four children, two sons and two daughters, survives him.

He began his business life as a clerk in the Jefferson Fire Insurance Company of New-York, at the age of sixteen, and in that position so won the esteem of the directors for ability and integrity that he was promoted to the office of Secretary of that Company when he was but little more than seventeen years of age. In this office he remained with increasing credit to himself and satisfaction to his Company for nearly seventeen years. During this

period his superior abilities and untiring industry made
him master of his profession, and pre-eminently helpful
in all organized effort for promoting the efficiency and
stability of insurance incorporations, while his conscientious judgment and decision of character qualified him for
leadership in all the relations of his business. He served
as an active member of the New-York Volunteer Fire
Department for several years, in order that he might learn
by personal observation the perils of the business to which
he was devoted, and the exposure to overwhelming disaster
to property owners which constantly menaced them. This
experience led him, in connection with other officers and
managers of Insurance Companies, to secure the adoption
of measures of reform in the construction of buildings, and
of methods of defence against conflagrations, such as an
ample supply of water and steam fire apparatus, &c., and
these public benefits have proven to be of inestimable value
and importance, not only to the City of New-York, but to
other cities of our country also. In respect of his practical
efficiency in the line of his profession, it may be said with
emphasis, that he was not only "abreast of his time," but
a pioneer in the march of reform and improvement. At
the close of 1852 the organization of the Continental [Fire]
Insurance Company of New-York was consummated. The
incorporators of this Company were among the most
prominent business men of New-York, who, feeling the
want of adequate indemnity against loss by fire, by which
the City was constantly menaced, and by which the
prosperity of its mercantile interests was embarrassed,
determined to establish a Company which would be equal
to the demand felt. The capital was fixed at $500,000,
nearly double the paid-up capital of any other Company
in New-York. Mr. HOPE was induced to leave the position
he had filled so acceptably and for so long a period in the
Jefferson, and become the Secretary of the new Continental
Company, in which office he continued until May, 1857,
when he was elected President of the Company, in place
of its first President, the Hon. WILLIAM V. BRADY, who
resigned. An implied condition of Mr. HOPE's acceptance

of the office of Secretary was, that the Continental would, at a proper time in the future, adopt what he regarded a most important system of business, which is known as the "Participation Plan," by which patrons of the Company were made to participate in the profits of the Company's business, without incurring any liability whatever. This plan had been thoroughly elaborated by Mr. Hope some years prior to this time, and he sought to give it practical effect. It was adopted by the Company, and went into operation July 1st, 1856; was prosecuted with remarkable success until, by the great conflagration in Chicago, in October, 1871, the soundness of the system was grandly proven, and its importance clearly demonstrated, by the preservation unimpaired of the reputation and solvency of the Company, while it paid one hundred cents to the dollar for every just claim, for losses aggregating more than $1,750,000, three and a half times its capital; neither of which results could have been realized without that husbanding of resources which the "Participation Plan," the outcome of Mr. Hope's sagacity, was intended to accomplish.

Devotedly attached to their chief officer, and proud of the splendid record the Company had made under his administration, the stockholders promptly adopted the recommendation of their officers and directors to re-inforce the position of the Company by doubling the amount of its capital, and paying into its funds the required sum of $500,000 within ninety days. About one year later the great fire in Boston occurred, inflicting upon the Continental a loss of $500,000. Here, again, the sturdy confidence of the Company in its chief was indicated by submitting to an assessment of forty per cent. upon its new capital, which required the payment of $400,000 more into its funds. On these occasions of stupendous disaster stockholders and other capitalists displayed their remarkable confidence in the reliability of the Company's management by subscribing in each instance more than twice the sum needed to meet the requirement.

To these distinguishing features of management must be

added what is known as "the New-York Surplus Law," under the operation of which, profits of a Company's business (which under the statute may be divided in cash to stockholders) are deposited with the Superintendent of the Insurance Department as protection to those policy-holders who are not involved, in case of an overwhelming conflagration. The wisdom, equity, conservatism and liber-ality of this valuable addition to the Insurance laws of our State would, of itself, perpetuate the honored memory of the underwriter to whom its existence is mainly due.

Notwithstanding the numberless exactions of his posi-tion, he found time for thought and helpful effort in con-nection with many important organizations, commercial, social and religious, to which he was chosen by the partial-ity of his acquaintances. He was a member of the Chamber of Commerce from 1857 up to the time of his death, Presi-dent of the American Baptist Publication Society, and a member of other kindred societies.

Such was the subject of our sketch as he was known to those with whom he became associated in his business. But that would be a very inadequate presentation of our subject, which should fail to notice that excellences of character which appeared in him in his intercourse with men in business, were the practical expressions of social, moral and religious qualities, which were the constituent characteristics of the man. The ideal of *true manliness* entertained by him was exalted. It implied a social order requiring personal probity, intellectual culture, commercial uprightness and refinement of manners; a moral code which was no other than the Decalogue; and a religious life whose absolute impersonation was He who, "while in the world, was the light of the world," and whose word of inspiration was, "Follow thou Me."

rest at Brooklyn, August 26th, 1886. To his loving friends this sculptured record of such a life seems as cold and heartless as the marble or granite on which it is inscribed. And when the history in its fuller details is all completed, the hunger of the heart will still remain unsatisfied. Mr. ROBINSON was a lineal descendant of men famous in the annals of New-England. If we go back six generations we find Governor WILLIAM ROBINSON, thrifty, revered and honored among the high officials of the State; and all down the line the record of the family is almost equally illustrious. GEORGE C. ROBINSON followed commerce on the sea, and was suddenly called from earthly life at Canton, China, at the age of 32, leaving five small children, of whom JEREMIAH was the eldest, to the care of the young mother, without the fortune he hoped to acquire for them in his life of adventure.

The boy remained with his maternal grandfather, JERE-MIAH NILES POTTER, who owned a large landed estate in South Kingstown, until he was twelve years of age, growing strong and sturdy in labor upon the farm, and receiving only such education as was given in the common schools of that day. He then served a little over two years in the grocery store of his uncle at Newport, spent two years more working in the field, and, at the age of sixteen, wringing a reluctant consent from his anxious mother, he came to New-York. This goal of his aspirations in 1836 was widely different from the great metropolis of the present day, but it always gave a chilling welcome to those who came to seek their fortunes at its hands, and its honors and gains were never to be had except by patient, persevering toil, and a pluck and energy that will not be denied. This temper and these gifts the boy brought with him, and by their exercise he wrought for himself a home for his adventurous feet.

After a long weary search in quest of employment, he at last found a situation in the store of E. P. & A. WOOD-RUFF, dealers in fish, salt and provisions. All that was promised him for his toil, early and late, and his untiring devotion to his employers' interests, was his board in the family of one of them, and he was to furnish his own wardrobe. But he was not daunted, and he rendered such faithful and intelligent service that he soon won for himself a more lucrative position. Many eyes were upon him, noticing his skill and fidelity, and he received many tempting offers to change his quarters, but he clung to the one establishment, and after four years became so essential to the business that he was taken into partnership. He was soon the real head of the firm, and continued so through all the changes of its members by death and retirement.

The story of his sagacity and enterprise in developing the river front of Brooklyn is too long to be told in this brief sketch. His association with the late WILLIAM BEARD in the purchase and improvement of warehouse and dock property, and the construction of the Erie Basin, which have added so largely to the commercial prosperity of the City in which he built his home, gave a fresh direction to his business activity, and largely augmented a fortune already ample for his support. He was also interested in the great East River Suspension Bridge, and was one of the pioneers in the promotion of that successful enterprise. From first to last, he was always the same active, wise, energetic man of business, kind and liberal to his workmen and employees, and true to all the interests committed to his hands.

This is but the bald outline of a career that was one unbroken success from boyhood to his maturer years; and it fails, after all, in revealing the man as he was cherished in the hearts of those who knew him best. In person, he was broad shouldered, deep chested, comely in face, dignified in his bearing, but in his home was gentle and simple hearted as a child. He was broad and liberal in his charities. He never acquired a dollar by those methods which increase the fortunes of so many who count their gains in millions. His enterprises were all in the line of legitimate business. His activities, if they brought gain to himself, were also useful to others, and every dollar of the large estate he left was honestly and fairly earned.

He had a strong helping hand for his fellows, in times of

financial peril and distress, and he stood in the community as a tower of strength and support in the days of business depression, when the hearts of so many failed them for fear. He did not grow hard and selfish as his riches increased, but more thoughtful and considerate of the welfare of others, with every added year of personal prosperity, and, down to the close of his earthly service, he maintained a name unsullied by a single stain.

Better still, and glowing with Heaven's own radiance, was his religious life and character. With deep humility and a generous forbearance in his treatment of others, he was always the consistent Christian gentleman. He was loyal to his faith, and was never ashamed to avow his attachment to truth and righteousness. But no pen can do full justice to such a life and character. Nor is a portrait needed for those who knew and loved him. They miss his firm and manly step, and the warm grasp of his friendly hand, but his memory is a constant presence both in the cherished home and the business circles adorned with his bright example. His widow followed him to the land of rest a few weeks since, leaving four affectionate children to mourn the departure of a fond and faithful mother. But they have a priceless inheritance in the radiance of a life no shadow can ever cloud. Its light went not out at the evening hour, but amid the golden glories of its setting sun it took on the immortality of an endless day.—DAVID M. STONE.

THOMAS B. CODDINGTON.

THOMAS BUTLER CODDINGTON was born at Perth Amboy, New-Jersey, December 5th, 1814. He was the son of JOHN and MARTHA CODDINGTON, and a descendant of WILLIAM CODDINGTON, the first Governor of Rhode Island. During his infancy his father was lost at sea, and when he was but seven years old his mother died, leaving two sons, DAVID, who lived only to attain the age of eighteen, and THOMAS, the subject of this sketch. After the death of his mother, a woman of more than ordinary character and intellect, he was cared for and educated by an only uncle, and his grandmother CODDINGTON. When about fifteen years of age, he came to New-York, and went into the office of JAMES A. MOORE, a white lead merchant, who took a marked interest in the boy, and during the few years he was with him, his house was open to him as a home. When about eighteen, having been provided with letters of introduction, he started for New-Orleans, but the cholera breaking out there, he returned in less than a year to New-York, and engaged in a commission business. In the year 1835 he formed the firm of T. B. CODDINGTON & Co., establishing himself in Broad-street in the metal business. The following year he married ALMIRA PRICE, daughter of the Rev. ELIPHALET PRICE, a Presbyterian Minister.

For a short time he made his home in Brooklyn, but subsequently removed to New-York. In 1854 he added the importation of bar iron and steel to that of metals, and later established a house in Liverpool, England, under the same firm name. In 1869 he went to England, and for several years resided with his family in London, returning to New-York in 1876. So long as he lived, he maintained his connection with the business he had founded, which had increased in magnitude and importance, until his firm had become widely known as one of the foremost houses in the metal trade.

During his business career of more than half a century, Mr. CODDINGTON displayed in an eminent degree the qualities which distinguished and adorned the best merchants of his time. He was remarkable for the quickness of his perceptions, his promptitude in action, and the courage and cheerfulness with which he met all the vicissitudes of commercial life; and, while his high character and abilities commanded the respect and confidence of those with whom he was brought in contact, his genial disposition, the kindness of his heart, and his ready sympathy and helpfulness, won their friendliness and regard.

His energy and sagacity, and his wide acquaintance

with men and affairs, caused his services to be desired by many corporations and societies, and led to his co-operation with them in an official capacity.

Mr. CODDINGTON was a religious man, and the influence of his unobtrusive faith was manifest in his life. He was a member and a vestryman of Grace Church, this City, to which he was strongly attached, and took an active interest in diocesan affairs, and in those of the Church at large. For many years he was a Trustee and Treasurer of the Trinity Public Schools, and, at the time of his death, was Treasurer of the General Convention of the Protestant Episcopal Church in the United States.

In all such relations he manifested the same ability and efficiency that characterized his conduct in other affairs of life, and made him a valuable counsellor and coadjutor in all the enterprises in which he was engaged.

Mr. CODDINGTON was a man of fine presence and unusual physical strength, and although he was then in his seventy-second year, his death, on the 23d of February, 1886, after a brief illness, was a surprise as well as a great grief to his many friends. He has left behind him an honored name, and a memory which is grateful to all who knew him.

GEORGE W. BLUNT.

GEORGE WILLIAM BLUNT was born in Newburyport, Maine, March 11th, 1802, and died in this City, April 19th, 1878, in the seventy-seventh year of his age. His father, EDMUND MARCH BLUNT, was a writer on nautical subjects, and publisher of "BLUNT'S Coast Pilot," the first edition of which was issued in 1796, and subsequently translated into most of the European languages. When his father retired from the management, GEORGE WILLIAM continued the publication until 1866, when it was sold to the Government. Mr. BLUNT followed the sea before he was fourteen years old, and gave considerable study to navigation. In 1822 he began business as a publisher of charts and nautical works, at the corner of Water and Fulton streets, in a building which stood on the site where the United States Hotel now stands. The business was moved from there to Water-street and Maiden Lane, and subsequently to Water-street and Burling Slip, and there continued, by EDMUND and GEORGE W. BLUNT, until 1866. The latter assisted his brother, EDMUND, in the surveys of New-York Harbor, Bahama Banks and George's Shoals, all of which were made on private account. The United States Coast Survey was not then in active operation. In 1834 Mr. BLUNT called the attention of the United States Government to the superiority of the Fresnel light for use in light-houses, and, upon the request of his brother, EDMUND, this light was subsequently adopted, and in 1852 the present Light-house Board was organized.

GEORGE W. BLUNT was selected in 1845 as one of a commission to organize the present system of pilotage for the Port of New-York. The Chamber of Commerce also elected him a Pilot Commissioner, which office he held at the time of his death. He was elected a member of the Chamber of Commerce April 5, 1842, and was highly esteemed by his associates. He was for five years a trustee of the Seamen's Retreat, two years a Commissioner of Emigration, President of the Commission for Licensing Sailors' Boarding Houses, a member of the Marine Society, one of the first members of the Union League Club, and the oldest director in the Manhattan Company. The greatest service Mr. BLUNT rendered this community was his untiring vigilance in preventing encroachments on New-York harbor, and urging measures for its protection and improvement; to these subjects he devoted much of his time. During the war he was one of a Committee appointed to examine applicants for the volunteer Navy, and at that time furnished the Government with able and competent officers. In other respects he was an active and earnest worker, and never grudged the service it was in his power to render in the interests of the public generally. Mr. BLUNT had two children, daughters, both of whom survived him.

JONATHAN GOODHUE.

THIS eminent merchant was born in Salem, Massachusetts, June 21st, 1783. He was the son of the Hon.
BENJAMIN GOODHUE, United States Senator from that
State for two successive terms. He was educated in the
best schools of Salem, which was then an important and
wealthy seaport.

In the year 1798, at the age of fifteen, he entered the
counting house of the Hon. JOHN NORRIS, of Salem, one
of the most wealthy and enterprising merchants of that
city, who was extensively engaged in trade with Europe
and the East Indies. Mr. NORRIS was held in high regard
for his great moral worth, his piety, benevolence and truth-
fulness. After five years of training in commercial pursuits, young GOODHUE was sent, by Mr. NORRIS, as
supercargo of one of his ships, to Aden, on the Arabian
coast of the Red Sea. There was no Suez Canal in those
days, and the voyage was made by way of the Cape of
Good Hope and the Isle of France, and thence up the Red
Sea. Including about six months spent at Aden, the
voyage occupied nineteen months. He reached Salem in
July, 1805, and in the following October made a second
voyage, to Calcutta, which terminated in October, 1806.
His intelligent observation and study enabled him to profit
greatly by these voyages, and to understand what cargoes
were best fitted to supply the needs of the peoples whom
he visited.

A year later, (November, 1807,) he removed to New-
York, to start in business for himself ; having the friend-
ship, confidence and patronage of his late employer, Mr.
NORRIS, of the Hon. WILLIAM GRAY of Boston, and JOSEPH
PEABODY, one of the most eminent merchants of Salem.
He bore, also, strong letters of commendation to the Hon.
OLIVER WOLCOTT, who was then engaged in commercial
pursuits, to ARCHIBALD GRACIE, and to General MATTHEW
CLARKSON, whose daughter he subsequently married.

His early career was marked by moderate success, which

9

would have been much greater, but for the long embargo and the subsequent war with Great Britain. When peace was declared in 1814, he despatched an express messenger to Boston, with instructions to proclaim aloud the good news at every town on the route. The messenger was received with great joy at Boston and elsewhere, and Mr. Goodhue's conduct in making this intelligence a public blessing, instead of using it for private and speculative purposes, won him the regard of all business men who knew him.

After the war, his commercial transactions were extended through all the ports of Europe, the East Indies, Mexico and South America, and his correspondents, who visited New-York and enjoyed his open-handed hospitality, became warmly attached to him. Amid all the vicissitudes of commerce and trade which affected the business of the great shipping houses of America, between 1807 and 1848, the embargo, the war with Great Britain, the fluctuations of the currency, the great financial panics of 1827 and 1837, and the Mexican war, the firm, of which Mr. Goodhue was the head, maintained the highest credit and the most spotless reputation. Wealth rolled in upon them, and it was used wisely and ungrudgingly, though always quietly, in aiding the unfortunate and the younger and weaker firms, and in the promotion of learning, science and religion. His kindness of heart was manifest in all his daily life. His domestic servants and his employees were strongly bound to him, and almost invariably remained in his employ, till they were obliged to retire from active life.

In politics, Mr. Goodhue was a Federalist of the old school, and from its principles he never swerved or departed in the slightest degree. As an importer, in the condition of our country at that time, he was, very naturally, a strong advocate of free trade. He was most thoroughly patriotic, and in all his commercial operations he was zealous for the honor of the nation's flag.

He became a member of the Chamber of Commerce April 15, 1817, and was active, though never obtrusive, in its deliberations. He retained his membership till his death. He was elected its President May 2, 1843, but declined the honor. At a special meeting of the Chamber, convened November 25th, 1848, on the occasion of his death, the following resolutions were unanimously adopted:

Resolved, That the Chamber of Commerce, and merchants of New-York, representing the unanimous sense of their body, record the death of JONATHAN GOODHUE, now no more of earth, with the sincerest grief, and with the highest respect for his virtues.

Resolved, That as a merchant his enterprise, his systematic attention to business, his unvarying good faith and fidelity, his unspotted honor and unstained integrity, entitle him to a lasting good name in the commercial annals of our country.

Resolved, That we equally declare our high esteem for his virtues as a man, for his kindness of heart, his liberality in useful public enterprises and his activity in works of charity, for his modesty, and also for his elevated Christian spirit, and for the unostentatious simplicity and blameless purity of his private life.

Resolved, That in common with the whole commercial community of this country, by whom he has been so long known and esteemed, we respectfully tender our sympathy to his mourning relatives and friends—and that these resolutions be communicated to them as a last mark of our respect.

At this meeting a Committee was appointed to procure a bust of Mr. GOODHUE, which was afterwards executed by the late HENRY K. BROWN, and is now in the Rooms of the Chamber.

Mr. GOODHUE had been from his early youth a member of the Congregational (Unitarian) Church in Salem, and had transferred his membership to the church of that denomination on its organization in New-York. His pastor,

Rev. Mr. (afterwards Dr.) H. W. BELLOWS, at his funeral, pronounced an eloquent eulogy on him, in which he did justice to his exalted Christian character. But, though faithful to his own church, his hand and heart were open to every effort to make men better, holier and wiser.

As a husband and father, no man could have been more devoted, loving and tender than Mr. GOODHUE. In a paper, written only a few months before his death, he gave wise and tender counsels and suggestions to those dear to him, and after avowing his readiness to depart, when it should please the LORD to call him, he subjoined this postscript : "I add, as a most happy reflection, that I am not conscious that I have ever brought evil on a single human being."

Mr. GOODHUE had suffered for nearly two years from symptoms of heart disease, and on November 24th, 1848, he passed away, suddenly, from that cause, not long after he had completed his sixty-fifth year, beloved and lamented by all who knew him.

GEORGE GRISWOLD.

GEORGE GRISWOLD, son of GEORGE GRISWOLD, and third of the name, was born at Giant's Neck, Lyme, New-London County, Connecticut, in the year 1777.

The ancestor of the family, MATTHEW GRISWOLD, emigrated from Lyme, England, in 1635, to Windsor, Conn.

GEORGE GRISWOLD, the subject of this sketch, removed to New-York City in 1796, having been previously a clerk in a store in Hartford. His elder brother, NATHANIEL LYNDE GRISWOLD, had preceded him in 1795, and conducted business under the firm of HAYDEN & GRISWOLD, which was dissolved in February, 1796.

The two brothers formed a copartnership in the beginning of 1798, the firm name being NATHANIEL L. & GEORGE GRISWOLD, which continued until the death of NATHANIEL in 1846. The business was carried on under the same name by GEORGE and his descendants until dissolved, January 1st, 1876.

The house soon acquired credit, and by industry and skillful management steadily advanced in wealth and influence. To NATHANIEL was assigned mainly that portion of the business that related directly to the care and management of their numerous vessels when in port, whilst GEORGE assumed the financial control and guidance of their general affairs. During the first five years their operations were on a very small scale, and consisted of commissions and speculations at home, and adventures to the West Indies. Afterwards they boldly embarked, at successive periods, in enterprises to every quarter of the world open to the commerce of the United States which appeared to offer a promise of success.

GEORGE GRISWOLD early rose to the very front rank of merchants for intelligence, comprehensiveness of view and signal ability. He maintained this position during the whole of his life.

Possessed of a vigorous intellect and strong memory, he was capable of severe and long-continued mental labor. His perception was clear and ready, his decision prompt, his action full of energy. His high integrity and sound judgment commanded public confidence, and led to his frequent selection for the office of arbitrator or umpire in the settlement of commercial disputes. He served as director in various corporations, insurance companies, banks and other associations connected with commerce, and in railroad companies when this branch of internal commerce began to assume importance, and ever discharged his duties with diligence and ability. He made the law of marine insurance a subject of special study, and his opinion on difficult cases is believed to have possessed for many years a weight not surpassed by any contemporary, lay or professional.

Whilst he was always largely and actively engaged in commercial enterprises, he was ever foremost in every benevolent and public-spirited undertaking. During the prevalence of yellow fever and the cholera he remained in the City and administered of his substance to the suffering. He was amongst the first to relieve those suffering from fire or other calamities, in other cities as well as his own.

Mr. GRISWOLD had a very extensive acquaintance with the leading men of all professions, and was on terms of intimacy with WEBSTER and his contemporaries.

His politics were ever conservative. Early in life he was a Federalist. He joined the Whig party at its formation, and followed its fortunes to the end. Although a zealous and efficient laborer in the political field, he never held a political or civil office other than that of Elector for the State of New-York, when General TAYLOR was chosen President of the United States.

Mr. GRISWOLD was elected a member of the Chamber of Commerce April 15th, 1817, and always took an active part in its affairs.

In person, Mr. GRISWOLD presented a fine specimen of the vigorous race to which he belonged. Nearly six feet in height, with broad shoulders and chest, erect, muscular and well balanced, his carriage was graceful, and his activity and strength seldom surpassed.

He died, after a short illness, at New-Brighton, Staten Island, on September 5th, 1859, in the 83d year of his age, and was buried in Greenwood Cemetery.

WALTER R. JONES.

WALTER R. JONES was the leading Marine Underwriter of his day, and contributed largely to the development of that department of commerce in the United States, particularly at the Port of New-York. He was the son of JOHN JONES, and was born at Cold Spring Harbor, Long Island, April 15th, 1793. The Cold Spring branch of the JONES family of Queens County, whose original seat was on the south side of the Island, whence all the sons of WILLIAM JONES emigrated, excepting the father of Chief Justice SAMUEL JONES, were originally gentlemen farmers and manufacturers. Their descendants, however, were naturally attracted to this City, in the building up of whose business and prosperity some of them took no insignificant part.

At the age of eleven, the subject of this sketch entered the store of his eldest brother, WILLIAM H. JONES, then in the flour trade. A few years later, through the instrumentality of his cousin, J. JACKSON JONES, he became a clerk in the office of the United Insurance Company, which was among the earliest of our City organizations to undertake marine risks, and where he served his first apprenticeship to the calling that engrossed all the subsequent years of his life. In 1824 he became an assistant to ARCHIBALD GRACIE, President of the first Atlantic Insurance Company. In 1829, after the discontinuance of this Company, and in conjunction with JOSIAH L. HALE, he organized the second Atlantic Insurance Company, with a capital of $350,000. Mr. HALE was President and Mr. JONES Vice-President, and the Company had a prosperous career until, in turn, it gave place to a third successor, bearing the name "Atlantic."

In the year 1842 the mutual system of insurance had come into favor. The substitution of the assured, for stockholders, as recipients of such dividends as might be realized from the business of underwriting, appealed to the interest of the merchants. Various difficulties and hazards were necessarily incident to the inauguration and conduct of such a system. But the experiment was in process of being tried, and Mr. JONES and his associates had faith in their ability to adopt it and carry it successfully forward. Accordingly, the present Atlantic Mutual Insurance Company was chartered and commenced business July 1st, 1842, with Mr. JONES as President and Mr. HALE as Vice-President. Not long afterward the office of Secretary was filled by JOHN D. JONES, who succeeded his uncle in 1855, and has ever since been the President.

The characteristics of WALTER R. JONES were untiring energy and industry, fidelity to duty, probity, accuracy and prudence. These qualities, together with the skill and experience gained in his previous training, were devoted

to the establishment and management of the new enterprise. Of the Company's standing little need be said here.
Its unquestioned credit and honorable repute have long
been recognized throughout the commercial world. During
the ten years, dating from January, 1844, the average of
annual dividend realized by its assured exceeded thirty-
three per cent., and at the time of Mr. JONES' decease, in
1855, the aggregate of these dividends, made in scrip to the
assured, had exceeded six millions of dollars. The firm
foundations on which the Company was thus established
remain unshaken, and its prosperity and usefulness in the
service of commerce have been uninterrupted.

While official duties claimed the time and attention of
Mr. JONES, they did not wholly debar him from other interests, which did not require his immediate personal care.
Among these interests, centred at Cold Spring Harbor,
were manufacturing industries and whaling ventures, under
the management of his brother, JOHN H. JONES. It may
be mentioned, as matter of local history, that in 1848 the
whaling fleet fitted out at Cold Spring numbered eight
vessels, having an aggregate tonnage exceeding three thousand tons, carrying about two hundred and fifty men, and
costing about a quarter of a million dollars.

The ready sympathy of Mr. JONES was also enlisted for
humane enterprises, when wisely planned, and especially
when associated with the sea. It was largely due to his
persistent effort that the Life Saving Benevolent Association was chartered in March, 1849, and was enabled to
initiate the improved system of Life Saving Stations on the
Atlantic coast. In short, he was never content to be idle
or to waste a moment possible to be employed upon some
useful task. At the same time his frank sincerity and un-
formal courtesy won for him a kindly place in the recollections of his associates and cotemporaries.

Mr. JONES was elected a member of the Chamber of
Commerce November 4th, 1834, and retained his membership until his death, which occurred in this City, April 7th,
in the sixty second year of his age.

LORING ANDREWS.

LORING ANDREWS was born on January 31st, 1799, at Windham, in White (now called Greene) County, in the State of New-York. His first American ancestor, WILLIAM ANDREWS, had been one of the companions of JOHN DAVENPORT in the settlement of the colony of New-Haven, in 1635, and his name appears on the records as one of the twelve men chosen to select from their own number the seven Burgesses to whom was to be entrusted the government of the infant settlement. WILLIAM's son, SAMUEL, who accompanied his father from England, removed with his own family, in 1672, to Wallingford, the first off-shoot of the parent colony, and but a few miles removed from it. The founder of the American family built the first church in New Haven, and after the migration to Wallingford, the name appears in many of the documents relating to the history of that community. The removal to Windham was made about the middle of the last century by LABAN ANDREWS, the grandfather of the subject of this sketch, and it was in Windham that LORING ANDREWS received his education, and underwent the early experience that was the foundation of his subsequent success in a larger sphere of action than the little country village afforded.

CONSTANT ANDREWS, LORING's father, was well remembered in Windham a few years ago, as having been a Justice of the Peace, a prominent Free Mason, a man of commanding presence, and of an ardent and enterprising temper. The family consisted of two sons and two daughters, the subject of this sketch being the second son.

Almost with the beginning of the century, began that movement to the then unknown "Great West," which drew with it the more adventurous spirits of the seaboard States. CONSTANT ANDREWS was one of these, and as he was a land surveyor by profession, the opportunities of a new country appealed to him with especial force. In 1817 he joined the westward march of the pioneers, leaving his family behind. LORING had already, in 1813, at the age

...rteen, apprenticed himself to FOSTER MORSE—one of
...rliest of the tanners who had been attracted by the
...n hemlock forests of the Catskill Mountains—serving
...he apprenticeship, which was completed in 1820. In
...eantime, his mother had died in New-York City, and
...her brother had followed his father to the West.
...n he found himself of age and a free man, young
...e at once took his way westward in search of the
...r and brother of whom for some years he had heard
...et tidings. The journey was then a great under-
...g for a youth of slender means, but he persevered
...e discovered that both his father and his brother had
...and been buried at Prairie-du-Chien.
...quest had occupied two years, and when the melan-
...eal of it had been attained, young ANDREWS re-
...l to New-York by the way of New-Orleans, and
...l at Hudson, (where one of his aunts was living,)
...ut and dispirited. His good aunt refused to let him
...her until he was restored to health and strength, but
...he was fully recovered, he determined again to seek
...ome in the West. From this purpose he was di-
...ly what he meant to be a passing visit to his old home
...ham. There he was warmly greeted, and his old
...er, FOSTER MORSE, offered him the management of
...f his tanneries, upon terms so favorable as to induce
...tle again in his birthplace. Until 1818, the busi-
...f tanning had been prosecuted on a small scale only,
...t year Colonel EDWARDS, of Northampton, Mass.,
...ed in Greene County the first of the great tan-
...which for nearly half a century, and until the
...had been stripped of their hemlock forests,
...ed the leading industry of the Catskill region.
...er was carted over the mountain roads to the town
...n, on the Hudson River, a long and wearisome
...and thence transported by boat to the City of
...York, at that time, and for many years afterward,
...market for the product. It was in 1822 that
...ANDREWS returned to Greene County, and seven
...he came to this City, which was to be his home

for the remainder of his life, to establish himself as a leather merchant, with a capital as yet small in money, but with a reputation for integrity and industry that secured him the confidence of the tanners of Greene County. It was not long before he took a prominent place among that body of solid and honorable men of the " Swamp," who were not less distinguished for their commercial honor than for their business sagacity.

LORING ANDREWS was to pass through one more trial on his way to prosperity. In 1832 he had formed a partnership with WILLIAM WILSON, in which GIDEON LEE and SHEPHERD KNAPP were special partners. The profits of the firm were large for several years, but the panic of 1837 came, and at the age of thirty-eight Mr. ANDREWS found himself once more penniless. But here there came to him a mark of confidence that not only reflected honor upon his special partners, but also emphasized the character for probity which he himself had earned. These gentlemen invited him to a conference, in the course of which they offered to let their money remain in his keeping, to be repaid, practically, at his own convenience, and with no other security than his word. The money was repaid in due time, and the success of LORING ANDREWS thenceforth was scarcely broken. For a great portion of the remainder of his business career he was alone, except when, during 1840, ABIEL LOW, of Boston, was his partner. In 1851 he admitted into partnership CHARLES GIBBONS, a young man who had risen from the ranks, and by his industry, perseverance and honesty had won the confidence of Mr. ANDREWS. In the latter years of his life Mr. ANDREWS was assisted in the management of his business by his two sons, WILLIAM L. and CONSTANT A., the firm name being LORING ANDREWS & SONS.

Mr. ANDREWS was described by his business associates as the soul of honor in all his transactions, and possessed in a remarkable degree foresight and independent judgment. He attested his great faith in the value of Swamp property by investing largely in it. He was one of the early directors of the Mechanics' Bank, one of the founders

of the Shoe and Leather Bank, and its first President.
He subscribed largely to the stock of the Atlantic Cable
Company, at a time when that enterprise seemed hazardous
to a degree which in these days it is difficult to understand,
or even to recall.

Mr. ANDREWS was elected a member of the Chamber of
Commerce July 6, 1865, and continued his connection with
the association to the close of his life.

In his social and more private relations, LORING AN-
DREWS was self-contained and somewhat reticent, but
kindly ; his benefactions were alike liberal and unostentatious. He died in this City, January 22d, 1875, in the
76th year of his age.

JOSHUA BATES.

THIS eminent banker and financier, to whose kindly
and generous offices America owes so much, was born in
Weymouth, Massachusetts, October 10th, 1788. His father,
Col. JOSHUA BATES, was one of the most estimable citizens
of Weymouth, but was not in prosperous circumstances.
He gave his children the best educational advantages, both
public and private, which Weymouth afforded ; and when,
at the age of fifteen, young BATES was placed in the
counting-house of WILLIAM R. GRAY, then one of the
merchant princes of Boston, Mr. GRAY says that his
father, in taking leave of him, gave him twenty-five
dollars, which was his whole patrimony. The boy was
faithful, intelligent, diligent, and strictly upright in
all business matters, and soon won the confidence of his
employer. Mr. GRAY had two business houses, one in
Charlestown, the other in Boston. When young BATES
was eighteen years of age he was put in charge of the
Charlestown house, and remained there three years, when
he returned to Boston, and for three years more was in
commercial relations with Mr. GRAY. In 1813 he formed
a partnership, under Mr. GRAY's patronage, with Capt.

BECKFORD, of Charlestown, under the style of BECKFORD & BATES, but, owing to complications arising out of the war of 1812, the business was not successful, and, at the end of three years, the copartnership was dissolved. Lieut. Gov. WILLIAM GRAY, father of WILLIAM R. GRAY, a great shipping merchant of Salem, had removed to Boston some years before, and in 1816 sent young BATES to Europe, as his agent. He conducted his business there very successfully, traveling over the continent extensively, and forming the acquaintance of the great commercial houses of Holland, France and Italy. From 1820 to 1826 he resided in London, and conducted negotiations with the great merchants of London, in behalf of the GRAYS and other American houses, and so great was the confidence he inspired, that when he was about to enter into partnership with Mr. JOHN BARING, January 1, 1826, one of the most eminent of these merchants, Mr. LABOUCHERE, voluntarily tendered him the capital he needed for the partnership. Two years later, in 1828, both Mr. BARING and Mr. BATES joined the great banking house of BARING BROTHERS & COMPANY, of which in a short time he became the active manager in all American and foreign affairs, and, on the retirement of Sir ALEXANDER BARING, (Lord ASHBURTON,) the senior partner. His thorough business abilities, his great knowledge of commercial affairs in all parts of the world, and his admirable tact and genial manners, made him a model banker. In the settlement of all American questions he was the supreme authority. He cultivated the most amicable relations with all the leading American bankers. While he never forgot for a moment his allegiance to his native country, and was always proud of his American citizenship, his relations were so cordial with the Governors of the Bank of England and the great London bankers, that he could obtain greater favors from them, than were accorded to any other banking house. He was always ready to render a service to America, and his first great opportunity to do so was not neglected. Mr. SAMUEL B. RUGGLES, long an honored member of the New-York Chamber of Commerce, thus stated Mr. BATES' services to New-York City and the country in 1838, in a speech before the Chamber, October 20th, 1864, called to take action on the occasion of his death. (We omit some passages, not necessary to the understanding of the subject.) At the time of the great financial panic in 1837, the Legislature of the State of New-York passed an act practically permitting the banks of the State to suspend specie payments for one year from May 16, 1837. Mr. RUGGLES was elected a member of the State Assembly in November of that year, and made Chairman of the Committee of Ways and Means, in that body. It was a part of his duty to examine carefully the resources of the banks, and especially their ability to resume specie payments in May, 1838. He was thus brought into communication with many of the most eminent bankers and financiers of the City and country. Among them, none possessed sounder financial knowledge, or clearer and more far-sighted judgment and integrity, than the late JAMES GORE KING, soon after President of the Chamber of Commerce, and the head of the great banking house of PRIME, WARD & KING, who were most intimately associated with the house of BARING BROTHERS & Co. Mr. KING was hostile to the act of suspension passed by the previous Legislature, and was determined to spare no effort to bring about the prompt resumption of specie payments in May, 1838. Meanwhile, Mr. NICHOLAS BIDDLE, then President of the "Pennsylvania Bank of the United States," (resuscitated from the old Bank of the United States, and regarded in many quarters as a high authority in matters of finance, wrote to Mr. RUGGLES, earnestly advising the prolongation of the suspension of specie payments, and asserting the inability of the banks to redeem their obligations in coin. The Committee of Ways and Means disapproved of Mr. BIDDLE's view, and consulted Mr. KING on the best means of bringing about resumption. He was so earnest in his belief in its necessity, that he went to Europe in the early winter of 1838, to aid in its accomplishment. How he

succeeded is told in the following letter, addressed to Mr.
Ruggles:

London, March 15, 1838.

Dear Sir:

I hasten to inform you that I have concluded an arrangement on the part of Baring Brothers & Co., and Prime,
Ward & King, with the *Bank of England*, for the shipment of one *million of sovereigns*, (in gold, of course,) by
the four or five first ships for New-York, from London and
Liverpool, and I trust and hope that upon their arrival
our banks, and those of the Atlantic Cities, will resume
and maintain specie payments, toward which result my
thoughts and efforts have been unceasingly devoted for the
last month. The service which I have thus had an opportunity to afford my own City and State, by aiding it in
taking the initiative in this great and wholesome measure,
affords me a satisfaction, in which I know that you and
my other friends will fully participate. This arrangement
was only concluded definitely this morning, but I com-
municate it with all dispatch.

James G. King.

To Samuel B. Ruggles, Esq.,
Chairman Committee of Ways and Means,
Albany, N. Y.

It was not till after Mr. King's return to New-York
that it was learned that Mr. Bates had not only readily
responded to Mr. King's proposition, which, without his
powerful aid and co-operation, could not have been accomplished, but mindful of the difficulties attending resumption, had insisted upon having another million of
sovereigns, ($5,000,000,) placed at the disposal of the
American bankers, if it should be required. In 1839 Mr.
Bates, solicitous for the rescue of the monied institutions
of his native land from embarrassment and dishonor,
offered, on behalf of Baring Brothers & Co., to advance
a large sum on State stocks, (which were not then readily
marketable in England,) for account of several banking

institutions of New-York City, and thus relieve them. This credit, though but partially used, contributed largely to maintain public confidence.

The result of the negotiations of 1838, so honorable alike to Mr. KING and to Mr. BATES, is now a matter of history. The first million of sovereigns, ($5,000,000,) with so much more in prospect, proved amply sufficient. The New-York banks all resumed early in May. Their example was generally followed throughout the Union, except in the case of Mr. BIDDLE'S Bank, which, after a vain attempt to carry an oppressive load of interior State stocks, finally went down and disappeared from the financial world.

But Mr. BATES' manifestation of the highest love for his country did not stop with these acts. When, in 1846, Great Britain and the United States were nearly ready to go to war on the Northwestern Boundary question, the British Government claiming, on very weak grounds, that the boundary line should be the 45th degree of north latitude, while the United States Government demanded the parallel of 54 40'; Mr. BATES, who had studied the whole subject very thoroughly, circulated among the members of Parliament, and his English friends, the very candid and able pamphlet of Mr. WILLIAM STURGIS, of Boston, who had devoted some years to the investigation of the question, and had explored the Northwest region in person. When Commissioners were appointed by the two countries, to settle the controversy and formulate a treaty, Mr. BATES was, at their joint request, appointed umpire, and his decision was accepted without hesitation and incorporated in the treaty. To his wise action we owe our possession of the Columbia River in all its course, and the magnificent territory of Washington, soon to be a State.

In the Northeastern Boundary question, settled by the AMERICAN treaty of August 9, 1842, Lord ASHBURTON, formerly a member of the house of BARING BROTHERS & Co., was the leading Commissioner on one side, and DANIEL WEBSTER, then Secretary of State, on the other; both were warm personal friends of Mr. BATES, (as was our then Minister, the Hon. ABBOTT LAWRENCE,) and all came to him for the history and geography of the boundary, which he understood better than any one else, and their final agreement was on the lines he had marked out.

In relation to his friendly action to us in the time of our civil war, the conclusion of which he did not live to see, we cannot express more fully the greatness of our obligations to him, than by quoting two of the eloquent resolutions adopted unanimously by the Chamber of Commerce, at the meeting on the occasion of his death ; these resolutions were offered by JOHN A. STEVENS, and seconded by JAMES BROWN :

Resolved, That this Chamber recognizes with cheerfulness, the long and able services given as fiscal agents of the United States, by the firm of which Mr. BATES was a member, and especially acknowledges the liberal, timely and valuable aid rendered to the Government, in its large transactions during the present rebellion, to all of which Mr. BATES, as senior partner, gave his personal assistance and influence.

Resolved, further, That not alone, or chiefly for what is already set forth, will the name of JOSHUA BATES be held in dear and grateful remembrance by all loyal Americans, but for that, in this our mortal struggle for national life, he has stood forth, with few around him, unwavering, unshaken, steadfast in his fidelity to his native country, unchanged and unseduced by aristocratic associations, or the blandishments of great wealth and power : a true supporter always of the integrity of the United States, and faithful to the cause of human liberty and progress among all nations.

We may add, what is not, perhaps, generally known, that to his influence over NAPOLEON III., who was under great personal obligations to him and his house, is due the abandonment of NAPOLEON's intention of declaring war against us in 1862. The Emperor had three grievances against us : our refusal to recognize MAXIMILIAN, our cap-

10

of the Confederate Commissioners, and the placing of the Count de Paris upon General McClellan's staff; and it required all Mr. Bates' skill and influence, to dissuade him from hostile action, but he succeeded.

It was natural that Boston, the place of his early business training, and Massachusetts, the State of his birth, should receive special gifts, as evidences of his affection; and so we find him founding the Boston Public Library by the gift of $100,000 in money and choice books, and in many other ways manifesting his regard for that city; but his heart was too large, and his philanthropy and patriotism too deep and broad, to be confined within State lines. His career was marked by comparatively few afflictions; he lost his only son, a young man of great promise, in 1834, by the accidental discharge of a fowling piece; and the death of his wife, to whom he was most tenderly attached, which occurred nearly thirty years later, was thought by his friends to have hastened his own. He died September 24th, 1864, at New Lodge, near London, England, in the 70th year of his age. Only one child, a daughter, survived him.

PETER COOPER.

This distinguished inventor, merchant and philanthropist, so well known throughout the land, was born February 12th, 1791, in what was then called Little Dock-street, now Water-street, near Coenties Slip, in this city. His mother was born on the site where St. Paul's Church now stands, at the junction of Broadway and Vesey-street. Both parents were devout people, and belonged to the Methodist Church. His maternal grandfather was Deputy Quartermaster-General in the War of the Revolution, and his own father was a Lieutenant in the Army at that time. The early education of Peter Cooper was very unlike that which his generosity has provided for many young men of to-day. At the close of the war his father began the manufacture

of hats in this city, and succeeded in amassing a small
fortune. Before PETER was eight years of age the father
moved to Peekskill, where he established a hat-factory and
small store. This business he sold soon afterwards, and
then engaged in the brewing of ale. From this he took to
brick making at Catskill, but as this proved unsuccessful, he
removed his family to Brooklyn, where a brewery was again
tried, but without success, and the family once more started
for the shores of the Hudson, where, at Newburg, the father
soon established another brewery, which, owing chiefly to
the exertions of PETER, was made a partial success. PETER
was then 16 years old. In 1808 he left his father's roof
for New York, intending to begin business as a brewer.
Lack of funds prevented him from carrying out his plans,
and he, therefore, apprenticed himself to JOHN WOOD-
WARD, a carriage-maker. For five years, the term for which
he was bound, he received $25 per year and board. He
was a close student, while other apprentices neglected
their opportunities. When, therefore, his apprenticeship
expired he was a very proficient workman, and the
appreciation of his master was manifested by an offer to fit
up a shop on the Bowery for him, and permit him to pay
for it when he was able. This offer Mr. COOPER declined,
on the ground that he did not like to begin life by bur-
dening himself with debt. He, therefore, left the coach-
making business, went to Hempstead, Long Island, and
there worked at $1.50 a day for a man who was making
a machine for shearing cloth. This was in 1812. In 1813
he married Miss SARAH BEDELL. At this time he had
saved sufficient funds to enable him to purchase the right
to manufacture a patent cloth-shearing machine. In this
he was successful. His inventive power and his close application now began to produce results: for at this period
he perfected a very important improvement in this machine. Commerce with England was stopped for some
time by the war, and Mr. COOPER realized a large profit
in his business; but when the war closed the demand
for his machine ceased, and he sold the patent to MATTHEW
VASSAR, the founder of Vassar College.

Mr. Cooper at this time made his first important venture in real estate in this city, by securing a twenty-years' lease of two houses and six lots, where the Bible House now stands (opposite the Cooper Union); and here he began the grocery business, and built four large wooden dwelling-houses. Shortly after, he purchased a glue-factory, with all its buildings and stock, and a leasehold right of twenty-one years of the site upon which it stood, in the old Middle Road, now Fourth Avenue, between 31st and 34th streets. This proved to be the foundation of the large fortune which PETER COOPER so honestly earned, and a large portion of which he so philanthropically spent. "COOPER's glue" soon became famous, and was of better quality than the imported product. He also manufactured whiting, prepared chalk and isinglass. When his lease expired, Mr. COOPER was considered a wealthy man. He built a commodious factory on Maspeth Avenue, Brooklyn, and there continued the manufacture of glue, until he reached his eightieth year.

Mr. COOPER's surplus capital was invested in various ways. He could command almost unlimited credit. Everybody knew him, and had confidence in his ability, enterprise and integrity. In 1828, with others, who afterwards proved to be irresponsible, Mr. COOPER purchased three thousand acres of land within the limits of the City of Baltimore. All the purchase-money was found by Mr. COOPER. By this transaction he secured the whole of the shore line of Baltimore, from Fell's Point Dock, for a distance of three miles. The manufacture of charcoal iron then began to engage his attention, and he erected a number of large kilns and a forge of novel design and construction. This property he sold to a Boston firm, and the Canton Land Company was then established, Mr. COOPER taking a large portion of his pay in stock. The stock of the Company appreciated in value so rapidly that Mr. COOPER was enabled to sell his portion; so that his Baltimore investment, after all, proved a paying one.

He built an iron-mill in 34th-street, in this city, but

in 1850 removed his business to Trenton, N. J., at which place he erected what was, at that time, one of the largest rolling-mills in America. Here he first introduced the manufacture of iron beams for fire-proof buildings. He was the first to apply anthracite coal to iron-puddling. Blast-furnaces were also built by him at Phillipsburg, New Jersey, and rolling mills, and wire-works, connected with mining operations in other parts of Pennsylvania and New-Jersey.

Mr. Cooper's inventive mind was continually at work. In 1830 he built a locomotive to demonstrate the feasibility of running trains round objectionable curves, and before this had invented an endless chain for the towing of boats on the canals. For nearly a quarter of a century Peter Cooper was a member of the Chamber of Commerce, and was honored by all his associates in the Chamber as a successful merchant and philanthropic citizen. For twenty years he was President of the American Telegraph Company, and was at its head when it controlled more than half of all the lines in the country. He also owned a large amount of stock in, and was President of, the New-York, Newfoundland and London Telegraph Company. His money and influence were also at the command of the promoters of the laying of the Atlantic Cable. Cyrus W. Field, the prime mover in this great project, was ably supported by Mr. Cooper during all the trying vicissitudes of that great enterprise.

The benevolent schemes of Peter Cooper have been so fully recorded that a passing reference to them will suffice here. The Cooper Union—that grand legacy to the students of science and art—is one of his great gifts, which will make his name known to future generations. Denied of educational privileges himself, he was determined to devote the savings of his life, if necessary, to the establishment of an Institute which should give to the poor an opportunity of securing that scientific knowledge which in after years they could put into practical use. The Cooper Union was begun in 1855, and in 1857 the building was transferred by its founder to the Trustees. The Institute cost $630,226. In 1882 another story was added, at a cost of over $100,000, and Mr. COOPER also made a special endowment of $250,000 for the support and increase of the free reading room and library. It is unnecessary here to explain the advantages this noble institution offers, beyond saying that its scope has been so enlarged as to provide for free courses in Natural Philosophy, Chemistry, English Literature, Rhetoric and Elocution, and many other useful branches of learning, including Art Schools for men and women.

In 1876 PETER COOPER was the nominee of the National Independent party for President of the United States, and conditionally accepted the nomination. He was also a promoter of anti-monopoly measures. His views on the currency question are well known. They were never very popular. His opinions on many economic subjects were collated just prior to his death and issued in book form. Mr. COOPER died in this City, April 4th, 1883, in the 93d year of his age, universally and sincerely mourned by all. His wife died in December, 1869. Six children were born to them, but four died early in life. The Hon. EDWARD COOPER, Ex-Mayor of the City, and SARAH AMELIA, the wife of the Hon. ABRAM S. HEWITT, are the two surviving members of the family.

JOHN DAVID WOLFE.

JOHN DAVID WOLFE was born in this City, July 24th, 1792. His grandfather, bearing the same name, was a native of Saxony, and emigrated to this country in the early part of the eighteenth century, and died here in 1776, leaving four children, the eldest of whom was DAVID WOLFE, the father of the subject of this sketch. DAVID WOLFE passed nearly the whole of his long life of eighty-eight years, on Fair-street, (now known as Fulton-) between William and Nassau streets, until the widening of that thoroughfare caused his removal to another section of the City. DAVID WOLFE took an active part in the entire War of the Revolution, and at the outbreak he was appointed by the Committee of Safety, under authority of the Provincial Congress, Captain of the militia company of foot in the City of New-York, on beat described by the City Committee as "beat Number 13," and served for several years as Assistant-Quartermaster of WASHINGTON's army. He was noted for the earnestness and promptness in the discharge of his duties, for which qualities he was highly complimented by General TIMOTHY PICKERING, his superior officer. After the close of the war, DAVID WOLFE engaged in the hardware trade. After a successful career he retired from business in 1816, and was succeeded by his son, JOHN DAVID WOLFE, who for a short time was in partnership with his cousin, under the firm name of C. & J. D. WOLFE; afterwards, until the close of his business career, was associated with JAPHET BISHOP, who married Mr. WOLFE's sister. The firm then was known as WOLFE & BISHOP, and their place of business was at the corner of Maiden Lane and Gold-street. Mr. WOLFE was one of the founders of the Chemical Bank and always a Director in that institution. He was also one of the earliest Directors of the Hudson River Railroad Company.

Mr. WOLFE retired from active business in 1842, having acquired a large fortune, which was afterwards augmented by judicious investments in real estate in this City. His life was thereafter devoted to charitable and philanthropic enterprises, to which he gave largely of his means, and aided by personal labor to make them a success. He was a devoted member of the Protestant Episcopal Church, and for several years a Vestryman of Trinity Church, afterwards a Vestryman, and, at the time of his death, Senior Warden of Grace Church.

He was President of the Prison Association of New-York, Vice-President of the Society of the New-York Hospital, Vice-President of the New-York Association for Improving the Condition of the Poor, Vice-President of the Society for the Relief of the Ruptured and Crippled, and an officer in other associations and societies having for their object the moral and religious elevation of the people.

JOHN DAVID WOLFE was a man of great benevolence, and his benefactions were as free from ostentation as they were far-reaching in their results. He never did anything parsimoniously. If he had pet charities, they did not shut out the claims of others upon his benevolence. Childhood in particular received from him personal attention. Several of the great cities of the West are largely indebted to him for their early educational advantages.

Mr. WOLFE was a patron of the various libraries and institutions of fine arts of this City. He was one of the founders, and a generous contributor to the American Museum of Natural History, and was its President at the time of his death. The Historical Society was his special beneficiary, and he always took an active interest in its affairs.

Mr. WOLFE was for many years a member of the Chamber of Commerce. He died in this City, May 17th, 1872, in the eightieth year of his age.

He left but one child, Miss CATHARINE LORILLARD WOLFE, recently deceased, who inherited not only his entire fortune, but his generous impulses, as her large and numerous charities abundantly prove. Her munificent gift to the Metropolitan Museum of Art of her entire collection of modern paintings has placed within the reach of our citizens, art treasures that will for ages preserve the memory of the donor.

With this noble gift, Miss WOLFE set apart the sum of two hundred thousand dollars, the income of which is to be expended by the Board of Trustees for the care and protection of the collection, and for making such additions thereto, from time to time, as the Trustees should deem appropriate.

BENJAMIN B. SHERMAN.

BENJAMIN BORDEN SHERMAN was born in Shrewsbury-town, Monmouth County, New-Jersey, November 8th, 1810. His boyhood was spent at Eatontown, to which place his parents removed a year after young SHERMAN's birth. He attended the Quaker school near that town, and was brought up in the Quaker faith. At the age of thirteen he commenced to study medicine, but ill health led to the abandonment of his studies.

In 1828, when eighteen years old, Mr. SHERMAN came to New-York, and found employment as clerk with CHARLES & OWEN WARDELL, wholesale grocers, at 45 and 47 Front-street. In 1833 he formed a partnership with CORNELIUS McCOON, and in 1842 GEORGE C. COLLINS was admitted to the firm. In 1847 Mr. McCOON retired, and in 1861 Mr. COLLINS also withdrew, when Mr. SHERMAN took three of his clerks into partnership, and the firm of SHERMAN, TALLMAN & Co. was formed. In 1864 Mr. SHERMAN retired from the wholesale grocery business, after an experience of thirty-six years. His high standing and ripe experience often led merchants to call upon him to decide disputed matters, and act as referee.

On January 1, 1865, Mr. SHERMAN became Treasurer of the New-York Steam Sugar Refinery, succeeding B. R. McILVAINE. For years he had also been connected with the banking interests of the City. On September 16, 1846, he was elected a director of the Merchants' Bank; and on May 27, 1859, was made Vice-President. He was also a director in the Metropolitan Bank from 1851 to 1858. But his best known labors in the financial world were in con-nection with the Mechanics' Bank, of which institution he was elected President, January 1, 1874, succeeding SHEP-HERD KNAPP. Under Mr. SHERMAN's management, the bank prospered, and fully maintained the high character it had borne under the management of his predecessor. In 1851 the Royal Insurance Company of Liverpool established a branch office in this City, and Mr. SHERMAN became one

direct ors and a trustee. He was prominent in the
'zation of the Central Trust Company of New-York,
was chartered in July, 1875, and served as a member
Executive Committee until the day of his death. He
was a director of the Mutual Life Insurance Company
my years.

ile Mr. SHERMAN never entered actively into politics,
he avored to fulfil the duties of a public-spirited citizen
nicipal and national affairs. When the rebellion broke
e was an uncompromising advocate of national unity,
as an outspoken supporter of the Government. He
actively in the organization of the Union League
an l was one of its most energetic members until
o e of the war.

to ok a great interest in the charitable institutions of
ity, and gave largely towards their support. He was
' the founders of the Home for Incurables, at Ford-
N. Y., and served as its Vice-President. He was Vice-
lent of the Juvenile Asylum, and of the New-York
, for the Prevention of Cruelty to Children, and a
' in the Eye and Ear Infirmary, in the Peabody
, and Treasurer of St. John's Guild.

ough brought up in the Quaker faith, Mr. SHERMAN,
s first coming to New-York, attended St. Paul's
h, and when Grace Church was established he became
d. attendant there. Subsequently he was appointed
tyman and Warden.

SHERMAN was elected a member of the Chamber of
e May 1, 1852, and always showed an interest in
a rs, and at times took part in its deliberations.

the early part of December, 1882, Mr. SHERMAN's
became greatly impaired, and he shortly afterwards
ed the Presidency of the Mechanics' National Bank.
ou h his health was never fully restored, he still
ued to take an interest in the various institutions of
he was a member, and was able to attend their
s until his death. He died suddenly in this City,
y 2d, 1885, in the seventy-fifth year of his age.

PRESERVED FISH.

PRESERVED FISH was born in the village of Portsmouth, Rhode Island, July 3d, 1766, and died in New-York City, July 23d, 1846, in the 81st year of his age. His father bore the name of PRESERVED FISH, and was a descendant of the Huguenots. He was a blacksmith by trade, and brought up his son to the anvil until the age of fourteen, when he apprenticed him to a farmer. A farm life did not suit the high spirited boy, and soon after we find him on board a whaling vessel, bound for the Pacific. Storm and tempest had no terrors for him, and he had so mastered the art of navigation that, at the age of twenty-one, he was made Captain. He commanded a number of vessels, and, by shrewdness and tireless energy, accumulated a fortune. He knew no fear, and once, when his vessel sprung a leak, and the crew, on the verge of mutiny, demanded his return to the nearest port, he refused to yield, and eventually brought his ship and cargo of oil safe to their destination.

Captain FISH left the sea in 1810, and settled in New-Bedford as a shipping merchant. CORNELIUS GRIN-NELL was his partner, and the firm was known as FISH & GRINNELL. Through some political disagreement he left New Bedford, selling his house and effects at less than half their cost. In two weeks after he was settled on a farm at Flushing, L. I., which he had purchased in order to devote himself to agricultural pursuits. He afterwards sold his farm and came to New York, where he was appointed Harbor Master. Here he became active in politics, and quite a number of lucrative positions were offered to him, all of which, however, he steadily refused. In 1815 he formed a partnership with JOSEPH GRINNELL, and as FISH & GRINNELL the firm did a large business. This house was among the first to establish a regular line of Liverpool packets, their ships varying from 340 to 380 tons burthen. In 1826 FISH & GRINNELL were succeeded by the firm of GRINNELL, MINTURN & Co. In that year

PRESERVED FISH went to Liverpool, and there formed a partnership with EDWARD CARNES and WALTER WILLIS, two English merchants, and carried on the shipping business for two years. He unfortunately lost by this connection, and returned to this City, being dissatisfied with the English methods of transacting business. His next partner was SAUL ALLEY, with whom he differed on an unimportant matter, which caused a dissolution of the firm in six months. He remained out of business for about seven years, when he was elected President of the Tradesmen's Bank, to the interests of which he devoted the remainder of his days. He was a member of the Chamber of Commerce from May 5, 1818, up to the time of his death.

Mr. FISH, with all his eccentricities, was an upright and distinguished merchant, and possessed many benevolent traits of character. He was married three times, but left no children. He was brought up a Quaker, but prior to his death became a member of the Episcopal Church. The story that PRESERVED FISH was picked up on the shore of the ocean when a child, and named PRESERVED in consequence, is pure fiction, and it is not necessary, in this brief sketch, to explain its origin. As before stated, his father's name was PRESERVED, and it is highly probable that the same name was given to the son, in order to perpetuate it in the family.

DAVID LEAVITT.

DAVID LEAVITT was descended from JOHN LEAVITT, of London, England, who came to America in 1628, and settled in Dorchester, Conn. DAVID's father was a wealthy merchant, a man of ability, and well and favorably known, not only throughout Connecticut, but also in this City. His son, the subject of this sketch, was born in Bethlehem, on the 24th of August, 1791. His parents earnestly desired to give him a liberal education, and he was fitted to enter

Yale College, but his early aptitude for business, and his desire to enter upon a mercantile career, led him to choose the office rather than the class-room. Before he was twenty-five years old he was well known as a man of energy, full of nerve and enterprise.

In 1814 he married Miss MARIA CLARISSA LEWIS, a most estimable lady, belonging to a well known family of Goshen, Conn. In 1823 Mr. LEAVITT became interested in the manufacture of white lead, and in that year went to reside in Brooklyn, where his business was established. About this time he was chosen President of the Fulton Bank, in this City. Later on he bought and assumed the management of the newly established ferry to New-York now the Fulton Ferry. He also became a trustee of the then village of Brooklyn, and an extensive owner of property in the neighborhood of the Heights. In 1838 he became President of the American Exchange Bank of New-York. During his Presidency of this Institution he performed good service to the State of Illinois, in reference to certain bonds held by the bank and its customers, whose value depended upon the completion of the Illinois Canal. He proceeded to England, and, pledging his personal credit, obtained loans which enabled that State to complete the canal, and eventually to pay the bonds, principal and interest.

In 1853 he built a country house in Great Barrington, Mass., and bought a large interest in and became President of the Housatonic Railroad, running through that country, and rapidly developed it.

When HENRY CLAY was nominated for the Presidency, Mr. LEAVITT was one of his most active and liberal supporters. He was a pronounced Abolitionist, though in no sense a leader in that cause.

Many young men were aided by Mr. LEAVITT in their struggles through life. In banking circles he was regarded as a safe and enterprising man, always disposed to help an honest embarrassed merchant, but in no case would he tolerate deception or disingenuousness in any form.

Mr. LEAVITT was an elder in the First Presbyterian

[...] of Brooklyn during the pastorate of the Rev.
[...] H. Cox, D. D., and some time later, until he
[...] from active business and took up his permanent
[...] in Great Barrington.

He died in the City of New-York, December 30th, 1879,
in the eighty-ninth year of his age.

FRANCIS SKIDDY.

FRANCIS SKIDDY was born in Cherry-street, New-York
City, February 10th, 1811. His early years were spent in
Paris, where he received his education. In 1830 he left
France for New-Orleans, and entered into business in that
City, which he continued until 1833; in that year he came to
New-York, and at once commenced his mercantile career as
a sugar broker, locating in Wall-street, a few feet distant
from the place he occupied for nearly four decades. He
soon gained prominence, and was generally regarded as one
of the shrewdest men in the sugar trade. He held an important interest in and connection with most of the large
transactions in sugar during the past twenty-five years,
and probably was as well acquainted as any man of his
day with the important movements and changes in the
handling of this great staple. He was a man of great force
of character, liberal, enterprising and scrupulously honest.
His business was very extensive. During the later years
of his life he took a very active part in financial institutions, having an interest in the Bank of the Republic, the
Central Bank, the Commonwealth, the Resolute and the
Commercial Fire Insurance Companies, and later, in the
New York Warehouse and Security Company. He was
also the chief promoter of the Missouri, Kansas and Texas
Railroad. For many years he was a director in the Mutual
Life Insurance Company, and also a director in the Pacific
Mail and in the Virginia and Old Dominion Steamship
Companies. For quite a period of his life, Mr. SKIDDY
was alone in business, but took into partnership, in 1848,

C. D. Chipnorn. This union was dissolved about three
years after, and John F. Carlisle then became a partner.
This partnership terminated at Mr. Carlisle's death,
which was caused by drowning at Long Branch. For a
period Edmund J. Wade and John R. Skiddy, son of
Francis, were partners, but this partnership was dissolved
about 1860. In 1863 Thomas Minford and George G.
Sivler became members of the firm, which was then
styled, Skiddy, Minford & Co., the name it now bears.
Francis Skiddy died in this City, May 1st, 1879, in the
sixty ninth year of his age.

GUSTAV SCHWAB.

Gustav Schwab was born in Stuttgart, Germany, November 22d, 1822. He came of a family distinguished for
its literary and scientific attainments, his grandfather,
John Christopher Schwab, having been invited by
Frederic the Great, of Prussia, to become a member of
the Royal Academy of Sciences and Professor at the
Military School in Berlin, and his father, Gustav Schwab,
the author of many works of prose and poetry, which to-
day endears his memory to numerous readers, both in
Germany and the United States.

Until the age of seventeen Gustav Schwab resided in
Stuttgart, enjoying the advantages of his father's refined
and cultured home, and pursuing the studies of the Latin
school of that City, which were to fit him for the duties of
his opening career.

Guided by a strong preference for mercantile pursuits,
and with the approbation of his friends, he entered the
counting-house of H. H. Meier & Co., of Bremen—a large
shipping and commission firm—where he served (as was
the custom) an apprenticeship of six years.

Energetic, enterprising and laudably ambitious, young
Schwab desired a wider field of opportunity and action,
and with that instinctive judgment which has guided to

our shores so many of his countrymen, he decided to make the New World his future place of residence.

In 1844, as soon as his term of apprenticeship was ended, he came to New-York and entered the office of OELRICHS & KRUGER, the correspondents of MEIER & Co. in the United States. There he remained for several years, and until the formation of the firm of WICHELHAUSEN, RECKNAGEL & SCHWAB, of which he was the junior partner, and which continued in business till 1859.

Meanwhile the firm of OELRICHS & KRUEGER had been succeeded by that of OELRICHS & Co., and in the year above named Mr. SCHWAB became one of its members, and so continued till the period of his death. Soon after his association with this firm it was appointed the New-York agents of the North German Lloyd Steamship Company, and to the thoroughness and efficiency of his management is largely due the eminent success of that Trans-Atlantic line.

In adopting the United States as the field where his enlarged and intelligent ideas could have full play, and for his home, it was the desire and aim of Mr. SCHWAB to give to it what he could of his time and his talents in return for the great benefits he was privileged to enjoy, and of which no man was more thoroughly appreciative. He soon became prominent in local works of charity and philanthropy, and many of the financial and commercial institutions of New-York asked for and received the assistance of his sound mercantile judgment in the operation of their affairs. He was a director, and for some time President of the German Society, founded in 1784, for the care and assistance of his foreign fellow countrymen in this City. He helped to found the German Hospital and Dispensary, and was one of its Board of Directors, and fulfilled the arduous duties of Treasurer until the fatal sickness came which terminated in his death. He was for some time a Commissioner of the Board of Education, and in all movements affecting the public welfare he took an active part, always giving that conscientious attention to matters of detail which made his service so very effective, and for which he was so justly noted. Among other institutions of finance he was the senior director and Vice President of the Merchants' National Bank, a director of the Central Trust Company, the Washington Life Insurance Company, and many others of a like character.

To the New York Produce Exchange he gave much of his valuable time, was one of its managers, and Chairman of some of its most important Committees; and he assisted in organizing, and continuously served as a Trustee of the Gratuity Fund of that institution. On March 1st, 1860, he became a member of this Chamber, and at once took a very prominent place in its counsels. His intelligent interest in its affairs, and in all the many questions of mercantile ethics which it discussed, was unfailing; and with a continuous liberality he gave of his time, and from the rich stores of his experience and scholarly attainments, whatever seemed most needful to minister to the solution of the problems he was called upon to expound.

The records of the Chamber bear abundant testimony of his great capacity for work; they are studded all throughout with his masterly reports, the last of which (relative to a subject in which he took the deepest interest, because of the benefits which he enjoyed under it,) sent into the Chamber, when he was too ill to come upon our floor and present it in person, protested against the proposed legislation by Congress to "Restrict Immigration into the United States."

In the mercantile world he was a power for great good. His solidity of character, his manliness, his sound judgment and unswerving integrity, together with his great willingness to do honest and hard work in furthering the commercial and charitable interests of his adopted city and country, won for him the universal regard and respect of his fellow-citizens.

Although apparently almost continuously occupied in secular and philanthropic affairs, Mr. SCHWAB found time for thoughtful and extensive reading. He was also a deeply religious man, and of the Protestant Episcopal faith, from

11

the inner piety of whose heart came a Christian humility that was a very beautiful and marked feature of his character. He was as courteous in manner as he was wise in counsel, as clear of discernment as he was open to conviction, and, with all, there was a quiet modesty in all he did and said as engaging as it is memorable, and so unique. Such was the character of GUSTAV SCHWAB.

Mr. SCHWAB died at his residence on Fordham Heights, New York City, on the 21st day of August, 1888, in the sixty-sixth year of his age. ALEXANDER E. ORR.

ELLIOT C. COWDIN.

ELLIOT CHRISTOPHER COWDIN was born in Jamaica, Vermont, on the 9th of August, 1819. His grandfather, Captain THOMAS COWDIN, of Fitchburg, Massachusetts, was a zealous patriot of the Revolution, and filled numerous offices of trust and honor, among which may be mentioned election for many successive years to a seat in one branch of the Legislature of Massachusetts. His father Elliot, his youngest son, was a child. His brother, General ROBERT COWDIN, now deceased, was one of those who inherited his grandfather's aptitude for military affairs, and on the outbreak of the war of the Rebellion led, as Colonel, one of the first regiments which came to the defence of Washington. ELLIOT, as a boy, came to the special care of his second brother, JOHN, an opulent merchant of Boston, who, at one period, took a marked interest in the politics of the State, and served at different times in both branches of the Legislature of Massachusetts. At his house ELLIOT resided, with various interruptions, for more than twenty years. He received the usual education of a youth destined for business life. At the age of sixteen he became a clerk with ALLEN & MANN, dealers in ribbons and millinery goods. Here he remained for about nine years. After the death of the older partner a new firm was formed, under the title of W. H.

MANN & Co., Mr. COWDIN, then twenty-five, entering the house as a partner.

In 1846 he made his first voyage to Europe as a purchaser of goods for the house. This was but the beginning of a series of journeys from New-York to Paris, Lyons, St. Etienne and Basle, which at last became so familiar a fact in his experience, that he came to consider taking passage in an ocean steamer as ordinary persons consider a trip on a ferry boat. At the time of his death he had crossed the Atlantic eighty six times.

It is curious that Mr. COWDIN was never in Paris at any time of his life, when the American colony there was aroused by an assertion of republican principles, that he did not take a prominent part in the consequent demonstration of American principles of government. It was his good fortune to witness the French Revolution of 1848.

In the spring of 1853 Mr. COWDIN dissolved his connection with W. H. MANN & Co., and established a new firm in this City, under the name of ELLIOT C. COWDIN & Co., with a branch in Paris. In the autumn of the same year he married Miss SARAH KATHARINE WALDRON, of Boston.

In the autumn of 1858 Mr. COWDIN had established his family in New-York, he, in the meanwhile, making his two yearly visits to France. He was one of those men who are seemingly never idle for a moment.

Although an ardent Republican in politics, and a man of strong convictions, as well as a facile public speaker, Mr. COWDIN did not appear very prominently before the public until the stirring times of the war, when he assisted in the foundation of the Union League Club, and through and with the Club exercised considerable influence in political affairs.

In the autumn of 1862 Mr. COWDIN was nominated, in the Eighth District of New-York, as the Union candidate, to represent that district in the national House of Representatives, and though not elected, ran largely ahead of his ticket. After the war had ended in the triumph of the national cause, Mr. COWDIN's warm and intelligent interest in public affairs hardly seemed in the least to abate.

He seemed both to understand and to perform public duty, and this understanding and performance of public duty he carried into all the complicated questions which came before the Chamber of Commerce, into the New-England Society, of which he was at one time President, into every well considered attempt to reform the municipal administration of the City of New-York, as well as into national and State politics.

Mr. COWDIN was one of the Commissioners of the United States to the Paris Exposition of 1867, and his report, made to the Department of State on silk and silk manufactures at the close of the Exposition, is a careful and thorough investigation of this important industry in all its branches. The report abounds with detailed statements of fact and conclusions, and has been extensively circulated in this country and in France.

In 1876 his friends in the Chamber of Commerce were desirous that he should accept a nomination to the Assembly of the State, in order that he might be instrumental in passing important reform measures. He was elected to this popular branch of the Legislature, and took his seat in that body January, 1877. At that time not only was party spirit singularly embittered, but, as a consequence, public spirit was at a low ebb. Mr. COWDIN entered at once on what may be called a campaign of reason and good sense against deep seated prejudice and fierce partisanship. He left the Assembly with the reputation of being the most hospitable and hard working member in it, but one who had anticipated the period when it was possible to establish useful and needful reforms. Probably he considered this period of his life, short as it was, as at once the most honorable and the most mortifying test to which his sense of public duty had been subjected.

Mr. COWDIN died in this City on April 12th, 1880, having reached the age of sixty-one years.

From the minute prepared by Mr. A. A. Low, and adopted by the Chamber of Commerce, May 6, 1880, we quote the following just estimate of his character, entertained by his fellow members:

" As a result of his long and repeated stay in Paris, Mr. Cowdin became widely known to many of our public men, and very intimately acquainted with BURLINGAME, SUMNER and WASHBURNE. His liberal hospitality, genial manners and cultivated tastes, brought around him other of his countrymen at home, who were equally conspicuous in public life with those above named. It may be said of him, as he once said of another, 'He enlarged and improved his mind by study and reflection; he dispensed a liberal hospitality; he cultivated enduring friendships; he won troops of friends by manners peculiarly genial and frank.'

" Mr. Cowdin became a member of the Chamber February 3, 1859, and he continued his membership during all the years of his subsequent residence in Paris.

" He was elected a member of the Committee on Home Trade and Commerce, May 19, 1870. He was elected a member of the Executive Committee, May 7, 1874, and as Chairman, May 4, 1876.

" How he met every appointment as a member of this body, and how he discharged his duties as Chairman of the Executive Committee, we all know; but as an incentive to others, as well as in justice to his memory, it should be recorded, that he was ever active, always interested, prompt, faithful and efficient.

" In the discussion of such public measures as have engaged the attention of the Chamber during these latter years, his efforts and influence were largely felt.

" An ardent spirit of patriotism, and a lively interest in commercial pursuits wrought in him with a worthy pride and laudable zeal for the advancement of every good and noble purpose.

" Bearing in mind the excellence of his character, his love of rectitude, his fidelity to duty, his efforts to do good, his success as a writer and speaker, and the peaceful and pleasant relations we were permitted for so many years to enjoy with him, this Chamber will ever hold in honor the memory of ELLIOT C. COWDIN."

KINLOCH STUART.

KINLOCH STUART was a native of Edinburgh, Scotland, born in 1775, and was in early life a large candy manufacturer in that City, but having endorsed for his brothers-in-law, builders, who failed, he surrendered his entire property for the satisfaction of the claims thus created. Notwithstanding this, however, there still remained due some seven thousand dollars, which he was unable to pay. Leaving Edinburgh, then in his thirtieth year, he arrived with his wife in New-York on the 13th of September, 1805, after a passage of fifty-six days. His capital, with which to start in life anew in a strange country, consisted of a robust constitution, indomitable energy, a clear head, stern integrity and one hundred dollars in money. In these days of cable telegrams and steamships it is difficult to comprehend what a forlorn hope the prospect of ever again seeing Mr. STUART or their money must have seemed to his creditors. But of one thing they were certain, and this was, that his integrity would not allow distance and difficulty of communication to weaken his sense of his obligations to them. How fully their confidence in him was justified, is shown by a parchment in the possession of his son ROBERT, bearing date 1812, attesting the receipt, by his eighteen creditors, of twenty shillings in the pound, and their appreciation of his conduct in devoting his earliest earnings, the fruit of close industry for sixteen to eighteen of the twenty-four hours (six days in the week) to the settlement of the outstanding indebtedness in Edinburgh. Three payments to the absent creditors were remitted in sums of one hundred pounds at a time, as fast as the money was earned, and before Mr. STUART had fully furnished his house. He did not wait to become rich before paying his debts. At the time Mr. STUART arrived in New York the yellow fever was raging among inhabitants, and for safety he decided to take up his residence at some other point. He went to Hudson, but that place presenting no profitable opening to his special industry, he returned to the metropolis in October, and towards the close of 1805 was living at No. 40 Barclay-street, (then a two story brick front house,) the upper part of which was occupied by LEMAIRE, a Frenchman, the architect of the City Hall. On the 1st of November, 1806, Mr. STUART removed to the house at the corner of Chambers and Greenwich streets, which he enlarged. At the time Mr. STUART came to live in New-York, the population of the City, according to the census, was seventy five thousand seven hundred and seventy persons. He resumed, in a small way, the business in which he had been so prosperous in Edinburgh, and through manufacturing a pure quality of candy, became so well known and successful that he made money rapidly, and took standing among the most reputable merchants of the City.

He continued in active business until the beginning of 1826, and died on the 29th of January of that year, aged fifty one. He left an extensive and rapidly increasing trade, and an estate, real and personal, valued at over one hundred thousand dollars. At the time of his death he ranked among the rich men in the City of New-York.

ROBERT L. STUART.

ROBERT L. STUART was the eldest son of KINLOCH STUART, and was born in the City of New-York on the 21st of July, 1806. After the death of his father, in 1826, he continued the business of manufacturing candy, until the 7th of January, 1828, when the firm of R. L. & A. STUART (the latter his younger brother) was formed. This copartnership continued unchanged for a period of fifty-one years, and until dissolved by the death of its junior partner, in 1879.

In 1832, R. L. & A. STUART commenced refining sugar by steam, and were the first successful operators in that industry, efforts by others in the same direction having resulted in loss, cessation or bankruptcy. The office of the firm at this time was at No. 169 Chambers-street, a building erected by them in 1831, and the first dwelling-house in the City into which gas was introduced, a main being laid from Greenwich-street for this purpose.

The five-story building, corner of Greenwich and Chambers streets, which the firm subsequently occupied, was erected by them in 1835. The nine-story building, corner of Greenwich and Reade streets, was put up in 1849. The large warehouses on the south side of Chambers-street were built by the firm, and first occupied for the storage of refined sugars.

In 1855-56, the manufacture of candy was discontinued, and sugar refining became the sole business of the firm. No work was ever done in the establishment on Sunday, nor were repairs made at the refinery on that day, or allowed to be made at outside machine shops. The same energy and perseverance in honorably meeting and overcoming obstacles which were dominant in the father were characteristic also of the sons. The hatred of everything spurious, which placed the manufactures of KINLOCH STUART above any suspicion of adulteration, made the product of R. L. & A. STUART a synonym for purity in the markets of the civilized world. During the Civil War the STUARTS gave their unqualified support to the Government, and were among the heaviest subscribers to the first million of the war loan—a significant proof of their confidence in the result of the struggle.

In 1872-73 the brothers retired from active business. In 1835 ROBERT L. STUART married MARY, the daughter of ROBERT McCREA, one of the old and wealthy merchants of New-York. Mr. STUART, after his retirement from active business, devoted his time principally to the work of philanthropy, in which he was most efficiently assisted by his worthy wife, whose name, like that of her husband, is found in connection with nearly every charity of New-York, and with many out of it.

Mr. STUART was a member of the Chamber of Commerce from June 2, 1853, a member of the Union Club for many years, and also a member of the Union League Club from its formation, in March, 1863. He was likewise connected with the Century Club, the New-York Historical Society, the American Academy of Sciences, the Museum of Natural History the presidency of which he resigned in 1880 and the Young Men's Christian Association, being President of the Board of Trustees of the last named at the time of his death. In the Presbyterian Hospital Mr. STUART was greatly interested, and was President of that institution. He gave to it in 1880 the sum of fifty thousand dollars, in addition to many previous gifts. Among other notable gifts of Mr. STUART, made in the same year as the above, are one hundred thousand dollars to Princeton Theological Seminary, a like sum to Princeton College, and fifty thousand dollars to the San Francisco Theological Seminary. Mr. STUART was a liberal but judicious patron of art, and his spacious mansion on Fifth Avenue is filled with many most beautiful paintings, marbles and bronzes. Deeply interested in all that related to the welfare of the City of his birth and love, and all good works at home and abroad, he won the respect, esteem and affection of the entire community. Mr. STUART died at his residence, in this City, on December 12th, 1882, in the seventy-seventh year of his age.

ROBERT McCREA.

ROBERT McCREA was a native of Scotland, born in 1764, but came to this country when a young man, and went into the business of importing dry goods. At that time both Alexandria and Newport were rivals of New-York in the importing trade.

Mr. McCREA was a man of sterling business qualities and sound judgment, and soon had a large and extensive trade, at one time having nine business partners in as many different cities of the United States. He was the first to import ingrain carpets into this country. Mr. McCREA married JANNETT, the daughter of the Rev. JOHN FUR-

GASON, and lived for many years on Spring-street, then the most fashionable part of the city. A man of genial disposition, generous almost to a fault, he was beloved and respected by all who knew him. At the time of his death, which occurred in 1837, in the seventy-third year of his age, Mr. McCREA was one of the most wealthy merchants in New-York City.

JOHN JACOB ASTOR.

JOHN JACOB ASTOR, the elder, was born July 17th, 1763, in the village of Waldorf, near Heidelberg, in the Grand Duchy of Baden. He was the youngest son of JOHANN JACOB ASTOR, a poor peasant, whose father had been in better circumstances.

The first years of his life were passed in poverty and privation, and, at the age of sixteen, he left his father's occupation and joined an elder brother who had settled some years before in London, and who subsequently became the head of the musical instrument warehouse of ASTOR & BROADWOOD. He set out on foot for the Rhine, and, resting under a tree while still in sight of his native village, formed three resolves, to which he adhered through life— to be honest, to be industrious, and never to gamble. He worked his passage down the Rhine on a timber raft, and, on arriving in London, received employment at his brother's factory. Here he remained three years, acquiring the English language and putting by some scanty savings for the time when he should be able to realize the project upon which his thoughts were fixed, of removing to America, where he had a presentiment of attaining great riches. In his later period of prosperity he often referred to these years as having been among the happiest of his life. In November, 1783, he embarked at Southampton, taking a stock of flutes and other musical instruments, which were to be sold at a profit. Upon arriving in New-York he found his brother, HENRY ASTOR, in possession of a con-

siderable fortune, acquired by supplying at first the British
garrison, and afterwards the meat dealers of the city with
cattle, which he bought in herds in the interior.

JOHN JACOB ASTOR soon busied himself in the fur trade,
to which his attention had been called by a fellow-country-
man, and in which large fortunes were being amassed. He
entered upon this new occupation with unremitting vigor,
and, at the end of ten years, had diverted the most profitable
markets from his competitors, and was at the head of a
business branching to Albany, Buffalo, Plattsburgh and
Detroit. Finding that London was a better market for
furs than New York, he chartered a vessel, put his brother-
in-law, WILLIAM WHETTEN, a ship captain, in command,
sold the cargo to great advantage, and returned with ASTOR
& BROADWOOD instruments, which, from their excellence,
were held in high reputation. Taught by this experience
he bought ships and engaged in the lucrative China trade,
sending vessels round the world on each cruise, carrying
furs to England, English manufactures to Canton, and thence
returning to New-York with tea. His business increased
immensely, but he superintended all parts of it personally,
and gave attention to the minutest details. His letters of
instruction to his agents were written with extraordinary
comprehensiveness and accuracy. It was his maxim, "If
you wish a thing done, get some one to do it for you; but
if you wish it done well, do it yourself." He meditated
long before acting, but a resolve once taken, it was executed without hesitation.

His greatest enterprise was the settlement of Astoria at
the mouth of the Columbia River, which is the subject of
WASHINGTON IRVING'S volume of that name. After the
famous journey of LEWIS and CLARK across the continent,
he dispatched traders and buyers to the Indian tribes of
Oregon and Dakota and the great lakes. The British
Northwest Fur Company opposed him to the utmost,
driving away his agents and voyageurs and claiming exclusive rights to the fur trade of the Pacific. In the face
of great difficulty the station of Astoria was maintained for
four years, and a treaty was signed by his agent and son-

in-law Bentzon, with Count Baranoff, on behalf of the Russian Government in Kamschatka and Alaska. In dealing with the Indians, and in his instructions to his captains relative to their intercourse with the savages, Mr. Astor was wise, humane and liberal. A significant corroboration to this statement is found in the conduct of Comcomly, the chief of the native Chinooks, who, upon the approach of a British sloop of war in December, 1814, offered to defend Astoria with his warriors, promising to inflict a sanguinary repulse upon the enemy. But unfortunately Mr. Astor had erred for once in his judgment of human nature, and had entrusted Astoria, with its fort, its magazines and its accumulation of valuable furs, to a renegade Scotchman named Duncan McDougall, who, for a bribe from the British Northwest Company, bade Comcomly dismiss his braves, and hoisted the Union Jack almost before he could be summoned to surrender.

In this remarkable enterprise Mr. Astor was actuated less by considerations of pecuniary profit than by the zest of a vast design, which had gradually developed in his mind, and which aimed at the exploration and civilization of the Pacific Coast, through the medium of commerce and colonization. The magnitude of his financial relations and the vigor and breadth of his self-trained intellect brought him into frequent correspondence upon the establishment and maintenance of Astoria, with the leading American statesmen of the time, but the Government gave no further encouragement or protection than its acquiescence in projects which were evidently to be so greatly to its advantage.

At the commencement of the present century Mr. Astor began investing the profits of commercial ventures in real estate upon Manhattan Island, whose immense future value he was one of the first to foresee. He bought meadows and farms in the track which the growth of the City would follow, trusting to time to multiply their worth. His rise to fortune was due to none of the curious windfalls and favoring chances which are popularly associated with his early years; the first half of his life was an arduous struggle, in which adversity and disappointment only stimulated him to further self-improvement, and to a broader and profounder study of the world. The practical cast of his character, and the principles of frugality and labor which his experience had instilled, made him impatient of indolence and sham and mendicancy. But he knew the value of wise benefaction, and by his will established the library which bears his name, and which his son and grandson have augmented, till their united gift to the City represents a million and a half of dollars.

Mr. Astor was a self-educated man, and his desire for useful information was a constant habit of the mind, and marked every period of life. He delighted in the society of men of letters and accomplishment. One of his most intimate friends, dating from the days of their service as directors of the Bank of the United States, was Albert Gallatin, and his frequent companion, and one who, at a later period, lived with him for several years, was Washington Irving. Through business relations he was interested in the chief banking institutions of the City, and in 1834, when the New-York Life Insurance and Trust Company was robbed by its cashier of its entire surplus, amounting to a quarter of a million, Mr. Astor saved the Company from an inevitable suspension, which, in those days, meant disgrace, by the gratuitous loan of an amount sufficient to meet its immediate needs.

After his retirement from active business, in 1822, he made several visits to Europe, residing on the continent, in all, nearly ten years. He acquired the French language, which he learned to speak and write fluently, was presented at the Court of Charles the Tenth, and devoted parts of two winters to the galleries and museums of Italy: the summers abroad were passed at a villa he owned on the Lake of Geneva, which he afterwards gave to his son-in-law, Vincent Rumpff, then Minister of the Hanseatic League at Paris.

Mr. Astor's last years were spent in repose and retirement, in the supervision of landed interests and in the society of a small circle of men of attainment.

His strongest trait was integrity. His private life was

blameless. His chief pleasure was in the simple recreations of his country home. By the force of his influence and example, he helped to give character to the society of his time.

In old age, surrounded by every luxury, and looking back across an eventful career, his thoughts reverted to the home of his boyhood in the humble little village of Waldorf; and by his will he made provision for the establishment there of an asylum for the sick and infirm, which, since its creation, in 1854, has alleviated suffering, and stood as a memorial of the love its founder retained to the last for his German fatherland.

Mr. ASTOR died in this City. March 29th, 1848, in the eighty-fifth year of his age.

SAMUEL B. RUGGLES.

SAMUEL BULKLEY RUGGLES was, for more than twenty years, one of the directing minds of the Chamber of Commerce. He was born at New-Milford, Connecticut, April 11th, 1800, and was descended from an old Colonial stock of English origin, inheriting, in full degree, that combination of ardor and perseverance which is characteristic of the New-England race. Gifted with rare intellectual powers, he was one of the most attractive of men. Ready in intelligence, felicitous in speech, and of a genial, kindly manner, he, from early youth, took his place among the intellectual magnates of the land.

Graduated from Yale College at the age of 14, he studied law as a profession, and was admitted to practice at the New-York bar in 1821. In 1838 Mr. RUGGLES was elected a member of the Assembly, from this City, and was chosen Chairman of the Committee of Ways and Means of that body. His report to the Legislature on the canal policy of the State, though derided at the time by political opponents as visionary and exaggerated, is one of the ablest of our State papers. Warm in expression and earnest in tone, its predictions, to use the writer's words at a later period, "startled the nerves of some of our worthiest citizens." Yet, not only were all of the estimates reached, but exceeded, within the period to which he had confined them.

His estimate in the report in question was, that if the Erie Canal should be enlarged, its tolls would reach the sum of three millions of dollars at the close of navigation in 1 49. The actual figures were over three and one-half millions. In that year, although the enlargement was not made, the number of tons carried to tide water was twelve hundred thousand. The movement reported for 1880 was over three millions of tons, valued at more than two hundred millions of dollars. This enormous increase was in no small measure due to the jealous and ceaseless care with which Mr. RUGGLES watched every act of the Legislature which threatened or concerned this great artery of internal traffic.

From the time that he first espoused the cause of the Erie Canal, until his death, there was no wavering in his devotion to the cause of internal improvements. His models, for admiration and imitation, were the famous FRANCIS EGERTON, Duke of Bridgewater, who constructed, at his own cost, the first canal in England, and DE WITT CLINTON, to whose energy and statesmanship New York owes its canal system, and the control of the traffic of the Lake country.

But while his fame is indissolubly connected with the canal system of this State, (he was Commissioner from 1828 to 18.. when he retired from the Board,) this was by no means the only sphere of his usefulness. Mr. RUGGLES was one of the original founders of the Bank of Commerce, in 1839, and took an important part in securing the passage at Albany of the General Banking Law, under which it was chartered, and for many years was a director of this institution. He was also one of the Commissioners with JAMES GORE KING and JOHN A. STEVENS to decide upon the route of the Erie Railroad. The records of the Chamber bear abundant testimony to his untiring industry and great sagacity, and numerous pamphlets from his pen show the range of subjects which attracted his attention. In 1852 he published a defence of the right and duty of the American Union to improve its navigable waters. In May, 1864, he delivered the address on the opening of the Metropolitan Fair in aid of the United States Sanitary Commission. The following July he was the orator on the occasion of the semi-centennial meeting of the graduates of Yale College, of the class of 1814, and of the Alumni of that Institution. The same year he published his report on the Resources of the United States, and on a uniform system of weights, measures and coins; this report he had previously presented to the International Statistical Congress at Berlin. In 1866 he represented the United States as Commissioner at the Paris Exhibition. In 1869 he was one of the delegates to the International Statistical Congress at the Hague. In 1871 he published a pamphlet entitled " Internationality and International Congresses; a Report to the Department of State;" together with a report to Congress on the comparative population and cereal products of the United States. In 1877 he addressed the American Bankers' Convention on the subject of American silver coinage, and made an earnest appeal for the " Dollar of our Fathers."

The last and crowning work of his life, however, to which he had given years of patient study of a most arduous character, was the " Consolidated Tables of National Progress in Cheapening Food," which presented, by decades and geographical divisions, the agricultural progress of the nation in cheapening the food of America and Europe. This important work was printed by the Chamber for distribution.

This brief sketch of Mr. RUGGLES would be incomplete without some mention of his identification with the growth of our City. At an early day he foresaw its wonderful development in population and boundary, and he was connected with some of its greatest enterprises. Although a lawyer by profession, his associations were, of choice, with the great merchants of this City, and his achievements and fame are our just heritage.

CORNELIUS RAY.

CORNELIUS RAY was of an old New-York family, the founder of which, JOHN RAY, emigrated to this country from Exeter, in the County of Devonshire, England, at the close of the seventeenth century.

CORNELIUS RAY was the son of RICHARD RAY and his wife, SARAH BOGERT, and was born in Smith-street, (now William street,) New-York City, April 25th, 1755.

Mr. RAY entered mercantile life at an early age, and became one of New-York's most prominent merchants. During the war of the Revolution, on the investment of the City by the British, he retired to Albany, where he married, on July 26th, 1784, ELIZABETH ELMENDORPH, the daughter of PETER EDMUND ELMENDORPH, of Kingston, Ulster County, in this State, by whom he had several children. Mr. RAY returned to the City when peace was restored, and again entered mercantile life. After the establishment of the Bank of the United States, he was chosen President of the New-York Branch, and continued in that office until the expiration of the bank's charter in 1810.

On April 20th, 1784, Mr. RAY was elected a member of the Chamber of Commerce, and its President May 6th, 1806, serving until May 4th, 1819, when he declined a re-election.

In March, 1817, through the efforts of Mr. RAY, the Chamber was aroused to renewed activity. Its by-laws were revised, and a large number of young merchants were elected members, who afterwards became prominent in its affairs. Though not a politician, Mr. RAY was a Federalist in principle and a consistent supporter of the Federal party. Being on terms of intimacy with prominent mem-

12

bers of that party, he was frequently called upon to preside
at its meetings.

Mr. RAY was long connected with and took an active
interest in the charitable institutions of this City. He was
one of the incorporators of the Society of the Lying-in
Hospital, which was established by Act of the Legislature,
passed March 1, 1799, one of its first Governors, and its
President for many years.

In his personal character and intercourse Mr. RAY was
kind and gentle, of high principles, and a merchant of
strict integrity. An affectionate father, a firm friend and
a sincere Christian, he left to his children at his death,
which occurred in this City January 18th, 1827, an untar-
nished name, which they will ever regard as their best
inheritance.

ROBERT RAY.

ROBERT RAY was born in the City of New-York July
14th, 1794. His father, CORNELIUS RAY, was President of
the Chamber of Commerce 1806-1819. ROBERT RAY was
graduated from Columbia College in 1813, receiving, four
years later, the degree of M. A. Although educated for the
bar, he never practiced law. After a trip to Europe he was
admitted a partner in the banking house of PRIME, WARD,
SANDS, KING & Co., and for many years was one of its
members. He was one of the founders of the Bank of
Commerce, and one of its directors from its organization in
1839 until 1841, having also served as Vice-President within
that period. In 1841 he resigned his office and went to
Europe, but on his return he was re-elected a director in
October, 1844, and served as Vice-President from May,
1848, until June, 1866, retaining the office of director until
his death, which took place at his residence in this City,
March 4th, 1879.

Mr. RAY's offices in various financial, commercial,
charitable and other institutions were quite numerous.

He was a trustee of Columbia College ; a director of the New York Life Insurance and Trust Company ; a Governor of the New-York Lying-in Hospital from 1834, afterwards Vice-President and President ; a trustee of the Lenox Library ; a director of the Eagle and the Sterling Fire Insurance Companies, and a director and afterwards President of Greenwood Cemetery. He was also a Vestryman of Grace Church, and its treasurer for many years. In 1835 he was a steward of the St. Nicholas Society, and for years a member of the Union Club.

Mr. Ray's active business career ceased on his retirement from the banking firm named. By his marriage, in 1819, with Cornelia, eldest daughter of Nathaniel Prime, he had several children. Mr. Ray was a man of the highest integrity, methodical in his business habits, somewhat reserved in manner, but genial withal. He never desired or held any political office, but nevertheless did all in his power to promote the welfare and prosperity of his native City.

JOHN C. GREEN.

John Cleve Green was born near Lawrenceville, New-Jersey, on the fourth day of April, 1800. His father's ancestors came from England, his mother's from Holland, near the close of the seventeenth century. Both families first settled on Long Island, but soon removed to New-Jersey.

His grandfather, George Green, married Anna Smith, daughter of the Rev. Caleb Smith, Pastor of the Presbyterian Church of Orange, and grand-daughter of the Rev. Jonathan Dickinson, first President of Princeton College. He settled in the township of Lawrence, entered the military service, as Captain, at the beginning of the Revolutionary war, but soon died, leaving four sons under seven years of age. The eldest, Caleb Smith Green, when sixteen years old, took entire charge both of his father's estate and of his younger brothers. He married Elizabeth Vancleve, a lady of amiable disposition, fervent piety, and great force of character. Their second son, the subject of this sketch, ever revered his mother's memory, and attributed to her early influence and wise counsel much of his subsequent success in life.

Mr. GREEN's early years were passed on his father's farm and in attending the schools of the neighborhood. In his fifteenth year he went to reside with the Rev. SELAH S. WOODHULL, his uncle by marriage, then settled in Brooklyn. After spending some time at school in that city, he entered the counting-room of N. L. & G. GRISWOLD, at that time among the most eminent shipping merchants in New-York. By his diligence, attention to business, and devotion to the interests of his employers, he soon gained their esteem, and attained a high position in their service.

In 1823, Messrs. GRISWOLD, being largely engaged in trade with South America and Spain, invited Mr. GREEN to visit those countries in the interest of their firm. To their inquiry, whether he would accept the position, he at once replied, "Yes, if your terms suit me." The terms were soon settled, and in a few days he embarked on the ship "Potosi," nominally as supercargo, but with full power to exercise a general supervision over the business of his employers at the various ports where their vessels touched.

After an absence of more than two years, one of which was spent in Spain, Mr. GREEN returned home in the spring of 1826, and in a few weeks embarked for South America and China, in the ship "Panama," with the same general commission as before, the voyage again occupying two years. From this time until 1833 he made an annual voyage to China, reaching Canton early in the fall, attending to the loading and despatch of Messrs. GRISWOLD's vessels, and at the close of the season returning home in the "Panama," the only ship in which he ever sailed after his first voyage.

In 1833 Mr. GREEN, while in Canton, preparing to return to New-York, was invited to join the house of RUSSELL & Co., whose senior partner was compelled to leave on account of his health. This invitation he accepted with some reluctance, limiting his engagement to three years from January 1st, 1834. The business of the house, already large, was greatly increased by the accession of Mr. GREEN to the firm as its acknowledged head. His perfect knowledge of the laws and usages of commercial life, his reputation for integrity, and his experience and skill in business made him a recognized leader in the sharp rivalry of the China trade. The partnership had scarcely terminated, and its affairs were still unsettled, when the mutterings of the storm, which in 1837 shook the financial world in both hemispheres, were heard in the East, and for the protection of his house, their numerous correspondents, and the safety of his own private fortune, he was compelled to remain in China two years longer. While failures were occurring in all parts of the world, the credit of RUSSELL & Co. remained unshaken; their liabilities in London, contracted in carrying on their enormous business, were fully discharged, and Mr. GREEN succeeded in removing his own funds to London and New-York without loss, thus closing his career in the East with a reputation for ability and integrity rarely equalled and never surpassed.

After his return home Mr. GREEN took a much needed rest from business cares, spending some time in the pleasures of social intercourse and in travel in his native land, making a careful examination of the resources and prospects of the Northern and parts of the Western States. In the fall of 1841 he married one of the younger daughters of GEORGE GRISWOLD. Domestic in his tastes, his house was his home, where he enjoyed the society of friends and ever dispensed the most generous hospitality. For some years Mr. GREEN continued to a limited extent his connection with the China trade, but at an early day his keen observation and sound judgment foresaw the wonderful influence which the railroad system of the United States would exert in the development of the country, and he gradually embarked in various railroad enterprises, always contributing an amount of capital sufficient to give him an influential voice in their management and control. As a director in these various roads, in the Bank of Commerce, and as trustee and President of the Bank for Savings in this City, and as manager in various charitable institutions, he ever gained the respect and confidence of his associates.

Though never holding office, he took a deep interest in public affairs, and during the Civil war his voice was ever raised, and his potent influence in moneyed corporations always actively exerted in support of the Government.

Mr. GREEN possessed a deeply religious temperament. From early manhood he took an active interest in religious, benevolent and charitable enterprises. Deprived by a mysterious Providence of all his children, his desire to aid the suffering and to do good to his fellow-men increased with his advancing years. Charity with him was not a mere impulse of the feelings, but a deep, abiding principle. He gave largely and wisely. Almost every benevolent institution of the City was a recipient of his generous aid, and to many of them he contributed his time and labor as well as his abundant means. To Princeton College, in his native State, he was a generous benefactor; her finest buildings and her rich endowment being largely due to his munificence.

Mr. GREEN became a member of the Chamber of Commerce May 5th, 1859, and so remained until the time of his death. He did not enter into the ordinary proceedings of the body, but on two memorable occasions: "the movement in behalf of the suffering poor of Lancashire," and that "in aid of Chicago in flames," he took a leading and conspicuous part. His stirring appeals and generous example on these occasions are among the cherished records of this association.

Mr. GREEN died at his home in this City on the 29th of April, 1875, in the beginning of his seventy-sixth year, with faculties unimpaired and a character unblemished, leaving behind him the record of a well spent life, and looking forward in the full assurance of hope to a happy immortality beyond the grave.

CHARLES H. MARSHALL.

CHARLES HENRY MARSHALL, one of the leading shipping merchants of New-York during the brightest period of American commerce, was for over thirty years a prominent and active member of the Chamber of Commerce.

He was born at Easton, Washington County, in the State of New York, April 8th, 1792. Both on the father's and mother's side he was of Nantucket descent. His paternal grandfather, BENJAMIN MARSHALL, a Quaker by faith, followed the sea, lived, when on shore, in Nantucket, and died in his home on that island. His son, CHARLES, who began life as a sailor on the deck of a Nantucket whaler, emigrated, in 1785, to Washington County, New-York, where he married, in 1786, HEPHZEBAH COFFIN, daughter of NATHAN COFFIN, of Nantucket, also one of the colonists who had taken up their abode in New-York. Of the seven children of their marriage, five sons and two daughters, CHARLES HENRY, the subject of this sketch, was the third. True to the instincts of their Nantucket lineage, all the sons took to the sea, and all became honorably identified as ship-masters, with the American merchant marine. CHARLES HENRY left home when only fifteen years of age, April 5, 1807, to seek his fortune as a sailor. He made his way to Nantucket, and offered himself to Captain SWAIN, of the ship "Lima," as able seaman for a whaling voyage. The Captain at first repulsed him, saying, "I want young men, but you are a mere boy and too light for my purposes." This so disheartened young MARSHALL that he could not conceal his mortification, on which the Captain relented, and said, "I will take you, my lad ; I dare say you will make up in smartness what you lack in size." Stimulated by this encouragement, young MARSHALL joined the ship's company with alacrity, and began his career as a sailor. He made several voyages before the breaking out of the war with England drove the American merchant vessels from the seas, and during the stormy period of the conflict devoted himself to study, laying the foundation of a good

English education, and forming the habit of reading, which he retained through life and which gave him always much pleasurable occupation. During a part of the year 1813 he taught school in a new settlement in the wilderness, fifty or sixty miles northwest of Easton, Washington County, N. Y., called Sollendagah, now the town of Northampton.

At the close of the war, in 1815, he resumed his calling as a seaman, and shipped as second mate on the ship "Mary," from New-York to Oporto. He became mate of the vessel before the end of the voyage. In 1816 he sailed in the Liverpool trade, first as mate of the "Albert Gallatin," a ship owned by JACOB BARKER, then as mate of the "Courier," owned by ISAAC WRIGHT and JEREMIAH THOMPSON, and before the end of the year obtained command of the new ship "Julius Cæsar," of which PHILETUS and GABRIEL HAVENS were owners.

In the "Julius Cæsar" he made a famous run from Charleston to Liverpool, in boisterous March weather, sailing a day later than the "Martha," a fast vessel bound to the same port, and commanded by an experienced master. The "Julius Cæsar" won the ocean race, arriving in the British Channel eighteen days after leaving Charleston and at Liverpool eighteen hours before the "Martha," exclusive of her day's start.

In 1817 the enterprise of a few shipping merchants in New-York led to the establishment of the line of packets between New-York and Liverpool known as the "Black Ball Line," and afterwards as the "Old Line" of Liverpool packets.

This was an advance step in the commerce of the country and marked the origin of regular lines of ocean passenger vessels to sail, interchangeably, from New-York to Liverpool on a certain day in every month throughout the year. The project originated with ISAAC WRIGHT & SON, FRANCIS THOMPSON, JEREMIAH THOMPSON and BENJAMIN MARSHALL, (a member of a different family from that of Captain MARSHALL.) The prospectus was dated "New-York, Eleventh Month, (November,) 27, 1817," and stated that a line of four vessels, the "Amity," the "Courier," the

"Pacific" and the "James Monroe," each of about 400 tons burthen, fast sailers, with commodious accommodations for passengers, would be despatched monthly, one from New-York on the fifth, and one from Liverpool on the first of every month. Contemporaneous with this circular were announcements, by other enterprising New-York carriers, of a new line of post-chaises to Philadelphia and a tri-weekly steamboat line to Albany !

The Liverpool packet line proved a success, and Captain MARSHALL became one of its most trusted and popular ship masters. In 1822 he took command of the "James Cropper," built for the line, a ship of 500 tons burthen, at that time quite a prodigy of size. In the same year he married FIDELIA WELLMAN, daughter of Doctor LEMUEL WELLMAN, of Piermont, N. H.

After twelve years of constant service, in command successively of the "James Cropper," the "Britannia" and the "South America," Captain MARSHALL, in 1834, left the sea to assume the management of the "Old Line," and after acquiring the interest of GOODHUE & Co., he became its principal proprietor.

During thirty years he retained the business, superintending the building of new vessels to replace the earlier and smaller ships, and many of the finest carrying vessels in our port were constructed and equipped under his practiced eye. The vessels thus added by him were the "Oxford," "Cambridge," "New-York," "Montezuma," "Yorkshire," "Fidelia," "Isaac Wright," "Isaac Webb," "Columbia," "Manhattan," "Harvest Queen," "Great Western" and "Alexander Marshall," ranging from 600 to 1,500 tons burthen. He carried the packet service to its highest point of utility and profit, and as it gradually gave way to vessels propelled by steam, he employed his ships in other lines of traffic, until advancing years compelled his withdrawal from active business.

He built and equipped one steamer, the "United States," a first class vessel of 2,000 tons burthen, and placed her on the route between New-York and Southampton, but after a few voyages she was sold to the Prussian Government during the contest between Denmark and Schleswig-Holstein.

Captain MARSHALL was distinguished in the commercial circles of New-York by his great independence, decision of character, sterling integrity, singleness of purpose and large public spirit. His sympathies were specially active as to every thing touching the interests of seamen, and of the commerce which they served. From 1851 to 1855 he was one of the Commissioners of Emigration. For several years he was Chairman of the Executive Committee of the Chamber of Commerce. For twenty years he was President of the Marine Society, and as such *ex officio* a Trustee of the Sailors' Snug Harbor, an institution over which he watched with the most unremitting assiduity. Holding this position virtually for life, and actually retaining it until his death, he would never consent to an election as President of the Chamber of Commerce, as the acceptance of that office, whose incumbent is also *ex officio* a Trustee of the Sailors' Snug Harbor, would necessitate his retirement at the end of the term from the latter institution, which was one of the objects nearest to his thoughts. The kindred and neighboring charities of the Seamen's Fund and Retreat and the Home for Seamen's Children shared with the Sailors' Snug Harbor in his constant care.

In 1845 he was chosen one of the Board of Commissioners of Pilots for the Port of New-York, and served in that capacity until his death.

In 1851, when the firing upon Fort Sumter aroused the loyal and patriotic spirit of the North for the defence of the Union, Captain MARSHALL was foremost in the efforts of the merchants of New-York to support the Government in every way in their power. As early as 1854 he had co-operated in the efforts made to prevent the repeal of the Missouri Compromise. In 1856 he voted for FREMONT and DAYTON, and was, from the first, an ardent member of the Republican party. He was one of the most active of the Union Defence Committee organized at the great meeting of citizens held in Union Square April 20, 1861, in the vicinity of his house on Fourteenth-street, over whose roof the flag which had waved over Sumter was raised and kept flying during the eventful days which followed that meeting while the first regiments were being hurried southward. He was active in the organization of the Union League Club, and in promoting all the measures by which it sought to strengthen the Administration in its great military and financial exigencies, and was serving as its third President at the time of his death.

Captain MARSHALL survived the successful issue of the war for the Union, and attended at Washington with a large deputation of his fellow-citizens on the occasion of the passage by Congress of the Constitutional amendment abolishing slavery and establishing freedom throughout the United States. Shortly afterwards he visited Europe for the last time, and on his return home, September 5th, 1865, was seized with an illness which terminated fatally on the 23d of the same month. At the next ensuing meeting of the Chamber of Commerce, held October 5th, a warm and touching tribute was paid to his memory and services, the record of which remains as a fit memorial to one who, at every period of his long and eventful career, had shown himself equal to all the tasks he undertook, true to every relation of life, and faithful, alike in private and public service, to every trust committed to his charge. --WILLIAM ALLEN BUTLER.

JAMES STOKES.

JAMES STOKES was born near the corner of Wall and William streets, in this City, on January 31st, 1804. His father, THOMAS STOKES, was born in London, England, and was the intimate friend and co-worker of ROBERT RAIKES, the founder of Sunday Schools, and of the Rev. JOHN VINE HALL, and the Rev. ROWLAND HILL, who formerly preached in Surrey Chapel, London. He was also associated with WILLIAM CAREY and others in the founding of the London Missionary Society.

THOMAS STOKES came to this country in June, 1798, and settled near Sing Sing, on the Hudson River, but afterwards took up his residence in New-York, and with his sons bought real estate on Broadway, near Rector-street, and elsewhere in the City, all of which proved very profitable. He was one of the founders and the first director of the American Bible Society and of the American Tract Society.

In 1837 JAMES STOKES married CAROLINE PHELPS, daughter of ANSON G. PHELPS, and afterwards joined his father-in-law in business, becoming a member of the house of PHELPS, DODGE & Co. He remained a partner until December 31st, 1878, when he left it to become one of the founders of the banking house of PHELPS, STOKES & Co. He was an eminently successful merchant, and, guided by his shrewd judgment, almost invariably made safe, investments. In politics Mr. STOKES was originally a HENRY CLAY Whig and Colonizationist, and afterwards a member of the Democratic party. He never held any public office. Mr. STOKES was an active member of the old Public School Society, an organization which was afterwards merged into the present Board of Education ; in this Society he had as associates PETER COOPER, GEORGE T. TRIMBLE and other philanthropic New-Yorkers. For many years Mr. STOKES was a consistent member of the Madison Square Presbyterian Church. In his impulses he was eminently charitable, and took a deep interest in the establishment of the Young Women's Christian Association, for the founding and maintenance of which he contributed largely, as he did also to the Young Men's Christian Association, of which he was a trustee. In all his business enterprises—which were very extensive—he was regarded as a man of the highest honor. He was President of the Ansonia Clock Company, the Ansonia Brass and Copper Company, a director in the Shoe and Leather Bank and in various other financial institutions. He was also largely interested in Pennsylvania and Michigan pine lands, and an active member of many organizations of a charitable and social character. Mr. STOKES died on Orange Mountain, New-Jersey, where he was temporarily staying, August 1st, 1881, in the seventy-eighth

PAUL SPOFFORD.

PAUL SPOFFORD was born in New Rowley, (now George-town,) Massachusetts, February 18th, 1792. He was sixth in descent from JOHN SPOFFORD, who, with others, came with the Rev. EZEKIEL ROGERS from England to this country in 1638.

After spending a few years in a country store, he embarked in business in Haverhill, Mass. There he made the acquaintance of THOMAS TILESTON, then editor of the Merri-mack *Intelligencer*. Much of the business there was what may be termed a barter trade. At times the articles taken, such as shoes, hats, &c., suitable for the South, would accumulate, and it was very desirable to find a ready outlet. Mr. SPOFFORD and his friend, Mr. TILESTON, decided to establish a commission house for that purpose, and in the spring of 1818 came to New-York and formed a partnership under the firm name of SPOFFORD & TILESTON. They soon became large shippers of domestic manufactures to various ports in the Gulf States, the West Indies and to South America. This profitable trade induced the firm to establish and maintain for many years regular lines of sailing vessels to the ports with which they had business relations. Meanwhile Spain had laid a heavy duty on our manufactures, so that the goods formerly shipped to Cuba could no longer be sent thither, but the firm had become well established as importers of coffee and sugar.

In 1838 England began to construct and run ocean steam-ships. American packet ships at that period had attained a world-wide celebrity for beauty of construction, speed and safety. Her success led our citizens to emulate in part her example; but as United States steamers were of light build, while the English vessels were constructed expressly for the service and were heavily subsidized, navigation of the ocean by steam, from these and other causes, made no progress in this country.

SPOFFORD & TILESTON, who had contributed to the building up of our mercantile marine, saw that the era of the sailing vessel was passing away, and that steam power would in the near future control the navigation of the ocean. After thoroughly convincing themselves that staunch, well-equipped and adequate steamships could be built in this country, they contracted with WILLIAM H. BROWN and STILLMAN, ALLEN & Co. for the construction of the steamship "Southerner," which made her first trip in 1846, and proved a success, weathering with perfect ease and safety some of the most terrific gales. A few months later the firm built the "Northerner," an equally fine vessel. This enterprise stimulated others to establish ocean steamship lines, and COLLINS, LIVINGSTON, VANDERBILT, LAW and others soon placed fine steamships on the ocean.

SPOFFORD & TILESTON also became the owners of a line of Liverpool packets, and their ships, the "Sheridan," "Roscius," "Garrick" and the "Siddons," are still remembered by some of our older merchants for their grace and beauty of proportion. But larger vessels were required, and the firm, therefore, substituted for those named, the "Webster," "Orient," "Calhoun," "Henry Clay" and others, which were then the largest of any engaged in the Liverpool trade. The firm also were among the first to fit up and despatch ships to California during the excitement there consequent upon the discovery of gold.

At the outbreak of the Civil war the firm of SPOFFORD & TILESTON were among the largest sufferers by the blockade of the Southern ports, and by the interruption of our commerce with the West Indies. Their heavy losses, however, did not cause them to waver in their duty to their country. At once they arrayed themselves on the side of the Union, and to the end of the conflict their faith remained unshaken as to the result. They spurned all temptation to put any of their vessels under a foreign flag, but, on the contrary, armed their Havana steamships, and obtained commissions in the United States Navy for their captains, and trusted to the skill and prudence of the commanders of their other vessels. Fortunately, with the exception of the steamship "Nashville," all escaped capture.

Although neither Mr. SPOFFORD nor his partner ever held political office, yet both often came into contact with and were greatly esteemed by the most prominent statesmen of the day. In 1864 Mr. TILESTON died, and though this loss of a partner and life-long friend was a severe blow to Mr. SPOFFORD, he nevertheless bore the strain well, and continued actively in the business until his own death took place, through paralysis, on October 28th, 1869.

Mr. SPOFFORD was connected with various enterprises. For years he was Treasurer and one of the Council of the New-York University, and a director in the Erie, Harlem and other railroads, and in several banks, fire and marine insurance companies. He and his partner, Mr. TILESTON, a sketch of whom immediately follows, were elected members of the Chamber of Commerce on October 1st, 1833, and their membership continued until death. Through a long business career the relations between these partners were the most cordial and happy, and the firm of SPOFFORD & TILESTON will always be associated with the development of the commerce of the nation.

THOMAS TILESTON.

THOMAS TILESTON, the business partner of the above named PAUL SPOFFORD, was born in Boston, Mass., August 13th, 1793. At the age of thirteen he obtained a situation in the printing establishment of GREENOUGH & STEBBINS, of that City, the salary being thirty dollars a year and board. As an apprentice he was diligent, studious and observing, and he soon became not only a competent type-setter, but a proof reader, employing his spare time in literary work, which brought him, pecuniarily at least, some success. Too close application, however, weakened his eyesight, and for some months he was unable to pursue his labors. About this period the junior partner in the publishing house of GREENOUGH & STEBBINS was changed, and GREENOUGH & BURRILL, the new firm, removed their business to Haverhill. Soon afterwards Mr. TILESTON bought out the interest of Mr. GREENOUGH, and the business was continued by BURRILL & TILESTON, the latter assuming the editorship of the Merrimack *Intelligencer*, of which the firm were the proprietors.

At the age of twenty-one he was selected by his old employers to superintend the printing of an American edition of King JAMES' Translation of the Bible, and this edition displays evidence of painstaking care and great ability. In 1815 he took entire charge of the publishing and printing business of the firm named. But the most important part of Mr. TILESTON'S career was yet to come. Prior to the war of 1812 Massachusetts was a commercial but not a manufacturing State. She bought liberally of English goods, and readily found a market for her surplus breadstuffs and fish. The State was opposed to a protective tariff, while South Carolina earnestly contended for it. The war of 1812 caused great changes, by which Massachusetts lost her market, her surplus capital was driven out of employment, and she became a manufacturing State. Haverhill became a manufacturing centre, and the merchants there having decided to establish a permanent agency in New-York, proposed to Mr. TILESTON, in conjunction with Mr. SPOFFORD, who resided in the same town, to proceed to New-York to receive consignments. This proposal was accepted, and thus the firm of SPOFFORD & TILESTON was formed in this City, in the year 1818, and its career is detailed at some length in the previous sketch of Mr. SPOFFORD.

In 1840 Mr. TILESTON was elected President of the Phenix Bank, and continued in that office until his death. His mind was evenly balanced, his industry knew no tiring, and his sagacity, skill and promptness gave him many advantages in mercantile transactions. Mr. TILESTON died suddenly, in this City, on February 29th, 1864, in the seventy-first year of his age. His forty-six years of active business life called for and deserved the following tribute which the Chamber of Commerce paid to his memory at a meeting held March 3d, a few days after his death :

During the last twenty years his influence in this Chamber and elsewhere has been constantly extended to those charitable and public movements and measures which have made our City justly celebrated.

Resolved, That in his decease the mercantile community has lost an estimable member, the young merchant a valued friend, and the City of New-York one of the active supporters of its commercial greatness.

Resolved, That in our varied forms of intercourse with the lamented deceased, we can all bear testimony to his industry, energy, sagacity and ability ; to the skill and courage with which he foresaw or adopted and entered into well-considered and productive plans of enterprise and improvement ; to the promptitude, punctuality and fidelity with which he pursued such plans and performed his engagements, and to his liberal public spirit.

Resolved, That after a long intimacy with him, we express with gratitude our appreciation of his virtues as a citizen and friend, his probity of character and his genial, social qualities.

COMFORT SANDS.

COMFORT SANDS was born at Sands' Point, on Long Island, February 26th, 1748. He came of an English family, that in former times had been most active in the settlement of Virginia and the Bermuda Islands, and a member of which, HENRY SANDS, had, in 1632, emigrated from Yorkshire and settled in Boston as a merchant, dying there in the year 1651.

13

HENRY SANDS brought with him a son or nephew, JAMES SANDS, who, in his eighteenth year, followed the celebrated ANNE HUTCHINSON to the Dutch settlements, near New-York, and when that lady, together with fourteen of her family, were murdered by the Indians, he took refuge in the Providence Plantations, seated himself in the Colony, and married the daughter of JOHN WALKER, a man historically distinguished as one of the eighteen persons associated with ROGER WILLIAMS in founding Rhode Island.

In 1660 JAMES SANDS, having sold his lands in Providence, joined Doctor JOHN ALCOCK and others in the purchase and settlement of Block Island. The history of his life there, so quaintly told by the old historian of the Indian Wars of New-England, shows clearly the sturdy character of one whose religious enthusiasm in early life had separated him from family and friends, and whose later life was passed as the leader and protector of an isolated community, always at war with French privateers, buccaneers and Indians.

In 1695 three of the sons of JAMES SANDS took up lands on Long Island, at what is now Sands' Point, and from JOHN, the eldest, descended, in the third generation, the subject of this sketch.

COMFORT SANDS was one of seven sons. He obtained such an education as was afforded by a good school at Hempstead, and, on his father's death, in 1760, he came to New-York, where, after some training as a clerk by his elder brother, he entered the counting room of JOSEPH DRAKE, a merchant then doing business in Peck Slip.

In 1769 he entered into business as a merchant, on his own account, a little later associating with himself CHRISTOPHER ROSEVELT as a partner, and in the same year he married Miss SARAH DODGE, the daughter of WILKES DODGE, and grand-daughter of THOMAS HUNT, of Hunt's Point.

During the very earliest stages of active opposition to the measures of Parliament, the name of COMFORT SANDS is to be found among those who guided and led the people into open revolution against Great Britain, for as early as 1765 he was of the small party which in the night removed ten bales of the obnoxious stamped paper from a brig just arrived from London, (then lying at the foot of Burling Slip,) and assisted in burning the paper on the beach, near Col. RUTGERS' place.

In 1769 he signed the pledge of the "Associated Merchants" not to import from Great Britain until the Acts imposing duties on tea, paints and glass should be repealed.

In 1774 Congress met in Philadelphia and resolved on a general "non-importation ;" and, to carry this into effect, created a Committee of Sixty, of which COMFORT SANDS was an active member.

In May, 1775, after the battle of Lexington, he was chosen one of a Committee of One Hundred, nominated by Congress to carry the public measures into execution ; and on the 7th of November, in the same year, he was elected one of the twenty-one members of the Provincial Congress, and served till July 1, 1776.

On the 10th of January, 1776, he was chosen a member of the Committee of Public Safety, and, at the request of the Committee, sent three vessels to the West Indies to procure powder, arms and medicines. The largest of the vessels he owned was taken on the voyage, the first vessel captured by the enemy in the war.

In 1776 COMFORT SANDS was again elected to the Provincial Congress, by which body he was unanimously appointed Auditor-General of the Province of New-York. In consequence of the resolution in Congress of May 15, 1776, a body of the most distinguished citizens of New-York was elected, COMFORT SANDS being one of the number, to form a Constitution for the State of New-York in particular, and the United Colonies in general. They assembled in New-York ; but the English having taken the City, they met as they could at White Plains and at Kingston.

In all these public trusts COMFORT SANDS had no hope of that reward which ever attends a successful military

career. His labors during the war were constant and
arduous, full of responsibility and weighted with care.

When the war broke out he was most happily situated
as to his private affairs, having already made a fortune
by mercantile ventures. He saw clearly that the path
of peace would lead him to the highest pinnacle of success.
The larger part of what he had already gained was invested
in ships, therefore, a war with the greatest naval power on
earth promised him only ruin ; but laying aside every consideration of self, he ventured all in the cause of the Colonies   his time, his efforts and his fortune ; and these gifts
which he so freely offered, his country as freely accepted.

COMFORT SANDS was one of these to whom the Government, during those trying times, looked most anxiously
for encouragement and support ; on whose efforts the Congress depended, for finding ways and means to carry on the
war ; to secure the public peace ; to sustain the armies in
the field ; to carry out such measures as would tend to
insure success, and finally lay broad and deep the basis of
an independent State.

In all political disruptions the temper and inclination of
the people must ever be a great factor in the desired solution of the problem of the settlement of the State. Apart
from military operations, success in revolution generally
depends upon a comparative few, whose wealth, faith and
courage are the powers which sustain a provisional government. It was the good fortune of the Colonies, during the
war of the Revolution, to possess a number of citizens
endowed with the highest character and abilities ; and
COMFORT SANDS was happy in being intimately associated
in his public duties with HAMILTON, JAY, LIVINGSTON and
others, whose names have become the synonym of all that
is noble, exalted and patriotic. With WASHINGTON he
was on friendly terms, and by him greatly respected. By
ROBERT MORRIS he was highly valued, as one on whom
the Government could depend in times of its sore financial
distress. To EDWARD LIVINGSTON he was as a brother,
acting with him at all times for the common cause.

The end of the war found COMFORT SANDS much crippled

in his resources, and, like many others, he continued to be long harassed in adjusting his claims with our Government, then in a chaotic state and almost bankrupt. In 1783, however, he was still a young man, but his abilities and public services had secured for him the friendship of the foremost men of the country, and he took rank as an important and influential citizen. He re-established his mercantile business on a larger scale, his ships being among the first to show our flag in foreign ports, and he lent his aid in promoting public institutions of utility to commerce and to the State.

On April 20th, 1784, Mr. SANDS was elected a member of the Chamber of Commerce, its Second Vice-President May 7th, 1793, and its President May 6th, 1794, and served in that office until May 1st, 1798.

With ALEXANDER HAMILTON he was associated in founding the Bank of New-York, and acted with him on the first Board of Directors. His own funds deposited in that institution from July, 1795, to November, 1797, amounted to $3,443,873, a phenomenal sum in those days, but illustrative of the vast mercantile business he had developed.

The date of the " Berlin Decree " of NAPOLEON found the ships of COMFORT SANDS at sea or in foreign ports. Many of them were seized and condemned, and this spoliation by the French proved his ruin. In June, 1801, he was declared a bankrupt under the harsh and unsettled laws of that day a settlement with his numerous and powerful creditors took place, and the final accounting yielded a surplus of $118,000, a result, the Court said, of which there was no other instance on record.

About 1786 COMFORT SANDS joined his brother in the purchase and development of an estate, consisting mainly of a large part of the site of the present City of Brooklyn, and that City still boasts, among those of her most distinguished citizens, the name of JOSHUA SANDS.

After the settlement of his estate in bankruptcy he retired from mercantile life, and passed much of his time at his country seat at the then small village of Newark, in New-Jersey.

His first wife having died in 1795, he married, in 1797, CORNELIA, the daughter of ABRAM LOTT, who had been Treasurer-General of the Province of New-York. By that lady he had three children, one of whom, ROBERT CHARLES SANDS, who died early in life, was distinguished for his learning and literary abilities. Of the children by his first wife, two sons died in France, and only by one son, JOSEPH SANDS, was the family continued in the male line.

In appearance COMFORT SANDS was tall, of a clear florid complexion and prominent features ; in character he was firm, open and unsuspecting, generous to friends, relatives and dependents, and liberal of his time and property in all matters pertaining to the public good.

In constitution he was perfect, knowing nothing of ailment or illness, and capable of performing any amount of work. His life was one long scene of industry and activity as a public man, as a merchant, and as the father of a very large family. He was well fitted for the times in which he lived.

Mr. SANDS died at Hoboken, New-Jersey, September 22d, 1834, in the eighty-seventh year of his age.

JAMES BOORMAN.

JAMES BOORMAN was born in Headcorn, County of Kent, England, April 23d, 1783, and arrived in this country, with his parents, September 1st, 1795. Within a year afterwards his father died, leaving a widow and five children, of whom JAMES was the eldest. It was the custom at that time for some merchants to take young men as apprentices, and to receive them as inmates of their families. JAMES BOORMAN, shortly after the death of his father, became connected with the firm of BETHUNE & SMITH, and resided with DIVIE BETHUNE, so honorably known in the early annals of this century. At the age of twenty-two he entered into partnership with Mr. BETHUNE, and continued in that relation for about eight years. At thirty he established the firm of

BOORMAN & JOHNSTON, and entered upon that career of mercantile success which lasted for more than half of a century.

This firm occupied a prominent place in the mercantile community, and it passed through all the vicissitudes of commercial life without a stain upon its character, or any impeachment of its integrity. For many years BOORMAN & JOHNSTON had almost the entire control of the Dundee trade, and their transactions in Swedish iron and Virginia tobacco were at that time on a gigantic scale.

Mr. BOORMAN was a man of high character, possessed of an indomitable will, guarded by sound sense and comprehensive judgment—qualities which, in their combination, made him a representative merchant of this country. Mr. BOORMAN was interested in many of the great enterprises of his day. He was the prime mover in the construction of the Hudson River Railroad, and was actively engaged in its affairs until the road was opened for traffic on October 3d, 1851. At the first meeting of the Board of Directors, held March 4th, 1847, he was elected Vice-President of the Company. On June 11th, 1849, he was elected President, which office he resigned October 7th, 1851, but continued a member of the Board of Directors. Mr. BOORMAN was also one of the founders of the Bank of Commerce, and his name heads the list of the first Board of Directors of that Institution. In 1855 he retired from active business, and devoted his leisure to the various charitable institutions of the City, in several of which he served either as President or Vice-President.

Mr. BOORMAN was a member of the Chamber of Commerce for nearly fifty years. On May 7th, 1839, he was elected Second Vice-President of the Chamber, and on January 10th, 1840, First Vice-President, and served until May 4th, 1841, when he declined a re-election. He died in this City January 24th, 1866, in the eighty-third year of his age.

JOHN J. PHELPS.

JOHN JAY PHELPS, one of the old merchants of New-York. was born in Simsbury, Conn., October 10th, 1810, in a house still standing and in the possession of his family. He was descended from WILLIAM PHELPS, an English emigrant of 1630, and could boast that all his ancestors in lineal descent were born, lived, died and were buried in the same old Connecticut town. In this line all were honest and reputable. One, JOSEPH, was sent thirty times to the Assembly of that State ; another, DAVID, was a Revolutionary Captain, whose adventures are a tradition of the family. Mr. PHELPS, in boyhood musings, made up his mind to a career of wider experience than that generally led by his Simsbury forefathers. So he set off at fourteen, with sturdy courage, to make his own way in the world. After the Connecticut fashion of the day, his first wish was to secure an education. To the regret of both, his father found it impossible to send him to Yale College, so the disappointed boy determined to seek his education in the next best school, that of the printing press. He went to New-Haven, found employment on the *Eagle;* was very homesick, but persisted ; wrote editorials, put them under the editor's door, and had much secret pride in seeing them used. He was industrious, moral and aspiring. He had nothing of youth, except its innocence and hope. It was not strange that he won. Before his majority he was enabled to buy the *New-England Review*, a journal of dignity and influence, published in Hartford, Conn. He conducted it, in partnership with GEORGE D. PRENTISS, who was afterwards the famous editor of the *Louisville Journal*. PRENTISS & PHELPS, boys themselves, gave employment in this office to various other boys, who rose to prominence. WHITTIER, the poet, was one of their best journeymen printers. Besides the *Review*, they published several books, notably the life of HENRY CLAY. Most of this biography was written by COLTON.

but many of the chapters were written by Mr. PHELPS himself. About this time he married Miss RACHEL PHINNEY, a daughter of Colonel GOULD PHINNEY, a wealthy glass manufacturer of Dundaff, Penn. This was the end of his literary career. He moved to Dundaff and joined with Colonel PHINNEY in his various enterprises. But literature, ceasing to be his occupation, became his pastime. He wrote nearly all the matter of a weekly paper printed in the village, delivered addresses on the fourth of July and other occasions, and was the one always sought for when village needs required a tongue or a pen.

Just as the consciousness of powers larger than the field took him from his farmer home, it took him from his wife's home, and, closing all business connections with Colonel PHINNEY, he went, with varied experience and respectable savings, to New-York. AMOS R. ENO, his cousin, accompanied him, and the two young strangers put up the sign of ENO & PHELPS and began, in an humble way, to sell dry goods to country merchants. Their honesty, ability and persistent devotion to their business made it, after STEWART's, the most influential firm in that branch. A score of large establishments sprang from the ruins, and there are many mansions on Fifth Avenue, now the homes of those who began their business life as clerks for ENO & PHELPS. The great fire of 1835 burned them out; but it was only a temporary halt in a triumphant progress. The firm of ENO & PHELPS was dissolved on January 1st, 1845, and both partners retired with fortunes thought large in those moderate days.

Mr. PHELPS was too young and active to retire yet from business, and he very soon afterwards, on January 1st, 1846, formed the firm of PHELPS, CHITTENDEN & BLISS, which imported and sold dry goods at No. 12 Wall Street. This adventure, too, was successful. Mr. PHELPS retired from it on January 1st, 1849, with larger resources and with a purpose to employ them, and to find his own occupation in buying and improving real estate in the City of New-York. Among the more conspicuous of these investments was the purchase of the Broadway Tabernacle, and of the crown of Murray Hill, on which latter, in connection with his kinsmen, ISAAC N. PHELPS and WILLIAM E. DODGE, he erected, in 1852-53, the large free-stone mansion, where he lived and died. He also built the large structure at Rector Street and Broadway, then the largest in the City, and various warehouses in Park Row, in Liberty, Church and Warren Streets and in other thoroughfares. He early recognized the value and beauty of free-stone and was the first to introduce its use into the City of New-York.

He found another field of activity, for which he seemed singularly well fitted, in promoting corporate interests that would benefit the City. Two of these were the Erie and the Delaware, Lackawanna and Western Railway Companies. He was one of the directors of the Erie at the time of its completion, and received the formal and engrossed thanks of the City for his share in that great undertaking. But it was in developing the great coal fields of the Lackawanna Valley, and constructing and managing the system of transportation, by which coal could be brought from them to tide water, that Mr. PHELPS showed greatest patience and sagacity and won highest praise. He was the first President of the Delaware, Lackawanna and Western Road, and maintained his connection with and supervision over it up to the time of his death. His life was a busy one in these directions. He was a director in the City, Mercantile and Second National Banks. Of the last two he was one of the founders. He was a trustee in the Farmers' Loan and Trust Company, in the United States Trust Company, in the Bank for Savings, now located in Bleecker Street, and in various other organizations of the kind. Of the best judgment, of an integrity beyond suspicion, he was a model trustee, and was constantly sought for to act in fiduciary capacities. While largely absorbed in these businesses, he never neglected the obligations which every conscientious citizen feels to society, the church and his country. At the breaking out of the war, the preservation of the Union became his chief concern. He aided by service on Committees, by generous contributions, and enthusiastically supported the Union League Club, whose object was to make loyalty fashionable.

In the Chamber of Commerce, the New-England Society, the Historical Society and all similar institutions he was a member.

He disliked the roughness of practical politics, but never failed to vote for and to contribute to the party he thought in the right. He ran for office once only. A contingency seemed to make it his duty to run for State Senator on a Citizens' ticket in the district where he lived. He received a good vote, but was not elected, nor did he expect to be.

He retired from business, as we have seen, at an early age. He resumed it temporarily and nominally for the purpose of adding the strength of his name to one of the remnants of his old firm, and for a year or two after the panic of 1857 the name of PHELPS, BLISS & Co. was seen on the front of 340 Broadway, the great mercantile palace he had built years before on the site of the Tabernacle.

Mr. PHELPS had worked too hard, and at fifty years of age his health was broken. He spent the last eight years of his life in travel, in study in the quiet of his library and in the enjoyment of the society of his friends. Of admirable capacity, of stainless honor, enjoying the respect of all and the affection of his friends, he waited patiently for his summons, and died peacefully on the 12th day of May, 1869, in the fifty-ninth year of his age. He was buried among his ancestors in Simsbury, Conn.

MARSHALL O. ROBERTS.

MARSHALL O. ROBERTS was one of New-York's most enterprising merchants and ship-owners. He was born in this City on March 22d, 1813. His father, OWEN ROBERTS, was a physician, and came to this country from Wales in 1798. Before MARSHALL was eight years old his father and mother died. At the age of fourteen he became a clerk in the ship chandlery of WILLIAM SPIES, at a salary of three hundred dollars a year. Three years later Mr. SPIES died, and his successor, finding young ROBERTS intelligent and useful to him in his business, continued him in his employ and doubled his salary. By extreme frugality MARSHALL saved a large part of his income, and at the age of twenty he was enabled to start business for himself. His store, which was also his home, was at Coenties Slip.

The Battery was then the fashionable place for the residences of the prominent merchants, who used to go at an early hour to Fulton Market for the family supplies. Passing young ROBERTS' store their attention was attracted by the industrious habits of the enterprising youth, and they were accustomed to stop and pass a kindly word, until finally they became so interested in his welfare as to offer him pecuniary aid when he saw an opportunity for a profitable investment. Through their assistance he was enabled to enlarge his business, and by degrees he obtained to a great extent the control of the Russian hemp market. By operating in Naval Stores and from his careful study of the Whale Fishery, he was able to supply the Government with oil at prices which defied competition. His unceasing vigilance, his acquaintance with the commercial needs of the country, his energy and fidelity to every engagement, gave him unbounded credit, and enabled him to undertake those enterprises which led to the accumulation of the large fortune he left at his death. From his building of the Hudson River steamer, "Hendrik Hudson," a marvel at the time, to the construction of the Texas and Pacific Railway, there was scarcely a project of steam navigation or railway transit in the United States in which he was not an active participant. The discovery of gold in California in 1849 gave full scope to his ability in foreseeing and seizing an opportunity for almost boundless profits from trade with that newly-acquired territory. He was one of the chief promoters of the Atlantic Cable enterprise.

During the Civil war Mr. ROBERTS was a firm supporter of the Government, and made liberal contributions towards raising and equipping regiments, and providing for the wounded. The poor always found in him a friend, and he spent large sums in numerous charities.

In early life Mr. ROBERTS took a deep interest in political affairs, and was known as a HENRY CLAY Whig. Between Mr. CLAY and Mr. ROBERTS the most friendly relations existed, and continued until the death of that illustrious statesman. Mr. ROBERTS was urged to accept several prominent offices under the Government, all of which he declined. In 1865 he consented to stand as the Republican candidate for Mayor of this City, and was believed by many to have been elected, but the result was decided in favor of his opponent by a small majority.

Mr. ROBERTS was an intense lover of art, and in him artists found a liberal and encouraging friend. In his large collection of paintings will be found many master-pieces of ancient and modern times. The portrait of Mr. ROBERTS is from this collection, and it becomes peculiarly interesting at this time, when the members of the Chamber are advocating measures for the restoration to its former prestige of the shipping of the country, for it should be remembered that the enterprise and sagacity of Mr. ROBERTS contributed in a large degree in making the United States in his day the first among the maritime nations of the world.

Mr. ROBERTS was elected a member of the Chamber of Commerce July 6th, 1865, and continued his membership until his death, which occurred in this City September 11th, 1880, in the sixty-eighth year of his age.

RUFUS PRIME.

RUFUS PRIME was born at No. 42 (now No. 54) Wall-street, in the City of New-York, January 28th, 1806, and was the second son of NATHANIEL PRIME, of the banking house of PRIME, WARD & KING. RUFUS PRIME entered Yale College in 1825, but left before graduating and entered mercantile life. Afterwards, with ARCHIBALD GRACIE, Jr., and JOHN C. JAY, he established the firm of ARCHIBALD

Gracie & Co., which conducted a general commission business for many years. At a later period he became a partner in the banking house of Christmas, Livingston, Prime & Coster, from which he retired in 1841. Mr. Prime was one of the founders of the Union Club of this City. For fifty-two years he had been connected with the Chamber of Commerce, having been elected a member October 1st, 1833. He died at his country home, at Huntington, L. I., October 15th, 1885, leaving four children--a daughter and three sons. Mr. Prime was a man of genial disposition, and although he led a somewhat uneventful life, he nevertheless took a deep interest in all questions affecting the general good of the community.

GEORGE T. TRIMBLE.

George Thomas Trimble, the eldest child of Richard and Ann (Roberts) Trimble, was born at Morrisville, Bucks County, Pennsylvania, August 17th, 1793.

His parents removed to Newburgh, N. Y., in 1800, and he was educated at the Newburgh Academy, the Friends' Boarding School at West Town, Pa., and the school of Dr. John Griscom, in Little Green Street, now Liberty Place, New-York City. Soon after leaving school he entered the counting-house of Buckley & Abbatt, flour merchants, in Front Street, near Dover, and remained with them until he became of age. In May, 1815, he began business on his own account as a flour and grain commission merchant at 25 South Street, and in August, 1817, became a member of the firm of Byrnes, Trimble & Co., composed of Thomas S. Byrnes, Silas Wood and himself. This was some years before the opening of the Erie Canal, when the chief supplies of breadstuffs for this market came from Pennsylvania and Virginia, and the firm for several years was among the largest receivers of flour and grain from tide-water, Virginia, Mr. Wood residing at Fredericksburg to promote that part of the business. They became, also, owners and managers of several merchant ships, and in 1818 established the second or "Star" Line of Liverpool packets, the old or "Black Ball" Line having been started a year or two earlier by ISAAC WRIGHT & SON and JEREMIAH THOMPSON. Mr. TRIMBLE became deeply interested in the management of these ships, for which his regular and punctual habits and somewhat masterful disposition well fitted him ; and to the zeal and energy with which he devoted himself to conducting the packet service is due no small share of the reputation attained by the old "Liverpool Liners."

In 1821 he paid his first and only visit to England, in the course of which arrangements were made to transfer the consignment of the line at Liverpool to WILLIAM and JAMES BROWN & Co., with which house his friend, JOSEPH SHIPLEY, had recently become connected. The relation then established grew into one of mutual esteem and confidence, and continued in unbroken cordiality as long as Mr. TRIMBLE remained in business.

Mr. BYRNES died in 1826, but the business was continued under the same name until 1831, when Mr. WOOD, having returned to this City to take an active share in its management, the firm became WOOD & TRIMBLE, and so continued until its final dissolution, September 11th, 1835, after the sale of their shipping interest to ROBERT KERMIT. Subsequently Mr. TRIMBLE became interested with some of his old captains in several transient ships, which he managed for a number of years, but retired from business entirely in 1848.

He was elected a member of the Chamber of Commerce November 6th, 1827, and took an active part in its affairs for twenty years, serving on its Committees, and visiting Albany and Washington on special occasions to represent the views of the Chamber on questions of legislation affecting the commerce of New-York.

He was, from conviction, a Free Trader, and, as such, was elected Vice-President May 2d, 1843, but declined to serve.

No notice of Mr. TRIMBLE, however slight, would be

complete without reference to his interest in the educational and charitable institutions of New-York.

In 1818 he became a trustee of the Free School Society, afterwards the "Public School Society," and for thirty-five years was unremitting in his devotion to the cause of common school education. He was Treasurer of the Society for several years and its last President, serving until its dissolution in 1853.

From 1823 to 1860 he was a trustee of the New-York Dispensary.

In 1846 he was elected a Governor of the New-York Hospital, and was President of the Society from 1858 until his death in 1872. By virtue of that office he became a trustee of the Roosevelt Hospital on its organization in 1864, when he was elected its Treasurer, and continued in charge of its finances for the rest of his life.

The only financial institution with which he was connected was the Bank for Savings, of which he was a trustee from 1854 to 1872.

He never sought an office, and never held one from which he received any pecuniary compensation or advantage.

Mr. TRIMBLE was by birthright and education a member of the Society of Friends, and his ideas of life were founded on their distinctive principles. He believed in moderation in all things, and, although "diligent in business," was not eager for gain, but gave freely of both time and money to such practical work as he thought conducive to the welfare of the community.

His uprightness of character and his faithful performance of every duty he assumed, gave him the respect and confidence of all who knew him. He died at his residence in this City, May 16th, 1872, in the seventy-ninth year of his age.

ISAAC SHERMAN.

ALTHOUGH few are more worthy of a place in the Chamber of Commerce, yet, if his wishes could have been consulted, it is doubtful if the subject of this sketch would have allowed his portrait to adorn its walls, so great was his aversion to personal distinction.

Mr. SHERMAN was a merchant of rare ability, and met with a full measure of success. He was born in Petersburgh, Rensselaer County, New-York, January 25th, 1818. His family removed to the western part of the State when ISAAC was quite a lad. In April, 1840, he engaged in the business of lumber and staves at Buffalo, and about 1843 he married Miss ELIZABETH WETHERELL, by whom he had two children, daughters, one of whom, the youngest, died at a tender age.

Being a prosperous business man, and having acquired a local reputation for sagacity and political knowledge, he was induced by his friends to run for member of Assembly from Erie County in 1845, and for Mayor in 1846 and 1847, but was beaten by his Whig competitors. These results seemed to satisfy his aspirations, as he never afterwards was a candidate for political office, although he was President of the Young Men's Library Association of Buffalo in 1849. This corporation, now the Buffalo Library, is the most prosperous literary institution in Western New-York.

After acquiring a moderate fortune, Mr. SHERMAN closed up his business, and, with his wife and daughter, visited Europe.

Coming to New-York in the spring of 1853, he purchased the stave business of the late WILLIAM DENNISTOUN, and associated with him BENJAMIN F. ROMAINE, forming the house of SHERMAN & ROMAINE. Four years later, JOHN P. TOWNSEND and HENRY WIBIRT, clerks of the house, were admitted to an interest in the business, though the firm name remained unchanged.

For nine years this firm carried on the largest business in the sale of rough staves for exportation that was ever

14

done in the country. In some years the quantity sold and
exported to nearly every foreign port amounted to
14,000,000, or equal to 240 full cargoes for vessels, each of
400 tons burden ; but as they were not always loaded by
full cargoes, about a thousand vessels per annum were
supplied with quantities sufficient for storage with other
merchandise and as dunnage throughout the ships.

In 1862 the house dissolved, Mr. ROMAINE retiring
temporarily from business. Mr. TOWNSEND founded the
present house of DUTTON & TOWNSEND, and Mr. SHERMAN
established the firm of SHERMAN & WIBIRT, which was
continued for four years, when they dissolved, and Mr.
SHERMAN finally retired from active business in 1866.

During Mr. SHERMAN's commercial career he was a
leader in his branch of business, and met with uniform
success. His keen insight and unerring sagacity made
him master of every situation, although giving little apparent attention to details.

Besides his commercial ability, he stored his mind with
useful knowledge ; he studied the political and legal history
of his country and the lives of its public men, and becoming a warm admirer of THOMAS JEFFERSON, adopted his
political creed for his own guidance.

He was a free soil Democrat in 1848, and became a Republican when it was a national party. He procured the
nomination of JOHN C. FREMONT for the Presidency, and
managed with ability his political campaign in 1856.

He admired the character of ABRAHAM LINCOLN, and
heartily favored him for the Presidency in 1860; after the
election, Mr. LINCOLN offered him the portfolio of Secretary
of the Treasury, but he preferred to be his counsellor without official designation, and it is safe to say there was no
person, outside the City of Washington, who rendered
more intelligent service, or whose opinions were oftener
sought by the President.

He opposed the bill offered in Congress, in 1861, to issue
legal tender notes to circulate as money, and suggested
heavy taxation in various forms as the best plan for raising
revenue to carry on the war, and only assented to the law,

after the immediate and pressing needs of the Government made it necessary.

He always believed that the necessity need not have arisen, had the taxes, which were afterwards levied, been imposed earlier, and maintained that the war could have been carried to a successful conclusion with currency on a specie basis without a violation of the Constitution. He considered the "greenbacks" (legal tender notes) a forced loan from the people, and urged their retirement by the Government after the close of the war, and that preparation should be made for resumption on a gold basis.

He joined the Union League Club the year of its organization, in 1863, and continued a member until his death : there his talks on financial topics were highly esteemed, and were listened to with pleasure. His reputation as an authority on the laws of taxation, in October, 1874, induced the Assembly Committee on Ways and Means, of this State, to request him to appear before it, when he made an exhaustive argument, which showed extraordinary knowledge and research, in which he favored the exclusive taxation of real estate and the franchises of a few specified moneyed corporations and gas companies. His fame as a political economist induced the Trustees of the University of Rochester, in 1880, to confer upon him the degree of Doctor of Laws, in which institution, some years before, he had founded a scholarship of political economy.

Mr. SHERMAN was frank and hearty in his manner, but his aversion to notoriety caused him to decline every office or place on Committees, either in the Chamber of Commerce, of which he was for many years a member, or elsewhere, but his advice and counsel were often sought and freely given ; the powers of his mind were extraordinary ; capable of grasping almost any subject, and none of importance were indifferent to him ; he was a true patriot, and had a high idea of public duty.

He died in this City, January 21st, 1881, leaving a widow and a married daughter.—JOHN P. TOWNSEND.

SIMEON B. CHITTENDEN.

SIMEON BALDWIN CHITTENDEN was born on the 29th of March, 1814, in the little town of Guilford, New-Haven County, Connecticut. He was the son of ABEL CHITTENDEN and ANNA HART BALDWIN. His family was founded in this country in 1639, by WILLIAM CHITTENDEN, a native of Cranbrook, County of Kent, England, who was one of the first settlers of Guilford. Mr. ABEL CHITTENDEN died while his son was still young, and the boy began his business life in his fourteenth year as a clerk in a store in New-Haven, whither he was persuaded to go by his pastor, under whom he was at the time preparing to enter Yale College. From that time his schooling was confined to such as he could give himself in the scant leisure of a life of hard work ; but it may be said here that this difficult schooling served to develop mental qualities of a very high order, and that both as a speaker and a writer in his maturer years he was the master of a clear, cogent, and often brilliant style, that his range of expression, the accuracy of his reasoning, the logical order of its development and the luminousness of his illustration were such as a trained scholar might envy. It may be added, also, that he showed throughout his life a keen appreciation of the value of education, and that the generosity of his gifts, when he had gained wealth, to promote education was only equalled by the intelligence and foresight with which they were directed.

After a few years of business in New-Haven, Mr. CHITTENDEN established himself in the wholesale dry goods trade in New-York in 1842, and remained in it until 1874, when he retired, shortly after his election to Congress from the Third (Brooklyn) District of New-York. During that time his career was an honorable and a prosperous one. He passed unscathed through the commercial and financial crises of 1846, 1857 and 1873, and won a reputation for scrupulous observance of his obligations, as well as for courage, sagacity and activity. He became connected with a number of financial institutions, was for nearly thirty-three years an active member of the Chamber of Commerce, and a Vice-President from 1867 to 1869 ; one of the founders of the Continental Fire Insurance Company and of the Continental Bank ; a Trustee of the United States Trust Company, a Director of the Union Ferry Company, and in several railway companies, and President of the New-Haven and New London Railroad Company. During the war for the Union he was one of the originators of the Union Defence Committee of New-York, and of the corresponding organization, the War Fund Committee, of Brooklyn.

In 1874 Mr. CHITTENDEN was elected to Congress for the short session of the 43d and the full term of the 44th Congress, and was subsequently re-elected to the 45th and 46th Congresses. He served in all seven years. In politics he was an Independent Republican. During this period, his party, though controlling the Presidency and the Senate, was in a minority in the House of Representatives. Mr. CHITTENDEN naturally took an active part in the discussion of the currency and fiscal questions which, from 1874 to 1881, held the attention of Congress and the country. His services to the cause of sound finance, not only at this time, but during the long and troubled period, from the close of the civil war to the time of his retirement from active life, were various and valuable. He had been familiar, at an early stage in his business career, with the banking system of New-England, and particularly with the methods of continuous redemption through the agency of the old Suffolk Bank. He had acquired a very clear and comprehensive conception of the functions of a credit currency, of the conditions of its safety and usefulness, of the limitations within which it could properly be employed, and of the obligations that it involved. His sensitive and vigorous conscience, which, in his personal affairs, made the scrupulous fulfillment of every contract of the most imperative importance, caused him to appreciate more clearly than most the duty imposed on all institutions claiming the right to use their notes as money. No one understood better than he the immense advantages to the community at large of currency of this kind. His keen and quick intellect perceived that it was absolutely essential to any adequate accomplishment of the work of exchange in communities so varied, so active, so widely scattered as those of the United States. But he perceived with equal clearness the dangers attending it. His conception of the principles of sound banking was the basis of his view of the duty and policy of the Government in dealing with the use of its notes as money.

In January, 1874, at the Baltimore meeting of the National Board of Trade, he outlined his view in the following resolution : "That all national banks shall be required to provide for the redemption of their notes in legal tenders at the chief points of specie imports and exports, and that the simplest and best method for securing an elastic currency will be found in the removal of all restrictions upon the circulation of national bank notes, secured, as now, by the deposit of United States bonds for the redemption thereof." In supporting this resolution, he explained that it involved the withdrawal and cancellation of legal tenders in proportion as bank currency was issued. These ideas were in part embodied in the subsequent legislation of Congress, but the provision for bank note redemption was not made complete, and that for the withdrawal of the United States notes was abandoned.

After his election to the House of Representatives, and when the restriction on bank issues, properly secured, had been removed, Mr. CHITTENDEN urged unceasingly and with great force the policy and the necessity of reaching real specie payments through the restoration of the right to fund United States notes in interest-bearing bonds. In February, 1876, he said : "A mountain of vicious legal tender debt confronts us. We can neither get round it nor provide for it in a lump. We must hew it away to the level of truth, honor and common sense, and there, and there only, can we stand to rebuild and restore the waste places. We must fund the legal tender debt. And why not ? Are these notes not an unnatural product ? Were they not born of an extreme exigency, now happily passed

away, when the noise of battle was on land and sea ? Was
it not explicitly provided when they were first issued that
they should at all times be fundable at the option of the
holder? Would their authors or Congress have tolerated
them for a moment but for such a promise ?"

Had this simple, effective and honorable course been
adopted, even at that late date, the country would have
been saved some serious evils, and the direct menace of
other and worse evils. Congress was not, however, to be
persuaded. It would do no more than it was forced to do.
The demoralization of paper money had so enfeebled and
confused the public mind and conscience that it could not
see, or, seeing, would not take the straight and narrow
way. Under the dictation of this perverted sentiment the
right to fund the United States notes had been repudiated,
the redemption and cancellation of the notes had been
stopped, and when the day for resumption under the Act
of 1875 approached, Congress weakly and wickedly ex-
punged the provision for the withdrawal of notes *pari
passu* with that of bank currency, and provided that the
notes redeemed after 1879 should be re-issued and kept
afloat. In this last provision Mr. CHITTENDEN'S clear
judgment perceived the crowning act of folly and bad faith.
On the floor of the House he exposed its nature again and
again, with convincing plainness of statement, and de-
nounced it with the most searching and indignant condem-
nation.

On the 19th of January, 1880, he said : "The United
States *owe* $346,000,000 of legal tender war debt, payable
on demand. We boast of paying it in good faith since
January, 1879, but in truth we *have not paid one dollar of
it yet*. We owe just as many dollars on that account to-
day as we did in May, 1878." "When legal tender notes
are presented and redeemed, what then? You say it is
honest payment of the war debt. I deny it. You do not
speak the truth. We boast of resumption for a full year,
but we have not paid a dollar of the legal tender debt in
that time ; not one. The moment my ancient ten-dollar
note, which I exhibited at the Speaker's desk two or three

years ago, was redeemed. Secretary SHERMAN straightway
forced a new loan of like amount from some other person,
and put the disgraced rag afloat again. Such is the law ;
the Secretary must obey it." "The individual, firm, bank
or railroad paying its debts, as the United States Government now pays its debt, would be without credit, exposed
to derision."

So convinced was Mr. CHITTENDEN of the viciousness of
the Act of Congress directing the re-issue of the "redeemed" legal tenders, in a time of profound peace, when
every condition was lacking that had been pleaded in
justification of the original issue in time of war, that he,
in agreement with Gen. BENJAMIN F. BUTLER, holding
the opposite view, brought a test case to secure a judgment
of the United States Supreme Court upon the constitutional authority of Congress to make such enactment.
The counsel employed by him were WILLIAM ALLEN
BUTLER, Esq., and the Hon. GEORGE F. EDMUNDS. The
decision was favorable to the authority of Congress, but,
in effect, it fully sustained Mr. CHITTENDEN's position,
that there was no authority in the Constitution for the
exercise of this power, for the Court was obliged to read the
authority into the Constitution by implication. It held, in
substance, that the Federal Court was possessed, as a sovereign Government, of all the rights of sovereignty exercised
by other Governments at the time it was established, unless
these were explicitly excluded ; that the right to make its
own notes legal tender was such a sovereign right, and
was not definitely forbidden, and was, therefore, possessed.
The judgment of the ablest and most authoritative Constitutional lawyers in the Union pronounced this doctrine to
be practically revolutionary, completely changing the nature of the Constitution. It was so. The sound common
sense, the trained perception of the business man, combined
with his rectitude, disclosed to Mr. CHITTENDEN the mon-
strous nature of this innovation. If, in later years, Congress
shall use the power thus recognized, putting the property
of every man at its mercy, in the mischievous manner that
is possible, it will be to the credit of the merchants of

New York, that one of the most earnest and one of the acutest of those who saw the peril in advance and fought it unwearyingly, was from their own ranks.

It is hardly necessary to add, that while in Congress Mr. CHITTENDEN opposed with all his influence the policy of the unlimited coinage of depreciated silver in legal tender dollars. It was largely due to his efforts that the restriction finally placed upon the coinage was adopted, and that the policy of the Treasury afterwards kept the coinage at the minimum amount of $2,000,000 worth of bullion per month.

The preceding is but a sketch in outline of Mr. CHIT-TENDEN's career, in which it has seemed best to give as much prominence as possible to his service in promoting those sound and honorable principles of financial policy to which the Chamber of Commerce has given its unwavering support. On the 14th of April, 1889, having just past his 75th birthday, Mr. CHITTENDEN died at his home in Brooklyn. With those whose privilege it was to know him intimately, he leaves, besides the memory of his unusual gifts and his valued service to his country and to the community in which he passed his life, the still more precious memory of a nature pure, simple, just and loving.—EDWARD CARY.

HORACE B. CLAFLIN.

HORACE B. CLAFLIN was born in Milford, Massachusetts, on the 18th of December, 1811. His father, JOHN CLAFLIN, was a farmer and owner of a general store ; a man greatly respected by his neighbors, well known throughout the neighboring country as Justice of the Peace and Member of the State Legislature, and reputed rich, in days when a large farm and a little ready money betokened affluence in a New-England village. His mother was an amiable and excellent woman, and taught her children many lessons of piety and of goodness. In boyhood HORACE exhibited much of the gayety and energy which distinguished him through-our life. His early comrades admired and loved him, and his schoolmaster became so deeply attached to him that he afterward followed with affectionate interest the progress of all his mercantile enterprises. When HORACE was well advanced in his studies, his father proposed to send him to College, but he preferred not to go. He felt confident, even then, that he should do something important in the business world, and he wished to enter it as early as possible. Accordingly, after graduating at the Milford Academy, he went into the paternal store, and worked diligently there in preparation for a broader field. When he was twenty years old his father gave him a thousand dollars, and he, in company with his elder brother, AARON, and his brother-in-law, SAMUEL DANIELS, (each recipient of a like gift,) bought his father out, and assumed the responsibility of the business. His first act, as manager of the store, was to pour on to the ground the stock of strong liquor, which, at that time, was generally considered a staple article of merchandise in a good country store. HORACE did not believe in selling intoxicating liquors, even for supposed family use, and he never was deterred by pecuniary considerations from acting up to his convictions. The following year, 1832, the young men opened another store at Worcester, Mass.; that town was better suited to HORACE's plans, and in 1833 AARON took sole possession of the Milford stock, and HORACE was master at Worcester. His mode of doing business there astonished the neighborhood. His energy seemed untiring, and his enterprise and good humor became proverbial.

His old school teacher, who had also removed to Worcester, writes :

"At the time he left Worcester I think all kinds of business in that place had become impregnated with the spirit of his business system. I do not think, with all the collisions which took place, he ever made an enemy who remained so twenty-four hours. Worcester was too small to carry out his plans. New-York had superior attractions and drew him away."

In 1837 he married AGNES, daughter of Colonel CALVIN
SANGER, of Sherbourne, Mass., and thenceforward every
hour that could be spared from his business was devoted
to his home. He was happy in all relations, but in his
married life pre-eminently. In 1843 he sold out his Worcester business, moved to this City, and, with WILLIAM F.
BULKLEY, formed the firm of BULKLEY & CLAFLIN, and
began business at No. 46 Cedar Street. Soon the energy
of the younger member of the house surprised the wholesale merchants of the metropolis, as it had startled the
retail dealers of Worcester. By 1846 the sales of BULKLEY
& CLAFLIN had risen to a million dollars per annum; and
in 1851, notwithstanding Mr. CLAFLIN'S strong anti-slavery
opinions, which drove away some Southern trade, the sales
amounted to nearly five millions. In January of that year
the firm moved to No. 57 Broadway, and in July Mr.
BULKLEY retired from mercantile life. Mr. CLAFLIN then
entered into a copartnership with WILLIAM H. MELLEN
and several juniors, under the style of CLAFLIN, MELLEN
& Co., and the rapid progress of the business continued.
Small profits, a low per centage of expense, hard work,
and the utmost liberality in credits, were Mr. CLAFLIN'S
rules, and the volume of trade increased so rapidly, that,
in 1853, it was necessary to seek more spacious quarters,
at No. 111 Broadway. There the firm found accommodations which sufficed for some years; but in 1859 the sales
had nearly reached ten millions, and another move had
to be considered. Then the great warehouse on Church
and Worth Streets and West Broadway was built, and in
January, 1861, the firm moved into it. The change was
unfortunately timed. In April the war broke out; a considerable portion of the assets of CLAFLIN, MELLEN & Co.
was cut off, or locked up in Southern accounts, and their
recently increased liabilities could not be met at maturity.
This was an almost crushing disappointment to Mr.
CLAFLIN; but when the creditors determined that his firm
could pay no more than seventy cents on the dollar, and
that per centage on long time, he made the best of the
situation, gave compromise notes to all who would accept

them, bought up outstanding claims for cash through the
help of friends, and soon was vigorously at work again,
determined eventually to pay his debts in full. Once more
he prospered. The extension notes were speedily paid,
and, before it seemed possible that it could be accomplished, he had accumulated a sufficient surplus to send a
check for the thirty per cent. which had been deducted in
settlement, with full interest on every dollar deferred.
Then he sought out all who had refused to accept compromise notes, but had sold their claims for cash, and to each
of them he made good all their loss, both of principal and
interest; so that no creditor of CLAFLIN, MELLEN & Co.
finally received less than dollar for dollar, with full interest
to the last cent. The business now increased more rapidly
than ever before. It was a time of excitement and of enterprise, and no undertaking was too great for Mr. CLAFLIN.
Sellers of merchandise knew that no lot could be too large
for him to buy, and they found out, also, that whatever
he bought was sure to be sold quickly and completely.
His ability to dispose successfully of the greatest accumu-
lations of goods without demoralizing the market, and his
personal popularity, gave his firm advantages which made
it easily outstrip all competitors in volume of trade. Mr.
MELLEN retired on the 1st of January, 1864, and at that
time the sales were nearly fifty millions of dollars per
annum. The style of the firm was then changed to H. B.
CLAFLIN & Co., and the business still increased.

Subsequently, in one year the sales of the CLAFLIN house
reached the enormous total of seventy-two millions of
dollars, and it is said that its sales for a single day
amounted to a million and a half of dollars.

His generosity to his associates, most of whom had retired with large fortunes, and his helpfulness to many
young merchants throughout the country, occasioned him
the distress of temporary embarrassment in the great panic
of 1873. He did not get needed accommodation then in
places where he thought he could rely upon liberal dis-
counts, and he was compelled to ask a short indulgence on
open accounts from the firm's creditors, to afford time for

the conversion of assets into money. Finding it impossible
to negotiate large amounts of the choicest of bills receivable
at any rate of discount, he made sweeping reductions in
the firm's stock of merchandise, and sold immense amounts
for cash at a great sacrifice, until the notes given in extension of open accounts were taken up long before maturity,
and the credit of the house was completely restored. In
this panic the direct liabilities of H. B. CLAFLIN & Co.
were very great, and the contingent liabilities much greater ;
but every note that bore their indorsement was paid at
maturity, and only a portion of the open accounts were
delayed in settlement some ninety days. The gathering
together and successful consolidation of the vast business
after the severe shock of 1873 was not the least of Mr.
CLAFLIN's achievements. A remarkable exemplification of
willingness to overlook injuries was shown at this time.
While he was most depressed by the great losses he was
making, the wife of a man who had outrageously imposed
upon his former friendship by fraudulently converting
funds intrusted to him, called upon Mr. CLAFLIN, told him
that she and her family would lose their home unless she
could raise several thousand dollars, and asked to loan her
the amount she needed. He disliked the woman, but he
pitied her, and, after some reflection, he handed her a
check for the money she needed, although he knew that it
would probably never be repaid, and it would benefit a man
who had practically robbed him of hundreds of thousands
of dollars. After 1874, Mr. CLAFLIN slightly relaxed his
attention to business, and, although still a regular occu-
pant of his office, he distributed some of his work among
his associates.

In 1877 he went to Europe for a short pleasure trip, and
on his return, as he stepped ashore, he said to one of his
sons : '' How glad I am to be back.'' ''Didn't you enjoy
the trip?'' '' O, yes, very much,'' he replied ; '' but I
should have had twice as good a time if I had stayed at
home.'' This was characteristic. Home was full of joy to
him, and he made it glad to all his household. Few men
have been so happy. His habits were of the simplest, his

health was perfect, and he was continually doing good and
spreading cheer wherever he went. There seemed no limit
to his benevolence. His hand was always open, and it was
a pleasure to him to give. The poor were as welcome to
him as the rich, and were treated with equal consideration.

He was deeply interested in the prevention of cruelty
to animals, and he gave HENRY BERGH great encouragement in the early stages of his noble work, when it was
meeting with little public appreciation. Indeed, he encouraged every earnest worker in any humane cause. Although sparkling with humor, yet he was filled with the
deepest and most helpful sympathy for all in suffering or
in trouble. Those who saw him casually never failed to
be impressed by his bright personality, and those who
knew him intimately appreciated the depth as well as the
brilliancy of his nature. The Rev. HENRY WARD BEECHER,
who knew the value of his friendship, testified :

" He has been to me a refuge, and more than ever he or
his own knew. I have been strengthened by him in days that
were weary and burdened. His face was never clouded,
and never turned from me—no, not for a moment."

And in a memorial sermon the great preacher said : " His
cheerfulness was unquenchable. He was like a bright
fire, that sends out flame and spark and warmth, not
because it is told to, but because it cannot help itself.
His thoughts rushed forth in endless streams like the
shining rays of a lamp. His head seemed to be a globe of
lambent flame. Full of merriment, quips and jests infinite,
he flung off his rattling and jocose spirits like sparks from
an unquenchable brand and this, too, without regard to
wind or weather, winter or summer, prosperity or adversity.
Whether in trouble of one kind or another, he flamed still
about the same. Indeed, I have sometimes thought that
it took the hard knocks of adversity to bring out all the
fire from the flint that was in him. Yet he was not a jester ;
he was not a mere sport-loving man. At hours of quiet no
man surpassed him in sobriety, in thoughtfulness, in out-
reaching questions with regard to destiny and life and im-

mortality. Sobriety of judgment, serious and conscientious views of life, were fundamental with him. To the end of his days, whatever might have been the outward play and coruscation, the jest and banter, at the bottom of all was a sincere belief in truth, in honor, in purity, in loyalty. Moral quality was everything with him. To the end of his life the inner stream of religious sensibility widened and deepened in him. In this, as in all his large benevolence, he shrank from publicity. In his very nature he abhorred ostentation ; and to him pretence, with all falseness and hypocrisy, was an unforgivable sin. His friendships were deep. He was loyal to them with a disinterestedness seldom seen in men, seldom even in women, who surpass men in loyalty of undying love. For these that were his friends nothing was too much. Again and again he periled everything that he owned to rescue a friend from danger. At one time I will mention no circumstance that shall point to the event except the fact—he made himself responsible for a million dollars to save a neighbor from bankruptcy ; and that at a time when his own affairs required the most searching care. A quarter of a million, a half million—what were they to him? He pledged them, he offered them, with the freedom with which one would give a cup of cold water to a child of those whom he loved ; and not to kindred alone, not to his own, but to neighbors and friends. He grew gentle and tender where men are apt to become suspicious and cynical."

It was fitting that this joyous spirit should walk through the valley of death without pain. On Thursday, the 12th of November, 1885, he suddenly became unconscious, and never spoke afterwards. On the following day he seemed to regain partial consciousness ; but a pronounced effusion of blood in the brain ensued, and on Saturday, the 14th of November, he peacefully breathed his last, in his city home on Brooklyn Heights. Rarely has a private citizen been mourned more widely. His name was known in nearly every city and town in the United States, and hundreds of eulogies of him appeared in the public press.

JEREMIAH MILBANK.

JEREMIAH MILBANK was born in this City, April 18th, 1818, was educated in its schools, and remained until his death a loyal and devoted citizen of New-York. For many years he was engaged in a large business which gave him the rewards which belong to wise forethought and diligence and good judgment. When he retired from it he still further proved his capacity in the larger enterprises which engaged his attention, and soon after became a Director in the Chicago, Milwaukee and St. Paul Railway Company, where, as one of the Executive Committee, he served with conspicuous ability in the management and development of its property. In the memorial records of that Company it is written of him : " He was always faithful, earnest and devoted in the discharge of his trust as Director, and his advice and counsel in regard to the management of the affairs of the Company were wise and prudent, and highly appreciated by his associates." Rochester University acknowledged his "great liberality" in contributing to its endowment ; the town in Dakota bearing his name was enriched by a church and a Public Library, which were his own gifts : and the Madison Avenue Baptist Church, of this City, in which he was a communicant, uttered this testimony by the lips of the Rev. Dr. CHARLES D. W. BRIDGMAN, the pastor : " A strong man has fallen who was well worthy of all the trust and honor we gave him. Wise, devout, generous, how can we speak of him, how can we think of what he was to us, without a sense of the mystery of his death ?"

Mr. MILBANK had breadth of mind. He swept a broad horizon. In the settlement of his plans he arranged for contingencies which a smaller mind would never have thought of. It was this mental reach, this ability to take in the whole field of action, with all the difficulties he would have to encounter, which lay at the foundation of the fortune he so steadily and amply built up. He was broad minded and practical. In addition to this, there was a conscientiousness which gave such a strength and dignity to his daily life as attracted the confidence of his fellow-men. Trusty is the word that supremely befitted him. He never separated himself from those who confided in his wisdom and honor. He guarded their interest; and so did he maintain his integrity under all circumstances ; that it was said of him "if he could have made a million dollars by a single act of dishonesty, he would have scorned the temptation." Such men constitute the true glory of the community and of the State, and not only because of their membership in the Chamber of Commerce, but because of their exemplary worth, their portraits are hung on the walls of the Chamber.

Mr. MILBANK died in this City, June 1st, 1884, in the sixty-seventh year of his age.

JOHN BROOME.

JOHN BROOME, ninth President of the Chamber of Commerce, merchant and statesman, was born in this country in 1738, of English parentage. His mother was of the old Huguenot family of LATOURETTE. Although he studied law with Governor LIVINGSTON of New-Jersey, in order to fit himself for the bar, he was induced by an elder brother to enter commercial life, and before the Revolution he and this brother, SAMUEL, commenced as importers of merchandise. Subsequently JOHN BROOME carried on business on his own account, and soon established a high reputation as a merchant, and acquired considerable wealth. Before the commencement of the war Mr. BROOME married a Miss LLOYD, of Lloyd's Neck, L. I. During the Revolution Mr. BROOME was a pronounced Whig, and stood loyally by his country through the whole of the trying scenes of that period. Like many of the Whig merchants of that day, he abandoned his business and residence in New-York while the City remained under British occupation, and removing to Connecticut he devoted his means and energy to fitting out

15

privateers for the destruction of British commerce. He returned to New-York when peace was restored, and it is recorded of him, to his great credit and good name, that he was among those citizens who, after the close of hostilities, paid in full, principal and interest, the debts he contracted in England during the war, when many regarded such debts as abrogated by that war. Mr. BROOME held several public offices, and his abilities and character seem to have been generally recognized. In 1775 he was a member of the Committee of Safety, and in 1776 he was a member of the Provincial Congress and of the Constitutional Convention of 1777.

He was elected President of the Chamber May 3d, 1785, continuing in the office until May 6th, 1794, and was one of the re-incorporators of the Chamber under the Act passed by the Legislature April 13th, 1784. He was for several years an Alderman of New-York when that office was considered one of honor and responsibility, and in 1784 was appointed City Treasurer. He was President of the New-York Insurance Company, the first institution of the kind incorporated by the State. In 1800 he was chosen a member of Assembly from this City, and, with his colleagues, General HORATIO GATES, HENRY RUTGERS and GEORGE CLINTON, contributed to the election of THOMAS JEFFERSON to the Presidency. In 1801 he was appointed one of the Commissioners of Bankruptcy, under the Act of 1798. In 1804 he was elected Lieutenant-Governor, and held that office up to the time of his death, which occurred in this City on August 8th, 1810.

JOHN BROOME was in many respects a remarkable man. He unquestionably wielded great influence in his day. Of upright character and marked ability, he possessed the confidence of his countrymen.

"Mr. BROOME's life, career and character," writes Dr. CHARLES KING, "are among those which the Chamber of Commerce may refer to with pride, as of one belonging for many years to their honored Association."

ROBERT H. McCURDY.

ROBERT H. McCURDY was born at Lyme, Connecticut, April 14th, 1800. His family was one of the best known in that State, his grandfather having been a prominent merchant there long anterior to the Revolution. He was fitted to enter the Sophomore Class of Yale College, and had determined to become a lawyer, but an elder brother having elected that profession, he was induced to abandon his design.

Mr. McCurdy arrived in New-York just before the close of the second war with England, and entered the employ of Mr. Lockwood, at that time a prominent dry goods merchant, who was in business in Whitehall Street. Among his fellow clerks in Mr. Lockwood's employ was the late Herman D. Aldrich, with whom he formed a strong friendship, afterwards augmented by a business copartnership, which continued until the close of his life.

So highly was Mr. McCurdy's capacity esteemed that in 1820 Mr. Lockwood, finding himself overstocked at the end of the season, sent him, although still under age, with a schooner load of goods to open a store at Petersburg, Virginia. The enterprise proved a success under Mr. McCurdy's management, and he remained South for several ensuing years.

About the year 1828 he returned to this City, and, with his former fellow-clerk, Mr. Aldrich, formed the copartnership of McCurdy & Aldrich, and entered upon the importing and jobbing of dry goods in Maiden Lane. The firm soon occupied a prominent position in that trade. In 1840 the late William Spencer was admitted to the firm, which then became known as McCurdy, Aldrich & Spencer, and soon after the house abandoned its jobbing and importing business and became exclusively wholesale, selling the products of many of the largest mills of the country, including those at Fall River, Mass.

In 1857 Mr. McCurdy retired from business. Each of

the partners had amassed a handsome competence, and the business of the firm was sold to Low, HARRIMAN & Co.

In 1858 Mr. McCURDY was the Republican candidate for Member of Congress from this City, but was defeated by his opponent, JOHN COCHRANE.

Mr. McCURDY rendered conspicuous service to the Government during the War of the Rebellion. At the outset of the agitation which followed the election of Mr. LINCOLN he was extremely anxious to do everything possible to prevent a civil war, and was a member of the Peace Conference which was held in Washington to avoid, if possible, any outbreak. His knowledge of the South led him to hope but little from the results of this movement; still he felt it his duty to try every possible means to prevent actual hostility. Upon the entire failure of this Conference he returned to this City, and when the war was opened by the firing on Fort Sumter he was among the first to see the necessity of a combination of all those in favor of the Union, regardless of past political antagonisms. He at once called a meeting of the leading citizens of New-York at his residence, No. 10 East Fourteenth Street, and there the measures were taken and the programme prepared for the great mass meeting in Union Square, which was the first manifestation of the united sentiment of the City of New-York upon the subject involved between the two sections of the country. He took an active part in the organization of the Union Defence Committee, and devoted his entire time and attention to its work. He also contributed materially from his own resources in aiding the Government to suppress the rebellion.

He was appointed a member of the State Committee for the erection of a monument on the battlefield of Gettysburg, Penn., and was very largely interested in its work.

Mr. McCURDY died in this City on the 5th day of April, 1880, within a few days of entering upon his eighty-first year. His business associate, Mr. ALDRICH, survived him but a few hours. It is seldom that such coincident circumstances occur as are presented in the lives of these two distinguished merchants. Born in adjoining States, almost at the same time, they commenced their life work together when boys under the same employer, became partners in business as well as intimate friends, lived side by side for many years, and finally died on the same day and of the same disease. Over their remains a dual funeral service was held, and both were simultaneously buried in adjoining plots in Greenwood Cemetery. It can be truly said of them that in life they were inseparable and in death were not divided.

Mr. McCurdy was not only an upright merchant, but he was a man of sound judgment and great business experience. He was connected with the direction of many of the leading financial institutions of this City, and was one of the earliest directors of the Mutual Life Insurance Company, and for many years was upon its Finance Committee, but never occupied any salaried office. He was a member of the Chamber of Commerce from August 1st, 1861, and in various ways rendered valuable public service in this Association.

JOHN CASWELL.

John Caswell was one of a large family of children of William and Mercy Buloid Caswell, and was born at Newport, R. I., December 6th, 1797. He came to New-York in the year 1811, being fourteen years old, and entered upon his life work as a clerk with his uncle, Robert Buloid, whose store was on Broadway, between Maiden Lane and Fulton Street. In 1820 the business was moved to Front Street, near Burling Slip, and was conducted under the firm name of Buloid & Finch. Upon the death of Mr. Finch, in 1822, John Caswell was taken into partnership by his uncle, and the name of the firm became Buloid & Caswell. After the lapse of several years, and after the death of Mr. Buloid, Mr. Caswell carried on the business in his own name ; but soon, having formed a partnership with his brother, Solo-

MON T. CASWELL, and other gentlemen, established the house of JOHN CASWELL & Co. about 1836, which was successfully carried on at No. 87 Front Street, until his death.

By his industry and assiduity he acquired a considerable fortune, and obtained an unblemished reputation for integrity, sound judgment and decisive action, while the firm of JOHN CASWELL & Co. became one of the representative business houses in the China trade.

In the words of one of his former partners, his characteristics as a business man are thus described :

" JOHN CASWELL was a modest, retiring gentleman, very diffident, not disposed to put himself forward in anything, but he was an eminently sagacious man, shrewd and keen in his judgment of men and their motives. He was seldom deceived, although he never refused credit to an honest, industrious man who knew his business well. He had many of the characteristics of a truly great merchant. Never hastily adopting an opinion until it was thoroughly investigated, he did not readily change unless convinced that he was wrong, and then he was great enough to admit the error and rectify it. He was distinguished for the probity of his character ; his word was his bond ; and in an intercourse of more than a quarter of a century with him as clerk, partner and friend, I never knew him to utter a falsehood or prevaricate in the slightest degree."

Mr. CASWELL was an attendant at St. John's Chapel, then at the Church of the Ascension, afterwards at Trinity Chapel, and was elected a Vestryman of Trinity Church, which office he held for many years until his death.

He was an intimate friend of the late Rev. Dr. WILLIAM A. MUHLENBERG, and was one of the founders and first supporters of St. Luke's Hospital in this City, and liberally aided very many of the charitable institutions of the Church with which he was connected. Few of those outside of the large circle who were recipients of his bounty, or were his chosen almoners, know how wise and discriminating but ample and generous were his daily charities and benefactions.

He was director in the Union Bank, United States Trust Company, Continental Fire Insurance Company and Second National Bank, besides having many other responsibilities of a fiduciary nature, in all of which he was active and conscientious in the discharge of his duties.

Mr. Cy will died in this City March 29th, 1871, in the seventy fourth year of his age.

DANIEL DRAKE-SMITH.

DANIEL DRAKE SMITH was born in the City of New-York August 29th, 1818. His paternal ancestors were English, and on the maternal side Huguenots. One of his ancestors in this country was JOSEPH DRAKE, who settled in Orange County, in this State, about 1750, and the family always cherished the tradition that this JOSEPH DRAKE was collaterally related to Sir FRANCIS DRAKE, the famous navigator of Queen ELIZABETH's time. Mr. DRAKE-SMITH's whole business life, extending over fifty years, was identified with the underwriting interest. He was Secretary of the Atlantic Insurance Company, and afterwards President of the Commercial Mutual Insurance Company, which he established in 1852. For many years he was Vice-President and afterwards President of the New-York Board of Marine Underwriters. On his retirement from active business in 1879 the Board of Trustees of the Commercial Mutual Insurance Company, of which he had been President from the time of its incorporation, presented him with a handsome and valuable testimonial as a tribute of their esteem. His judgment upon questions of marine insurance was generally regarded as sound, and his opinions were frequently sought by those engaged in that business in this and other cities, and in fact he acquired distinction as one of the most accomplished underwriters of the country, while his uncompromising integrity and strict fidelity to duty were prominent traits of his high character. Mr. DRAKE-SMITH was also a writer of ability on economic and political questions, possessing a clear and vigorous style, and during the latter part of his life he translated from the Latin and published "Spinoza's Ethics," which was regarded by competent judges as an excellent work.

In 1883 the Mayor of the City appointed Mr. DRAKE-SMITH a Rapid Transit Commissioner, and as Chairman of the Commission he performed very effective service for the City.

He will be long remembered by the Sandy Hook pilots for the active and aggressive interest he took in defending the retention of the compulsory pilotage system.

During the Civil war he was an earnest supporter of the Government, and his voice was heard from many platforms in his country's interest, urging his fellow men to the performance of their duty as patriotic citizens.

He was a member of the Chamber of Commerce from May 6th, 1858, up to his death, and took part in the discussions on most important public and commercial questions, his wide and extended learning enabling him to throw much light upon intricate and controversial subjects, which the Chamber was called upon to consider. He also served on several of the Chamber's Standing and Special Committees. Mr. DRAKE-SMITH resided in this City until 1863, when he removed to Englewood, N. J., where he died on February 8th, 1887, in the sixty-ninth year of his age.

JACOB BARKER.

JACOB BARKER was born in what is now the town of Perkins, Swan Island, in the Kennebec River, in the province, now the State, of Maine, December 17, 1779. His parents were members of the Society of Friends, at Nantucket, and removed from thence to Maine in 1772. He was a distant

cousin, on both the father's and mother's side, of BENJA-
MIN FRANKLIN, whom he greatly resembled, in form and
feature. His father died April 26, 1780, when JACOB was
about four months old. After the peace of 1783, his
mother returned to Nantucket, reaching there in April,
1785, where he enjoyed the advantages of the excellent
schools of the island till he was in his eighteenth year,
when, like most of the enterprising Nantucket boys of
that time, he came to New-York to seek his fortune. He
entered the counting-house of ISAAC HICKS, an eminent
New-York commission merchant, in 1797. He remained
with Mr. Hicks, greatly to their mutual satisfaction, until
the close of 1800, when he entered into partnership with
JOHN BARD and JONAS MINTURN as commission merchants.
He was only twenty-one years of age, full of energy, and
of great physical courage and enterprise, and he soon took
the whole business upon his own shoulders and combined
a shipping business with it; a year later he was the owner
of four ships and a brig.

He was a tireless worker, and before the war of 1812 was
declared, he had become a thorough student of political
economy, an attorney at law, a banker, a State Senator,
and the largest ship-owner in the United States, except
WILLIAM GRAY, of Boston and Salem. His ships traversed
every sea. He established a house in Liverpool, and his
business connections with most of the European States were
very extensive; with Russia, especially, he had established
a very large trade. His transactions, in the purchase and
sale of ships, with foreign governments, were of immense
extent, and were almost all made with their Admiralty
officers. He also took contracts with our own Government,
supplying our light-houses with oil, when Mr. GALLATIN
was Secretary of the Treasury. When ROBERT FULTON was
building his first steamboat, Mr. BARKER imported for
him, at his own risk and on his own account, the first
marine steam engine brought into this country, and held it
for him, until he could raise the necessary funds to pay
for it.

While he was State Senator, the Senate, under the old

Constitution, sat as a Court of Errors : Mr. BARKER delivered an opinion in an insurance case, in opposition to that of Chancellor KENT, and his opinion was sustained by the Court. He was so thorough a student of the laws and principles of trade, commerce and finance, in their relations to the policy of the Government, that he became an ardent politician and political leader, and carried all the zeal of his earnest and restless nature into his political life. He espoused the cause of JEFFERSON, advocating the purchase of Louisiana, and subsequently defending the Embargo and Non-importation Acts, though he was convinced, that with his extended commercial and shipping business, the immediate result to him would be great and heavy losses. He was too patriotic to let this certainty outweigh the conviction that his country would be benefited by a firm resistance to the encroachments of Great Britain and France on her commerce. He at first opposed the war of 1812, but when it was declared, he supported Mr. MADISON's war policy. His ships were all captured during the war; but his fortune was still ample, and in 1813, finding the Government distressed for funds, he obtained subscriptions for two million four hundred thousand dollars, subscribing one hundred thousand dollars on his own account ; and the next year, learning that the ten million loan advertised found few or no takers, with his subscription and his other arrangements to the same effect, he was prepared to offer to the Treasury an additional loan of five million dollars more, to sustain its credit.

After the battle of Bladensburg, at the request of President MADISON's wife, Mr. BARKER and ROBERT G. L. DE PEYSTER took from the President's house the original portrait of WASHINGTON, by STUART, to preserve it from being seized by the British. They fell in with the train of the American army, then retreating from Washington, and continued with it till nightfall, when they stopped at a farmhouse near the banks of the Tiber, passed the night, and deposited the portrait there for safe-keeping. After the war was over, Mr. BARKER returned to the farmhouse, and, re-claiming the picture, returned it to Mrs.

MADISON, who placed it in the new White House, as soon as it was re-built, where it remains to this day.

After the war he established the *Union* newspaper, to advocate the election of DE WITT CLINTON. He founded the Exchange Bank in this City in 1815, and became largely concerned in stocks. He was again elected to the State Senate, and there, was among the first to advocate the construction of the Erie Canal, as well as other measures proposed by Governor CLINTON. He continued to take an active interest in politics, and in 1820 was the first man to nominate ANDREW JACKSON for the Presidency. He sustained him, also, in 1824 and in 1828. In 1834 he removed to New-Orleans, where he again engaged in banking, and, being admitted to the Louisiana bar, speedily became a political leader there, but, true to his early training in the Society of Friends, he would neither hold slaves nor support slavery. This bold and fearless stand undoubtedly diminished his fortune, but he never wavered in his position. He was an old man (eighty-two years of age) when the Civil War commenced, but though remaining in New-Orleans, he opposed the Rebellion. In 1865 he was elected to Congress from that city, but, owing to the Reconstruction difficulties, was not permitted to take his seat. In 1867, with his great fortune lost from the vicissitudes of the war, he removed to the home of his son, ABRAHAM BARKER, in Philadelphia, where he died December 26, 1871, at the age of ninety-two years.

ALFRED S. BARNES.

ALFRED SMITH BARNES was born in New-Haven, Conn., January 28th, 1817. His father was the proprietor of an inn located in that part of the town known as Barnesville, and was a man of probity and Christian character. His mother was a MORRIS, of Huguenot descent, for whom her son, ALFRED, always cherished the tenderest recollections, as it seemed to be her life work to guide her children with love in all the Christian graces. Owing to a large family,

ALFRED was sent away to a boarding school at nine years of age, and there received his rudimental education. Upon the death of his father, in 1827, he returned home and remained with his mother several years, when he was placed under the care of an uncle living near Hartford. Here he united farming and schooling, but soon became restless to enter a business. His uncle endeavored to interest him in the shoe-making trade, but, not having a taste for the occupation, he shrunk from it, and aspired to a position in a book store. In 1831 the way was opened to him to enter the book store of D. F. ROBINSON & Co., of Hartford, as errand boy, and with all the enthusiasm of his nature he entered upon his duties there, at thirty dollars per year, with a home in the family of Mr. ROBIN-SON included. The firm removed to New-York in 1835, and there he completed his clerkship.

In 1838 Mr. BARNES, then a young man of twenty-one, became acquainted with Professor CHARLES DAVIES, the mathematician, and the result was a copartnership under the firm name of A. S. BARNES & Co., for the publication of the latter's books. They removed to Hartford and opened business in a store about fifteen by twenty feet. Professor DAVIES furnished the material for the books, and Mr. BARNES published and went about introducing the same into the schools of the country, so far as the travelling facilities of that day permitted. Professor DAVIES remained a partner till 1848, and was succeeded by EDMUND DWIGHT, who continued only a year or two, and was in turn succeeded by HENRY L. BURR, a brother-in-law of Mr. BARNES, who remained a partner till his death in 1865, since which time Mr. BARNES' five sons and a nephew have successively been admitted to the firm, and now carry on the business.

In 1840 the firm of A. S. BARNES & Co. removed to Philadelphia, and, after four years, removed again to New-York, where it has since remained. Mr. BARNES gave untiring attention to the affairs of the business for over fifty years, and his wise judgment in all matters pertaining thereto was one of the chief factors in its success. The list of publications has been mainly school books, (although some digression in other lines has been permitted, but only incidentally,) and embraces now over eleven hundred titles. The schools of several generations are familiar with the firm's imprint, and it is hardly necessary to recall the names of the more popular books. DAVIES' Mathematics have been more widely used, probably, than any other series extant, the aggregate sale of the series to date having been at least ten million copies ; a safe estimate of the total out-put of the house to date would be at least seventy-five million copies. Mr. BARNES would never permit an unworthy publication to emanate from his house, nor would he employ a man who did not impress him by an upright and gentlemanly bearing, and he was seldom deceived. Always genial himself, he sought to have pleasant feeling prevail throughout his establishment, and by absolute fair dealing the house has earned for itself an enviable reputation. For some years he was special partner in the publishing house of POTTER, AINSWORTH & CO., which, since his death, has been merged into the house of which he was the head.

In 1857 and 1861, periods of money stringency, he felt the clouds gathering about him, but by prudence and the confidence of his friends he passed safely over the troubled waters.

Mr. BARNES chose, as between money spending and money giving, the latter, and he seemingly gave with unstinted hand to the numerous charities that favorably presented themselves to him. Perhaps no better monument to his habit of giving could be mentioned, than the beautiful edifice he caused to be erected at Ithaca, N. Y., for the use of the Christian Association of Cornell University.

Mr. BARNES was a member of the Chamber of Commerce from April 27th, 1865 ; he was also associated as Director or Trustee in the Hanover Bank, Home Insurance Company, Dime Savings Bank of Brooklyn, Provident Life Insurance Company, Fidelity and Casualty Company, Trustee in the Brooklyn Polytechnic Institute, Packer Institute and Cornell University, and in the Long Island Historical Society ; and with various railroads and other institutions, thus proving his untiring energy and interest in promoting all healthful and progressive enterprises. In the elevated railroads he was one of the pioneer investors, and although his original associates withdrew from the enterprise upon the failure of the endless-chain idea, he remained a steadfast believer in an elevated mode of transit, and was a Director of the New-York Company up to within a few years of his decease.

In benevolent societies and church affairs his name often appeared, indicating that his time was not entirely occupied with matters temporal. The title so often applied to him of "Christian merchant," in all that it implied, accurately describes the man.

He married, in 1841, HARRIET E. BURR, a daughter of General TIMOTHY BURR, of Hartford, to whom were born ten children, five sons and five daughters, all of whom survived their parents. Mr. BARNES died in Brooklyn, February 17th, 1888, at the age of 71 years.

JAMES BROWN.

JAMES BROWN, for a half century the head of the eminent banking house of BROWN BROTHERS & CO., was the fourth and youngest son of ALEXANDER BROWN, a wealthy and enterprising linen merchant of Ballymena, County Antrim, Province of Ulster, Ireland, and was born in Ballymena on February 4th, 1791. About 1798 the elder BROWN migrated to Baltimore, and established a warehouse for the sale of linens there. He sent his sons to England to be educated, and, on their attaining their majority, took them into partnership. His business becoming extensive, and some ventures made during the Peninsular War and in the stormy times preceding our war of 1812, having proved largely successful, ALEXANDER BROWN resolved to establish branch houses for the sale of his linens. The firm now became ALEXANDER BROWN & SONS, and the eldest son, WILLIAM, who had returned to the old home in Ireland for a visit, established, in 1810, a branch house in Liverpool, which, in 1815, assumed the name of WILLIAM & JAMES BROWN & Co. Subsequently the firm name was changed to BROWN, SHIPLEY & Co. Mr. WILLIAM BROWN accumulated a large fortune, was elected a member of Parliament, and with a liberal spirit which did him great honor, established the Free Library of Liverpool, to which he gave half a million of dollars. On his retirement from business he was created by the Queen a baronet. The next son, GEORGE, remained with his father in Baltimore: JOHN A. became the head of a branch house in Philadelphia, and JAMES, the youngest, was sent to New-York in 1825. In 1826 the house of BROWN BROTHERS & Co., still in the linen trade, was founded in New-York. It was composed of ALEXANDER, the father, WILLIAM (afterwards Sir WILLIAM) in Liverpool, JOHN A. in Philadelphia, and JAMES, then thirty-four years old, in New-York. At the close of 1838 the firm sold out their linen business, and thenceforth devoted themselves exclusively to banking, in which, indeed, they had already been profitably engaged. Their character for integrity, financial ability and liberal dealing, as well as their abundant means, soon made them the representative banking house in this country. When the financial panic of 1837 came on, the firm held American bills for a very large amount, including four million dollars of protested paper, and other engagements in England to the amount of ten millions more. They were abundantly solvent, but the panic was raging in Europe as fiercely as here. The large amounts of American securities held by the firm, though good, were not available at that time, and it was almost impossible to draw bills or remit specie to England. There was a consultation between the brothers, and WILLIAM was deputed to go to the Bank of England and ask that a committee of their ablest financiers should be appointed to investigate the condition of the American banking house, and, if they were satisfied, that the Bank should make them a loan sufficient to carry them through. The committee was immediately appointed, and, after examination, reported so favorably that the Bank of England granted them a credit of five million pounds, or so much of it as they might need. At the end of six months the loan was repaid, and from that time their credit and reputation, both in Europe and America, stood higher than that of any other banking house having American connections. From that time to the present, the circular letters of credit of BROWN BROTHERS & Co. have been as current in every part of the world as the notes of the Bank of England. They have now their branch establishments, all carefully managed, in Boston, Philadelphia and Baltimore, and their representatives in New-Orleans, as well as in most of the principal cities of the world.

JAMES BROWN withdrew wholly from public and political affairs, to devote his whole powers to the consideration of the problems of finance and the conduct of his vast business. Though of genial manners and a most kindly nature, he suffered no interruption or intrusion upon his time during business hours, and his faithful servant permitted no access to his private office, without his master's explicit permission. Yet he found time for aiding and guiding great charitable and philanthropic institutions amid his busy life. He was for many years President of the Association for Improving the Condition of the Poor, and an active and leading Director of the Bank for Savings in Bleecker-street, a Vice-President or Director of the American Bible Society, of the Union Theological Seminary, of the Presbyterian Hospital and other charitable institutions, and in the charities of his own church he was always a large, though never an ostentatious, giver. He had been the Senior Elder of the University Place Presbyterian Church for many years.

For twenty years and more before his death Mr. BROWN had withdrawn from the more active duties of his banking house, but his interest in it continued till his death, which occurred in this City, November 1st, 1877, in his eighty-seventh year. Mr. BROWN was twice married. His first wife was a daughter of the Rev. Dr. BENEDICT, of Plainfield, Connecticut. Three daughters survived her. His second wife was a daughter of the Rev. Dr. JONAS COE, of Troy, who survived him. By this marriage he had three children, two sons and a daughter.

The Chamber of Commerce, of which body Mr. BROWN had been a member for more than fifty years, was informed of his death the same day, whereupon a Committee was appointed, consisting of A. A. LOW, WILLIAM E. DODGE and SAMUEL B. RUGGLES, to prepare resolutions of respect to his memory. At the meeting of the Chamber, held December 6th, the Committee reported the following, which were unanimously adopted :

Resolved, That the demise of JAMES BROWN bids us pause amid the activities of business to add another name to the roll of our honored dead ; the name of one whose life, gathering brightness with length of years, has shed lustre upon the commercial character, not of our city only and of sister cities, but of the United States, the name of him who, as partner of the house of BROWN BROTHERS & Co., has extended American credit to the remotest quarters of the globe, and vitalized our relations with the commercial world.

Resolved, That it becomes us to bow with resignation to the will of GOD, who, in the fullness of years, has withdrawn from our Association one of its oldest and most esteemed members, whose presence in this Chamber, although marked by an unostentatious reserve, imparted dignity to its proceedings and strength to its resolves.

Resolved, That we will cherish the memory of our late associate, and, making record of his long, useful and exemplary life — a life eminently conspicuous for its munificent charities — we will hold this record sacred in our keeping as long as the love of rectitude, philanthropy, patriotism and Christian gentleness shall endure.

Resolved, That without recounting Mr. BROWN's manifold virtues, but sharing with the church, with society, with the community at large in a common loss, and par-

16

taking of a common grief, we will send to the family of the deceased a copy of these resolutions as a token of our respect for the departed, and of our sincere condolence for the bereaved.

CORNELIUS VANDERBILT.

CORNELIUS VANDERBILT was of Holland-Dutch stock, and his remarkable career makes him one of the most prominent figures in the commercial history of the second half century of the Republic. He was born near Stapleton, Staten Island, New-York, May 27th, 1794. His father was CORNELIUS VANDERBILT; and he was a great-grandson of JACOB VAN DER BILT, whose ancestors first came to this country from Holland in 1650, and settled on Long Island.

Like many of the men who have had a successful business career in New-York, his early life was spent upon a farm; but the energy and enterprise which were the distinguishing characteristics of his career, impelled him, at the age of sixteen, to more venturesome pursuits. He seems to have instinctively foreseen that the great opportunity in the development of the new country was the business of transportation. He began by carrying laborers across New-York Bay, from New-York to the fortifications at the Narrows, in a small sail-boat; and in two years he had become the owner of several small craft, and captain of a larger one. During the war of 1812 his venturesome spirit made him better known, and gave him greater income. He furnished supplies by night to two forts near New-York, and was selected by the Government officers for expeditions which required special skill and daring. At the age of nineteen he married SOPHIA JOHNSON; and on his twenty-first birthday he was the proprietor of an established business and the owner of a capital which amounted to nine thousand dollars. He invested this in the purchase of a part interest of a steamboat running from New-York

to New Brunswick, New-Jersey, and became her captain.
In seven years from this time, and about 1824, he had
secured full control of the most important steamboat line
running out of New-York, known as the "Gibbons" line;
and, three years later, he leased the ferries between New-
York and Elizabethport, New-Jersey. From this period
began the expansion of operations which continued without interruption or failure until the close of his life. He
soon had steamboats running upon the Hudson River, and
on Long Island Sound to Hartford, Providence, Norwich
and New-Haven. He practically controlled for many years
water transportation between New-York and Hudson
River and New-England points.

In 1849 he made a new departure. The discovery of gold
in California had led to immense immigration to the Pacific
coast. To meet and stimulate this he established a steamship route from New-York to San Francisco, crossing the
Isthmus at Panama. Railroading was then in its infancy,
and the plains and mountains between California and the
borders of civilization in the East an unexplored territory,
filled with hostile Indians. The three steamers which he
placed upon the Atlantic, and four upon the Pacific side,
gave him a control of the business between the Atlantic
seaports and the Pacific slope. In 1855 he established a
Trans-Atlantic line, but, after a trial of six years, abandoned it. During the Civil War, in 1861, when the whole
country was alarmed at the prospective damage to our sea-
coast cities from the rebel ram "Merrimac," he presented
the steamship "Vanderbilt" —then the finest steamship on
the ocean to the Government. In recognition of this
gift, at the close of the war, Congress voted him a gold
medal. In 1864 he became convinced that the business of
transportation by water had culminated, and the opportunities of the future were in railroads, their operation and
extension. He therefore disposed of all his interests in
steamboats and steamships. His prominence and distinction during these many years as the owner and commander
of a large merchant fleet had given him the popular title of
"Commodore," by which he is best known.

It was characteristic of Commodore VANDERBILT that whatever he determined to do he entered upon at once. He immediately secured a control of the stock of the New-York and Harlem Railroad Company, and became its President; and the next year he also bought a majority of the stock of the Hudson River Company and assumed its management. He was the first to discover that the success of a railroad line was in the control of the direct connections upon which it must rely for its business. He, therefore, immediately began the purchase of the stock of the New-York Central; and in 1869 consolidated it with the Hudson River Railroad, forming what is now known as the New-York Central and Hudson River Railroad. He became the first President of this corporation. He had practically rebuilt the Harlem Road, and he now turned his attention to the improvement of the consolidated line; under his management two additional tracks were constructed west of Albany: the Grand Central Depot, St. John's Park Freight Station, and the Grain Elevators on the Hudson River at Sixty-fifth street were erected: and the magnificent entrance into the City, by viaduct and tunnel, through Fourth Avenue, laid out and completed. To secure the permanence and growth of the New-York Central's business with the vast commerce distributed at Chicago, he purchased a controlling interest in the Lake Shore, Canada Southern and Michigan Central Railroads; and these made the New-York line by the New-York Central and the north and south shores of the lake to Chicago.

The Commodore gave fifty thousand dollars to the Rev. CHARLES F. DEEMS to purchase the Church of the Strangers in this City and for its mission work. He founded the VANDERBILT University at Nashville, Tennessee, to assist in the educational development of the South, and endowed it with a million of dollars. His fortune at the time of his death was generally estimated at one hundred million dollars, all of which he left to his eldest son, WILLIAM HENRY, except four million dollars, which he bequeathed to his daughters, and eleven million dollars to WILLIAM HENRY's four sons. Mr. VANDERBILT was a very hand-

some man, and one of the most striking figures in his old
age in New-York. He died in this City on the 4th of
January, 1877, at the age of eighty-two years, retaining
his physical vigor and mental energy to the last.

WILLIAM H. VANDERBILT.

WILLIAM H. VANDERBILT was born in New-Brunswick,
New Jersey, May 8th, 1821. He was the eldest son of Commodore VANDERBILT, and was educated at the Columbia
Grammar School. He began his business career early in life.
At the age of seventeen he entered the office of the then
famous firm of bankers and brokers of which DANIEL DREW
was the head. He married when he was twenty Miss KIS-
SAM, the daughter of a well-known clergyman of the Dutch
Reformed Church. Close attention to his duties in the
office and over work impaired his health to such an extent
that in 1842 he settled upon a farm on Staten Island which
belonged to his father. It was here that the sterling
qualities which afterwards won his success were first manifested. The Commodore had strong opinions of the value
of self reliance, and the discipline which only comes from
working one's own way in the world. WILLIAM H. was
left entirely to his own resources, and accomplished the
difficult task of not only earning a living off his farm,
but of making it profitable. He also became active in
political affairs and matters of general interest on the
island, and after a short time was widely known and respected as an energetic, public spirited and successful
citizen. The Staten Island Railroad Company became embarrassed, and Mr. VANDERBILT was selected as the one
best qualified to manage its business and bring it out of its
difficulties. By general consent he was appointed Receiver,
and began his career as a railway officer and director. He
speedily developed superior business ability, and it was
not long before he had liberated the Company from its
troubles, and put it upon a paying basis. The Commodore

was so much impressed with this demonstrated capacity that he called him from the island and placed upon him very large responsibilities. He appointed WILLIAM H. Vice-President and Executive Officer of the New-York and Harlem, and afterwards of the Hudson River Railroad. The situation was a difficult and trying one, as much was expected both by the public and his father. But in a few years the railway men of the country recognized in him a railroad manager of unusual talent. Upon the consolidation of the Hudson River and New-York Central, he was called to the direction of the affairs of the new Company, and entered upon activities which resulted in his becoming one of the most important and powerful factors in the railway system of the United States.

The death of his father left him in control of the lines between New-York and Chicago by the New-York Central, and of the Lake Shore on the south and the Michigan Central and Canada Southern on the north shore of the lake. He inherited the bulk of his father's vast fortune, and immediately bent his energies and resources to extending and strengthening the system which was to honor and perpetuate the name of VANDERBILT. By securing a controlling interest in the Chicago and North Western and the Chicago, St. Paul, Minneapolis and Omaha, he reached the great wheat belt of the Northwest, and covered the territory between Chicago and the Missouri River, and on towards the Pacific. The West Shore and Nickle Plate roads had been constructed parallel with the Central and Lake Shore, and threatened the serious impairment and possible ruin of both properties; but he first successfully fought this unjustifiable invasion of territory fully and satisfactorily served by existing roads, and then purchased the one for the Central and the other for the Lake Shore. Time has demonstrated the wisdom of this policy.

Soon after the consolidation of the New-York Central and Hudson River Roads, Mr. VANDERBILT became impressed with the importance of a permanent entrance into the City of New-York, and a central terminus which would be equal to the large and rapidly increasing passenger traffic of the line. The Grand Central Depot was constructed, and connected by a depressed road, tunnel and viaduct, with the bridge across the Harlem River. By this improvement the New-York Central secured the unequalled advantages of four tracks into the heart of the City, and a station so located as to give the Company the best position of any of the Trunk lines for passenger business between the West and the Metropolis. This work will remain an enduring monument to his wisdom and foresight.

The labor strikes upon the railroads of the country, in 1877, were the most serious ever known. They stopped the movement of most lines, suspended travel and paralyzed business. Mr. VANDERBILT managed, with great skill and diplomacy, to keep his roads open.

The Granger excitement and the increasing agitation for restrictive legislation against railways convinced Mr. VANDERBILT that it was a mistake for one man to own the controlling interest in any great transportation line. It aroused antagonism and invited attacks. By one of the best managed and most successful combinations ever formed, he was able, in a single transaction, to sell two hundred and fifty thousand shares of the stock of the New-York Central and Hudson River Railroad Company for thirty millions of dollars. In 1883 he resigned his official positions and transferred the supervision of the VANDERBILT system to his sons, CORNELIUS and WILLIAM K. VANDERBILT. CORNELIUS was made Chairman of the Board of Directors of the New-York Central and Hudson River and the Michigan Central Railroads, and WILLIAM K. was Chairman of the Board of Directors of the Lake Shore and Michigan Southern, and subsequently, also, of the New York, Chicago and St. Louis Railroad.

Mr. VANDERBILT was generous and public spirited. In 1884 he presented to the College of Physicians and Surgeons of the City of New-York five hundred thousand dollars, for the purchase of land and the erection of buildings. This gift contributed largely to the higher education of physicians, a subject in which he was deeply interested. He also gave five hundred thousand dollars to the VANDER-

BILT University, which had been generously endowed by his father. He gave the money which secured from the Egyptian Government the gift of the Obelisk, and brought it to New-York and placed it in Central Park.

Mr. VANDERBILT died in this City on December 8th, 1885. By his will he left a million of dollars to various charities, sundry bequests to friends, ten millions of dollars to each of his eight children, and the residue of his estate to his sons, CORNELIUS and WILLIAM K. VANDERBILT.

HANSON K. CORNING.

HANSON KELLY CORNING, oldest son of EPHRAIM CORNING, was born in Hartford, Conn., on the 9th of July, 1810. He was a direct descendant from SAMUEL CORNING, who came from England about 1630, and settled in Beverly, Massachusetts, where he was chosen one of the selectmen in 1665. EPHRAIM CORNING removed his family to Alexandria, Virginia, while HANSON was yet a child, and there he grew up and received his education.

At eighteen years of age he entered the office of his uncle, EDWARD CORNING, who was engaged in the hardware business at Albany, New-York, where he remained for three years, when he was sent, in 1831, by the concern of E. & L. CORNING, (composed of his father and uncle, who had established themselves in New-York, and were among the earliest American merchants to engage in trade with Northern Brazil,) to Para, Brazil, charged with looking after their interests and enlarging their business. He remained in Para for four years, during which period he consigned to New-York what was probably the first shipment of India rubber in the shape of shoes and toys. They were made by the natives in the India rubber forests ; were very unwieldy in form, but possessed of extraordinary wearing qualities, and were the forerunners of the important business now carried on in India rubber boots and shoes.

In 1835 Mr. CORNING returned to New-York to take the place vacated by the retirement of his uncle, LEONARD CORNING, from the concern, which then became EPHRAIM CORNING & SON, and established at No. 74 South Street, where they and their successors remained for more than thirty years. In the same year he married EMMA B. DOR-RANCE—a union which continued a source of great happiness until the end of his life.

The discovery by CHARLES GOODYEAR of the process for vulcanizing India rubber stimulated the manufacture of India rubber goods, especially boots and shoes, to an enormous extent, and the importing of Para rubber in crude form gradually increased, until it became a great trade. The facilities which Mr. CORNING had established during his residence in Para enabled the firm to hold a leading position in the business as it developed, and under the old firm name of EPHRAIM CORNING & SON until 1849, (when his father retired,) and his own name, H. K. CORNING, until 1859, when the concern was changed to H. K. CORNING & SON by the admission of his son, EPHRAIM L. CORNING, he maintained the supremacy as importer of Para rubber, and extended his business to Maranham, Rio de Janeiro and Rio Grande do Sul. In 1867, by reason of impaired health, he retired from active business.

Prosperity followed Mr. CORNING's business career from its beginning, except during the panic of 1837, when EPHRAIM CORNING & SON were embarassed, owing to the magnitude of their business, and were forced to make a compromise with their creditors. In less than five years afterwards they paid every creditor in full, principal and interest—an action so rare in business records as to be worthy of mention.

From the time of Mr. CORNING's retirement he devoted himself, as he had long been doing, to philanthropic work of very varied character, not only among institutions in New-York and elsewhere, but privately in hundreds of households, where his kindly interest and ready help lightened the cares and increased the comforts of the needy.

Mr. Corning was elected a member of the Chamber of Commerce March 2d, 1854, and continued his connection with it up to the time of his retirement from business.

In the simple Christian hope in which he had lived he died on the 22d day of April, 1878, in this City, leaving behind him the blessed memory of the just. His wife survived him for precisely six months.

GEORGE WASHINGTON.

George Washington, the "Father of his Country," was born in Washington Parish, Westmoreland County, Virginia, near the junction of Pope's Creek with the Potomac River, February 22, (February 11, Old Style,) 1732. He was the son of Augustine Washington. Augustine Washington was a wealthy planter, and was twice married; his first wife, Jane Butler, bore him four children, of whom, two sons, Lawrence and Augustine, reached maturity. The second wife, Mary Ball, brought her husband six children, of whom George was the eldest. His father owned two or more large plantations, and removed, in George's early childhood, to the one situated in Stafford County, nearly opposite Fredericksburg. Before he had reached the age of twelve years his father died. He inherited the Stafford County property, and his elder half-brother, Lawrence, received the large estate on Hunting Creek, afterward known as Mount Vernon. His early education was somewhat defective, but he showed a strong predilection for mathematics, for which he had a private teacher. His half-brother, Lawrence, was his guardian, and on leaving school, at the age of fifteen, he resided for some months with his brother at Mount Vernon. Lawrence had married a daughter of William Fairfax, the wealthiest planter in Virginia, and for some time President of the Executive Council of the Colony. George was inclined to a military or naval career, and, probably, through the influence of Lawrence's friends, a midshipman's warrant in the English Navy was procured for him, but the mother opposed it so strongly that he relinquished his purpose. The next year, however, he was appointed Surveyor to the immense estates of Baron Lord FAIRFAX, that eccentric nobleman having determined to take up his residence in America, and being then on a visit to his kinsman, WILLIAM FAIRFAX. The task was an arduous one for a boy of sixteen years, but young WASHINGTON gladly accepted it, and for the next three years he roughed it on the frontier, encountering many dangers and hardships.

In 1751 the Virginia Militia were put under training for active service against France, and WASHINGTON, although only nineteen years of age, was appointed Adjutant, with the rank of Major. In September of that year he accompanied his brother, LAWRENCE, who was in failing health, on a voyage to the Barbadoes. They returned early in 1752, and LAWRENCE, dying soon after, named his half brother as one of the executors of his great estate, and made him the presumptive heir of the Mount Vernon property, which soon after came into his possession, by the death of LAWRENCE's infant daughter.

When Lieutenant Governor DINWIDDIE arrived in Virginia, in 1752, the militia was re-organized and divided into four military districts. The northern district was the most important of these, and of this, GEORGE WASHINGTON, then just twenty-one years old, was commissioned by the Governor, Adjutant-General. In November of the same year he was sent with only one companion on the perilous enterprise of penetrating to the French post of Le Boeuf, on French Creek, near Lake Erie, and of demanding, in the name of the King of England, that the French should withdraw from this territory. To reach this point it was necessary that they should traverse, for hundreds of miles, an unexplored region, inhabited only by Indian tribes known to be hostile to the English. The expedition was, of course, unavailing, and its only good result was, that WASHINGTON's report to Governor DINWIDDIE was sent by him to London, and published. The Assembly of Virginia authorized the Executive to raise a regiment of three hundred men, to maintain by force the asserted rights of the British Crown over the territory claimed. The command of this expedition was given to Colonel JOSHUA FRY. At the urgent request of his friends, WASHINGTON was commissioned Lieutenant Colonel of the regiment. The expedition met with varied fortunes, but not being sustained by promised reinforcements, and Colonel FRY having died on the route, Colonel WASHINGTON, after defeating an advanced party of the French and intrenching himself in a fort, (Fort Necessity,) which he had thrown up on the "Great Meadows," was obliged, being attacked by an overwhelming force of French and Indians, to capitulate and surrender his artillery, July 4, 1754. In the winter of 1754–55, orders were received for "settling the rank of his Majesty's forces, when serving with the provincials in North America." These orders were so insulting to the provincial officers that WASHINGTON and many others indignantly resigned their commissions. WASHINGTON retired to Mount Vernon. Here, in the spring of 1755, he was found by General EDWARD BRADDOCK, who had been commissioned to make a formal campaign against the French on the Ohio. General BRADDOCK had heard of WASHINGTON's services in the vicinity of Pittsburg, and of his thorough knowledge of the theater of operations, and he endeavored to persuade him to join the expedition. WASHINGTON would not consent to go in any other capacity than as a volunteer aid-de-camp. The result of this campaign need not here be particularized. He saved the shattered remnants of the line army, and brought them off the field, where BRADDOCK and all his chief officers had fallen. The Virginia Assembly passed a bill directing the enlistment of sixteen new companies for the defence of the province, and commissioned WASHINGTON as Commander-in-chief of all the forces raised and to be raised, in the Colony, with authority to appoint his own officers. The next three years were years of many disappointments to Colonel WASHINGTON. The British Government sent over Lord LOUDON to be Commander-in-chief of the British forces in the Colonies. WASHINGTON laid before him a detailed account of the operations thus far undertaken against the French on the Ohio, and specified the causes of their failure. He urged an active campaign with larger forces. Lord LOUDON would not listen to his plea. "Canada" he said, "was the point to be attacked," and so far was he from giving any aid to the Virginia provincial troops, that besides requiring from them their full quota for the northern expedition, he ordered them to protect their own frontier, and to send aid to South Carolina, against Indian raids in that colony. WASHINGTON, almost in despair, urged upon the Virginia Assembly the enactment of a more stringent militia law, and a large increase in the number of her regular troops. These measures the Assembly was unwilling to grant, and he was compelled to defend an Indian frontier of about four hundred miles, with a very inadequate force. In 1757, Gen. ABERCROMBIE succeeded Lord LOUDON, who had accomplished nothing. The new General committed the control of the Middle and Southern Provinces to Gen. FORBES, who decided to undertake an expedition against Fort Duquesne. WASHINGTON urged a quick advance over the old Braddock road, and an early campaign, but Gen. FORBES determined to construct a new road farther north in Pennsylvania, much longer, and so difficult of construction that the army, which had started in April, did not reach its rendezvous in the Alleghany Valley till late in November. WASHINGTON and his provincials led the advance, and his forces took possession of the ruins of Fort Duquesne, November 25, 1758, the French having evacuated and burned the fort the night before. WASHINGTON changed its name to Fort Pitt, and having repaired the fort, and left two hundred of his regiment to garrison it, marched the others back to Winchester, and himself proceeded to Williamsburg, Va., to take his seat in the General Assembly, of which he had been elected a member. As Indian hostilities had ceased, with the expulsion of the French from the Ohio, WASHINGTON resigned his Commission as Commander-in-Chief of the Virginia forces, determined to devote himself thenceforth to a civil career. Soon after resigning his Commission, he married,

January 17, 1759, Mrs. MARTHA (DANDRIDGE) CUSTIS, a young and beautiful widow lady of great wealth, (the MARTHA WASHINGTON of a later period,) and for the next fifteen years devoted himself to the cultivation, enlargement and improvement of his magnificent estate of Mount Vernon, interrupted only by his annual attendance in winter upon the sessions of the Colonial Legislature at Williamsburg. This season of rest was diligently improved by WASHINGTON, in careful study of every department of military science, till the gallant Colonel of the frontier service, in 1754–1758, had qualified himself thoroughly for much higher commands in the war, which he felt was soon to come. In the Legislature of the Colony, too, he had constantly urged the enlargement and thorough drilling of the militia.

The first premonitions of the coming conflict came from the North. Thus far, Virginia, under her Royal Governors, had had little experience of oppression, while New-York and Boston, especially the latter, had been grievously wronged, and subjected to gross and cruel insults and outrages. These culminated, in 1774, in the closure, by Act of Parliament, of the port of Boston. WASHINGTON was the leader of the Virginia Legislature, and as he foresaw that the rod of the oppressor, if unresisted, would soon be laid on the backs of all the Colonies, he showed the Legislature and the people of Virginia, that " the cause of Boston was their cause." Virginia led the way in calling a Congress of all the Colonies to meet in Philadelphia, September 5, 1774, to secure their common liberties, if possible, by peaceful means. In this Congress, GEORGE WASHINGTON represented Virginia as her first delegate. Its remonstrances and appeals exhibited the highest abilities, as well as the loftiest patriotism. In October, the Congress dissolved, but recommended the Colonies to send delegates to another Congress in the spring of 1775. Meantime, several of the Colonies had felt it necessary to raise local bodies of troops to repel the insults and aggressions of the British forces, of which considerable bodies were stationed in or near the larger seaport cities. The battles of Concord and Lexington had been fought, and the evidences that the British Cabinet were determined to force a bitter conflict were overwhelming. Among the earliest acts of this Second Congress, which met May 10, 1775, and of which WASHINGTON was again a member, was the selection of a Commander-in-Chief of the Colonial forces. This high and responsible office was unanimously conferred upon GEORGE WASHINGTON. Fully comprehending the peril, sacrifice and labor it involved, he accepted it, June 19th, 1775, but upon the express condition that he should receive no salary. He would keep an exact account of his expenditures, and expect Congress to pay them, and nothing more. He repaired immediately to Boston, near which the battle of Bunker Hill, between the British troops and the besieging provincials, had been fought, June 17, 1775. General GAGE was occupying Boston with a large force. WASHINGTON was not in a condition to attempt an active siege of the city, but it was an excellent opportunity to thoroughly train and discipline his army for future effective action, and he fully improved it. The general feeling among the American people was, that the British Government, finding them a unit in their resistance to the attempted oppressive measures, would recede from them, and that the old condition of amity and peace would be restored. Very few in the summer and autumn of 1775, believed that a revolution would be necessary. But the British Cabinet and Parliament seemed bent on driving the colonists to independence. They would not receive the petition of Congress; they ordered the bombardment of the town of Falmouth, (now Portland, Me.;) they prohibited trade with the Colonies, and authorized the capture of their vessels; they seized and impressed into their navy, American seamen in great numbers along the American coast, and in every way sought to goad them into open revolt. Thus provoked and insulted, the American leaders soon began to consider whether independence was not desirable. Even WASHINGTON, calm, cool and self-poised as he usually was, wrote from the head of the army, in May, 1776: "A reconciliation with Great Britain is impossible. When I

took command of the army, I abhorred the idea of independence, but I am now fully satisfied that nothing else will
save us." While WASHINGTON did not dare to assault
the British troops in Boston, he compelled them to evacuate that city in March, 1776, by a masterly blockade of all
their sources of supply. General HOWE made his way
toward New-York, which he occupied about September 1st,
after defeating the American army in the battle of Long
Island, August 27, 1776. He also occupied the Lower
Hudson soon after, and WASHINGTON was obliged to retire
behind the Delaware River, with a small, ill-provided army ;
but by the surprises of Trenton and Princeton, he regained
much of his lost ground in New-Jersey. How he kept his
army in the field—so ill-clothed, ill-fed and ill-paid were
they is a mystery not easily solved. There was no central government, having authority to raise men, provisions
or money. In 1777 78, the sufferings of the army were
terrible. At Valley Forge, only a day's march north of
Philadelphia, they were in need of all things, and WASH-
INGTON's private fortune was heavily drawn upon to supply their imperative needs. Yet in the former year
occurred the successful battle of Bennington, the two
battles of Saratoga, and the capture of BURGOYNE's
army ; and during the latter, Sir HENRY CLINTON was
compelled to evacuate Philadelphia, and the severe but
indecisive battle of Monmouth, N. J., was fought. Later
in the year, the British captured Savannah. In 1779 and
1780, the fortunes of war were against the American Commander, especially at the South. North Carolina, South
Carolina and Georgia were overrun and held by the
British troops, while BENEDICT ARNOLD's treachery had
nearly cost WASHINGTON the control of the strongholds on
the Hudson. But the campaign of 1781 restored the prestige of American arms. TARLETON was defeated at Cow-
pens, S. C. ; CORNWALLIS was crippled at Guilford Court
House, and defeated at Eutaw Springs ; MARION and his
partisans cleared North Carolina and most of South
Carolina of British troops, and CORNWALLIS, coming north
to join Sir HENRY CLINTON, was hemmed in at Yorktown,

Va., by WASHINGTON and ROCHAMBEAU, and compelled to surrender his whole force, about 8,000 men, October 19, 1781. This virtually ended the war. On November 30, 1782, a preliminary treaty of peace was arranged at Paris ; the definitive treaty was signed September 3, 1783, and between July, 1782, and November, 1783, all the cities occupied by British troops were evacuated, New-York City last of all. On December 4, 1783, at FRAUNCES' Tavern, (still standing on the corner of Broad and Pearl Streets, February, 1890,) in this city, WASHINGTON took leave of his officers in an address full of affection and patriotism, and on December 23d he resigned his commission to Congress, then in session at Annapolis, Md., and retired, without regret, to his beloved home at Mount Vernon.

He had, before resigning his commission, addressed a circular letter to the Governors of the several States, calling their attention to the necessity of some changes in the Constitution, under which the war had been carried on. This was the old Articles of Confederation which had proved so imperfect a reliance, during the seven years of conflict. It was for the modification of this that WASHINGTON was so anxious ; and during the three or four years that followed the close of the war, his correspondence on this subject was very extensive, and he was much gratified when, on February 21st, 1787, Congress called upon the States to send delegates to a convention at Philadelphia, for the purpose of revising the Articles of Confederation, "to render the Federal Constitution adequate to the exigencies of the Government and the preservation of the Union."

This Convention met May 14, 1787, and continued its sessions till September 17. WASHINGTON was a delegate, and was unanimously chosen President. The members were the most eminent statesmen in the country. It was decided to have an entirely new Constitution, rather than to attempt to revise the old Articles of Confederation. Two parties were developed in this Convention, both equally patriotic, but differing widely in their views in regard to the organization and powers of the nation. One

17

party wanted a strong Central Government, and would have been willing to strip the States of all powers, except those of merely local administration; the other party desired only a very slightly modified Confederation, with plenary powers for the individual States. Both parties were extremists, and their advocates were obliged to make concessions, until the *juste milieu* was arrived at in the present Constitution and its earlier amendments. WASHINGTON presided with impartiality, and, though inclined to a strong government, he was so just and judicious that while he exerted a powerful influence over the action of the Convention, he disarmed all hostility, and secured a unanimous adoption of the Constitution by the eleven States represented in the Convention. On its adjournment the harder task remained, of securing its ratification by at least nine States, which number was necessary for its adoption. In this work WASHINGTON labored zealously, with voice and pen, yet with such patriotism and delicate regard for the feelings and rights of others, that he won all hearts. In the autumn of 1788 eleven States had given in their adhesion to the new Constitution; and, by Act of the old Congress, the first Wednesday of January was designated for the election of the new Congress and the Electoral College; the first Wednesday of February for the College to meet and choose the new Executive; and the first Wednesday of March as the time, and New-York City as the place for the meeting of Congress and the inauguration of the first President.

For the first President it would have seemed treason to the people to mention any other name than WASHINGTON's, and he was unanimously elected. Of his inauguration, which did not take place till April 30, 1789, we have had every possible detail narrated, in the recent Centennial Anniversary in our City in April, 1889. His first term as President was largely devoted to the perfecting of the details of the new organization, and passing the necessary statutes for putting it in complete operation, the establishment of the Supreme Court, and the creation of the Departments of State, Finance, War, Navy and Justice. There were no definitively formed parties, and only one occasion for the exercise of the veto power. North Carolina and Rhode Island both accepted the Constitution in 1790, on which events WASHINGTON heartily congratulated Congress and the country.

In 1792, at the second election for President, he was desirous of retiring, but the people would hear of no other name, and he yielded to the universal wish, and was again elected by the unanimous vote of every Electoral College. During the two terms, 1789–1797, three States, Vermont, Kentucky and Tennessee, were added to the Union, and there was great growth and development in all the States, while there were no discords to mar the harmony of the new Republic.

At the third election, in 1796, WASHINGTON was again most urgently entreated to take the Presidential chair, but positively refused. He felt that two terms were sufficient, and he longed for the quiet and rest of private life. For forty-five years of his active life he had been almost constantly engaged in the service of his country, his State or his Colony.

In September, 1796, just before the election, he issued to his countrymen his memorable "Farewell Address," which, in language, sentiment and patriotism, was the most admirable legacy he could have left to the nation he had created. In March, 1797, he returned to Mount Vernon to spend his remaining days in a well earned quiet and peace. His administration of the government for these two terms had been far more successful than even the most sanguine friends of the new Republic had dared to hope. The finances of the country had been relieved from embarrassment, the public credit was fully restored; every department of industry was quickened into new life; the revenue derived from imports had proved a bond of union to the whole country, and had produced astonishing results upon the trade and commerce of all the States. The exports from the Union had risen from nineteen millions to over fifty-six millions of dollars per annum, while the imports had increased in a like proportion. The progress of the States in their new career, in self-government, intelligence and education, was exceedingly encouraging, not only to the friends of liberty in this country, but to their sympathizing allies abroad.

Once more was the nation's hero called from his well earned repose at Mount Vernon, to serve his country, and, patriot that he was, he accepted the trust. In 1798, a war with France seemed imminent, and he was called by Congress to take command of all the United States forces, with the rank of Lieutenant-General. He had just commenced to organize his troops, when a treaty of peace was signed between the two nations, and put an end to all further action. WASHINGTON died at Mount Vernon, after a short but severe illness, December 14, 1799, in the sixty-eighth year of his age. The whole country was enshrouded with gloom, by the sad intelligence of his death. The mourning was universal. Men of all parties in politics and of all creeds in religion, not only in all States of the Union, but in foreign lands, united in paying honor to the memory of the man who was "first in war, first in peace, and first in the hearts of his countrymen." His remains were deposited in a family vault at Mount Vernon, and the estate has since become the property of the nation.

We close this sketch with the following extract from the eloquent address, delivered by the Hon. CHAUNCEY M. DEPEW, at the Centennial Celebration of April 30, 1889 :

"No man ever stood for so much to his country and to mankind, as WASHINGTON. *　*　*　*　*

"He, with unerring judgment, was always the leader of the people. MILTON said of CROMWELL: 'That war made him great, peace greater.' The superiority of WASHINGTON'S character and genius were more conspicuous in the formation of our government, and in putting it on indestructible foundations, than in leading armies to victory, and conquering the independence of his country. 'The Union in any event,' is the central thought in his farewell address, and all the years of his grand life were devoted to its formation and preservation. He fought as a youth with BRADDOCK, and in the capture of Fort Duquesne, for the protection of the whole country. As Commander-in-Chief of the Continental Army, his commission was from the Congress of the United Colonies. He inspired the movement for the Republic, was President and dominant spirit of the Convention which framed its Constitution, and its President for eight years, and guided its course until satisfied that moving safely along the broad highway of time, it would be surely ascending toward the first place among the nations of the world, the asylum of the oppressed, the home of the free."

MOSES TAYLOR.

MOSES TAYLOR, for fifty years a merchant and banker, was born in New-York City, at the corner of Broadway and Morris Street, January 11th, 1806. He was of English stock ; his great grandfather, who bore the same name, having emigrated from London in 1736. Mr. TAYLOR's father, JACOB B. TAYLOR, was for several terms an Alderman for the Ninth and Fifteenth Wards; in the days when a seat in that body was regarded as a high honor, and a position to be sought after by men of character and intelligence.

MOSES attended the best schools the City then afforded, but though an obedient and industrious pupil, business had for him greater charms than study ; and, at the age of fifteen, he became a clerk in the large mercantile and shipping house of G. G. & S. HOWLAND. He remained with this house more than ten years, and his industry, integrity, energy and foresight made him invaluable to his employers. When he was twenty-six years of age he had accumulated fifteen thousand dollars, and with this small capital he set up in business for himself, in modest quarters, at No. 44 South Street ; selecting the West Indies, and particularly the Cuban trade, as his specialty. His business was prosperous during the next two years, but in December, 1835, occurred in New-York the first great

fire of the century, and his warehouse and goods were
swept away. Nothing except his books of accounts was
saved. He opened an office the same day, in the basement
of his house in Morris Street, and soon after procured temporary quarters in Broad Street, and resumed business
with speedy success. He also made arrangements with
his landlord, while the ruins were yet smouldering, for the
re-building, on a larger scale, of the warehouse, No. 44
South Street, which he subsequently purchased, and occupied for nearly fifty years.

In 1855, Mr. TAYLOR was elected President of the City
Bank of New-York, which office he held up to his death.
Under his control the affairs of the Bank were managed
with great financial skill, and it safely outrode the panics
which seriously embarrassed many other banking institutions. Mr. TAYLOR was a member of the Committee of the
Associated Banks of the City of New-York, which, in
1861-62, made large loans to the Government to sustain its
credit, then greatly imperilled. Securities exceeding two
hundred millions of dollars in value passed through the
hands of this Committee, and it was largely due to their
prompt support that the nation was saved from threatened
financial disaster. Mr. TAYLOR was untiring in his efforts
to maintain the credit of the Government, and his advice
was sought by the Secretary of the Treasury on many
trying occasions.

Mr. TAYLOR was one of the directors of the Company
to lay the first Atlantic Cable, and its Treasurer. He
was largely interested in the coal lands of the Wyoming
and Lehigh Valleys, Penn., and the owner of large blocks
of mining and railway stocks of that region. He was
President of the Lackawanna Coal and Iron Company, and
held a considerable interest in the Manhattan Gas Company, of this City; was connected with the Georgia
Central Railroad, the Western Union Telegraph Company,
the Farmers' Loan and Trust Company and other financial
institutions. He died in this City May 23d, 1882, in the
77th year of his age. His immense fortune at the time of
his death was estimated at forty millions of dollars.

ROBERT B. POTTER.

MAJOR-GENERAL ROBERT B. POTTER was the son of
ALONZO POTTER, Bishop of Pennsylvania, and SARAH
MARIA, daughter of ELIPHALET NOTT, President of Union
College, N. Y. He was born at Boston, where his parents
were at that time temporarily residing, in July, 1829, and
died at Newport, R. I., February 19th, 1887. Educated at
Union College, the breaking out of the war found him en
gaged in a chamber practice of the law. He at once began
a training for the military service, and attached himself
to a regiment; joining, under the three years' call, the
"Shepard Rifles," which was shortly consolidated with
other similar organizations into the 51st New-York Volunteers. Young POTTER was mustered Major of this regiment
on the 11th October, 1861. At Annapolis, to which they
were sent, the regiment organization was completed by the
appointment of EDWARD FERRERO as Colonel, POTTER
as Lieutenant-Colonel, and CHARLES W. LE GENDEL, a
French gentleman, resident in America, as Major.

This regiment, from the fact of POTTER's connection
with it, became the special charge of the merchants of
New-York. A Committee was formed, whose headquarters
were in the rooms of the Chamber of Commerce, which,
by the sums of money for extra bounties raised among the
merchants and bankers of New-York, kept its ranks full
from its marching to its disbandment at the close of the
war, a procedure by which its officers were maintained
in the service; and, one after the other, in turn promoted
to Brigade and Division commands.

In February, 1862, the Brigade to which the 51st was
attached was embarked, under command of Brigadier
General RENO, for service on the Carolina coast. In that
month they attacked Roanoke Island, and POTTER led his
men first over the Confederate works. In March he par-
ticipated in the capture of Newbern, where he fell shot
through the body. In the same engagement Major La

GENDRE was dangerously hurt by a ball through the mouth.

In May, POTTER returned to his regiment as Colonel; FERRERO having been promoted Brigadier-General. In July the 51st was assigned to the Ninth Army Corps, BURNSIDE commanding. In August, RENO's command, with POTTER's regiment, was sent to re-enforce POPE in Virginia, and was constantly in service till the second Bull Run.

On the re-organization of the army under McCLELLAN, the Ninth Corps, under RENO, was assigned to the Army of the Potomac, and in September were engaged with LEE at South Mountain ; POTTER's regiment forming the head of the attacking column. In this engagement RENO fell. Following the enemy's line of retreat, POTTER led his men in person across the Antietam Bridge. In December he, with his regiment, were engaged at Fredericksburg in support of a battery, and so exposed that they lost a fifth of their number in ten minutes.

In March, 1863, Colonel POTTER was promoted Brigadier-General for gallant service at Fredericksburg, and ordered to the Department of the Ohio, which BURNSIDE commanded, with headquarters at Cincinnati. Here POTTER was named President of the Commission which tried and convicted VALLANDIGHAM, for treasonable conduct within the lines. In June, General POTTER marched with PARKE into Kentucky, and was assigned to the command of the Second Division. LE GENDRE, now its Colonel, had joined his regiment. In July, his superior officers being too ill for service, General POTTER found himself in command of the Ninth Corps, and made his headquarters at Lexington. Marching to Knoxville, he was appointed, in general orders, to the command of the Ninth Corps, which was already virtually under his orders. In the defence of Knoxville he was especially distinguished, both by his manœuvres in the field against LONGSTREET's column of relief and in the seige, the brunt of which fell on his command.

After the relief of Knoxville, POTTER joined BURNSIDE

in the East and engaged in the recruiting of the Ninth Corps, in which POTTER secured the aid of his many friends in the Chamber of Commerce, the New-York Stock Exchange and the New-York Produce Exchange. He was now assigned to the command of the Second Brigade of the Second Division of this corps, but in consequence of the illness of General PARKE, POTTER held the command of this division, first by seniority, and later by assignment, till the close of the war.

He was hotly engaged during the battles of the Wilderness, in one of which Colonel LE GENDRE received a dangerous wound in the face, losing an eye. POTTER's division followed the movement to the south of the James River, and was posted in advance within eighty yards of the enemy's line at Petersburg. It was his command that was engaged in the Mine of Cemetery Hill Fort, and on the Court Martial which sat on this unfortunate affair he was the only officer, of all engaged, who was exempted from censure. In the close engagements which followed he was constantly in action. In the final attack on the Petersburg lines, in March, 1865, he carried the works opposite to his command by assault, and was reforming his line, when he fell, shot through the body by a ball from a shrapnell shell. He was taken to the Jones House, where, as he lay between life and death, he was visited by President LINCOLN, then on his way from City Point to Petersburg.

In July, 1865, on the disbandment of the Ninth Corps, General POTTER was assigned in the new arrangements to the command of the district of Connecticut and Rhode Island, with headquarters at Newport. On the day of his (second) marriage he was commissioned by the Secretary of War, Mr. STANTON, full Major-General. In January, 1866, he was "honorably mustered out of the service of the United States." He was subsequently appointed Colonel of the Forty-ninth Regiment of Infantry, U. S. A., but declined.

General HANCOCK said to the author of this sketch, "that General POTTER was one of the twelve best officers in the United States service— West Point graduates included."

General GRANT, in his Memoirs, speaks of him in terms of praise.

At the close of his service he was appointed Receiver of the Atlantic and Great Western Railroad, a position of the highest responsibility and trust. At the end of this engagement he passed several years in Europe, endeavoring to recruit his shattered health. The close of his life was spent at Newport, where he died.

As a soldier he was brave and dashing to a fault, always ready to lead, and with a coolness under fire which never failed him. He was in private life a charming companion, kind of heart, and accomplished in varied ways.

It is because of his intimate relations with the merchants of New-York that his bust finds a suitable place in the Art Gallery of the Chamber of Commerce. The bust is the work of WILLIAM CLARKE NOBLE, of Newport, R. I., from measurements taken from the face after death, with the aid of a sketch and photographs, and is considered by his family and friends a highly satisfactory representation of this distinguished officer in the vigor of his health. It was presented to the Chamber of Commerce in February, 1890, by a number of gentlemen, officers of the army, members of the New-York Bar, to which he belonged, and merchants, members of the Chamber.

INDEX TO BIOGRAPHICAL SKETCHES.